BU
UNIV.

Kamrynn Bellary

The Ravenell Dynasty Trilogy

Book One
Enduring Love

© 2022 **Europe Books**| London
www.europebooks.co.uk | info@europebooks.co.uk

ISBN 9791220131612
First edition: November 2022

Enduring Love

This book series is dedicated to all ladies on Earth, who endeavour a world of equality, diversity, and inclusion; and who believe in love and romance, and have taken a chance at love, only to have experienced heartbreak, but yet, maybe if even only deep down, still believe in the possibility of true love.

This story and book series is a work of fiction.
All characters, and situations are purely fictional.

This fiction story series is for adult audiences, and contains elements of human life, including love, sex, violence, sexual assault, abuse, rape, death, grief, and spirituality.

Chapter One

Deirdre wrestles with sleep, tossing and turning thinking of Nicolaus. She breathes deep as she eyes the fireplace mantel that holds pictures of the two of them. They have been a couple since she can remember. The photos show them throughout the years, lovingly looking upon each other, displaying the engagement ring. However, the pictures seem empty to Deirdre because she has never given Nicolaus a wedding date.

Deirdre Omari is a well-known Austin, Texas lawyer of Greek and African American mixed heritage. She is successful, beautiful and confident, with the physique of a model. The love of her life is the dashingly handsome Nicolaus Ravenell, who has made a name for himself as a Sergeant Major on a special force unit in the military. Deirdre and Nicolaus have known each other all their lives, and have been in love since their teen years.

As Deirdre has a restless sleep, dreams enter her mind like movie scenes for each year when Deirdre confirms her love for Nicolaus with tears in her eyes, as he asks her to marry him on their engagement day anniversary. They have now been engaged for ten years. They are so happy, with sunlight shining behind them. She can feel their love for each other, their want and desire for each other. She can feel their future, when suddenly, Nicolaus' mother, Ceil Ravenell, appears above them, floating as if she were a witch. Her elegant black dress sways in the non-existent wind, and the sunshine has now left them, replaced with darkness and black clouds. Ceil floats towards them holding a placard of the iconic Estonian Ravenell family crest. She pushes the placard in their faces without words. She laughs as she places it on their heads, hurting them, and then …. Deirdre sits up in fright, awake, out of breath, looking around. Suddenly, she hears the birds singing. She looks to the extensively large window in the expansive Ravenell mansion, to see it is morning. She breathes deep to calm herself down, realizing it was only a dream. A damnable telling dream, but just a dream.

She looks at the clock to see it is half past eight, and jumps out of bed. Nicolaus is arriving back home from a mission today. The family is going to the ceremony for which Nicolaus will receive another medal of honour. Deirdre and her mother have rooms within the Ravenell home, upon Nicolaus' insistence. The mansion is so expansive, it could be considered a castle, except Austin, Texas does not have any castles. As Deirdre bathes and readies herself, she can hear that the Ravenell mansion is buzzing with life and excitement.

Deirdre checks her looks in the mirror. She smooths the sexy brown dress that clings to her body. The dress runs below her knees, but shows no skin. She checks her hair, and sees her mother, Constance, behind her in the mirror. "Oh Mother, I am so excited to see Nicky! I've missed him so much." They greet each other with a morning kiss to opposite cheeks.

Constance Omari is an older woman and appears much younger than her age. She strongly admires her daughter, who inherited her brown skin and wavy hair. Constance lost her husband, Cecil, and twin daughter, Abigail, years ago. She has never remarried, keeping her devotion to her beloved Cecil. She lives in a beautiful home Deirdre bought, they share it together. However, she does enjoy her time with the Ravenells, having history with their family, and due to the strong bond between Deirdre and Nicolaus.

"You look beautiful as always, daughter."

Deirdre blushed, "Thank you, Mother."

"You should give Nicky a date today. He's patiently waited ten years to marry you. I worry so much when he is away … that something could happen while he is on mission …" Deirdre quickly turns to stop her mother's words, afraid she may jinx him or something.

"Mother, don't. Please …"

Rachel, Ceil's sister enters the room. Rachel is as beautiful as Ceil, and treats Nicolaus as if he were her own son. She and Constance have been lifelong friends, and she has high hopes of Deirdre marrying Nicolaus.

"Your mother is right. You need to give Nicky a date, in the not too far off future. You two virgins need to start making those babies!"

"Auntie Rachel!" Deirdre chuckles with shock at the frankness of Nicolaus' dear aunt.

"Well, it's true! Those beautiful babies are just waiting and waiting to get here." She turns to Constance. "I've always known when your daughter and my angel get together, their babies will be beautiful. But Jesus, now I'm getting old, it will be harder for me to run after 'em."

The ladies laugh.

Constance scolds Deirdre, "Well … how long you gonna keep the man waiting? I know Nicky loves you. He'd do anything for you, and he'd wait because you want him to, but …," she shakes her head, "ten years is many years, Deirdre. That's forever for any man to wait to be with a woman."

"We both have been working on our careers, and …" Deirdre pauses in her explanation, "I know his mother doesn't want us to be married."

Rachel put her hands to her hips, "Ah, you can't let Ceil scare you away from love. It's my Nicky you'll be spending your life with, not my sister! She'll get old and die off anyway."

"Rachel!" Constance was shocked at her candour.

The ladies laugh again, and make their way to the sitting room.

"Well … and then what?" Rachel continued, "Benji runs around like he's half crazed, falling into any woman that will part her legs …"

Constance wasn't sure what was wrong with her friend. "Oh my God! Rachel, you are so blunt today!"

"Well! We all know babies aren't coming from him. I'm actually shocked we haven't had any surprises where Benji's concerned."

Benjamin, Nicolaus' younger brother, enters the sitting room, and kisses Rachel on her face, greets Constance, and quickly takes Deirdre's hand, holding onto it.

Benjamin is handsome but lazily kept, with an unbuttoned shirt, nice trousers, and tousled hair. His personality is reckless and irresponsible. Benjamin has no imagination except when it comes to women. He refuses to work and lives off the family.

"Why am I hearing my name thrown around?" Benjamin asks of the lovely women in his presence. He proceeds to gently kiss Deirdre's hand, his lips lingering, tasting her.

"Oh, we are just talking about families and babies," Rachel answered.

"Hmm. I'll never fall into that trap," frowning of the thought. He changed his face as his attention landed on Deirdre. Still holding her hand, "Deirdre, will you ride with me? I want to talk to you." He looked upon Deirdre as if he wanted to kiss her, no disguising his want for her in the presence of her mother.

Deirdre puts her arm against Benjamin's chest in a defensive move, as suddenly he is much closer to her than he should be. "Oh Benji, I don't know …. What are you up to?"

"Please, I just want to talk," he begged her.

Deirdre sighs, feeling mischief in the air. "Well, you promise not to make any strange detours? I don't want to miss any part of the ceremony."

Benjamin smiled at her, his hands suddenly holding her, "I promise! You won't miss anything."

Ceil Ravenell, the matriarch, enters the room. She glides across the floor and goes directly to her beloved Benjamin, separating him from Deirdre, and plants a kiss on his cheek. Her beauty does not match up with her volatile attitude or the covert loathing for her oldest son, that seethes from her pores. Ceil proceeds to button Benjamin's shirt, and runs her hands through his hair to make it look neater.

"Why so much chatter?" Ceil harshly asks everyone.

"Oh Ceil, aren't you excited that Nicky is returning today?" Rachel asks her.

"Not really. It's more peaceful around here when he is gone."

"Well, we are very excited!" Rachel defends her Nicky, not liking Ceil's attitude.

Ceil looks upon her sister with disdain. She frowns, then snaps, "Rachel, why are you even here?"

Rachel looks at Ceil with surprise. "Well of course I'd be here to help welcome Nicky home."

Nigel Ravenell follows his wife, and enters the room. He bends his tall frame to greet all the ladies with a loving kiss. It is clear to see from where his sons get their handsomeness. Nigel's rich heritage of Moorish ancestry, mixed with African Americanism, provides chiselled features to his looks. Nigel comes from a wealthy family, and his match to Ceil, who's of a historically aristocratic family of Estonian origins, make them a power couple, especially in the city of Austin.

Rachel does not take her eyes off him as he greets her last with a kiss. This does not go unnoticed by Ceil.

"Of course, you'd better be here for Nicolaus!" Nigel tells Rachel with a smile. "I am so proud of him! Getting another distinguished medal for valour. He's done so much for our country."

Deirdre touches Nigel's arm, and nods her head in full agreement. She is suddenly pulled away and out the door by Benjamin.

"Well, let's get this over with," Ceil states begrudgingly.

"Dwight and Alexander will meet up with us at the ceremony," Nigel informs the family.

"Francesca will meet us there as well," Rachel says of her own daughter.

The family head out the door into their vehicles. Benjamin opens the door to his Italian sports car for Deirdre. Constance and Rachel ride together in a black American luxury car; they have a driver. Nigel and Ceil get into their black limo, and then the family caravan pulls away from the mansion.

After about five minutes, Benjamin speeds his Italian sports car past the family cars on the wrong side of the road. After passing the cars, he jumps over to the correct lane, and speeds off.

"Where on earth is he going with that girl?" Ceil asks annoyed.

"That girl?" Nigel frowns. "Ceil, I hope you can tamper down your tone a little. This is a happy day, after all. What's bothering you today, anyway?"

Ceil eyes him harshly, without speaking, as Nigel busies himself getting them both drinks. Ceil takes her drink, and downs it quickly. "That girl bothers me."

Nigel's frown grows deeper. He does not like where he knows this conversation is headed. "Ceil, would you please stop. Deirdre is a young, successful woman. She will officially be part of our family one day. She is a good match for Nicolaus."

Ceil scoffs. "I don't need your explanation! She and Constance are always around. What do they want? I am tired of taking care of them."

"My God, Ceil, really? Constance losing her husband was your doing, remember? You made sure Cecil was run off. We owe Constance! Deirdre has nothing to do with it, she was a newborn baby at the time."

"Well …" Ceil shrugged, as if she didn't care.

Nigel continued to defend the Omari ladies, "Let us not forget that it was Constance that took great care of my mother when she was on her death bed. The least we can do is provide for her, and celebrate her beautiful daughter. They are just like family."

"Well, they are not family! And will never be, if I have any say in the matter," Ceil grumbled.

"You have got to stop this!" Nigel was desperate to get a handle on this before they reached their destination. "And stop being so nasty towards Nicolaus. You have been abusing him and punishing him since he was a child. This has all gone on for too many years now.

I thought we had an agreement, that Benjamin was our new beginning."

"Well, I don't know what you expect!" Ceil sniped at him.

"I expect you to be reasonable and abide by our agreement! I have begged your forgiveness a thousand times. You have to let the past go so we can all move forward. It was a one-time mistake, Ceil, decades ago."

"A mistake that produced Nicolaus. And betrayed me …"

Nigel grabbed onto Ceil and held her firmly to him. "I'm sorry," he sincerely apologized again, wanting this to end. "I have been faithful to you ever since. What more can I possibly do?"

"You want to know what you can do? Get rid of him! Send him away somewhere! Declare Benjamin the first true heir and send that bastard away."

Nigel looks at her in shock. Slowly, he releases her from his arms and pours another drink. "What do you mean, Ceil?" he asked, eyeing her, wanting clarity, and trying to find time to recover from the shock of her words, something he'd never heard from her before.

"Just what I said. Nicolaus is illegitimate."

"Nicolaus is not illegitimate! He is my son."

"But he's not my son. Benjamin is our new beginning, so he should be the first heir. Bring him into the company so he can take over when you retire."

Nigel half laughs. "Benjamin? My dear Ceil, what you propose is … unimaginable, frankly," Nigel gives a slight pause in thought. "Benjamin doesn't even go to the office. Benjamin does nothing. He is reckless and lazy! He wants no part of inheriting the company. Besides, Dwight would never agree to it."

Dwight Collins is co-founder of their company and Nigel's devoted friend. They built the healthcare business, Villamae Medical Corporation (VMC) together from the ground up, years ago, and have turned it into the multi-billion-dollar company it is today. Nigel and Dwight are racial opposites, both born into established millionaire families, and came together in the cause of helping others. They are both proud to be in the position of giving their sons this great legacy. Dwight's son is Alexander, who is a lawyer, and is also Nicolaus' best friend. It is intended that they take over the company for their father's one day. However, Dwight and Nigel have not yet discussed their plans with anyone.

Nigel continues, "What has Benjamin even done? What does he do with his time all day, every day?"

Ceil knew Nigel was right, but was not about to admit it. She fiercely defended her son, wanting him placed above Nicolaus where she felt was his rightful inheritance. She snapped at Nigel, "Do not speak ill of my Benjamin!"

Nigel ignored her reaction, "But Nicolaus … now Nicolaus is a natural leader. He's intelligent, having accomplished his Master of Business degree while leading his men. He is pious, decorated, will get any task done, and everyone loves him. Benjamin, I'm not so sure … he could even lead anyone. On his first day in the office, we'd probably be sued for sexual harassment."

"Ha! So, Benjamin loves women. Hell … like father like son. That apple didn't fall far from the tree."

"Ceil, don't insult me. Are you saying I chase skirts like our son? That I am a womanizer and sexually harass women, like our son?"

"You have the virility of a lion when it comes to women. Must be that Moorish DNA of yours," she attempted to add another insult, "and obviously, you have passed it down to Benjamin. So, he has a healthy appetite for women. He should still be first heir!"

"Oh for God's sake! Healthy and respectful are two different things. Benjamin has absolutely no self-control for a man his age. He just can't keep his hands off women."

Ceil waives his comments away. "That is beside the point. We can always help him get a grip. I want his standing to be first heir, and I want Nicolaus gone!"

"Jesus, Ceil, Nicolaus has been gone. For twelve weeks!"

"I want him permanently gone."

Nigel looks at Ceil in shock and a little fearful of what her steely stubborn nature might do to bring about her thoughts. He shakes his head, "That's just not going to happen, Ceil. I need Nicolaus here." Ceil's cold stare rushes Nigel to another drink.

Chapter Two

Deirdre gripes as Benjamin veers off the road, away from the family caravan, "Ah, Benji, you promised you would not do this!"

Benjamin smiles, feeling in complete control, "It will just be a minute. I just want to talk to you."

Deirdre frowns. "I thought that's why I'm in the car with you! Benji, I don't want to miss the ceremony," she makes clear.

Benjamin pulls the car over, off the nearest exit on the Mopac freeway, to the side of the road, next to some foliage, and a beautiful open field, with neighborhoods nearby. He gets out the car and opens the door for Deirdre. He helps her out of the car by the hand.

Still frowning and feeling uncertain of his motives, Deirdre asks, "Benji, what's this about?"

Quickly, Benjamin takes Deirdre into his arms, and embraces her. Feeling bold, his hands run over her body, at last grabbing her buttocks and pulling her tightly against him.

Deirdre pushes against Benjamin's chest in shock, as not even Nicolaus has ever touched her in such a way. Not sure what he is trying to do, Deirdre pushes against his chest again, but cannot break his hold on her as he gropes her again. Deirdre feels herself become slightly angry, "Benji, what are you doing?"

"You know I love you," Benjamin declares. "I've asked you so many times, but I won't stop asking until you say yes. Deirdre, I want you to marry me!"

"Benji." Deirdre pushes against him again, unable to get loose. "Why are you doing this? Please just stop. Please … let me go," she tries to wriggle herself out of his arms. He's too strong for her.

"I can be so much more to you than my brother. I can do more. Mother would leave you be if you were with me."

Not giving up, Deirdre continues to struggle against Benjamin, "Benji, please!"

Her pleads go ignored. "I would love you so much more." Benjamin force kisses Deirdre's mouth, as she struggles against him. Having enjoyed her predicament, he loosens his grip and lets her free, with a smug smile on his face.

Deirdre steps away from him, touching her mouth. She feels shocked at his aggressive behaviour. His flirtations had never gone this far before. She straightens herself.

Feeling emboldened, Benjamin continues, "You're not going to marry Nicolaus anyway.

You may as well admit it to yourself, Deirdre. He's been stringing you along for ten years. It's a mystery to me because I don't understand how he could possibly not have you."

Deirdre stops at his comment and looks at him. "Wait a minute, Benji. You've got it all wrong. It's me that's been making Nicky wait. And he has waited, with respect and patience, for ten years." Deirdre stops again, as if she had an awakening. "Ten... years," she says slowly as if she hadn't realized the time span, although she'd just talked about this with her mother and Aunt Rachel. Timidly, she touches Benjamin's chest gently, afraid he might grab her up again. "Benji, I'm flattered at your offer, and I love you too, but... I love you like a brother, nothing more," she tells him sternly, wanting to make her point. "And it could never be anything more," she adds for emphasis. "I love everyone in Nicky's family, how could I not?" she reasoned. "Nicky is special, he's my soulmate! We were born to be together. It's our destiny. He is the love of my life!"

"Yeah, yeah," Benjamin blew off her devotion for Nicolaus. "But, what if something happened to Nicolaus? Like he didn't come back from one of his fancy missions."

"No, Benji. Don't even say that," Deirdre frowned, having heard this for the second time today.

"Really. If he weren't here. Would you consider marrying me? I would take care of you, even if you didn't love me. I will always love you, Deirdre," Benjamin's mouth slipped on these words, without the feeling or passion from his heart.

Deirdre shook her head negatively, knowing that Benjamin only wanted to bed her. "I can't imagine ever marrying anyone else," she told him, hoping to quash any thoughts he had of ever being with her.

Deirdre walked to the car. "Now Benji, please, let's go. My darling is arriving. I must be there to greet him." Without any more words, she put herself into his car, and closed the door.

Chapter Three

Tears well in Deirdre's eyes as she proudly watches Nicolaus receive another military medal. The family stands with the crowd of other military families on the main site at the Fort Sam Houston Joint Military Base in San Antonio, Texas, in the space where deployments and returns occur. There are women, men, mothers, fathers, teens, children, and babies of all races, creeds, and colours there to meet their military service family member returning from deployment.

Benjamin holds Deirdre close, and gently rubs her back and shoulders, not to make her feel uncomfortable, but not able to keep his hands off her, just as Nigel had earlier described. Of course, at a time like this, his actions are inappropriate. "You okay?" he asked her sweetly.

Deirdre nods, with a big smile on her face, her tears streaming. She listens as Nicolaus' accomplishments and accolades of bravery are stated. Nicolaus stands straight and tall to receive his accommodation.

Deirdre looks over to Nicolaus' parents, who are standing next to her. Ceil is scowling. Nigel is beaming proud, as are her mother and Rachel. Dwight and Alexander are smiling, as they watch Nicolaus be honoured. Deirdre looks at Benjamin, whose grip has tightened on her. When she meets his gaze, he looks as though he wants to kiss her again. Horrified, Deirdre quickly turns her attention back to Nicolaus.

Francesca, the brother's fun-loving cousin, and Rachel's daughter, worms her way between Benjamin and Deirdre, to save Deirdre from Benjamin's advances. She kisses Deirdre's face, and drapes her arms around Deirdre's neck, in the space in front of Benjamin. "I got you sis! I got you," she whispers to Deirdre.

"Thank you," Deirdre whispers to Francesca, sighing with relief as she receives another kiss from her. She leans on her for support.

Benjamin huffs, annoyed, but steps back, holding onto Deirdre's arm.

Nicolaus has a tall muscular frame. His intelligence and sharp eyes grab people's attention. His handsome face usually carries a charismatic smile that makes women croon over him, dreaming he was theirs, despite his continually serious nature. He is overly loyal, and true to his word due to his high integrity standards. Women gravitate towards him, sensing his qualities of humility, courage, gallantry, and kindness. Nicolaus is pinned. He stands in line next to seven other comrades, who were also pinned and celebrated.

As the ceremony ends, and Nicolaus makes his way through the crowd to his family, he is greeted by many people he knows. He is hugged, receives handshakes, and is bombarded with kisses from grateful military wives, because they know that he has delivered their husbands back home to them safely.

Suddenly, Nicolaus is swarmed by the press. He excuses himself and runs to Deirdre, the press following close behind. Without hesitation, Nicolaus scoops Deirdre into his arms and twirls her around as if she were a doll. Deirdre is joyful in his arms, she giggles with delight. They embrace tightly, and smack lips.

"Look at that spectacle!" Ceil complains.

The loud sound of press cameras and flashing photo lights swamp the couple. Jealously, Benjamin stares at Nicolaus, watching him hold onto Deirdre.

Nicolaus can feel his brother's eyes. "You made it Benjamin! Thanks for being here!"

Nicolaus tries for a hug, while clinging to Deirdre, but Benjamin does not reciprocate.

"Yes, I escorted Deirdre, and I …"

"Thank you! I'll take it from here!" With Deirdre in tow, Nicolaus is off to greet other family members. Deirdre looks back at Benjamin apologetically, then shrugs, glad to be with Nicolaus.

Nicolaus kisses Deirdre's mother, who hugs him tightly. Then Rachel jumps him with love, and holds him tight. He wipes her tears, and kisses her, with light laughter. Nigel hugs his son with pride, and gives a man pat to his back. Dwight greets him as well.

Francesca jumps into Nicolaus' arms, and covers his face with kisses. "I missed you so much my cousin. So glad you are home and safe."

Nicolaus returns her kisses and plants her feet on the ground, laughing. Alexander and Nicolaus hug in brotherly love.

Nicolaus steps up to hug his mother, but is stopped by her hard cold stare. He touches her forearm instead. "It's so good to see you, mother," he tells her happily.

"I cannot say the same," Ceil delivers her words with a mean streak. Her demeanour is not unexpected.

"Okay," Nicolaus responds, pretending not to be bothered by her rudeness, as the press is all around them. Ceil removes herself, and stands next to Benjamin. The press go crazy with pictures of the couple, as Nicolaus is surrounded by love.

"Sergeant Major Ravenell, welcome home and congratulations," a press lady tells him, ready to get her story.

"Thank you."

"Our viewers want to know when the two of you are going to tie the knot?" Live cameras and microphones are swiftly put before the couple.

Nicolaus looks at Deirdre with great love. "Well, when Deirdre is ready, then we shall wed. Simple as that."

"Any wedding dates set?" the reporter pressed for details from the couple.

"I'm ready," Deirdre says into the microphone with a smile.

Nicolaus looks to Deirdre, taken aback, "Wait … what? You're ready?" A joyful sound came from him, "You have a date for me?"

Deirdre nods with a huge smile, feeling relief for finally having decided, "Yes … yes, I have a date for you. Yes!"

"Oh my God! Wait a minute, … I haven't forgotten what day it is."

Before everyone, as a large crowd has gathered around to see what is happening, and the live video cameras, and photo cameras which now seem non-stop, Nicolaus hands his award certificate, award box, and equipment to Alexander, and then drops to his knee. He takes Deirdre's hands. "This is the anniversary day of our engagement … ten years ago. Deirdre … I cannot imagine my life without you. I could not do anything in my life without you. We have been in each other's life since we were children, and there is only room in my heart for you. Only you. Having you in my life has made me a better person."

Rachel cries tears at the romance. She hugs Constance to her.

The crowd reacts positively. Nicolaus continues, "I know having you as my wife, I will be more blessed than I already am. And... as much as I love you now, I don't know how, but our love would only grow more. Deirdre Omari, will you please walk with me, side by side to eternity? Will you marry me?"

Women in the crowd gasp and swoon at his romantic words.

Uncontrollable tears of joy fall from Deirdre's eyes. She nods, "Yes! Yes! I will marry you. Yes … on June 15th!"

Nicolaus stands, and swoops her up again, twirling her, making her laugh with joy. The crowd goes crazy with laughter, clapping, gasping with pure joy. The couple is quickly surrounded.

"This spectacle really needs to end," Ceil says nastily.

Anger is about Benjamin. "Damn it!"

Ceil looks over to Benjamin and is confused at his reaction. Frowning, "What's wrong with you?"

"I love Deirdre, mother. I want her."

Ceil scrunches her face. "Do you know how ridiculous you sound right now? Really!

Why would you want her, when supposedly she is your brother's fiancée? That girl is not fit for either of you. I really must do something to remove her."

"No! Just leave her alone. I will win her."

Ceil rolls her eyes and shakes her head. "I promise to find you a suitable mate. It's not Deirdre. We will find you someone better."

Harshly, "Mother, you're not listening!" Benjamin looks at Ceil and his aggression softens. "I know what I want, and I want Deirdre."

"Words of a childish man. If you had Deirdre, you wouldn't know what to do with her!

She would drive you to madness. No! I know best. Leave it to me dear."

Benjamin briefly stares at Ceil as she walks away before he can say anything else. His determined gaze returns to Deirdre, and he watches her as she interacts with Nicolaus. Deirdre's eyes catch Benjamin's gaze, feeling him watch her, she gets uncomfortable, and turns her back to him, and focuses on Nicolaus. Subtly, she checks over her shoulder for him, and he is gone.

Chapter Four

The family is seated at the dining table for Nicolaus' return luncheon, joined by Rachel, Constance, Deirdre, Francesca, Alexander, and Dwight, Ceil and Nigel each at the respective heads of the French marble dinning table. The servers give each person a plate, filled with hot, southern, comfort food.

Nicolaus and Deirdre intermittently hold hands, and every now and then Nicolaus kisses Deirdre's hand, as he admires her with much love, between bites of food. Benjamin eyes them jealously, feeling his lust for Deirdre increase. He downs a drink and taps his glass for the server to provide him an immediate refill, which he downs the new drink, without taking his eyes off Deirdre.

Ceil notices Benjamin eyeing the couple, and is not pleased with his behaviour. Then she notices her sister staring at Nigel, as he is in conversation with Dwight.

All this negative behaviour is getting under Ceil's skin, bringing her aggravations to the surface.

"Thank you, mother, for all of this. I didn't expect such a fuss. I was just going to grab lunch with the guys," Nicolaus tells Ceil.

Ceil nods with a half-smile, but says nothing.

Rachel is sitting next to Nicolaus, and touches his free hand, closest to her. "We are so glad you are back home, and that you are safe, Nicky."

"Thank you, Auntie Rachel."

Alexander, a professional lawyer with his own practice, has green gem eyes that have a sparkle of mischievousness. He observes the light caramel skin of his best friend, wishing he had the charisma and piety that Nicolaus carries naturally and daily. "Nicolaus, we have a lot to catch up on."

"That's right! Before I left you were working on a big case", Nicolaus remembered. "You go to court yet?"

Alexander nodded. "It got complex. We'll talk about it later. I don't want to bore everyone here."

Francesca jumped into the conversation. "Can you tell us anything about your adventure? Where were you?" Francesca has maintained her British accent due to her childhood and teen years at boarding school in London, and her continued education of anthropology at Cambridge. She is independent, a wicken, a professor who walks and looks like a model, and she says what is on her mind. Her hobby is genealogy. She has always found herself in the role as advisor, especially in family matters.

Nicolaus chuckled, "Well … I wouldn't exactly call it an adventure. You know I can't say much, but we were somewhere in Switzerland."

"Switzerland? Jesus, you're like a fucking James Bond." Her British accent made her comment humorous, and most everyone laughs.

Rachel frowns, "Professor Francesca Olivia Kiviste! Such language!" Most everyone laughs again.

"Well, he is."

Nicolaus chuckles. "No, I'm not. We always work in teams, for whatever mission we are given."

"Did you kill anyone? I want the scoop! An ambassador? High prized target? Enemy of the country?"

"Francesca, you know the drill. I can't tell you any of that. Let's just say, it was a peacemaking mission."

"And your enlistment is coming up again. Three weeks, right?" Nigel thought he'd slowly bring up the subject.

Nicolaus scoffs with surprise, "You remember? Yes, in three weeks. We've been so busy, I haven't even thought about what I want to do, or where I want to be."

Nigel looks at Dwight, then to Nicolaus. "I don't want you to re-enlist, son."

Benjamin gets the server's attention and makes demands, "Get me more bourbon, and fill the glass this time."

Francesca is sitting next to Benjamin. She grabs his empty glass from his hands. "Benji, you're already drinking too much. I don't want to see none of your antics today."

Benjamin snickers and kisses at her. Francesca rolls her eyes, knowing its already too late. She watches as his gaze returns to Deirdre.

Deirdre sees Benjamin's behaviour and feels uncomfortable. She tries to ignore him, and listens to Nicolaus.

Nicolaus frowns with intrigue. "You don't want me to re-enlist? Why not, father? What do you mean?"

"We'll talk after lunch."

Nicolaus nods. His attention returns to Deirdre. He smiles at her, and then leans to kiss her forehead.

Immediately Ceil points to Nicolaus and Deirdre, "Enough of that!" she says of their display of affection. "Why were there so many press people at the ceremony?"

Nicolaus shrugs and frowns. "Good question. I don't know."

"And you two were sure quick to announce your plans to the world."

Rachel interrupted Ceil's chiding of the couple. "It was so romantic!"

"It was embarrassing!" Ceil reprimanded them. "And it will be on television, and in all the papers."

Nicolaus corrected Ceil, defending their actions, "I would tell the world how much I love this lady, and anyone who will listen." He reigned kisses on Deirdre's hand again. She looked at him feeling his love for her.

"That is so sweet," Rachel agreed.

"No one asked you Rachel," Ceil told her spitefully. She then turned her attention back to the couple in love, to land into them. "You have not come to me and ask my permission to marry. It's a family tradition that the mother picks a bride for her sons. This tradition has been in our family since the time we were in Estonia, in the 16th century."

Dwight did not like where he thought this topic may be going, as he'd known Ceil a as long as he'd known Nigel. He also wanted to help defend the couple, whose love was undeniable. "16th century Estonia, huh? Well … that's a rich heritage, Ceil, but everyone knows that Nicolaus and Deirdre are getting married." He frowns, "They've been engaged for ten years!"

"Engaged for ten years without my permission!" Ceil sniped.

Constance touches Ceil's arm, to try to calm her.

"Ceil, dear, it's okay. No harm is meant. It's refreshing to see these two lovely, young, intelligent, and successful people, in love. They are devoted to each other, and have been since they were children."

Ceil jerks herself away from Constance. "Devoted," she repeats the word as if it were a bad thing. "Where is your devotion to this family?" she snaps at Nicolaus.

Nicolaus frowns at Ceil, feeling she may be up to something. "Haven't I proven …"

Ceil cuts Nicolaus off, "I'm tired of you disrespecting me! And disrespecting this family!"

Nicolaus sits back into his chair, and sighs. Now he taps his glass at the server, nodding, pointing to the alcoholic beverage across the room. He looks at his watch, realizing the good feeling of the moment only lasted about thirty minutes. Almost a record for their family gatherings.

"Auntie Ceil, Nicolaus and Deirdre are just madly in love," Francesca tries to reason with Ceil. "They haven't seen each other for twelve weeks. Surely, you understand about love. You're married."

Silence falls over the table with all eyes on Ceil, waiting for her answer. "No one asked you Francesca! You're just like your mother, budding in where you're not wanted."

"Mother! Please!" Nicolaus opposes Ceil's treatment of everyone.

"Please what?"

"I appreciate you Francesca, and I always need your advice. I appreciate all of you."

"Don't try to cut me off and change the subject," Ceil refused to let it go.

"Ceil, we all just want to enjoy this celebration. There is no need for any of this, now is there?" Nigel tells her.

Ceil slams the table with her fist and stands in authority. "I will not be quieted!" Ceil slams the table again and points to Nicolaus. "You dishonor me by making your announcement to the world, and never have asked my permission. Who the hell do you think you are?"

Quickly, Nigel stands and goes to Ceil, wrapping his arms around her to drag her from the room as she continues to chide and yell at Nicolaus, "Ceil, come on dear." Her voice diminishes the farther away she is taken into the mansion.

Nicolaus frowns, with hurt on his face. He takes another drink. "I am so sorry everyone, I must apologize for my mother. I'm not sure what that is about. Hopefully, it will be done soon."

Alexander happily, changes the subject. "Yes! You two have June 15th to worry about. That's what … eight weeks away?"

Deirdre nods with a huge smile, feeling better now that Ceil is not in the room, "Yes, I think that will be enough time to get the invitations out and to get everything ready. Don't you, Nicky?"

Nicolaus is preoccupied with thinking, and looks distant. He doesn't respond until Deirdre hugs his arm. "What … yes, yes," he nods, "hmhum, should be enough time. But … regardless …," he gives Deirdre a big teasing smile with an eyebrow lift. Laughter engulfs the room.

Benjamin is not amused. He stands in a drunken state, almost knocking his glass and the plate from the table, which Francesca quickly catches. He rudely stumbles from the table out the room. The excited talk about the future wedding continues.

Chapter Five

Everyone gathered into the main sitting room after lunch. Nicolaus and Alexander are seated across from Dwight and Nigel, Deirdre next to Nicolaus. Everyone has an after-dinner drink in their hand. Drinking good alcohol is the family thing they all do together, often.

Nigel and Dwight nod to each other, being on the same page in deciding to make the offer to their sons official. Nigel especially wants to make the offer official before all the family, since Ceil was beginning to turn against Nicolaus.

Nigel downed his drink, stood by the rather large fireplace, and got right to the point, his attention directed to Nicolaus and Alexander. "Look, Dwight and I have been making plans for the future of the company. And we have decided we are ready to give it over to the both of you. We want both of you to operate it as co-partners, just as we have done all these years. You would both be Vice Presidents."

Alexander chokes on his drink mid-swallow, the announcement fully taking him by surprise. The bourbon tries to exit his nose, and he coughs loudly and painfully.

Nicolaus pats Alexander's arm with concern, frowning, "You alright?" He hands Alexander a napkin to wipe his face. Alexander nods and wipes his mouth and eyes, with another barking cough.

Ceil is deeply frowning at her husband. She folds her arms in disagreement, still in a frenzy from earlier.

Nicolaus is also frowning at his father, in disbelief, "Operate the company? You mean take over for you?"

Dwight jumps up and stands next to Nigel, "This is a great time for both of you to come in, as changes are being made, and it will be right before the merger."

Rachel clasps her hands, "Oh, that's so wonderful. Wonderful!" she exclaims happily.

Nicolaus and Alexander look at each other with slight frowns, then back to their fathers. They both begin talking over each other.

Nicolaus shakes his head, still in disbelief, "Father ... I couldn't ... I don't know enough."

At the same time Alexander says, "How could I possibly do this?"

They both stop. Alexander nods to Nicolaus so he can speak first.

Nicolaus looks at Deirdre, then to everyone present, then back to Nigel, "Father ... I don't know anything about running the business. Besides, I haven't even decided about my re-enlistment, and ..."

Nigel interrupts Nicolaus, "I don't want you to re-enlist. Your place is here now. I want you to stay. You and Deirdre should get married, as you have been planning. Nicolaus, this is your time to step into your role at the company. Dwight and I will teach you both everything we know. We will make sure you and Alexander are fully developed into the role."

"I mean, it sounds nice", Alexander begins, "and ... it's truly an honour ... that you want us to follow in your footsteps. Really. I mean ... wow ... but ... what am I supposed to do with my law firm?" Alexander reminds them of his own commitments.

Dwight answers with his arms in a wingspan, "Sell it. Keep it. Whatever you like. But I need you now, son."

"Wow!" Nicolaus takes a drink, feeling this is a huge ask from his father, making him feel uncertain. "I don't know father … what … what about Benjamin?"

Benjamin steps forward to get himself out of the equation, "Oh hell no! I agreed to help with the fundraisers in two weeks, like we do every year. That doesn't mean I want to run anything." Briefly, he looks at both of his parents, "I'm sorry, but leave me the hell out of this!"

"As you can see, Benjamin has no interest, nor the mindset for this." Nigel met Ceil's glare at the confirmation of what he told her earlier.

"Your father is right Nicolaus. You are a natural leader. Both you and Alexander will do great!" Rachel agreed and wanted to be sure to place her encouragement for Nicolaus to assist his father.

This made Ceil step forward to negate Nicolaus' abilities, "No! Nicolaus is right! You should not offer him Vice President. He has done nothing to earn it! He has not even been here! Benjamin should be …"

"Oh, and Benjamin has earned the privilege to be Vice President?" Nigel asked Ceil sarcastically. Then he quickly placed his attention to Nicolaus, trying to squelch any further comment Ceil may have. "Nicolaus, I want you to succeed me. Dwight and I have discussed this, and he is in agreement. You succeed me, and Alexander succeeds Dwight."

Dwight nodded, "And you and Alexander have got to come in now, while we are still at the helm, so we can teach you all we know."

Francesca stood with a high chest and a hand on her hip, "Wait a minute … what about me?" she asked jokingly to make a point, "If they don't want it, I'll step in Uncle Nigel! What you need is a woman to take control and get that work done! I'm your woman!" she laughed, and Deirdre and Rachel giggled with her.

Constance pulled her back to her seat, "Francesca!"

Benjamin slowly slips out of the room, unnoticed.

Alexander wanted further clarification, "You want us to give up our careers?"

"Yes!" Nigel happily claps his hand one time. "This is the future we are talking about, not only for the company, but for our families! Stand with us and lead VMC into the future! It's where you both belong!"

Ceil stepped forward, ready to barrage insults on Nicolaus. "I don't agree! This is not a good fit for Nicolaus. You should follow your heart and stay with the military. The military is where you should remain! Away from here! Anyway, you will get bored. And you don't know anything about healthcare, now do you? You would utterly fail. You are indecisive, and divisive, and can't even handle simple family matters. You should stay abroad and continue your military life."

Deirdre and Francesca gasp at Ceil's harsh words.

Francesca reacts to Ceil's comments, "Damn! Auntie Ceil, that's just bloody mean."

Nicolaus scoffed at Ceil's comments, "I understand how you feel about me mother … thank you," he told her.

Now Rachel steps forward to defend her beloved, "Really Ceil? Nicolaus, don't listen to her. You should give it a try. You are a natural leader, and your father clearly wants you to succeed him."

Now Ceil angrily focuses her attacks on Rachel, "Rachel, you stay out of this! Benjamin should be the successor, and you know it."

Nigel wants to qualm the bickering, "No, Rachel is right. Don't listen to your mother, Nicolaus! Listen to what I'm telling you. I need you to stand with me. And as Dwight has pointed out, now is the time!" Nigel pours himself another drink and takes a swig, "Look, we know it's a lot to process. Don't make a decision now. Both of you take time to think about it. Let us know in a few days. Okay?"

Nicolaus and Alexander stand, and hug everyone except Ceil, who has retreated from the room, seething in anger.

Chapter Six

Later, Nicolaus and Alexander find a moment alone in the mansion drawing room to take a breather away from everyone, and to discuss the proposal of their fathers. The drawing room has overdramatic features, with a golden colour scheme, an arched cathedral like ceiling, and a large fireplace. The windows are draped with golden curtains. The furniture even has a golden theme. Nicolaus collapses in the nearby chair with a sigh. Alexander sits across from him.

"Did you see this coming?" Nicolaus asked.

"I had no idea they were even thinking about this. I mean, my father mentioned maybe one time he was thinking about retiring, but he never said anything about me succeeding him at the company."

Nicolaus nods, with folded arms, in thought. "I wonder what brought this on."

"You know they're serious!"

"Yes, I … can tell. Adamant." Nicolaus sighs in thought. "What are you gonna do?"

"Honestly, I'm not sure. On one hand, how could I not take on what my father asks of me, and carry forward a million-dollar corporation he helped create? But … on the other hand, I have built up my law firm, how do I just walk away from that?"

"Yeah, I know what you mean. My father doesn't ask much of me, and this could be the last thing he ever does ask of me. How could I turn him down? But giving up my military career is like … giving up my independence." They sit in silence for a while, thinking about what to do, periodically glancing at each other.

Alexander breaks the silence, and begins a chain of thoughts. "I suppose … this could be … a really good experience."

"We would be learning and applying new skills. And hey, we'd be working together!"

"Right? And how hard could it be?"

"I could settle down with Deirdre."

"We could make some real change to help lots of people."

Nicolaus nodded in agreement. "We'll have to put up with my mother, though. She is on the board, you know."

Suddenly Alexander began spewing company statistics, "Fifteen thousand employees; over two hundred fifty thousand patients; one point three million prescriptions …"

Nicolaus looks at him frowning, "Is that VMC?"

Alexander nods, "I help my father put together the annual shareholders report." He gets quiet again with thought, before saying, "I suppose I could hire someone to run my firm."

"Alexander, if we say yes, there's no turning back."

Alexander nods, "Let's do it! I'm all in."

Nicolaus nods in agreement, "Okay. I'm all in."

Chapter Seven

An auburn sunset streaks across the cloudless, open sky, as a warm night settles on the city of Austin. Deirdre and Nicolaus find time alone at the mansion pool. With romance in the air, Deirdre sits next to Nicolaus on the pool lounger, which barely fit both of their bodies. Her small frame is on the left half of his body, atop of his left leg; the leg that does not give him a slight limp. His arms immediately surround her in a sweet full body cuddle. Deirdre melts into Nicolaus, feeling weak with overwhelming love for him. Nicolaus smiles, while eyeing her sexily dressed body, as she had changed into her beige, chiffon beach robe. It was ankle length, but daring, with a slit from the high thigh, and one couldn't tell if her beach robe was covering something underneath or not. Nicolaus held her soft, delicate body in his muscular arms. He'd missed her while he was gone, thinking of her every night. He couldn't wait to get home to hold her again. He loved how she has always fit specifically in the space of his middle chest.

Deirdre felt so safe in his arms, knowing he would totally respect her. She never could explain that rush of weakness and excited love she always felt in his presence, it was just there. She never could hide it, and everyone saw it. Moreover, it got worse when he touched her, or caressed her, as he sweetly did now, gently and respectfully rubbing her back or her arm.

Deirdre smiled and a tear fell from her eye when Nicolaus sweetly kissed her hand. "I missed you so much while you were gone. I wish we could have talked every day. I missed having you near me," she told him.

Nicolaus smiled at her, and kissed her tear away. "Babe, you know I missed you!" He kissed her hand again. "You're so beautiful. I've missed everything about seeing you… your hair, your lovely scent, your eyes … your soft skin, …" Nonchalantly, he took in her sweet scent, which made his senses go wild. He wanted to kiss her again, and again, and again, and again.

Deirdre felt herself wanting to cry at his words and actions, at his presence, at the essence of him. She adored him so much. He was her heartbeat, her breath. They flowed together like a bird's wing on the wind. He saw her emotion, and kissed her hand again, then kissed her forehead. Deirdre wanted more of him. She leaned in for a mouth kiss, and he didn't disappoint her. The kiss was gentle and undemanding. "Thank you," she whispered to him, her hand feeling on his muscular chest. "Thank you for being you, babe. You know, I appreciate how you have never tried to …" she stopped herself, thinking about how different he was from Benjamin. She wasn't sure she should continue.

"Never tried to what?" Nicolaus wanted her to continue.

Deirdre met his searching eyes. "You've never tried to force yourself on me. All this time we've been together … ten years," her voice drifted with that number, as she realized again the span of time, "not once …." She looked in his eyes, "You've waited so patiently."

"I would never force you to do anything. Wait a minute … Deirdre … did something happen? You okay?"

Deirdre smiled, but didn't answer.

Nicolaus tilted his head, and squinted his right eye, as he did when he was putting invisible pieces together in his mind. "Did Benjamin bother you while I was gone? Or my mother … was she ridiculous?"

Deirdre sighed and frowned at his questions, wondering how he could possibly know. She looked at him, and shook her head in a lie, believing if she didn't say the words, it wasn't exactly lying. Anyway, he'd just literally gotten home, and she certainly didn't want to burden him about Benjamin's bad boy behaviour. Especially after he'd just gotten a hammer dropped on him by his father. Instead, she relaxed against him, and breathed. "So did you and Alexander decide what to do about your father's offer?"

"Yeah, we both think our fathers are serious. I mean, I do understand that they want to retire. They've worked hard for many years, you know. They have to leave the company in someone's hands."

"So, you're on board?" Deirdre took his large hand in hers. Her small fingers attempted a squeeze, but barely fit around his hand.

"Well … yeah. It's going to be a lot to learn. And it's not going to be easy putting up with mother though."

"No, but I know you will be great in the role. You'll do good babe, and be a real help to your father and the company. It will be more good that you can do, than bad to endure from your mother. I think in the end, it will all even out."

Nicolaus nodded in agreement. He smiled at Deirdre and kissed her hand, knowing she being by his side has always made him stronger. "Babe, you sure you want to go through with the wedding plans?"

Deirdre chuckled, sitting up to face him. "Yes! I'm positively sure!" She sighed. "Though I do still have concerns about your mother. I really think she doesn't want us to be married. After all this time, I have never figured out why, but … she just doesn't like me."

"Babe, it's not you. It's me she's against. And I'm not sure why she said those things earlier. She's never said that to me before. I don't know what's going on with her, but hopefully it will all blow over by the time we walk down the aisle."

Deirdre chuckled again, feeling as though she didn't care why Ceil was upset. She was so glad to have Nicolaus holding her. "Well, regardless, I think we should move forward.

We don't need our parent's permission. It's time for us to get married." As Nicolaus nodded in agreement, she leaned forward for another kiss. Lovingly, he grasped her lips with his, gently kissing her mouth.

Chapter Eight

As night fell, Nigel and Ceil were in their bedroom on the other side of the mansion. Nigel was fuming, and frankly, embarrassed by Ceil's behaviour towards Nicolaus earlier.

"You have got to stop treating Nicolaus so poorly, Ceil. You embarrassed him in front of other people at least three times today."

"Nicolaus is an embarrassment to this family!"

Nigel frowned deeply, "Ceil, you've got to stop this."

"Stop what?" she asked sharply, providing Nigel with her dark, undivided attention.

"Badgering him at every turn! You punish him every day of his life since he's been here.

It's got to stop! He's a grown man, Ceil. A decorated man. He's adored by hundreds of people. His country celebrates his achievements. It appears you are the only one on earth that dislikes him."

"You don't know what you're talking about. I don't punish him. I've done no such thing!"

"Really, Ceil?" Nigel frowned at her denial of the truth, "I remember plenty of instances." Nigel's memory was strong, as he remembered details of Ceil torturing Nicolaus from the time, he was brought home. His mind quickly had remembrances:

Nigel was talking to Constance about Ceil's erratic behaviour towards five-year-old Nicolaus. Constance believed Ceil was too harsh with him. That's when they heard Nicolaus wail, like never before, sending them racing towards the direction from whence the sound came. Nigel walked into the large kitchen to find Ceil beating Nicolaus about the legs with a metal fire poker rod. She was angry and chastising him for playing with Deirdre against her wishes. Four-year-old Deirdre is crouching in the corner in silent horror, and three-year-old Benjamin watches, taking it all in. Nigel could see that his son's right leg looks mangled, while he tried to crawl away from Ceil. Nigel pulls Ceil off Nicolaus, and the child collapses on the floor, absorbing the hatred and the pain delivered by his mother. Not done with her punishment, and looking crazed, Ceil escapes Nigel's grasp and runs to kick Nicolaus in the stomach. Benjamin runs to Ceil, crying, and confused; not understanding why his mother is upset. Then as if a deranged woman, Ceil hugs Benjamin to her as if he were hurt, and walks out of the kitchen with him in her arms, clung to her chest, telling him everything will be fine.

"When Nicolaus was five, you damaged his legs, giving him injury for life," Nigel reminded Ceil.

"He had to learn to listen," Ceil defended herself.

Then at another time, when young Nicolaus was six years of age, Nigel remembered Ceil harshly slapping Nicolaus across the face, knocking his loose teeth onto the floor, and daring him to speak or cry.

Deirdre is again present, and frightened, she has retreated, crouching in the corner for safety. Benjamin watches the exchange.

"When Nicolaus was little, you have slapped his face so hard his teeth flew right out of his mouth."

"Ah, those teeth were loose and going to naturally fall out anyway," Ceil responded.

Nigel is shocked at her uncaring and unremorseful attitude to her incredulous past behaviours. So many abuses his mind remembered:

Nigel helped Deirdre clean up Nicolaus, at the young age of eleven, after Ceil, in a rage, launched glass ob-

jects at him, in a continuous flow to ensure she injured him.

Then another time, Nigel lost the argument with Ceil for Nicolaus wanting to study to be a priest at the age of fourteen. Ceil accused Nigel of being a weak father for not putting a stop to his idea of becoming a priest. Ceil manipulated Nigel into siding with her when she belittled him, telling him he did nothing to support her in their marriage and said, "Why did I even marry you if I have to do everything myself?" Nigel being stunned by her statement, ran after her when he realized she had stormed out of the room towards Nicolaus' bedroom. As Nigel got to the entrance of the flung open French doors to Nicolaus' bedroom, he witnessed Ceil demand the fourteen-year-old justify why he wanted to study scripture and become a priest, when their family was not about that. As Nicolaus looked up from the religious manuscripts and books on the table in front of him, he honestly answered her question. Nigel watched as Ceil harshly slap Nicolaus across the face for answering her. When he tried to clarify, she slapped him seemingly as hard as she could, knocking him back, daring him to speak. Deirdre happened to be present for this abuse as well, and was sitting at the table, next to where Ceil was standing, frozen with fright at Ceil's behaviour. Nigel was motionless as Nicolaus looked to him for help. Nigel felt that if he stepped in, it would only anger Ceil farther and feed her abuse of him, so he remained silent and unmoved, to Nicolaus' disappointment. The commotion brought Benjamin around, and they all observed the mean actions of Ceil as she placed the religious books and papers to a roaring fire in the bedroom fireplace. With hands on hips, Ceil sighed and smiled with satisfaction, watching the items burn. Nicolaus was devastated for quite some time.

Two years later, Nigel had a hard time calming Ceil's rage, as she hunted for Nicolaus, threatening to separate his male genitalia from his body with a pair of garden shears, once she learned that he had proposed marriage to Deirdre.

"You have tortured him all his life! You have given Nicolaus weak nerves. Sometimes I hear him vomiting after a tussle with you. You even mocked him when he told us he wanted to join the military. Telling him they wouldn't want him because of his leg. The leg that you injured," he yelled at her. He sighed to calm himself, "You've told him on more than one occasion that he'd never amount to anything, and yet look how amazing he's turned out. He received another commendation today, Ceil. He's done great on his own! The country respects him, and he deserves your respect as well."

Nigel poured himself a drink. After swallowing it down, he looked at how the light of the chandelier played upon his glass, and said, "So no, this all must stop now. Today! After all, one day he's going to be running this family."

Ceil pointed at Nigel in his face, "No, he will not run this family, or anything else! Not as long as I am living. I despise Nicolaus. He disgusts me! And you have no room to criticize, this is all your doing!"

Nigel slammed his glass down on the wet bar in their extensively large bedroom. "Look Ceil, I understand that your issues with Nicolaus are my fault. I acknowledge it, as I have done before. We have to get this smoothed out. Nicolaus is going to succeed me. We both know, between our two sons, it has to be Nicolaus."

"No! I will never agree to it. Never!"

"Ceil, why are you fighting this so? You heard Benjamin. He wants nothing to do with helping at the office or learning the business or running the business. Nicolaus has the brain for this, not Benjamin. Why is this so hard for you?"

Without answering, in a huff, Ceil turns her back to Nigel and walks out of the bedroom.

Chapter Nine

Two weeks later there is chattering of invited guests and some press figures inside the large conference room in the elaborate skyscraper with windowed walls that overlook the Lady Bird Lake in downtown Austin. Lady Bird Lake is named after Lady Bird Johnson, the first lady of the 36th United States president, Lyndon Baines Johnson, of Texas. Inside the luxury office building, the Villamae Medical Corporation headquarters is housed.

Nicolaus surprises Deirdre, as he gently twirls her to face him. As always, her beauty brings uncontrollable joy to him.

Deirdre gasps with delight. Her arms go around the man she loves. "Hey babe! When did you get here?"

Some members of the invited press rush over to take pictures of the couple. Nicolaus and Deirdre try to ignore them.

"Just now," Nicolaus tells her, "I couldn't wait to see you!" Nicolaus holds her by the waist with both hands, and looks into her eyes, wanting to whisk her away. "You ready for all of this? To be in the spotlight?"

Deirdre looks surprised at his questions, and gives a short sigh, "Seriously, babe … not really. But here we go!"

Nicolaus nods and smiles, and takes Deirdre's hands and kisses them. "I love you … so much. You look incredibly beautiful."

Deirdre notices the press, and gives him a quick frown and negative head shake, feeling bashful.

A well-known woman of the local press, Jeune Tran, rushes over to the couple, glad to get them alone, smiling. "Deirdre and Nicolaus, I wonder if you'd let me interview the both of you about your engagement, virginity, and pending marriage."

Nicolaus looks to Deirdre, then to the woman, and frowns a little. "Well ... I ... wouldn't really feel comfortable talking about that. I mean ... why would you want to write about that?"

Jeune picks up on his meaning, "Your virginity? Oh I think it's inspiring! It will be good for young people to have an example of waiting. You two are the perfect couple."

"Hmm, I don't know."

Deirdre touches Nicolaus on the chest, smiling at him, "I'll be glad to take care of it, honey." Then she turned to Jeune, "Yes, I understand your angle. Uhm, why don't you meet me at the bridal shop when I'm picking out my dress. And you can get pictures too!"

Jeune was surprised at her answer. She quickly nodded, "Oh, wow, thank you, that would be great!"

Deirdre chuckled, "Pictures of the shop and stuff, not the actual dress, right, cuz he can't see it yet," she giggled, while thumb pointing at Nicolaus.

Jeune smiled with her, still nodding, "Oh yes, of course." She gave her business card to Deirdre. "Here's my card, my name is Jeune Tran. Please, just call me when you are ready."

Deirdre takes the card, feeling excited about the prospect of helping young people, "Okay, no problem."

Nigel walks into the room with the confidence of success. All press members withdraw from Nicolaus and Deirdre to place attention to Nigel as he goes to the front of the room.

Deirdre turns to face Nicolaus again, "See honey, I'll take care of it!"

Nicolaus cannot resist kissing her hands again, wanting to kiss her mouth. "You complete me babe. I love you."

Deirdre whispers with a smile, "I know you do. I promise, we'll talk after I'm done here."

Their hands linger before parting.

Nigel stands before the crowd of people, next to the curved board room table, dressed in his expensive suit, as always. He signals for the room of staff, family, guests, and press to silence, and it does. The room is decorated with balloons, flowers, and expensive party favours.

Nigel looks for and finds his ladies amongst the crowd. Deirdre is smartly dressed in a tight black dress. Ceil wears an Italian designer mid-calf dress, and Rachel wears a berry coloured, sexy tight dress with a heart shaped bodice. Elsa, his assistant and Deirdre's close friend, is extremely clever, with a heart of gold, walks with high confidence and the essence of a fashion model. She is sharply dressed, with her flowing hair pulled back from her face, held by an elegant barrette. He smiles to see her attending the crowd.

"Thank you all for being here today," Nigel began, "This is our kick-off of Charity Week at Villamae Medical Corporation." The audience claps and cheers. "Yes, yes!! We are excited! I would like to turn your attention to Ms. Deirdre Omari, a brilliant lawyer, who is gracing us with time away from Senators Craig and Durban." With a smile, Nigel waives to the senators in the crowd, then continues. "Deirdre has put her talents towards our charity week events, and it doesn't hurt that one day she will officially be part of my family. Deirdre …." Nigel opens his arms to welcome Deirdre to the microphone. He kisses her cheek and steps behind her.

Deirdre steps up to the microphone. "Thank you, Mr. Ravenell, Pops!", she jokes with nervous laughter. The crowd responds with smiles and light laughter. "Welcome to all! Yes, as you know it is part of the VMC mission to provide resources to those who need our life saving services and may not be able to pay for it. VMC gives back to the community in a big way, every year. So, every penny we fund raise this week will go towards medical insurance for underprivileged people and uninsured children, to directly help communities we serve."

The audience claps, and heads are nodding at the noble work of the organization.

"Let me quickly run down our fundraising agenda of the week for you. We begin today with the annual *Clash of the Ravenells* at the Medieval Festival. Our very own Nicolaus and Benjamin will battle it out, for entertainment, of course. They have both been working really hard to be ready for today." Deirdre leads the audience to clap for the brothers.

"Then we have the *Walk in Her Shoes For a Day* event, where all the men of our corporate office will wear women's shoes all day! And just for fun, during lunch they have the *Save My Baby* challenge while wearing those shoes, they get to climb a fire truck ladder to save a baby doll from falling out of a window." The guest and press members gasp at the thought of such an event. Deirdre nods in understanding, "Yes, that is going to be great fun for us ladies to watch!" Laughter ensues throughout the room.

On Wednesday, we have our *Rocky Road Ice Cream Social* at the Eastside Community Centre, where all the Ravenell family will serve ice cream.

"Thursday is our *Golfing with the Stars Tournament,* at the Eastside Golf course, just off Martin Luther King road and Highway one-eighty-three.

And Friday night is our *Annual Charity Gala* at the Performing Arts Centre, and we do expect to have big name stars in attendance. We have received five hundred RSVPs, the largest number ever!" The audience claps, people smile, and there is some chatter. "Yes! We are so excited! We know this week will be a great success, and you are a part of helping us make it all happen! Thank you!" Deirdre turns and kisses Nigel on the face, handing him the microphone.

People in the audience clap, and then audience mingling begins.

Ceil is standing next to her sister, Rachel, who is looking across the room and smiling at Nigel. "What are you doing?"

Rachel is caught off guard by Ceil. Quickly, she snaps her thoughts from the past and sees her sister. She keeps her smile on her face, despite Ceil's look of hate.

"Stop looking at my husband like you want to devour him."

Rachel gasps, offended by her accusation, "I am not doing that!"

"Why are you even here, Rachel?"

Giving Ceil a surprised frown, "What? I attend every year! You know that, Ceil."

Nigel senses the trouble and quickly crosses the room. "Ladies, ladies, not here or now please. There are cameras and reporters all around us."

Both women sigh and stop talking to each other.

Rachel smiles at Nigel, "You look great Nigel! This place …" her hands spread about, "looks great! Really great!" Rachel beams with joy. She looks at Nigel with immense love.

"We can thank Deirdre and Elsa for that. They pulled it all together. Have done an incredible job. I think everyone will love the activities too!"

Nigel places a kiss to Rachel's forehead and grabs Ceil's hand. "Speaking of activities … we have to get going to the festival for the Ravenell Brawl!" Nigel holds Ceil by the hand and elbow, ushering her out the room, and towards the limo.

Deirdre watches and sees Nigel's signal that it is time to leave. Deirdre touches Elsa on the shoulder. "Elsa, I have to leave now. You remember what to do to close out, right?"

Elsa smiled at her, "Of course! Don't worry! I've got this! Tell Benji I wish him luck!"

Deirdre gives her a hug, and quickly catches up to Nigel as they leave the press in the conference room.

Chapter Ten

Nigel and Ceil are seated together at the back of the limo, across from Deirdre. Nigel takes a drink from his glass, while Ceil looks upon Deirdre with disdain.

"When do you plan on getting a real job?" Ceil goads Deirdre.

"Excuse me?" Deirdre says, as she frowns at Ceil in disbelief. She rolls her eyes and tries to ignore the rude question. It's the first thing Ceil has said to her since they were in the vehicle.

Ceil continues with her rudeness, "I'm sure you heard me dear. Your ears are working fine. When do you plan on getting a real job? A career. We have done a lot for your family, and I am ready for you to start carrying your weight."

Nigel interrupted his drink, "Ceil, please!" He touches Ceil's leg for her to stop, aware that Ceil picks on this child whenever she can.

"Mother Ceil, I have a real career. And I quite enjoy working at the state capital."

"No dear, that is not a real job! And stop calling me mother! You may call me Mrs. Ravenell!"

For a moment, Deirdre looks shocked, but then quickly removes the expression from her face, remembering Ceil's behaviour can be unpredictable, and threatening.

Ceil continues, as she wants to drive the spike home. "And I want you to stop hanging on my son all day. It's time for you to move on. I told you both, you do not have my permission to marry," she told her sternly.

Nigel frowns, shaking his head for her to stop, but said no words. He knew Ceil could not be serious.

Deirdre sits up straight with nervousness, deciding to do what Nicolaus has always warned her not to do ... confront Ceil Ravenell. Deirdre looks around the enclosed limo, and bites her lip, realizing this could get awkward. "Mother Ceil, I have never understood what the issue is between us. I truly love your son, and have for years. I have no doubt that we should be together for the rest of our lives. We want to be married. Somehow, it seems that you are against us being together."

Ceil gives a cold stare at Nigel, as if she were offended that Deirdre questioned her.

With the silence, Deirdre continued, "I have done my best to do everything I can for you. And ..."

Ceil interrupts, sitting forward as if she might pounce Deirdre, pointing a finger at her. "Let me stop you right there. Right there! First of all, how dare you even think you have done anything for us! On the contrary, it is us who have done for you. And if you don't know your facts, you best go check with your mommy. Secondly, you will only be part of this family if I choose for you to be a part of this family. This ain't no free for all, where you can just walk in and do whatever you want. Its whatever I say!"

Nigel grabs Ceil's arm and hand, to try to subdue her before things get out of hand, "Ceil, please ..."

Ceil jerks herself away, and continues. "And third, you do not have my permission to marry my son. Nicolaus will marry whom I say, when I say, and where I say. It is not up to either of you! That decision is up to me!"

Shock reigns over Deirdre again. She wasn't sure what to say. Words stutter, and stumble out of her mouth, as she fishes for an apology that she felt she didn't owe. "Well ... I ...I'm ... I wasn't ..."

Laughing to mask his embarrassment, Nigel pulls Ceil back to calm her. "It's okay Deirdre." Nigel laughs to try to ease the distress he saw on Deirdre's face. "This woman is like a lion with cubs, isn't she? She forgot to mention me! Didn't she?"

Ceil points at Nigel, wrestling out of his grip of her, scowling at him. She wants him to understand that she was not kidding. "I'm not playing! He will marry whom I say …"

"We both make such big decisions." Nigel pats Deirdre's leg to assure her. "Don't worry, you're on the very short list, and I'm pretty sure you will get that job too!" He winks at her to lighten the mood.

Deirdre sighs with a nervous smile, and feels awkward. She stares out the window at the passing vegetation and frowns in wonder if Nicolaus is aware that his mother is serious about picking his bride. She bites her lip, frowning, fearing the bride is not intended to be herself. Nigel asks about the itinerary, and Deirdre is relieved to go over every detail with them, as the limousine continues down the road to the Medieval festival.

Chapter Eleven

The Ravenell limousine pulls to the front gate of the festival grounds. Nigel exits the limo and assists Ceil and Deirdre out. They observe the happenings of diverse people, many of whom are wearing traditional medieval costumes. Many rush to the window to pay for tickets and enter the gate. There is also bustling activity over the whole Medieval festival fair grounds, shops, booths with trinkets, items and information for sell. To look down the road, it seems there are several hundred people walking along the fair grounds. A huge ferris wheel can be seen far away towards the back of the long stretch of street. Mostly adults of all ages are in attendance. Nigel, Ceil, and Deirdre are escorted through the entrance gate.

Benjamin and Nicolaus had already arrived and are preparing on opposite sides in the same area of the large event tent where they will compete. The audience begins to enter and take their seats for the charity event.

Both brothers are assisted by friends, backstage, to dawn their medieval under armour costumes. Nicolaus observes the props of a heavy shield and a fake sword. He notices the weight of the sword in his hand, and the thickness and heaviness of the shield. He frowns, then looks to his brother.

"This is kind of heavy," he tells Alexander, a bit worried.

"I heard they were specially ordered. Probably thought the two of you would enjoy having an authentic shield."

Nicolaus smiles, but then his worried look lands on Benjamin. "Yes, but, this may be too much for Benjamin."

"Awh, it's all in fun. It won't hurt him to get a taste of real military combat."

On the other side of the backstage, Benjamin slaps his friend's hands away and lightly shoves him.

Giggling, his friend informs him, "Odds are against you buddy!" He attempts to help Benjamin straighten his costume again, only to be shoved back.

Benjamin sees Nicolaus looking at him while speaking to Alexander. He assumes he is the subject of conversation. Agitated, Benjamin walks across the tent, up to his brother, ignoring Alexander. "I hope you are ready for me to kick your ass in front of everyone," he taunts Nicolaus to his face. "I'm so sick of you. I'm sick of being in your shadow! I'm sick of being compared to you! I'm sick …"

Nicolaus puts a strong hand to Benjamin's chest. "Benjamin, save it for out there."

Rudely, Benjamin slaps Nicolaus' hand away, and turns and goes back to his side of the tent, rejoining his friend.

"What the hell was that?" Alexander asked in dismay, watching Benjamin walkaway.

Nicolaus touches Alexander's shoulder to quiet him, while watching his brother throw a temper fit as the crowd noise grows louder and the announcer takes the stage. "Nervous energy. He is just trying to get ready."

The brothers are announced, and they enter the stage from the opposite ends of the tent. As they walk onto the stage, Medieval music is blasted over the loudspeakers. Nicolaus steps up to close the gap between them, and smiles with an attempt to hug his brother by the shoulders as the crowd noise is loud at this fundraising event. Benjamin pushes Nicolaus away, and gets into a fighting stance. The crowd cheers louder at his antics. The referee stands between the brothers, states the rules of the competition, lets the brothers shake, and the game begins.

In anger, Benjamin quickly lunges at Nicolaus, and misses because Nicolaus is quick on his feet, and he jumped out the way. Benjamin is driven by his anger to draw blood from his brother. He lunges at Nicolaus again, and misses when Nicolaus jumps back.

Nicolaus twirls around, and they clash their shields and grip each other in a muscle lock, pushing against each other, trying to knock the other off balance.

Nicolaus tries to offer brotherly advice, "Focus yourself Benjamin. Concentrate your anger into your moves."

Benjamin shoves Nicolaus off him. "I don't need your advice." Sweat is already pouring down his face, unlike Nicolaus, who appears calm and collected.

The brothers clash again. The crowd goes wild. Nigel, Ceil, and Deirdre are led to a VIP section, away from the crowd. They have great seats, and can clearly see Benjamin and Nicolaus through the glass in the air-conditioned luxury room.

"I am so sick of you!" In a dirty move, Benjamin delivers an unexpected punch to Nicolaus in his face, hitting his eye.

Nicolaus stumbles back, as punching is not part of the competition. The referee momentarily pushes Benjamin back. Nicolaus frowns at Benjamin, letting him have that cheap shot. As the competition resumes, Nicolaus stumbles again, as Benjamin uses an illegal move, kicking at Nicolaus' forever damaged knee.

Nicolaus shoves Benjamin away from him, and cries out in pain, "Awh!!"

He looks at Benjamin as if he is asking for war.

Deirdre's hand is over her mouth with more shock of the day, "Oh my God! Why did Benji kick Nicky in his bad knee?!"

Ceil smiles, and speaks over the loud crowd noise "Let's see if he can take Nicolaus down this year! I told him to play dirty!"

"No, Mother Ceil, he could really hurt Nicky!" Deirdre looks frowned, wanting to stop this whole thing, afraid of what might happen.

"Well ..." Ceil responded, not caring.

Deirdre sighed hard in frustration, "Ah!"

Nicolaus initiates the next clash, almost running through Benjamin. The brothers lock, and it quickly becomes clear who the stronger brother is, although there are crowd shouts and chants for each brother. Benjamin begins to buckle, but is not willing to go down so quickly. "No! I'm sick of everyone thinking you are better. You are NOT better than me!" In a clearly illegal and insane move, Benjamin headbutts Nicolaus.

The crowd cheers turn to gasps. The referee blows his whistle, but the brothers ignore him. Nicolaus is stunned that Benjamin would headbutt him. He throws down his sword, and wipes the blood he sees dripping from his forehead. In anger, Nicolaus throws down the shield, as he understands Benjamin wants a real fight. He beckons Benjamin forward with hand gestures after getting into fighting position.

"Oh no!" even Nigel sees this is going too far.

The referee blows his whistle again, and stands between the brothers.

Benjamin also throws down his gear, and lunges for Nicolaus after knocking the referee to the ground. Benjamin makes contact with Nicolaus' torso. They both go backward, falling onto the ground.

The crowd goes wild again, as now this has turned into a wrestling match. Benjamin tries to throw punches at Nicolaus, but they are blocked by Nicolaus' forearms. Nicolaus wrestles himself on top of Benjamin, not letting him get anywhere through his kicking, jerking, and maneuvering. When Benjamin tires himself out, Nicolaus pulls him to his feet, and swings him to the other side of the stage. Limping on his hurt leg, Nicolaus goes after Benjamin, to teach him the lesson he asked for. Nicolaus delivers one punch then another.

Ceil stands in upset, "That brute!" she says of Nicolaus.

Just then, the unmistakable sound of gunfire is heard ringing through the stands. Everyone stops, and looks around. A man is standing on the stage with a long barrel shot gun pointed into the air. Suddenly, loud screams are heard from the crowd, and then everyone scatters from the bleachers. Chaos, confusion, and extreme fear is within the people as they run for their lives.

Security guards quickly enter the VIP room, "Mr. and Mrs. Ravenell, we must go! This way please!" Without hesitation or argument, Nigel, Ceil and Deirdre follow security. Deirdre tries to turn back to see Nicolaus, but is ushered on by the security guard. The crowd is still scattering.

The gunman focuses his attention on Benjamin, who has now taken cover behind a podium that had been moved to the side of the stage. Nicolaus is close to Benjamin to protect him. "Benjamin Ravenell," he yelled, "you are never going to sleep with my wife again ... or anyone else's wife. I'm gonna make sure of that!" The gunman points his gun towards the two brothers. With quick thinking, Nicolaus grabs the discarded shield, just as the next shot rings out. Benjamin hides behind the podium, with his head exposed just enough to watch as Nicolaus walks towards the firing gun without fear.

With angry adrenaline, Nicolaus uses the shield to deflect each bullet fired from the gun until he is close enough, then sends the shield like a gigantic frisbee disk towards the gunman.

The shield hits the gunman knocking him to the ground. In an instant, Nicolaus is on top of the guy, and puts his arm over his neck, shocking him and making his breathing difficult, but not enough to kill him, just enough to subdue him.

"Drop the gun, you bastard," Nicolaus demands, "Drop it!"

The gunman's arm is outstretched on the ground. His hand opens and the gun drops as Nicolaus applies pressure to his neck.

"What the hell is wrong with you, firing that gun in a crowd of people at a fundraiser?" Nicolaus continues with anger, "I should rip your head off right here with my bear hands!"

Several security officers arrive on the scene. One of the officers runs over and kicks the gun away, out of reach range of the gunman. It takes two security men to pull Nicolaus off the gunman. Another two security officers grab the man and lift him off the ground to detain him. Nicolaus struggles against the security officers before he gets ahold of his emotions.

"Okay, sir, thank you, we've got it from here," the officer tells him. Nicolaus continues to struggle against them. "Sir, sir," he yells to get Nicolaus' attention, "we have it, thank you," he tells him sternly. "Thank you, Major, thank you." He recognized Nicolaus' military rank, knowing it would get him to calm down.

Nicolaus calms himself. He turns to check on Benjamin. "Benjamin, Benjamin," he calls. There is no answer, and no sight of Benjamin. Nicolaus limp jogs to the outside of the tent area. He sees police cars and the press arriving. He sees Deirdre and his parents, and goes over to them, glad to see they are okay. "Where is Benjamin?"

Deirdre shakes her head, "Benji saw us and then he just took off running."

Nicolaus looks around for Benjamin. There was no sign of him. He attends to the police officers on the scene who need to talk to him about what transpired, as others are interviewed as well. Nigel handles the press.

Chapter Twelve

Later at the Ravenell mansion, Nicolaus happens to be near the foyer in the front room when Benjamin returns home. Benjamin seems okay and smells inebriated, with a scantily clad woman on his arm. Benjamin becomes immediately bothered when he sees Nicolaus. Nicolaus, however, wants to confront Benjamin as soon as he sees him. Benjamin sends the woman up the stairs ahead of him, and instructs her to wait.

She flirts with the handsome Nicolaus on her way up the stairs, "Well, hello there." Knowing who Nicolaus is, she eyes him, and gets close to him in passing.

"Hello." Nicolaus tells her, saying no more, unless she continued the conversation.

She does not. She floats up the stairs with a sexy hip switch, following Benjamin's instructions.

It is well after midnight. The brothers look pitiful as they both have cuts and bruises on their faces, and Nicolaus has an ice pack strapped to his knee. The liquor wreaks strongly on Benjamin, as they stand in the corridor in front of the huge heart shaped staircase.

Nicolaus grabs his dishevelled brother by the arm. "What the hell happened out there today, Benjamin? Who was that man with the gun?" he asks, deeply frowning.

Returning the deep frown, Benjamin aggressively pushes Nicolaus' large frame to release himself, "Get off me, man! I mean what I said. I'm sick of you, man!" Benjamin stumbles, having trouble standing.

"Jesus, Benjamin, I hope you didn't drive yourself home," Nicolaus is not liking this behaviour in his brother.

"Don't fucking try to tell me what … what to do," his words slur as he half yells at Nicolaus.

Nicolaus is still frowning, "Benjamin, why are you so angry with me? What's going on with you?"

Benjamin sighs to calm himself down. Afterall, Nicolaus did save his life earlier today. He does owe his brother an explanation. "I'm just sick of being in your shadow. Okay?" he says through gritted teeth, with less animosity.

"Yeah, you said that earlier. You're not in my shadow!"

"I am in your shadow!" he yells, feeling himself ready to go off again.

Nicolaus sighs, ignoring his statement, wanting to get to what occurred today. "Why was that man coming after you with a gun? He was arrested, but I was not allowed to talk to him." Lowering his voice, not to offend Benjamin's lady friend, "He said something about you sleeping with his wife. Is it true...what he said?"

Benjamin shrugs his shoulders, not answering. "Why did you even save me?"

Nicolaus frowned, "What? You just want me to stand around and watch while some guy pumps bullets into you? Well, that's not going to happen." He steps towards his brother. "Benjamin …"

"You should have let him shoot me."

Nicolaus frowned, feeling helpless. He wanted to give Benjamin a hug, but could see he wasn't open to such a gesture. "Benjamin, come on ….. Now I know something is wrong! You're drinking too much!" Instead of trying to hug his brother, he puts his hand on Benjamin's shoulder. "Talk to me." He wanted to reach Benjamin. He knew he needed it.

However, Benjamin pushes Nicolaus away again. "No! I'm not one of your little soldiers you can order about. Just leave me the fuck alone!" Benjamin yells at him, then storms out the corridor, and up the stairs.

Nicolaus sighs, confused, not understanding what is going on. He has a worried look on his face, as he watches Benjamin stumble up the stairs, and harshly grab the woman by the waist, whisking her off to his bedroom.

Chapter Thirteen

The next day was busy and frenzied for the Ravenell family. The In Her Shoes fundraiser was to begin at eleven in the morning, so preparations had to begin early. Since the VMC offices were on the top floors of the high rise where the headquarters resided, Deirdre had arranged the rental of windowed offices on the second floor, not too high off the ground.

Two fire truck ladders lifted up into the open building windows. Below in line, were brave men, stern in their masculinity, standing in women's heels, ready to climb the ladder to save a baby doll, after having paid their donation. Nigel and Dwight are the first men to climb on the fire truck ladders in heels. Staff and women below laugh, but also cheer them on, as unbalanced, but carefully they climb.

There are two open windows, side by side, divided by wall space, to the same office suite. Nicolaus and Deirdre are in one window to hand the baby doll to the participant. Ceil, Elsa, and Benjamin are in the other window.

Nigel and Dwight receive the baby doll, and hold it up for the crowd to see. The crowd below cheer enthusiastically. Then begrudgingly, they climb back down the ladders muffling statements of being too old for this type of activity.

Movement of people climbing up the ladders and arriving at the window is about every ten minutes with the fire fighters responsible for the people on the ladders. During down time, Deirdre and Nicolaus are flirting and kissing, getting on Ceil's nerves. Nicolaus whispers in Deirdre's ear, making her laugh. He embraces her from behind and kisses her neck. Deirdre lovingly cackles.

Benjamin obsessively watches Deirdre. Eventually, Deirdre notices Benjamin and suddenly grows shy, as he makes her feel uncomfortable.

Elsa watches Benjamin with a prang of jealousy, as she is determined to have more than a light touch of flirt from Benjamin. Elsa is ready to reveal her secret devotion and strong attraction to Benjamin. She taps him on the shoulder, and meets his turn with a smile. "You know, if you are truly pining for a woman, I am so available to you!" Elsa pulls herself into Benjamin to whisper in his ear, so Ceil could not hear. "I would do anything for you Benji. Anything."

Benjamin looks at Elsa and playfully grabs her into his arms. He breathes the perfume on her neck, with his eyes on Deirdre, and places a gentle kiss on her cheek, as if to save her for later, then releases her. He then goes back to staring at Deirdre with heightened desire.

Nicolaus looks back and sees Benjamin staring at them. Frowning, "You okay, Benjamin?" Benjamin does not move or answer. "Benjamin, what's wrong?"

Ceil quickly snaps at Nicolaus, "Enough of that! Mind your business! Leave him alone!

Maybe like me, he is sick of seeing you and Deirdre carry on in an inappropriate manner!"

Nicolaus gives a "I'm sorry." He looks at Deirdre with love, "I have an indelible need to hug this woman!" They chuckle together and give each other a peck kiss.

Nicolaus cools down his attention to Deirdre, and attends to the man that made it to the window. Benjamin also tends to the man at his window. During another down time, Benjamin stares at Deirdre again. He wants her to feel him, although he knows it makes her uncomfortable.

Nicolaus walks over to him, and stands before his eyes, not liking his behaviour. "What's wrong with you Benjamin? Did you get hurt yesterday?"

Ceil steps between the brothers, as if they were fighting. "Enough of this I said Nicolaus. Leave him alone!"

Nicolaus does what is asked of him.

After another three sets of men, an angry man wanting revenge appears in Benjamin's window. In pretence of reaching for the baby doll, he punches Benjamin in his face, landing himself inside the window, on top of Benjamin. Nicolaus sees this, and stands to wait to see what will happen.

The angry man punches Benjamin several times in his stomach and torso, naming women for each punch. "This is for Annette." Next punch is to Benjamin's eye, "And for Mandy." The next punch is to his torso, "And for Barbara." The punches are too much for Benjamin. He cannot recover to defend himself. He takes each punch. Each blow makes him weaker. "And for Hattie."

In anguished haste, Ceil signals to Nicolaus, waiving her arms for him to help, "Don't just stand there, you fool, help him!"

Nicolaus shrugs his shoulders and sighs. He effortlessly grabs the man around his neck and shoulders and pulls him off Benjamin. With his full strength, he pulls the angry man, who is now huffing and tired, to the other side of the room. Nicolaus holds him back as he tries to go after Benjamin again.

"Stop it!" Nicolaus shouts at him, slamming him against the wall to get his attention. "What's going on?"

The angry man sees Nicolaus, and seems to now be broken. His arms are restricted by Nicolaus, but he tries to point to Benjamin, his voice breaking, as if he might cry now, "He's been having an affair with my wife." The angry man sighs heavy, then shouts, "My wife!

And has tricked my daughters!"

Nicolaus sighs hard. He looks at his brother, frowning. He returns his attention to the angry man, shaking him to calm him down, "All right, all right! Are you sure?"

"Yes!" he shouts. "Of course, I'm sure! Its him," he tries to point to Benjamin again with restricted movements, as Nicolaus has not let up on him. "That's Benjamin Ravenell. It's him." Suddenly, the man gets emotional, and sinks to the floor. Nicolaus lets him slide to the floor, but remains before him, so he would not get away or harm anyone else.

Security rushes into the office suite, after hearing the commotion. "We've got this sir!"

Nicolaus looks at the security guard, "Hey, you didn't notice him before he came up the ladder?"

"Sorry sir! Nothing seemed out of the ordinary."

As the security guard helped the man up to his feet, and detained him, taking the man out of the office, another security guard rushed in.

Ceil is on the floor, next to a wreathing Benjamin, crying for him, as if he were a child who was horribly hurt. "Oh, my Benjamin. My Benjamin."

Nicolaus walks over, as Deirdre tries to help.

Ceil lashes out at them, as if she is unhinged, "Get away from him!! Get away!!"

Nicolaus puts his hands up, and pulls Deirdre away. "Get my brother an ambulance," he tells the security guard. The guard nods and makes the call. After Benjamin is transported, with Ceil and Elsa by his side, Deirdre and Nicolaus finish the time left for the fundraiser.

Chapter Fourteen

The following morning, the Ravenell family members are eating breakfast in the luxurious family breakfast room. Deirdre and Francesca are present, both sitting on either side of Nicolaus.

Benjamin is present with the girl Nicolaus met the other night; however, the other family members have not seen her before. Despite she still being scantily clad, and overly attentive to Benjamin, kissing his facial bruises, Benjamin does not bother to introduce her. It's obvious he does not intend to keep this young lady around. As this is Benjamin's normal behaviour, of which Ceil does not approve, no one takes him to task for courtesy.

"I'm sorry, I didn't get your name," Francesca loudly asks in her heavy British accent of the half-naked woman who is busy touching on Benjamin.

The loudness of Francesca's voice got her attention. "Hmmm, oh, my name is Andy. Short for Andrea." She nods, "Nice to meet you."

Francesca looks at her strangely, wondering if she understands that Benjamin thinks she's a toy to be thrown away.

Nicolaus sees her reaction and touches her arm with a slight head shake and a soft "Hm hum", so that she doesn't get in the middle of it.

Francesca rolls her eyes and sighs. Suddenly, Francesca presents two jars of ointment, one for each brother. "I made some natural ointments for your cuts and bruises, after the festival fight, I thought you might need it." Francesca touches the large bruise on Nicolaus' forehead, and his bruised eye. Like a warrior, he does not cringe, though his injuries are sore. "I heard you two were really going after each other. Not exactly what that charity fundraiser is supposed to be about," she chastised them.

Nicolaus looks at the ointment. He smiles at Francesca, ignoring her statement. "Thank you, Francesca." He places the jar in front of his plate, and Benjamin does the same, thanking Francesca. Nicolaus continued, "Father, we really need to rethink the security set up for these charity events. We especially need more detail around Benjamin."

Deirdre nods in agreement. "And there will be a lot of celebrities at the golf tournament tomorrow."

Ceil starts in on Nicolaus, "What makes you think you are in charge of security?

Or anything when it comes to my Benjamin?"

Nicolaus is slightly shocked at her question, "Wow! Well … considering I had to save Benjamin … from a gunman … that actually intended to kill him, and after what happened yesterday, I think I should have some say in the matter."

"This is all your fault! You bring out the worst in your brother."

Nicolaus looks at Ceil in disbelief, "Ah! How is this my fault?" He frowned, "I'm not the one running around town womanizing at any chance that presents itself," agitated, he directed the words towards Benjamin.

Benjamin stops toying with Andrea and looks up at Nicolaus, but says nothing.

Ceil was not going to let Nicolaus get away with that remark, "You think you're so smart. Coming in here, and ordering people around, like we are your little army. You think you have all the answers."

Nicolaus shakes his head, "No, I'm concerned about Benjamin's safety, mother! We need better security to protect him. Frankly, to protect everyone, because of his behaviours."

Nigel clears his throat loudly, "Yes, Nicolaus, I was thinking the same thing."

With offensive anger, Benjamin stands, angrily looking at Nicolaus, then looks at Deirdre, and leaves the room in silence, pulling Andrea behind him by her arm.

"Now look what you've done!" Ceil yells at Nicolaus. She throws her cloth napkin onto the table and leaves the room to follow after Benjamin.

"But Auntie Ceil …," Francesca calls out.

"Francesca, just let her go," Nicolaus tells her.

"But she forgot to thank you for saving her precious Benji. You both could've gotten shot!"

"Wouldn't be the first time for me."

Deirdre looked shocked, never having heard about this, "What Nicky? You've been shot before?"

Nicolaus nods.

Nigel looks at him stunned as well, "Son …?"

Deirdre touches his arm in concern, frowning, "Nicky, you've never told us."

"I know. I'm fine."

In Francesca fashion, without missing a beat, "Who the fuck are you? I feel like I don't even know you anymore! You're a fucking cyborg."

Nicolaus chuckles, "Francesca, I'm not a cyborg."

"A fucking shape shifter?"

They all burst out in laughter at her scientific fantasy references. Nicolaus points at Francesca playfully, "Francesca, stop."

"Uncle Nigel, you need to call Manfred," Francesca tells him.

"Who's Manfred?" Nicolaus asks.

"He was part of my security detail while I was abroad. He's damn good! A Native American that doesn't miss a thing! You can trust him with your life!"

Nigel nods, "Yes, I think you're right. I'll contact him today. Nicolaus, I know it's a big ask, but I want you in charge of security, despite what your mother says."

"Well, yeah!" Francesca agrees.

"Father, I ..."

Deirdre nods in agreement, touching Nicolaus' arm.

"Okay. I'll do my best."

Deirdre smiles, "We know. And your best will be more than enough."

Chapter Fifteen

Later the same day is the Ice Cream Social fundraiser at the Eastside Community Centre. There are lines of people with money in hand, ready to donate to the cause.

The Ravenell family are stationed at the tables, each with hats, plastic aprons, and gloves to serve up the ice cream. Elsa is at the front of the line, receiving the money. Nicolaus rearranged the set up so that people pay one by one, before approaching the table for ice cream. He also hoped this would help with crowd control.

Nicolaus stands next to Ceil on his right, and Benjamin to his left. Nigel is to the right of Ceil. Deirdre was away making preparations for the golf tournament.

People are courteous and all is going well until an upset woman appears before Benjamin. Her name is Marcy, a strikingly beautiful woman with dark braided hair and dark skin. She receives her ice cream from Benjamin, but does not take her eyes from him, as if she is waiting for something. "Benji, don't you remember me?"

Benjamin smiles nervously, trying to recall this woman's name. "Ah ...sure ... ah!"

"Benjamin, you don't remember me?"

Giving up, Benjamin smiles and shakes his head, "I'm sorry. I can't place you."

Marcy squinches an eye with a slight head tilt, "You were just with me, Monday night."

Benjamin gives her a blank stare, trying to remember. That was the night he was very drunk, after the man with the gun tried to shoot him, before he went to the bar to pick up Andrea.

Marcy grows angrier at his blank stare. "You don't remember? You promised we'd go to Vegas to get married. We were supposed to leave today," she says louder, to make him remember.

"Okay, okay, I remember." Benjamin touches her arm, "calm down."

"What's my name Benjamin?" Marcy folds her arms and waits for his answer.

Other people are getting their ice cream from Nigel and Nicolaus. Nicolaus sighs and watches the interaction, waiting for the trouble to follow. Ceil starts to move from her station to assist Benjamin. Nicolaus' hand is quick to her forearm to prevent her from moving, then he whispers, "Mother, let it be. There are too many people to make a scene. Just let it play out."

Ceil tries to jerk her arm away from Nicolaus, but smoothly, without incident, he won't let her jerk away from him.

Marcy gets louder, frowning, now tapping her foot, "You can't remember my name? Maybe that's why you didn't call me like you said you would?"

Benjamin realizes Marcy is very upset with him, and that he probably did do something along the lines of what she is saying, however, he cannot remember. "Please, I'm sorry, just give me your number again, and I will …"

With great anger Marcy slaps her ice cream in Benjamin's face, turns and leaves.

Humiliated, Benjamin turns from the crowd of onlookers who gasp.

With all her might, Ceil jerks herself away from Nicolaus' hold. "Don't you ever touch me like that again!" she tells him angrily. She leaves her station to attend to Benjamin.

Nigel and Nicolaus keep working the crowd.

The next woman steps forward, "I would rather have my ice cream served by you, any day, babe!" she tells Nicolaus. "Can I have a picture with you?"

"Sure!" The woman uses her phone to take a selfie with Nicolaus.

The next woman is bolder towards Nicolaus, "How about a kiss?"

Nicolaus shrugs with a smile, "Sure!" The woman kisses Nicolaus on the cheek.

Suddenly, women toss their money into Elsa's hands, breaking the line, they crowd rush over for their turn with the handsome Nicolaus Ravenell.

Nigel giggles, shakes his head with pride, and keeps serving.

Chapter Sixteen

Later that evening, Deirdre enters the sitting room alone and sees Benjamin standing with a scantily clad woman. Surprisingly, this woman is different from the woman who had breakfast with them. Benjamin, unashamedly has his hands all over this woman, as he intensely gazes upon her seductively.

"Oh, I'm so sorry. I didn't mean to interrupt. I wasn't aware …."

Benjamin looks at Deirdre delightfully, and quickly responds, "Don't be silly. Please," he reaches for Deirdre's hand and nods at the woman to dismiss her.

Deirdre takes Benjamin's hand, as he pulls her to sit next to him. Not letting go of her hand and without hesitation, he takes her delicate hand to his lips, and gently and lingeringly kisses it, peering into her eyes. His seductive mood has not changed. Benjamin takes Deirdre's other hand, and he looks upon her with gladness for having her to himself. As he kisses her other hand, arousal is about him. Deirdre gets uncomfortable and takes her hands from him.

"You were looking for me?" Benjamin continues, not taking his eyes from her.

"Yes, actually. Nicolaus is very worried about you."

Benjamin slightly shakes his head, "Let's not talk about Nicolaus. What about you, Deirdre?"

Deirdre takes a breath, knowing she has to be careful. She nods with a smile, "Yes, actually, I am worried about you too, Benji. Are you okay? I mean, really, okay?" she touches his torso, and then his face, thinking he must be sore, seeing the bruises.

Benjamin smiles, and takes her hand to kiss it again, "Better, now that you are here."

"Tell me what I can do for you at the golf tournament."

Benjamin sighs with a smile, still holding her hand. "Marry me."

Deirdre rolls her eyes. Not this again! "Benji." Her tone implies she wants him to be serious.

Benjamin draws closer to Deirdre and is intoxicated with the beautiful smell of her. Being close to Deirdre, he does not hide his increased desire for her. "Do you realize how much I truly love you? You have no idea how much I want to make love to you ... what I want to do to you ... to please you."

Deirdre fears the uptick in his behaviour, and gets nervous, as he is suddenly upon her. His arms are wrapped around her.

"Benji." She begins the struggle of trying to get out of his arms. As Deirdre struggles against Benjamin, she has somehow ended up on his lap, in his cobra grip, her back against him. He deeply kisses her neck, sending chills through her, making her breathe hard, while his hand squeezes her breast. "Benji, stop" she protests, "Let me go now."

Suddenly, Benjamin releases her. Deirdre jumps from his lap and quickly leaves the room. Benjamin watches her leave, and smiles naughtily at her reaction.

Meanwhile, across town, at the exact same time that Benjamin is assaulting Deirdre, Nicolaus and Manfred meet with the security team to increase the security detail for Benjamin's safety.

Nicolaus started off with positivity, hoping to get the men more aware of their duties. "Hey guys, I really appreciate the good job you are doing making these events safe for everyone attending. I am a little concerned about my brother, though, with these attacks on him lately. Tomorrow's golf tournament is a huge deal. There will be lots of important people, celebrities and the press."

Manfred reiterates, "It's going to be important that we tighten up security."

The men agreed, "We understand, Sir," the Security Lead was the voice for the group.

"Great, because I have a bad feeling something may happen," Nicolaus told them.

"So, tell me, what can we do about communication if something should happen?"

"Sir, we usually communicate by phone. We call if there is a problem."

Nicolaus shakes his head in disagreement. "If something is happening on the eighteenth hole, and you guys are at the entrance, or the exit, or God knows where, I'm supposed to call?" He shakes his head again. "That's not efficient guys. What can we do differently?"

"Well, we can wand everyone as they enter, and check all purses for gun safety," one guard offered up.

Nicolaus nodded, wide eyed, thinking they were going to do that anyway, "That would be smart. Let's keep that in the plan. What else? What about communication? We need to keep it simple."

The security staff look to each other for ideas, but none voiced one. They were stuck on the idea of their cell phone communications.

"What about walkie talkies, guys?" Nicolaus offered. "I know it sounds cheesy, but they work. It's easy, and efficient for such a large area. They work off the same towers as the cell phone technology."

Manfred agreed, "Walkie Talkies may be cheesy, but having them will be helpful.

And we will have more than one channel of communication."

The Security Lead nodded, "Yeah. But we don't have any."

"I'll get 'em. And set 'em. Let's just meet thirty minutes early to have a practice run," Nicolaus told them.

"Yes sir! Not a problem!" the Security Lead was glad for the solution, and figured it would work.

"Let's make sure my fiancée's event goes smoothly, and that my brother or others don't get hurt."

"Yes sir!"

Chapter Seventeen

Nicolaus and Deirdre were to meet for dinner at eight that night. Nicolaus arrives at the famous Eastside Eatery restaurant just as he saw Deirdre's car pull up. Nicolaus drove his black American sports car into the space just behind Deirdre's car. He jumps out, and meets Deirdre at her sports car, and opens the door for her. He helps her out, and places a kiss on her forehead.

Nicolaus frowns, sensing something is wrong. "Babe, you okay?"

Deirdre nods, "I'm fine," she lied to him, again. She was shaken after the second sexual assault of Benjamin. How could she possibly tell Nicolaus about what Benjamin was doing? She was afraid if Nicolaus knew, he'd kill him. Literally, kill him.

Nicolaus frowned, not liking this. It was the second time he knew she was putting him off. He hoped if he pushed a little, she would tell him. "Honey, I know you. What's happened?"

Deirdre touches his face, hoping to convince him, "Nothing. I'm fine."

"Did my mother say something inappropriate to you again?"

Deirdre shakes her head, wishing he'd drop it, "I'm just tired … and … worried about Benji."

Nicolaus jumped right on her words, "Benjamin?" He frowns with a head tilt, "Did Benjamin do something to you? Is he talking smack to you? Did he touch you or hurt you? I know he's been behaving strangely towards you."

There it was, that thing that frightened her about telling him what Benjamin was really up to. Deirdre touches Nicolaus' chest, "No, no, nothing like that," she lied, yet again.

Nicolaus took ahold of Deirdre's arms and looked into her eyes, "Deirdre … you'd tell me if something was happening, right?" He sensed something was occurring. It worried him.

"Oh, it's nothing like that. I'm just … worried about him, that's all."

"Okay," he held her to him, feeling unsettled. "I'm worried about him, too."

Deirdre was glad to be in his arms, as it made her regret of lying to him, ease a little. "I'm sure it will all work out."

"Well, let's try to get through the next few days, and then we can work on Benjamin." Deirdre nods, and Nicolaus places another kiss to her forehead, making her warm inside.

They enter the restaurant, and are immediately recognized by staff and patrons who waive to them, but no one bothers them. Their mood lightens as they place their order.

"I'm so excited that Mr. Havenshire, himself, is catering our gala tomorrow night."

"Honey, I know these next few events are going to be big! I made some security changes, and …"

Deirdre touches Nicolaus' chest, "Whatever you think best. You know I completely trust your judgment."

Nicolaus smiles, "You're something else, lady!" He kisses her face, and gently and lovingly kisses the side of her mouth. They are interrupted by plates of barbecue chicken and chicken fried steak. "Wow! This is great! Thank you so much!" he tells the server.

The couple begins to eat. Taking in the moment, Nicolaus admires Deirdre with great love.

"I love you," he tells her sweetly.

Deirdre feels like she wants to cry tears of joy at his sincere words. She gently touches his face. "Nicky, you are so wonderful. I can't believe you've waited ten years to be with me," she tells him again. "In all this time, not once have you ever stepped out on me with someone else, or even tried to force yourself on me."

"No, never! I would never hurt you like that."

Deirdre chuckles to keep from crying, "I'm sure you've had plenty of opportunities to be with another woman, and ..."

Nicolaus interrupts her, frowning, "Where is this coming from? If you want me to wait longer, I'll wait longer. All that matters to me is that we are together. That you be my wife, and always in my life. I'd never make it without you, babe."

"I just ..."

Nicolaus takes Deirdre's hand, and looks her in the eyes. "No. No, it's only you."

He looks down, then returns his gaze to her eyes. "Stop worrying." He kisses her hand gently. "My dream will come true on our wedding day." He smiles, then gently kisses her face again.

Deirdre sighs to relieve stress. "You know, your mother is definitely against us getting married. She seems very adamant about it. She made it very clear to me."

"Trust me, it's not about you, it's about me. As beautiful as my mother is, I have never understood why she hates me so much. It's always been that way with her, as far back as I can remember. But you know what? We are not going to worry about her. We are not going to listen to anything she spews at us. My father loves you, and wants you to be part of the family."

"Nicky, I just think that … sometimes when a woman says things, you have to listen. Your mother believes she's in control of you."

"But she has always found the opposite to be true."

"I don't know, Nicky. She was pretty adamant."

"Don't worry babe. It will be okay. We are getting married."

Chapter Eighteen

Nigel saw how upset Ceil was, and he was sure she was upset about Nicolaus.

She seemed to be more obsessed with Nicolaus, than usual, despising his every move.

"Ceil," he called her gingerly, "you okay?" sitting next to her on their luxurious bed.

"No, I'm not actually. Did you see how Nicolaus man handled me today? He let that woman embarrass my Benjamin." She crossed her arms as she mulled over events.

"Now Ceil, it's a little disingenuous to say Nicolaus man handled you. Isn't it?"

"He grabbed my arm …"

"He held your arm. Hmhum. But you know, he was right. There were too many people for things to get out of hand. Better for there to be one incident, than all those ladies jumping in to defend her, then we'd have a brawl on our hands. Anyway, perhaps Benjamin deserved a little embarrassment, to the least, after what he did to that young lady."

Ceil frowned at Nigel, unable to defend Benjamin's actions. Suddenly, she flicked her arm in the air in frustration. "Ah, this is all too much! That girl has scheduled too many events, too much public exposure, too much …"

"Okay, okay," Nigel put his arm around Ceil, drawing her up to him. She didn't resist. She seemed tired, and laid her head on his shoulder. Nigel kissed her forehead. "I'll tell you what, why don't you sit out the golf tournament tomorrow. Let us men handle everything."

Ceil nodded, taking Nigel's hand in hers. She felt a headache settling over her.

"Yes, I was thinking that." She sighed, "And you can bond with Benjamin, and think about which leadership position you want to place him in to help you run the company."

Nigel cringed his teeth, frowning, hoping they were not going down this road again. "Well, okay," he simply said, hoping she'd drop the idea. He kissed her head again. "Why don't you get into bed?" He assisted her in standing, and walked her to the head of the bed. "What can I get you, dear?"

"Bourbon please," she touched her head, "I'm not feeling well."

"Of course."

Nigel left her presence, and Ceil got into bed. She couldn't stop thinking about how she wanted to get back at Nicolaus for what he did today. How dare him think he can just grab her, and stop her. Her thoughts of vengeance against Nicolaus were growing exponentially each day. She knew whatever plan she came up with, had to be cunning. Now that she wouldn't be rid of him since he was not re-enlisting, and she could not get Nigel to send him away, she would have to come up with something that would drive him off.

She'd been through more than enough raising him, after Nigel brought him home when he was a baby, and insisted that she take care of him. Imagine that! Asking her, the matriarch of this family with a royal blood line, to take care of his illegitimate child, he'd conceived with her own sister. It wasn't her fault that Rachel hadn't the wits about her to care for her own child. Nigel had sworn Ceil to secrecy, not wanting Nicolaus to know what really happened. She knew one day, when the time was right, she would tell Nicolaus the truth, and watch his face melt into confusion and hurt. But now was not that time. She had to come up with a plan that would be shrewd, something he would be forced to endure, and be unable to untangle.

Nigel arrived with her bourbon. Ceil swallowed the two ounces with a head throw back, and settled down for sleep to encase her. The blood throughout her body immediately began to warm, placing a smile on her face. Soon she drifted to sleep.

Chapter Nineteen

The golfing tournament was held at the Eastside Golf Grounds the next afternoon. Many celebrities from all over the country attended to help raise money for the VMC cause. It also didn't hurt that Deirdre makes plenty of celebrity connections through her work for the senators. As the start time of the tournament drew near, many celebrities arrived by limousine, some drove themselves, while others made a rowdy entrance on motorcycles.

Nigel, Nicolaus, Benjamin, Dwight, and Alexander stand together on the golfing green, greeting everyone as they arrived and were getting ready to play. Several outlets of press are present, and are set up on the putting green for this great human-interest story.

Hundreds of everyday people, who didn't mind paying one thousand dollars a ticket, have entered the tournament for a chance to golf with celebrities. Mingling has already begun.

Suddenly, just about tee time, a man appears before the Ravenell men. He is holding a golf club as if it were a baseball bat, and without words, he begins swinging it wildly, though directed at Benjamin, trying to hit him. The crowd of Ravenell men jump back as the man continues to go after Benjamin.

The man aims the club at Benjamin's back. "You scoundrel!" he yells at Benjamin. "You took advantage of my Maddie, and my daughter Anita!" he yelled for all to hear.

Just as the swing comes towards him, Benjamin moves out the way, the club just missing him. Without hesitation, the man aims the swing of the club for Benjamin's head, but misses again.

Benjamin moves away from the line, dodging the swinging club. The man is determined to get Benjamin. Smartly, Benjamin takes off running away from the crowd.

The man pursues him, shouting obscenities while chasing him. "Come back here you fucking coward. Stand and fight, like a man! You can fuck my wife and daughter on the same day, but you can't fight?"

Shaking his head in a controlled pissed mood, Nicolaus pulls a walkie talkie from his back pocket and reaches security. He turns from the crowd to talk, keeping his eyes on the scene. "Where are you guys? A man is attacking my brother. He's being chased by a guy who wants to hurt him with a golf club."

Manfred rushes over to Nicolaus' side, as he sees what is happening.

Nicolaus listens to the walkie talkie, not liking what he is hearing. "What's your ETA, guys?"

Sighing, Nicolaus turns to Manfred, and hands him the walkie talkie. He then nods to Alexander, and at full speed, they take off running after the two men. The man swinging the club cannot catch Benjamin, but he still swings the club, trying to hit him. All actions on the green have stopped, as the press records the event, and guests and celebrities watch the scene. Nicolaus charges, and takes the man down to the ground in a tackle made for the game of football. The man fights to get up, but Nicolaus and Alexander hold him down until security arrives. Manfred radios in their location.

The crowd loudly cheers them. "Now that's excitement!" a celebrity golfer comments.

Security finally arrives and detains the man. As Nicolaus and Alexander return to their fathers, they are encircled and greeted by the golfers, and rounds of drinks are bought at the mobile sidebars. With great embarrassment, Benjamin slinks away, while Nigel satisfies the questions of the press, as the golf tournament gets underway.

As the games begin, Nigel and Dwight are golfing and delightfully chat with the celebrities and important people. Nicolaus walks around with Manfred and checks on security, but also finds time to be with Deirdre to chat with celebrities; their marriage date being the height of conversation. Despite what happened earlier, the fundraising event is successful.

Later that evening, in the Ravenell mansion library, Nicolaus pulls Deirdre close to him as he speaks to his father. Smiling, "Father, that was a great fundraiser today. My God, and all those folks will be at the gala tomorrow? Exciting!"

Nigel swallowed his drink, "Yes! I'm not sure how Deirdre pulled all this off!"

Deirdre smiles with humility, "I'm just so glad it is all working out. And yes, one more event tomorrow. Everything is in order."

Nigel smiles and nods. "There will be over five hundred very important people in attendance, and lots of press, probably more press than there was today."

Deirdre nods in agreement, and touches Nicolaus on the leg. "Babe, people are paying a lot of money for the gala. Even more money than they paid for the golf tournament today."

"We can't have any mishaps tomorrow." Nicolaus looks at his love. "I'll run an even tighter ship tomorrow." All three stand and hug. Deirdre is excited.

Deirdre and Nicolaus exit the library, his arm tightly around her. Nicolaus walks Deirdre to her bedroom door. His embrace turns into a hurricane of love as he wraps Deirdre into his arms against his body. Deirdre lays her head on his strong chest, accepting his love, knowing he will not demand anything of her, nor will he accost her sexually. Suddenly, he lifts her chin for a kiss. His kiss is gentle, but gets a little more persistent as he tastes her warm mouth and tender lips. Nicolaus loves how Deirdre automatically responds to him. He breaks the kiss, giving her time to breathe, and then goes in for another one.

Deirdre feels herself melting into him, her love, her man, her life. She would never be able to resist him. He pulls away, breaking the kiss again, making her open her eyes, they both breathe heavy.

"Well, well, you two love birds going at it, huh?" Benjamin's voice interrupts their sweet moment.

Deirdre tries to pull away, but Nicolaus holds onto her, pulling her closer.

"Benjamin," Nicolaus says. He sighs with frustration, as he wanted more kissing and hugging on his lady. He lets Deirdre go, opening her room door for her. Their hands linger, as she enters the room, then he closes the door, securing her safely inside. He knocks on the door, then only after hearing the lock, does he address Benjamin. "What's going on brother? You all right? You kinda disappeared on me today."

"Well, you can see that I'm all right," he replied sarcastically.

"Okay, well … what happened, who was that guy? Another husband of one of your rendezvous women?"

"He is a loser. A dude that, obviously, can't perform in bed. You know, if there weren't so many sloppy husbands around, I wouldn't have to take on these women."

Nicolaus laughed at his absurd comment, which reminded him of something his mother would say. "Wow!

Oh, so now you're a Casanova? My God Benjamin, that's a lot of sex you're taking on, if that's the case. I hope you are using protection. You're either going to get something, or bring a baby around."

"You, Mr. Virgin Soldier Man, trying to tell me what to do about sex? Really?" Benjamin faked laughed at the irony. "Give me a damn break! You've never even seen a tit, let alone pussy. Don't fucking lecture me, Nicolaus!"

"Look, all I'm trying to say is … be careful."

Benjamin looked to the door of the room that held Deirdre. "Whatever. Is your plan to stay a virgin forever or you gonna hit that in there?" he nodded towards the door.

Frowning, Nicolaus stood before the door, as if to keep him from even looking at it, "Don't talk about Deirdre like that."

"Virgin pussy is the best," Benjamin declared. "After that love scene I just witnessed, I'm sure Deirdre is hot and wet, just waiting for …"

Nicolaus pushed his brother on the chest to get his attention, "Knock it off, Benjamin."

"I'm just saying …"

"You don't need to say anything about Deirdre. You have enough to worry about with all these men coming after you, trying to kill you. Maybe you need a better way of meeting women. There's lots of single women in Austin."

Benjamin gave Nicolaus a mischievous smile, "Maybe what I really want is not out there."

Nicolaus didn't catch what Benjamin was actually hinting at, his lust for Deirdre.

"But you have to be serious about looking, Benjamin."

"Oh, I can be serious."

Nicolaus put his arm around Benjamin's shoulders and ushered him out of the hallway. They went to the kitchen, a thing they'd done since their youth. Kitchen staff were still present. They provided a dessert snack to the brothers.

Nicolaus invited the staff to sit with them, and they each snacked on the apple pie that was left from the day. Sitting with the staff was something Ceil did not approve of, and she often chastised Nicolaus for it. However, Nicolaus did not like treating the staff as the servers they were, he treated them as people, with families, wants and needs.

Something else he and Deirdre did for the staff each year was provide Christmas gifts for them, or large cash bonuses, depending on what they were going through, despite the fact that the staff was paid fairly well for their work at the mansion.

Manfred happened to be walking by, and Nicolaus asked him to join them. As the group sat, the staff talked about their children, and laughed at Nicolaus' witty comments. This is one of those times when Benjamin admired Nicolaus. Benjamin felt like he was part of the group, and he knew that Nicolaus had included him easily and purposefully to make him remember how they used to be somewhat closer than they were today.

After thirty minutes of fun, the men were ready to turn in for the night. Nicolaus stopped Benjamin at the top of the stairs and told him, "Benjamin, if ever you need to talk, … I'm … here for you," he offered.

Benjamin smiled at him, feeling the sincerity. "Yeah, thanks. I'll see you tomorrow."

"Good night then."

Chapter Twenty

Ceil and Nigel are in their bedroom, Nigel, tired from the golf tournament, glad to climb into bed. Though he noticed Ceil was not getting ready for bed, but was pacing the room. He knew that eventually, she would say what she was upset about, as she had heard what had happened earlier.

"He did it again!" she complained. "He embarrassed my Benjamin. Again!"

Nigel sighed, half laughing, "You mean he saved your Benjamin!" His frown is deep, "My God, what has Benjamin done that all these people are after him?"

Ceil denied what she knew was true. She knew it was Benjamin's womanizing behaviour that was bringing trouble to his door. "Benjamin is just popular. People are envious!"

"Popular in the wrong way, perhaps! We have got to get a handle on this before Benjamin really gets hurt. Nicolaus will not be around every day to save his ass."

"None of this ever happens when Nicolaus is not here. Why would it suddenly be happening now? I tell you, its Nicolaus! He has orchestrated all of this!" she spurted illogically.

Nigel frowned again, "But Ceil, why would Nicolaus do that?" He wanted to make her see her own folly thinking.

"So, he can appear to be the hero."

"Oh Ceil. That's not Nicolaus."

"He's trying to hurt my Benjamin!"

"But he's putting his life on the line to save him. Anyway, Nicolaus is not trying to take accolades for any of this." Nigel sighs heavily with concern, "Perhaps this has been happening for some time, and we just didn't know about it."

"Benjamin would have told me."

"Ceil, are you sure?"

"Of course, I'm sure! I know my Benjamin! He would have told me if he was having trouble like this."

Nigel shakes his head negatively, not believing Ceil. "I am so glad Nicolaus has agreed to stay and work with us. We really need him home. Benjamin is not going to be of any help, especially not with all this going on."

Ceil immediately was upset that Nigel would just dismiss Benjamin out of hand in such a manner. "No! Benjamin is the one who should work beside you. He should inherit the company. Let Nicolaus run off and play soldier boy all he wants."

"Soldier boy?" Nigel sounded offended. "Ceil, our son is a high-ranking officer in the military. I guarantee you, he is not playing anything. He serves with honour and distinction, and you should be proud of him, instead of having such spite for him. There is always a place for Benjamin, but we need Nicolaus to run things." He felt agitated, "And we really cannot have this discussion again!" he told her, finally standing up for Nicolaus. "We both know that between our two sons, Nicolaus is the leader. He will take care of the company. And whether or not you like it, Ceil, one day Nicolaus will be in charge of this family." Ceil was standing near, and Nigel took her hands to pull her close to him.

Ceil jerks her hands away from Nigel. "No! I will never agree to it. Never!" refusing to give in to the notion of placing his illegitimate son above their Benjamin.

Nigel bit his bottom lip in frustration, "Well, whether or not you agree Ceil, it will be Nicolaus who shall succeed me," he told her harshly, as if to end the discussion.

Seething with great anger Ceil turns her back to Nigel, and leaves the room, slamming the large, heavy door.

Chapter Twenty-One

The Performing Arts Centre sits across the street from the beautiful Auditorium Shores in downtown Austin. The Friday summer night sky was dark, clear, and full of cosmic stars. The centre itself was filling up with celebrities.

A banner for the VMC Annual Gala is prominently displayed at the entrance of the centre. The magnificent smell of the famous Eastside Eatery's catered food is apparent, as it fills the air, making mouths water and bellies bristle. Important people of the city, such as the mayor, city council members, commissioners, educational dignitaries, judges, and others, as well as famous celebrities are dressed fancily for the gala. People are sitting at formal tables being served food, while others are eating, and others are walking around chatting. A contemporary band is on the stage providing light musical entertainment.

Nicolaus is near the main entrance of the great hall of the centre, dressed nicely, with security ear buds and equipment.

Francesca has always kept up with fashion trends and is fashionably dressed. She walks over to Nicolaus in the dark centre that is lit with fluorescent overhead lighting, and the flames of table candles. She touches Nicolaus on his shoulders, "Ah, my strong, sweet cousin! Always working!"

Nicolaus looks over his shoulder and is happily surprised to see Francesca. "Francesca! Hey!" he hugs and kisses her. "Wow! You look amazing!"

"Thank you, my darling. Uncle Nigel got you working, I see."

Nicolaus gives a slight frown with a smile, "Yep, and then some! Whoa!" he suddenly notices Francesca's tall, burly, date. "Who's your friend?"

Francesca is all smiles, "Nicolaus, I want you to meet my new friend, Byron, he is here on business with Dwight. And he seems to be one of your biggest fans! Ever since I met him, he's been going on and on about Nicolaus this, and Nicolaus that. I'm like, Nicolaus? Nicolaus who?" she laughs. "He almost fainted when I told him I was related to you." Byron and Nicolaus nod and shake hands. Francesca continued, "Byron is in pharmaceuticals, all the way from Latvia."

Byron smiles and nods.

"What? Wow! What brings you to Austin?" Nicolaus asks.

"Business, of course. With VMC." Byron speaks with a thick European accent, and broken English. "I work for Drone Pharmaceuticals. And then the beautiful Francesca inviting me to this wonderful event. What a cause of greatness! Very smart, move for business. No?"

"Yeah," Nicolaus nods, "my father's idea."

"Byron is learning English very well." Francesca explains. "You know about Drone Pharmaceuticals? Ever heard of 'em? That's the merger everyone keeps talking about," she explains to Nicolaus.

Nicolaus nods, preoccupied with security, "Hmm? Sounds familiar. I believe so. My father has mentioned a merger."

"VMC well known in Latvia, as model company to make us better. What honour meeting you Nicolaus. I have followed your military exploits and intriguing you next moves," Byron says happily, showing his excitement to meet Nicolaus.

Nicolaus is surprised, "You follow my military career?"

Byron nods heavily, "Yes, yes. You family success fascinate. I think everyone in Latvia. So, course, we want to know everything about all of you."

Nicolaus smiles, still surprised at his words, "Wow! I had no idea."

Nicolaus' attention is suddenly interrupted and turned away by a happening on stage. As the singing group finished their set, the voice of Benjamin is heard. He frowns, "Ah, excuse me." He kisses Francesca. "Let's catch up more later. I've got to take care of this."

Francesca carts Byron away.

Nicolaus is shocked and pissed at the same time, "Unbelievable!"

Benjamin grabs onto the microphone, clearly in a drunken state of mind, and not a scheduled part of the show. As he speaks his words are slurred. "Eh.... Everybody! Thanks! Thanks for being here, man. I just, I just ...." For a moment, he forgot what he was going to say. "Oh yeah, I'm Benjamin, the less known and other half to the well-known brother Major Nicolaus Ravenell." Benjamin, stumbles a little, almost loosing balance. The press move in to take pictures.

At the mention of Nicolaus' name and military rank, the audience cheers for Nicolaus and begins clapping.

Blinded by the stage lights, Benjamin points into the audience at the sound of clapping, "Yes!" he agrees with them. "And I just want to read a poem I wrote for you all."

Nicolaus speaks into his earbud to security, "How did my brother get on that stage?"

Someone shouts from the audience for Benjamin to get off the stage. Benjamin points to the audience again,

"I gotcha' buddy. I gotcha." He clears his throat. In his drunken bid for attention, he continues, "The poem is called 'In the Shadow of My Brother'. I had another poem called, 'Life is Secondary', but I decided this one was better."

Nigel was surprised and frowning, never having known his youngest son was a secret poet. Who knew? He noticed that Ceil seemed as surprised as he was, but she did not move or say anything. He looked around for someone to get Benjamin off the stage, and relaxed when he saw that Nicolaus was talking to someone in a radio. He knew he was already on it. Nigel took a drink and watched with the rest of the audience. He saw that press cameras were flashing like crazy. He only hoped Nicolaus would take care of this quickly, and without much drama.

As the large amounts of ingested alcohol made Benjamin studder and stumble over the words of his poem, more people were yelling for him to get off the stage. Bravely, or maybe stupidly, Benjamin continued to read, ignoring the jeers and shouts from the audience.

Wanting to yell at the staff, but trying to remain calm, Nicolaus instructed them, "Get him off stage. Find Deirdre so she can transition, and get him off."

"Yes sir," the staff answered, "but what if he is in the middle of ..."

"What?" Nicolaus' patience was gone. He talks through gritted teeth, trying not to yell, "I don't care if he is in the middle of a sentence, get him off that stage! Now!" Nicolaus changed the radio to a different channel to instruct a different staff member, "Hey, Joe, let's turn off the stage mic for a minute or two. Thanks!"

Suddenly, Benjamin's microphone is cut, but he keeps reading. Deirdre enters the stage and the audience claps. Manfred helps staff gently escort Benjamin off the stage.

Deirdre smiles and keeps the show rolling, "Wow! Let's give a hand clap for that wonderful introspection from the one and only Benjamin Ravenell!" Deirdre leads the audience in clapping, a sure fire way to transition from disaster to the next act. "I am so sure you will enjoy the next act, they travelled all the way from Dallas to sing just for you. Let's give it up for the Texas swing band, Delicate Roses!"

The stage curtain opens, and a female band dressed in yellow begin to sing contemporary music. The audience loves it; laughter and dancing ensues. Nicolaus sighs with relief.

Nicolaus meets up with Manfred, "Manfred, please take my brother to the house, and have somebody stay with him. Make sure he's all right."

Manfred nods with a smile, appreciative that Nicolaus trusts him, "Sure thing."

Deirdre walks through the crowd to find Nicolaus while the band is singing. She sees Rachel who takes her hand, and they walk together. Deirdre and Nicolaus see each other, and he walks to meet her and Rachel. "That was quick thinking babe. Thank you!" she tells him.

Nicolaus kisses her hand, and Deirdre is off to take care of business. Rachel visits with Nicolaus for a few minutes and is then invited to dance. People, including celebrities are dancing to the music, eating, and having fun.

Meanwhile, it takes about a half hour for Manfred to escort Ceil and Benjamin back to the Ravenell mansion. Once he sees they are secured, he leaves them to head back to the centre, to continue his work beside Nicolaus.

Benjamin heads straight for the liquor, and begins to pour a rather large drink.

Frowning, Ceil walks over and takes the drink out of his hand, "Don't you think you have had enough for tonight?"

Benjamin looks at Ceil, gets another glass and pours another drink. "Don't tell me what to do mother!' he tells her angrily, "I get enough of that from Nicolaus." He swallows the full drink, and slams down the glass on the sidebar counter. "Damn! Sometimes, I get so sick of him! Sick of him!" The booze fuels his anger as his anger fuels his drinking. He pours another glass and downs it quickly, as if it has magical powers to make him feel better. "Geez! I'm starting to ..."

Ceil smiles, and finishes his sentence for him, "Hate him?"

Benjamin covers his face, feeling confused. He gets emotional and wants to cry, but holds back. He does have feelings of hatred, but doesn't want these feelings. After all, Nicolaus is his only brother, and he did save his life a few times this week. And he is the military hero of the family. But why, oh God, why does Nicolaus always come off as the one that is better? The good one. The smart one. The strong one. The brave one. The pious one. The one that is in control. The one who has Deirdre's heart. Why?

Ceil takes the glass from Benjamin. She removes his hands from his face, and hugs him to her, knowing he is embarrassed and probably feeling shame. "It's all right son. We'll fix him. I promise you that." She vows action against Nicolaus. "He will run away from here when I get done with him!"

Chapter Twenty-Two

The gala continues at the Performing Arts Centre. Deirdre takes the stage again.

"Such wonderful entertainment tonight. Let's have another round of applause for The Delicate Roses!" Deirdre leads the audience in applause, and then continues. "Yes!" she says excitedly. "And before I bring out our final act for the night, I want to again thank each and every one of you for attending our annual gala. Please keep us on your schedule each year, as it is truly you that help families. Your donation will go directly to the medical insurance fund, and families in the VMC service areas will have the opportunity to obtain affordable healthcare. Truly it is a blessing to see children who need transplants, or who have cancer or kidney disease receive the quality treatment they need because of your donations. Thank you." Deirdre happily sends air kisses to the audience. The audience clap and cheer.

"And now without further ado, we bring to you these wonderful young ladies, out of Houston, who want to be the next big girl group of the decade. Ladies and gentlemen, Twelfth Harmony!" The audience stands to their feet with loud applause and cheering. The dance floor space fills up very quickly. Twelfth Harmony sing their harmonic hip hop songs to the audience's delight.

After a set of six songs from Twelfth Harmony, the gala ends with balloons and confetti falling from the ceiling. After another thirty minutes, the staff begin to usher the guests out of the centre. Rachel and Francesca find Nicolaus and Deirdre to give pleasantries and kisses upon leaving, as they are escorted by Nigel and a few celebrities he is conversating with.

After everyone is out of the centre, Deirdre and Nicolaus embrace as the long night ends.

"Babe, you really did a great job. This was fantastic!" He pecks Deirdre's lips, then kisses her forehead, and then kisses her hands.

"Thanks babe! I'm exhausted! Ready to go?" she asks him.

Nicolaus nods, "Let me make sure the guys have everything under control."

Deirdre smiles at his commitment to the security of the place, "Okay, I'll get my things. No rush! I want everything to be right for Pops."

An hour later, as Nicolaus and Deirdre arrive at the mansion, everyone is gathered in the library: Nigel, Ceil, Francesca, Rachel, Alexander, and Dwight. Nigel steps up to Deirdre and kisses her on the forehead lovingly, "Such excellent work this week. Each event was wonderful! You've earned a place on our volunteer of the year wall! Thank you so much, we couldn't have done all this without you!"

Ceil groans with approval.

Deirdre returns the hug, "Thank you Pops! It was great professional experience for me as well! Staff is still counting, but I believe we will hit over a million in donations. So exciting!"

Nigel looks at her surprised, "Wow! We have never raised that much before. Deirdre ... I'm speechless. That's ... incredible!" Nigel looks to Ceil and Dwight approvingly.

"Babe, that's wonderful!" Nicolaus tells her. Everyone else says their congratulations with joy of the results of her work.

Nigel smiles, "Well ... now, without a doubt, you'll have to be part of the family!"

Nicolaus gets alcoholic drinks for everyone, and hands them out. He sits next to Deirdre, pulling her close.

Nigel takes a drink in thought, "Son, you did an outstanding job on security tonight. Not one problem ... well besides Benjamin on stage ... but even that was handled very tastefully, and quickly. Outstanding!"

"Thanks Father! I will go by early to make sure everything is as it should be with the clean up and all."

"Thank you. Wonderful!" Nigel looks to Ceil again, his eyes reminding her of their conversation about Nicolaus getting things done, and leading properly.

"Which brings to mind," Nicolaus remarks, "Francesca, introduced me to Byron, of Drone Pharmaceuticals, father. You and Dwight are working with him?"

Nigel nods, "Yes, yes, Byron Vinters. We have just begun working on the merger deal with Drone Pharma."

Ceil was standing in the background, and then suddenly appears next to Nigel, with intense interest, "Byron is here, in Austin?"

Francesca nods with a smile, "He's a real cutie, Auntie Ceil!"

"Well, let's talk about that later. Son, right now, I want to focus on the two of you." Nigel opens his hand towards Nicolaus and Deirdre.

"I just want to confirm for everyone present, that we all know that you two make a great couple!"

Deirdre giggles lightly. Nicolaus smiles at her, and grasps her hand, remembering what they had discussed earlier about Nigel's thoughts on their marriage plans.

"I mean it," Nigel continued. "And Nicolaus, ... wait ... where is Benjamin? He is supposed to be here with us right now."

"He is probably out somewhere with his girlfriends. He mentioned he was going to some club on Red River," Ceil told them. Then bitterly, she added, "Probably licking his wounds from the public humiliation he was given again tonight."

Nicolaus and Nigel both shake their heads, not wanting to get into it with Ceil.

Actually, Benjamin is passed out drunk, half dressed, on his bed upstairs. Three girls are present in his oversized, luxurious bedroom. Quietly, they are going through his things, the drawers, and the clothes closets. They take his money and his credit cards. Laughing, they take some of his clothes. This would be a security breach, except Benjamin had invited the girls over for wild sex capades, however, he is so drunk, he didn't make it passed getting undressed.

"Well … as I was saying … you must know we are looking forward to your wedding day. And Dwight and I look forward to both Nicolaus and Alexander joining us at headquarters for training, to move into their roles as co-Vice Presidents."

Elation and sounds of joy come from everyone present … except Ceil. Nigel notices this, and quickly he grabs Ceil's hand and takes Dwight by the shoulder, and continues his assertions, "The three of us, couldn't be prouder of the three of you!"

Upstairs, the girls quietly leave Benjamin's room with stolen items, giving him a kiss on his head, laughing for having left lip stick stains on his face so he would remember they were there. The girls descend the stairs, and find their way to the back door of the mansion, leaving unnoticed.

Chapter Twenty-Three

Three days later, Nicolaus, Alexander, and Dwight are in Nigel's VMC office. His office has a pristine view of downtown, through the glass walls. You can see across the lake that runs through the middle of the city. Nigel is staring out the window, thinking about the future, when Nicolaus interrupts his thoughts.

"So, the company seems to be well known in Latvia. Byron says we are a model company for them."

Nigel swirled on his heel, as Dwight was nodding. "Yes, they have tuned into us, and we are so glad. Since our federal trade commission thinks we will have a monopoly on healthcare if we own pharmacies, they blocked our bid to purchase national pharmacies here in the U.S. So now we have set our sights on European pharmaceutical markets."

"Yes," Dwight agreed. "That's why we are in negotiation with Drone Pharmaceuticals in the first place. We want pharmaceutical contracts in Europe. We believe we can get a really good deal. And this contract will not only give us a footing in Europe, but we also hope to open new technological advances for the company as well."

Nigel waved his arms about, "In fact, Ceil wanted to go to Latvia with Byron to tour their company. She took Francesca with her this morning. While there, they will be going to her ancestral home in Tallin, Estonia. Francesca was extremely excited about going. She is making videos for Rachel, for all of us really."

Byron was true entertainment on the long flight to Latvia, especially after the marathon run they did in the New York airport to make their connective flight from Austin. They had one more connection to make in Amsterdam, before landing in Riga, Latvia. Once off the plane in Riga, both Ceil and Francesca noticed the crisp air, despite it being mid-day in June.

Ceil left Francesca to herself at the hotel, promising an adventure and the opportunity to meet her Great Aunt Clara in Estonia. In the meantime, Ceil made her way to Drone Pharmaceuticals with Byron. As planned, he gave her a tour of their operations, and the factory.

Ceil found herself impressed, and did believe this was a good deal for VMC. Having seen everything, she was more convinced than ever that her plan against Nicolaus would work.

Byron led Ceil into the large conference room, where she met with Andrejs Drone, CEO of Drone Pharma Group. Andrejs gentlemanly shook Ceil's hand, then pulled a chair for her to sit at the conference table.

"Mrs. Ravenell, we have honour to meet you," Andrejs said in his Latvian accent and broken English. He is a tall, thin man, with salt and pepper thick hair, slicked back, with comb lines present. He has a friendly face, with a large white tooth smile, and he smelled of sexy aftershave or cologne. He is casually dressed in a dark blue suit, with a mauve coloured shirt and no tie, his shirt opened mid-chest. Other executive team members, including Byron, join them in the conference room, placing food and drink on the large, maple wood table.

Andrejs continued, "Would you like for us to contact Mr. Dwight Collins to join us in these contract discussions? As I assume that is why you are here."

Ceil smiled, "No, no, it is not necessary to contact Dwight. I know my being here is a surprise. Your kindness and hospitality are well noted. Thank you. I have controlling shares of VMC. I am in charge now. And yes, you are correct, it is the contract negotiations that brings me here."

Andrejs smiles with a laugh, "Yes ma'am, we are very eager …very, to make this a good solid contract." The other executives laugh with him, and nod in agreement. "We want this contract to last for many, many years into future."

Ceil nods, also smiling, feeling like she is about to get what she wants, "Yes, I know, and that is why I'm here! I love your eagerness. I also want a solid contract. In fact, I understand that sometimes you like to negotiate based on the customs of your country."

Andrejs poured himself and Ceil a drink. He placed the glass of wine before her.

"Yes, we do! Ah, if appropriate," he added as an afterthought. "What do you have in mind?"

Ceil mischievously smiles, "An arranged marriage."

Andrejs is astonished, "Marriage?" He looks at his team members, as they look amongst each other, then to Ceil at her unusual business request. Andrejs nervously laughs, rubbing his chin in thought, realizing the ease and potential for profits this type of transaction will bring to his company.

Ceil pushes him, excitedly leaning forward, "Your daughter, Marguerite, she gives you troubles. Yes? You have a hard time keeping her in line, making her behave … or so I've heard. Believe me, I understand how it can be with these young people. Well … I think she will do nicely for my Nicolaus."

"Marguerite?" Andrejs sounds surprised, knowing of Nicolaus and his stellar reputation. "Oh, no," he laughs nervously, not sure what she is up to. "You do not know what you ask for. She is fiery … how you say … wild

… mustang …. She will be very harsh for your Nico-laus… not proper."

"Oh, I've done my research about her. I know she is exactly what I want."

"Is not your Nicolaus already to wed?"

Ceil waived away his question, as if he were being silly or absurd. "You let me worry about Nicolaus."

With slight hesitation, Andrejs does more thinking. Then with more nervous laughter, he nods in under-standing. "So, you want arranged marriage? My Mar-guerite to your Nicolaus." He watches Ceil as she nods and smiles. Andrejs nods and grabs Ceil's hand to shake it. "Yes, we can do that!"

Ceil nods and smiles again. She raises her glass to af-firm their understanding. She sits back in satisfaction, and takes a sip of the Latvian wine. The team moves to draw up the contract as Ceil and Andrejs work out the rest of the details.

Chapter Twenty- Four

When Ceil returned to the hotel, Francesca thought she was a little too happy, and this caused her concern. However, as they went out on the town to sight see, and have dinner, Francesca put away those thoughts, hoping Ceil really just needed the getaway and was enjoying being close to her childhood home.

The next day, they took a train to Tallin, Estonia. The countryside was breathtaking, with views of the Baltic Sea, the lush forests and vegetation, and the medieval style town.

Francesca was shocked when they arrived at Ceil's ancestral home. The huge castle had a beautiful stone exterior that lasted through the ages. The castle looked like it was out of a fairy tale, with rounded walls, three stories high, on a hilltop that probably once overlooked rolling grassland, which was now covered with red roofed houses and structures, all the way to the sea. Francesca had her phone camera going. After entering the huge gates, they drove up a winding cobble stoned way, which one could imagine used to be the horse road to the gate entrance to the huge doors of the castle.

"Auntie Ceil, I never imagined such a place in your history," Francesca exclaimed.

Ceil smiled, "Yes, yes. Your mother and I spent time here as children, before we were carted off to America. Francesca, there is a beautiful walking garden in the back of the property. You must be sure to capture images of it." She clasped her hands together, "You will just love it! I'm very sure, you will love it!"

As Francesca exited the limousine that carried them up to the door, the size of the castle swallowed her and Ceil. It was looming and huge. Once inside, despite its draftiness, Francesca was shocked to see similarities of the Ravenell mansion, such as the large double staircase upon entrance, and the tall fireplaces. The Ravenell mansion had shoulder high fireplaces, however, this castle had fireplaces so big, a person could fully stand inside, and still have a huge space for headroom. Inside the castle was exceptional, just as the outside. It had survived fully intact all these decades, and was completely functional.

They were greeted by house staff who took them to a large room off to the side, which had a hefty fire roaring in the large fireplace. The inside of the castle had no reflection of the weather outside. Ginormous windows provided plenty of daylight, but cool air drafts flowed through the whole of the castle, making all the rooms cold, despite it being warm outside.

This room held large family portraits on the gold trimmed white walls, along with modern and antique furniture that mixed nicely together. Before Francesca could explore the portraits, a feeble elderly woman appeared before them.

"Auntie Clara!" Ceil greeted her with a hug and a kiss.

"Ceil? Is that you?" Clara patted her on the back and then the shoulder.

"Yes, Auntie Clara, it's me, Ceil."

"Why, my, my! Sellest on aastaid, aastaid, kui nägin sind viimati!" she told her in the traditional Estonian language, that it had been years since she'd seen her last.

Ceil looked at her surprised, and raised her finger to her mouth in thought, trying to remember how to translate in Estonian for conversation. Then it came to her.

126

"Jah, tädi, ma elan Ameerikas." (Yes, Auntie, I've been living in America.) "Pidage meeles?" (Remember?)

Clara nodded with laughter. She held her hands out towards Francesca, in a bid for her to get a hug. "Kes see ilu on? Kas ta on sinu oma?" (Who is this beauty? Is she yours?)

Francesca leapt to the space of her newly found ancestor, happy to meet her. She didn't know what to do, not understanding the language, and ended up with a curtsy and laughter. After all, they were inside a castle. Clara grabbed hold to her, and hugged her tightly.

"No Auntie Clara, this is Francesca, Rachel's daughter!"

"Rachel? Ah!" She hugged Francesca again.

"So nice to meet you ma'am!"

"Francesca, this is your great Aunt Clara. She is your grandmother's sister."

"Amazing!"

"You are ilus … beautiful, chil'."

Francesca nodded with a slight bow. Her great Auntie Clara smelled of gingerbread cookies, or a similar sweet bread. Her frame was bent, and her gray hair had stray whisps. She must have been a centurion, or close to it. She walked with a cane, as the castle was large, and had many stairs.

Clara used her strained eyes to look past Francesca for the others. "Teised?" (The others?) "Nicohls … Bennie?" She pointed to Francesca. "Teised? Your Nicohls."

Francesca quickly got over her shock that Clara knew about them. "Oh, Auntie Clara, you are mixing us up. You mean Nicolaus and Benjamin, are Ceil's sons. Yes, they are well."

Clara smiled, then shook her head. "Nicolaus. Your Nicolaus," she insisted.

"My Nicolaus?" Francesca was trying to understand.

Clara nodded with a smile, thinking she finally understood. "Yes, your Nicolaus."

Ceil stepped in, touching Francesca, "Auntie Clara, Nicolaus and Benjamin are just fine."

The servers brought tea, tarts, and cakes for them to enjoy. Francesca began to film again. She was delighted at the interior of the castle. She was sure to capture Auntie Clara, and Ceil in her decent, nice element. It was a side of Ceil she did not see often. It was as though her Auntie Ceil was where she belonged, here in Estonia, and was out of place in Austin, Texas.

She seemed regal in this setting.

After the snack session, Francesca continued to tour the castle, while Clara and Ceil caught up with each other in the Estonian language.

The large wall portraits came into her viewing screen. Suddenly, she noticed how all the family members seemed to resemble each other. Each image held a family member that posed for their portraits, looking every bit of royalty they were. Shock coursed through Francesca as she came upon a portrait of a tall, handsome warrior. He was the only one dressed as a warrior, obviously, an especially important person to the family. He held a shield and sword, in a defensive stance, as if he were not posing for the picture. As she stared at this portrait, she certainly felt as if Nicolaus himself was staring right back at her, only having a lighter shade of skin colour. In disbelief, she pulled down her phone and used her eyes to look at the portrait. Yep, that's what she saw. Nicolaus, from the past, looking at her, full on, in the present. She didn't understand what she was looking at. How can this be? Her Nicolaus, as Auntie Clara called him, resembled Nigel, and Nigel was not of Ceil's family, was he? Francesca frowned, and studied the portrait. She took pictures, "No bloody way!" she exclaimed.

And then another amazement. Another portrait, of the same man. She looked back at the other one to be sure, then compared the faces. Yes, it was the same man, this time he was posing, with a woman at his side. A woman who Francesca could swear looked just like … Deirdre. "What the …?" She studied it closer, and was unable to deny what her eyes were showing her. She began to freak out a little, "Auntie Ceil!" she called, not taking her eyes from the portrait, afraid it would change if she did so.

Ceil and Clara were across the large room, "Auntie Ceil!" she called louder.

Ceil rushed over, and Francesca pointed to the portraits without words at first, wanting to get Ceil's reaction. After a minute of Ceil's silence, Francesca finally asked, "Who are they? How can this be?"

"Oh Francesca, I thought you hurt yourself!" Ceil looked upon the portraits as if it was no big deal. "Okay, well, yes, what of it?"

"Auntie Ceil!"

Ceil sighed, "Okay, that is Nicohls, whom Aunt Clara was referring to."

"Wait a minute … Nicky is named after Nicohls? This man?" Ceil nodded, and Francesca frowned deeply, feeling frustration arise. "But … Auntie Ceil, he was a warrior or some kind of soldier."

"Yes."

"Ah … but Auntie Ceil, you were against Nicky joining the military, you laughed at him."

Ceil frowned, unable to explain this away, "Oh, that is a different situation."

"Okay, but how is it that Nicohls looks exactly like Nicky, or that Nicky looks exactly like Nicohls?"

"Well, Francesca, as you can see, all our family look alike," she waived her hand over the portraits. "It's our Kiviste family DNA. We have dominant genes. That is why we all look alike. Don't you see yourself up there?"

Francesca nodded to her question, as she could see her face in the ancestors on the wall, and then she continued to probe, "But Auntie Ceil, Nicky and Benji look like Uncle Nigel."

"Well," Ceil took a step back, "perhaps you think so, but you have not had any other relevant information to compare them to. But now you do!"

"Okay, but ... what about that picture. Who is that woman?"

Ceil knew who she was referring to. She glanced at it, "Yes, that is Nichol's wife. They called her DeeDee, but I believe her name was Mari." Ceil gave her a slight smile and went back to her visit with Clara.

Francesca's freaked out mental status calmed a little, but she was amazed over the picture of Nicohl and DeeDee. She took several pictures, and continued on her castle adventure. The staff led her to some of the upstairs bedrooms and provided her some history of the family.

After an hour touring the castle rooms, great dining hall, the ballroom, and the kitchen, the staff took Francesca to the gardens out back. She was absolutely taken aback by the beautiful, romantic garden grounds. She felt as though she was back in time. There was a maze of flowers and bushes, with flowered trees everywhere. The air smelled thick of gardenia, her favourite flower.

There was a gazebo in the middle of it all. Francesca went to the gazebo, and sat, enjoying the warm sun on her skin. Her phone battery died, just after she captured it all.

She laid prone on the cushioned bench and fantasized about living in such a place. She wanted to take it all in.

Francesca's thoughts returned to that portrait of Nicohls and DeeDee. Did they really call that woman DeeDee? DeeDee? Mari? Can that only be a coincidence? What the hell? Why had their parents never discussed this with them? Why is it that Ceil is against Nicky and Deirdre marrying? Does this castle have something to do with their pending marriage? Francesca decided she was going to befriend the helpful castle staff to have a bridge to this place after returning home. She was determined to get her questions answered.

Chapter Twenty-Five

The following day Deirdre was steadily working in her office at the state capitol building.

Suddenly, her secretary is standing in the doorway, "Ms. Omari, you have a visitor.

He says it is urgent."

Deirdre sighs without looking up, keeping focused on her computer monitor. "I have to finish this brief. Unless it's Nicolaus, ask them to come back in about two hours."

"I promise I won't take too much time."

Deirdre looks up at the sound of Benjamin's voice. She nods to the secretary to let him in. "Benji, what are you doing here?"

Without hesitating, Benjamin drops to one knee and opens a ring box. "Marry me, Deirdre."

Deirdre sighs slightly, and frown smiles, "Benji. What are you doing?"

"I love you. Marry me."

Deirdre did not move from behind her desk. She didn't want to chance Benjamin grabbing onto her. She sighed heavily, then giggled, "Well … I don't know, did you ask Nicky about this? Did he clear you to ask this of me?" She giggled again, hoping bringing up Nicolaus would send him scurrying away, angry, but away.

Benjamin stood, sighing, "This is not a joke!" he said with slight anger. He took a breath to calm down. He didn't like that Deirdre returned her attention to her work. From the other side of her desk, he attempted to close her laptop, but Deirdre was quick to put her hand on the keyboard so it couldn't be closed.

"Look Benji, I appreciate that you love me. Really, I do … I appreciate you. You know Nicky and I are to be married in two weeks. You know this. So please, I'm asking you … stop this. Just stop."

"No. He doesn't deserve you."

Deirdre scoffed. "You mean I don't deserve him!" She sighed, pushing the button on her desk, "Benji, you can't change what's going to happen. It's sweet of you to offer to marry me, but I intend to marry Nicolaus. He is the love of my life. I can't imagine life without him, and you are just going to have to accept it. Okay, hon?" She opened her laptop, feeling quite the lawyer, "but I have got to get this brief completed, I have a deadline. Nicky and I will see you later at the house. Maybe we can talk more than."

The secretary rushed in. "Do we need security, Ms. Omari?"

Deirdre looked at Benjamin, who was certainly angry, "Well, Benji, do we need security?"

Benjamin backed away, looking sheepish, "No, no, I'm leaving."

He turned and left her office, and left the building, knowing if he made a commotion at the capitol building, he'd be quickly subdued and arrested.

"Just make sure security escorts him off the grounds. I don't want any surprises when I leave for home," Deirdre told her secretary.

Deirdre picked up the phone to call Nicolaus, but decided against it, since this time Benjamin did not attempt to touch her. She didn't want to burden Nicolaus with this, after all he was just getting started at VMC, she was sure he had way too much to worry about already. She believed this would all be over and done with Benjamin once she was married to Nicolaus. She dialled Elsa, and encouraged her to reach out to Benjamin, and get him to take her out. Deirdre figured that if she could get Benjamin's mind preoccupied about someone else, it would take his obsession off of her.

Chapter Twenty-Six

Three days later Deirdre is at a popular shopping mall in Austin, at a bridal shop that gives personal service to all their patrons. With her mother present, Deirdre stands on the pedestal admiring the fitting of the white wedding dress on her slender physique, in the slew of mirrors before her. She has longed for this day for so many years, the happiness inside her wants to bubble out. Deirdre runs her hands over the heart shaped bodice that has a sheer front veneer. The dress is covered with beads. The train is made of chiffon, with beaded flowers. "What do you think of this dress mother?"

Constance stands behind Deirdre, while uncontrollable tears fall from her eyes as she is ecstatic for her daughter. "You look so beautiful! That one is the best dress you've tried on."

Deirdre smooths the bodice that fits her perfect figure. "You like how this one looks mother?" Deirdre looks the beautiful dress over in all the mirrors.

Suddenly Jeune Tran, the reporter Deirdre arranged to meet at the bridal shop has arrived and chimes in, "Yes, I agree, you look very beautiful in that dress, Deirdre. Like a dream!"

Deirdre turns at the sound of the familiar voice. She sees the camera and a well-known reporter standing next to Jeune. Deirdre offers her hand with a smile, "Ms. Tran, you made it!" The women shake hands.

"Yes! And I hope you do not mind, but I brought with me a friend of mine who would also like to cover your story. Deirdre this is Tamron Ha…"

Deirdre interrupts, star struck, "Tamron?" putting her hand to her chest in disbelief. "You want to cover my story?"

Tamron smiles with her bright, toothy, celebrity smile, "When Jeune told me about your story it's so inspiring; waiting ten years to marry the man of your dreams, the man you love. Saving yourself especially for him … I think everyone should have a chance to know your story."

Deirdre was shocked, "Really? Wow! Okay!"

Jeune turned to Constance, "And this must be your mother." She gently grabs Constance's hands, "It's a pleasure to meet you."

Constance nods and introduces herself, also a little star struck, "Constance Omari. Likewise, it's a pleasure to meet you. And an honour to meet you Tamron! We didn't know this was such a big thing."

Tamron also takes Constance's hand, "I think your daughter can inspire young girls across the country. Especially with handsome Nicolaus waiting for her, as well. We did some checking, and he really is on the up and up about that. There is no one else but Deirdre in his eyes!"

"Oh yes, Nicky is an honest man and true to his word." Constance sighed, "When he sees my daughter in that beautiful dress … tears will come to his eyes as they have mine."

Jeune takes Deirdre's hand and has her twirl a little, "Now Deirdre, although I would really love to get a shot of that dress, I have instructed my crew to only get shots of the shop, and of you from the neck up, so we don't put any bad vibes on your wedding."

"Oh, thank you!"

Jeune nods with a smile, "You really do look spectacular in that dress. I hope it's the one you have chosen."

"Thank you. Mother and I had just agreed on this one."

The four women sit down on the luxury furniture of the bridal shop for the interview. Jeune provided instruction as the crew set up and set the lighting. "Now, we'll go live, but just relax and be yourself. Don't worry about looking at the cameras, just look at us!"

Tamron began the interview, providing the background story for the audience. She then turns to Deirdre, "Why ten years? That is a long time to wait to guard your virginity."

"They should have been married years ago," Constance jumped in.

Deirdre smiled, feeling nervous, realizing this was an international show, "Yes! Nicolaus and I are both virgins, it's true and I say that proudly! The timing just hasn't been right for us to marry. Nicolaus asked me to marry him when we were very young ... we were teenagers. We both love each other very much, and I have always wanted to marry him. And then he began his military career, and I began my law career."

The next question went to Jeune, "What about Mrs. Ravenell, Nicolaus' mother? We hear she is a difficult person."

Deirdre smiled to cover her surprise at the blunt question for the international viewers. She hoped Ceil was not watching. "Well ... she's very sweet, really." Deirdre saw Constance side eye her at that lie she just told. Deirdre placed her hand to her mother's leg so she would not comment, then continued, "She knows what she wants and usually gets what she wants, that's all.

Sometimes people call a strong woman 'difficult', really."

Tamron continued on about the family, "So you get along well with Mrs. Ravenell? And she agrees to you marrying her son?"

"Oh yes, I get along with all the family. We are all close. Nicolaus and I have known each other since we were children. I have loved Nicky for a long time, and I'm excited for us to be married."

On the other side of the world in Latvia, the Drone sisters, Penelope and Marguerite, are watching Tamron's international show interview of Deirdre, live on television, in their lavish mansion. Penelope is the older Drone sister. She is short and plump in body, and usually has a strong unpleasant smell. Her hair is done up in a swirled bun on-top of her head. Enchanted, she watches Deirdre, wishing it were herself instead. She has been in love with Nicolaus Ravenell since she learned of his existence. Marguerite was blessed with a tall, thick body, and has very plain looks. Opposite her sister, she sometimes wears her long hair down about her shoulders. Her manner is abrupt and uncaring, and she is terribly spoiled.

"This is the man father is forcing me to marry?" she observes magazines that feature Nicolaus and Deirdre her father brought for her to study. "For his business venture?" she yells spitefully. "He is just trying to get back at me!" For a brief moment, Marguerite has a memory of rocking naked on top of Vlad in the stables, almost reaching orgasm. And then she is horrified when she looks up to see her father. She climbed off Vlad, and covered herself, running from the stables, no words exchanged with her father. He'd never brought it up again, as if it was an unspeakable thing. Frustrated at the memory, she yells again, "Ugh!" She looks at Nicolaus again, and has absolutely no desire for him.

Annoyed, Penelope turns up the volume of the television, to drown out Marguerite's moans and whines.

Jeune continues the interview, "What do you think it will be like to be married to Nicolaus?"

"Heavenly!" is Deirdre's answer.

Andrejs walks into the room. Marguerite is quick upon him, her anger unabated, "Penelope, stinks again." She shouts at her sister over the loud television, "Penelope, go clean yourself!" Then Marguerite throws the magazines to the floor at her father's feet in a rage tantrum. "This is garbage!" she tells him enraged in her broken English. "I refuse to go through with marriage, trust fund or no! I am no man's sheep for trading! Not even yours. I am woman, I demand respect." Rudely she pushes past her father, and storms out of the room.

Penelope continues watching the interview, as Tamron asks Deirdre, "What advice would you give to any young girl who may be dating someone today?"

"Value your virginity! In fact, put a high value on your virginity. Once you give it away, you cannot get it back. So only give it to the right person, at the right time, under the right circumstances. And only we, us ladies, determine all three of those terms."

"Well said!" Tamron smiles.

Suddenly the bridal shop doors are thrown open. Benjamin bursts in, and runs over to Deirdre. Everyone is stunned as he grabs Deirdre into his arms. Being a breath's kiss away from Deirdre, he says, "I'll do what my brother doesn't have the guts to do, go beyond local media." He turns to the reporters, "I will declare my love for this woman on international television."

"Whoop! What is going on here?" Penelope exclaimed, getting closer to watch what was happening in the interview.

"Which camera?" Benjamin asks, holding on to Deirdre. Jeune and Tamron point to a camera, as Deirdre struggles against Benjamin's cobra hold. He looks at Deirdre, and then into the camera, "I love this woman, with all my heart. And I want the whole world to know it. I would do anything for her."

Deirdre frees herself, standing, as Manfred swoops in, grabbing Benjamin.

"Sorry ladies, everyone," Manfred apologizes. "I'm so sorry Ms. Omari," he looks to Deirdre, understanding Benjamin has just ruined their meeting, not realizing they were being televised. "He is inebriated again, and he got away from me. So sorry ladies."

In a flash, the men are gone, but Benjamin's voice lingers and can be heard off camera.

"I love you, Deirdre! I love you! Marry me! I can give you a better life. Marry me!"

Tamron puts her hand to her head, not sure what just happened. "Who is that?" she asks of anyone, as they are still rolling live.

"Benjamin Ravenell, Nicolaus' brother," Jeune answers. "Now this is indeed interesting. Deirdre, what was that about?" she tries to pull a just as stunned Deirdre back into the interview. Did that really just happen on international television?

Constance stands, shaking her head, knowing she has to try to protect her daughter, "Oh no! Oh dear, dear! Please turn off those cameras now. We are done here." Constance consoles Deirdre as she bursts out in tears.

Tamron and Jeune are astonished to have to end the live interview. "Well, sometimes we can see that love can be complicated," Tamron tells the audience. "We'll try to follow up and bring an end to this story." The camera crew fades the live session out.

Constance takes Deirdre to the back room, away from everyone. Only minutes later, Constance comes out alone, to end the session with Jeune and Tamron, apologizing and promising to send them invitations to the wedding as she escorts them out of the bridal shop. Deirdre is still shaken when Constance returns to her. Constance notices Deirdre's phone is ringing. She sees it is Nicolaus calling, and that Deirdre isn't answering it, nor will she let her answer it. Deirdre knows that Nicolaus was watching the interview, and is afraid of what he might do to Benjamin. Deirdre does not want to be the cause of their strife. She is also afraid of what Nicolaus might think of her. Would he think she went behind his back while he was away? Looming larger is the fact that Benjamin publicly humiliated her with his foolishness, before an international audience, tarnishing not only her reputation, but the reputation of Nicolaus as well. Deirdre doesn't know what to do. She feels paralyzed by uncertainty, while tears streamed down her face.

Chapter Twenty-Seven

Nicolaus was not only appalled, but outraged by the behaviour of Benjamin he'd just witnessed in the live interview. Immediately, his rage was interrupted by phone calls of support and similar alarm from his friends, his military buddies, and several celebrities from across the country. Apparently, everyone was watching Deirdre's interview, as she made this unusual public appearance to tell their love story.

Nicolaus' worry was magnified when Deirdre did not pick up the phone. Why hadn't he seen this coming? His suspicions of Benjamin's behaviour towards Deirdre were now confirmed, and he was mortified. Knowing his brother, he knew what he saw was a symptom of what was really going on.

He only hoped Benjamin had not brought harm to Deirdre. He felt as though he failed to protect her from his brother's harassing and predatory ways. Part of the outrage he felt was hurt that Deirdre didn't trust him to tell him what was happening, so he could protect her.

"Where is he right now?" Nicolaus came upon Manfred with fury, looking for his brother as Manfred entered the house. It had been a half hour since the interview fiasco. "Why haven't you answered my calls?"

Manfred held Nicolaus by the shoulder, "Nicolaus, let's think about this. You can't go chasing after Benjamin when you're upset. You know you'll hurt him. Your father would not want …"

Nicolaus turned from him, "Are you going to tell me where he is or not?" he yelled at Manfred.

Manfred looked around with a frown, "Where is your father?"

Nicolaus stepped up to Manfred's large frame, "Leave my father out of this. This is between me and Benjamin." He stepped back, trying to calm himself, "Where is he?"

Manfred sighed, shaking his head, "I'm sorry, he got away from me again. Your brother is a …"

"So where is he?" Nicolaus interrupted, pressing him sternly, knowing that Manfred knew how to find Benjamin.

Manfred sighed heavily again, shaking his head, afraid he was going to regret telling him. He pulled out his phone. "I put a tracker on his car, so I could keep an eye on him." He looked up at Nicolaus whose stance was of a soldier, ready to move on the word. He sighed, "Look, I'm going to tell you, but Nicolaus, I expect you to remember your father and honour him. Benjamin is your brother." Nicolaus nodded one time, and waited for the information. Manfred sighed again, "he's heading south down Mopac freeway, just passing Steck Avenue. And …" Nicolaus was gone before he looked up. "Oh God!" he felt dread, and hoped the brothers would not get hurt or end up in the hospital. Immediately, Manfred sought out Nigel.

Speeding his car down the freeway, it was not long before Nicolaus spotted Benjamin's silver Italian sports car. In close proximity, Nicolaus trailed Benjamin to his usual hang out on Red River, downtown.

As Benjamin gets out of his car, he is immediately accosted by Nicolaus. With great strength and vigour, Nicolaus grabs Benjamin and slams him against his car, wanting to punch him, but restrains himself. Benjamin struggles against Nicolaus, but cannot get away.

A crowd of people are watching and begin gathering, as they recognize the brothers.

"What the hell are you doing? Who the hell do you think you are, putting your hands on Deirdre?" Nicolaus grilled him angrily, shaking him through a fistful of clothing. "I saw you make a drunken fool of yourself at the end of Deirdre's interview today. What the hell do you think you're doing?" shaking him more. Full of anger and adrenaline, Nicolaus uses his other hand to punch the car, right next to Benjamin's head, leaving a dent in the soft metal. Benjamin continues to struggle against his brother, but cannot get loose. "Everyone saw it! I'm getting calls about you from across the country. Ms. Winfree even called me! You're a damn laughingstock!" he yelled in Benjamin's face.

Finally, Benjamin jerks himself away from Nicolaus and stands erect. "Oh, you mean I did what you are too cowardly to do, put action behind my love for Deirdre. Now she knows I'll do anything for her."

Nicolaus angrily grabs Benjamin up again, inches from his face, suddenly aware of the audience, "Love? You better mean you love her as a sister because she is going to be your sister-in-law."

"No, I …"

Not letting him finish his sentence, Nicolaus angrily slams Benjamin hard against the car again, intermittently shaking him to put emphasis on his words, "I better not ever see you disrespect Deirdre like that again. And I sure as hell better not ever hear any of this bull crap from you again."

Benjamin jerks himself free of his brother's grip again, only because Nicolaus let him get loose. Disappointed and finding this event sobering his thoughts, he understands that it's his fault that he has now broken that rekindled bond he'd found with Nicolaus a few weeks ago.

Feeling embarrassed, and waiting for Nicolaus to strike him, as he can see that he wants to strike him, Benjamin goes all in, "Or what?" he shouts at Nicolaus, "You'll do what?"

In a calmer tone, Nicolaus replies to his question, "You don't want to know what. Believe me."

"Oh, wow. Ewwh, that's really scary," he mocks Nicolaus. "That threat is about as empty as your support for Deirdre today."

"I don't owe you any explanations, but I will tell you that Deirdre wanted to handle that interview herself.

That was her time to shine." Nicolaus' anger bubbles up again, causing him to shout, wanting to punch Benjamin, "And you ruined it for her!" Aggressively, he grabs Benjamin up again, "I don't know what's in that screwed up brain of yours about Deirdre. Whatever it is, you'd better clear it out! If you ever put your hands on her again … you don't want to know what I'll do to you." Harshly, he pushes Benjamin away from him, and turns to leave. In an afterthought, Nicolaus turns and grabs Benjamin up again, "Give me your keys!" he demands of his younger brother.

"No, I'm not giving you my keys."

Without waiting, Nicolaus harshly searches Benjamin and takes his keys, then angrily sets demands on him, "You're not to drive drunk anymore. You're going to kill someone! Get a ride home."

Nicolaus slams himself inside his car, screeches the wheels, and speeds away.

Chapter Twenty-Eight

Nicolaus returned to the mansion, hoping Deirdre might have returned, but he saw that she had not, and was greeted by an anxious Manfred and Nigel.

"I'm sorry son, Deirdre has not returned," Nigel told him.

Nicolaus sighed and frowned at Manfred, "I told you not to bother my father about this."

Nigel touched Nicolaus' shoulder, "No, he was right to notify me of what was happening. I'm sorry to say I did not see the interview, but Ceil saw it. The media has been calling like crazy. They want comments and interviews but never mind about that. What of Benjamin, is he ..."

"Don't worry, I didn't hurt him." Nicolaus lifted Nigel's hand and placed Benjamin's car keys in his palm. "He's out of control, father."

"He's spoiled, is what he is," Nigel replied down spirited.

"You mean he acts like this all the time?" Nicolaus is still frowning, and now pacing. He didn't know where to put his upset.

"Your brother is nothing like you, Nicolaus. Benjamin is reckless, and ..."

"What have you done to my Benjamin?" from nowhere, Ceil suddenly appeared and ceased upon Nicolaus.

Nicolaus sighed, shaking his head, "I'm going to check on Deirdre. Excuse me, mother, father." Nicolaus abruptly left, not wanting to get into his mother's drama, leaving her to Nigel and Manfred.

When Nicolaus arrived at Deirdre's home, Francesca answered the door, pulling him in with a kiss to his

149

cheek. He saw that Elsa and Rachel surrounded Deirdre in the back sitting room. Constance quickly walked over to him, shaking her head negatively.

"Mother," he quickly kissed her forehead, taking her hand "how is she?"

Constance shook her head negatively again, "No, it's not a good time Nicky. She's devastated."

Nicolaus did not remove his eyes from his beloved, "Oh … I must see her." His body automatically went in the direction of Deirdre, but Constance stood in front of him to stop him, while Francesca pulled back on his arm. Constance put her hand to Nicolaus' chest, "Nicky, she needs time."

Constance's interruption of his movement brought his attention to her. "No, I must see her. Please!" Nicolaus touched her shoulder, and without waiting, he went directly to Deirdre.

She flew into his arms, and he wrapped her in his love. Nicolaus touched Rachel's arm, "Thank you for being here Auntie Rachel," he told her softly. "Elsa," he whispered her name with a nod, then eased Deirdre to the other side of the room, so they could talk.

"Did Benjamin hurt you, babe? Did he hurt you?" His mouth kissed the top of her head, as he held her tightly, wanting to protect her from the world.

"Did you hurt him?" she half whispered, half afraid of the answer. She knew Nicolaus would understand she was asking about Benjamin.

"No. I didn't hurt him. I'm not gonna lie, I wanted to hurt him, but I didn't." He frowned, we had strong words though," he gave a hard sigh, the emotions still raw on him. "Deirdre did he hurt you? You alright?" he asked her again.

150

Deirdre sighed, "No, not in my body. But my God, what are people going to think? What must you think?" she could not look him in the eye.

Nicolaus just held her, their bodies against each other. "What do you mean? Everyone saw what I saw. He basically barged in on that interview, and grabbed you on live tv. I got calls from all over the country, people are shocked at his behaviour. They know it's not you. Ms. Winfree even called to give her support to you."

Deirdre looked up at him, frowning, "Ms. Winfree?"

Nicolaus met her gaze, "Yes, babe, Ms. Winfree. And as for what I think, … I'm … I'm so sorry. I … I failed you. I didn't protect you …"

"Protect me? My God, Nicky, it's not your fault. You shouldn't have to protect me from Benji. Anyway, you've been on the other side of the world," she slipped her thoughts.

Nicolaus caught her comment because now he was being overly vigilant, "Wait, so this isn't the first time this has happened?" Deirdre froze, not wanting to answer him. She saw anger in his face, though he tried to mask it. "Damn, I should have seen this coming," he said under his breath, mad at himself. He put his attention back on Deirdre, "You should have told me, Deirdre." He sighed, pulling her close.

"I didn't want to burden you with this. You have enough to worry about, Nicky."

He broke their embrace, and held her chin as he gently chastised her, "You don't get to decide that. With Benjamin, he has to be checked right away or he will keep pushing. You promise me Deirdre, that if anything ever happens again, if he even looks at you funny, that you will tell me. Promise me." He gently wiped the tears from her beautiful face, the tears that didn't seem to belong there.

Deirdre nodded, "Yes, I promise," she softly agreed.

Nicolaus sighed, and held her tightly again, trying his best to wrap her up in his love.

He kissed her head, until her mother and Rachel pulled her away from him.

Francesca grabbed onto Nicolaus' arm, having grave empathy for both of them, wishing Benjamin behaved better, though he never did. From the time they were children, Francesca remembered that Benjamin was always harassing or assaulting some girl, known or unknown to him. She believed he had a problem of self-control. Though, self-control was not his only problem. Being horribly spoiled increased his jealousy of others, and his sense of entitlement. She felt that her Aunt Ceil did not teach Benjamin properly, though as she tugged on Nicolaus' arm, she did ponder on the reason why these two brothers had such different behaviours. Perhaps because one was starved of a mother's love while the other was smothered with a mother's love.

"How are you doing through all of this?" she asked Nicolaus.

Nicolaus sighed, and found his way to a nearby counter stool. He sat down, feeling disheartened, adrenaline still running through him. He shook his head, "I need somewhere to put all this negative energy."

"Nicky, you need to get to where you are grounded. When you go on a mission and have all that pent up energy, what do you do?"

"After a mission, once we are back at base I would usually work out."

"Well, I think, right now you need peace. You know, peace of mind. What gives you peace?"

Nicolaus looked at Francesca as if she were a genius, "Of course, you're right! I need to go see the Bishop."

Nicolaus gave Rachel, Elsa, and Constance an additional thirty minutes of support to Deirdre before he grabbed her hand and asked her to go to the church with him. Nicolaus drove straight to the historic church they were to be wed in. The church was located on Martin Luther King Jr. Drive, and was the church that both Nicolaus and Deirdre frequented, and greatly financially supported because of the work they did in the community. Once inside the historic frame, the blue carpet welcomed everyone, and carried them forward to the front of the church before the altar. Their hands never parting, Nicolaus led the action, sitting in the front pew.

Deirdre knew it was the silence, peace, and love of the church that made tears seep from Nicolaus' closed eyes. She hugged on his arm, resting her head on his shoulder. She knew he must be emotionally exhausted. He began to pray, at first in Latin, then in English. Deirdre closed her eyes, and focused on his words, his tenderness, his giving spirituality, as he first prayed for others, for her protection, then for peace in his own spirit. Soon, they were joined by the church Pastor, and then also by the Bishop, both men prayerfully laying their hands on them, to heal their pains. The praying grew louder and intense. Deirdre felt herself get emotional, though she didn't know why. She cried as the prayers intensified.

Then, as sometimes happens with Nicolaus during these visits with the Bishop since he was much younger, and unbeknownst to his family, he was touched by what some may call holy love, or the holy spirit, or universe power. The spiritual power ceased him, shaking his strong muscular body, making him semi-conscious, not able to get off the floor, his mouth still uttering prayers. As he was wrapped in this holy energy, everyone stepped away, and let him live through it. The pastor once told Deirdre, 'Never interrupt the energy! He may be receiving some type of healing, or divine intervention, or divine messaging or instructions!' She watched over him to ensure his safety.

After several minutes, it was done, the energy was gone from Nicolaus. He sat up, looked around, and quickly understood what had happened. The men helped him up to his feet, then the Bishop blessed the couple with a holy anointing on their foreheads, and sent them off with more prayer. They left the church wrapped in each other's arms.

Nicolaus looked at the sky. There were still some hours of daylight before sunset. "You up for a dip, babe? I need a cleanse."

Deirdre giggled, pulling this complicated man she loved closer to her, forgetting her troubles. "Sure, hon, whatever you need." She didn't know why, but she felt that everything was going to be okay. Perhaps it was the prayers. Perhaps it was because she could see that Nicolaus felt better. Perhaps being in the church made her extremely mindful of her upcoming wedding. Perhaps she felt that everything was okay simply because she was with the man she truly loved.

Nicolaus drove through the stop and go traffic of the Austin city streets. When they arrived at Hippy Hollow, the optional nude park, there were only a few people present this evening. Nicolaus and Deirdre went to their favourite spot, which they usually had to themselves. They stripped off their clothes down to their undergarments, leaving them on nearby rocks, and hand in hand ran into the water. The fresh stream water was very refreshing and exactly what Nicolaus needed. He floated on top of the water as if letting his troubles sink off him to the bottom of the lake, as he enjoyed being one with nature. Unable to be apart for long, they were soon in each other's arms. Nicolaus kissed his fiancé, "I love you so much. I can hardly wait until we are married. I just want you to be my wife, and walk with me all the days of my life. I love you, Deirdre."

Deirdre was safe in the arms of her man, her love. She responded to every kiss he gave her. Each time he caught her lips in his, she was overwhelmed with emotion. She was ready to be his wife, to give him her all. Finally, they would be together in commitment, in love, and in physical union.

They stayed in each other's arms, in the water, until the sun began to set.

Chapter Twenty-Nine

All were gathered at the mansion for dinner, as Deirdre phoned her mother and told her to meet them there. After she and Nicolaus showered in their separate rooms, they joined everyone downstairs.

Francesca pulled out the video of Ceil in Estonia and showed both Nicolaus and Deirdre. Nicolaus was happy to see Ceil smiling and looking as if she was enjoying herself. He agreed with Francesca, "Yes, she does seem to be in her element. I cannot remember the last time I've seen her so happy."

"The castle is so beautiful," Francesca told them. She hit Nicolaus on the forearm, "I can't believe you haven't been there, with all the traveling you've done."

Nicolaus shrugged, "When you're on a mission you can't exactly go sightseeing. We all have to stay together, and protect each other, and stay focused."

"Well … you ain't on mission now! You two should go here for your honeymoon. And you need to meet our great Aunt Clara while she's still here. She sure knew about you Nicky! She right out asked about you."

Deirdre's eyes lit up. She nodded, "Yes, we should go, Nicky."

"And then I found this!" While the family was waiting for Benjamin, Francesca was using her time wisely. She showed them the picture of their ancestors.

When Nicolaus saw the photo of Nicohls, he took her phone to get a better look. Frowning, "He looks like … me."

"He looks exactly like you," Deirdre agreed.

"Oh no, there's more." Francesca scrolled to the next photo, "Wait for it …" she slowly revealed the photo of

Nicohls and his wife, with a beaming smile on her face. "Can you believe this?"

Deirdre looked slightly taken aback, "What?" She and Nicolaus looked at the photo closely, "Oh my God! I've got an ancestor from Estonia too? What? Mother ... Mother, come see this."

"Yes, Nicohls and DeeDee," Rachel confirmed.

"Auntie Rachel, you know about this?"

Rachel nodded, "We all know about it."

Nicolaus frowned, "But ... you've never told us ..."

Rachel's eyes went to Nigel, then back to Nicolaus. She nodded slightly, and said no more, only touching his front shoulder, looking upon him with love. There was so much she hadn't told Nicolaus, and so much she wanted to tell him.

The air of mystery was interrupted by Benjamin's entrance. He was still fall down drunk. He stumbled in the front door, with an unknown woman, whose clothes were skimpy at best.

Nicolaus immediately went over to Benjamin to help him up. Benjamin begrudgingly accepted the help. Then Nicolaus forced him up the stairs, towards his bedroom suite.

Constance saw that Ceil was about to stop Nicolaus. She touched Ceil's arm, "Ceil, it's okay, let him." Ceil stopped her movements, looked to her, then to Nicolaus. Constance reassured her, "He's not going to hurt him, Ceil. He didn't hurt him earlier. The boys need to talk," she explained. "Trust him."

Ceil sighed, heeding Constance advice. She nodded, "It won't matter soon anyway. None of this will matter."

Constance frowned, not understanding what Ceil was talking about. They sat down together on the sofa, and watched the two brothers go up the stairs, Nicolaus using his strength to practically float Benjamin without effort. Ceil seemed different to Constance tonight, calmer than she had been for a long time.

Rachel and Francesca went to the half-naked, ivory skinned woman, who was looking around the mansion. "And you are?" Francesca was appalled at these women who continued to show up with Benjamin.

"Slit!" she batted her eye lashes that enhanced her blue eyes. She held her hand out for a lady shake to Francesca.

Francesca did not take her hand, but frowned, trying to understand, "Slit?"

She nodded, "Yes, they call me Slit."

"Who calls you Slit?" Francesca couldn't believe it. "What is your name?" she asked her as if she were simpleminded, as she figured she must be.

"Everyone calls me Slit. That's my name!"

"Oh!" Francesca looked to her mother, then nodded to the woman. "Slit, you need a sweater or some kind of covering."

"No thank you, I'm fine."

"No, that wasn't a question. I'll be right back."

Francesca went into one of the nearby closets, and came back with a full-length sweater, that one wears outside in autumn. "Here you go, put that on, and button it up, like … all the way up," she demanded of the woman with a polite smile.

Upstairs, Nicolaus was holding onto Benjamin, who began to resist. Nicolaus turned on the shower water, and he put his brother into the space. Benjamin sunk in a sitting position, with delayed reaction to the cold water pouring on him. Suddenly, he felt the water, and tried to fight it, but could not. Nicolaus let the water run for a few minutes, then turned it on warm for Benjamin. Benjamin was then able to stand, and Nicolaus helped his younger brother out of his clothes, Benjamin again resisting. Nicolaus giggled at his actions, having assisted many of his comrade soldiers and those under his command in the same condition several times before. Nicolaus continued to assist him out of his wet clothes. "Relax, relax," he told him. Once he got Benjamin completely nude, he closed the shower door, "Freshen up," he told him. "Everyone is waiting on you for dinner."

Benjamin let the warm water rush over him, making him feel better, but he found himself wanting to cry. He had that confused feeling about Nicolaus again. Why was he being so nice? Why was he being so helpful? Benjamin quickly washed up and turned off the water, only to find his older brother holding a towel for him.

Not having forgotten the earlier scene today, Benjamin jerked the towel from him, "What do you want?" he asked rudely, with suspicion of Nicolaus' actions.

"Look, I just want to apologize for how I came at you earlier. I was angry when I saw you manhandle Deirdre. I shouldn't have come at you that way, ... Manfred tried to stop me. I could have ... should have handled the situation better. I apologize for my rough behaviour towards you."

Benjamin looked at Nicolaus who seemed sincere, but he didn't want to let him off the hook that easily. Why should he? "Yeah, so you think you can threaten me, and then words make everything normal again?"

Nicolaus looked down, sighing, regretful for what he'd done. He looked Benjamin in the eyes again, being a man, owning up to his mistake. "You're right. I was wrong. My actions were ... inappropriate. And for that

I'm sorry." He touched Benjamin on the shoulder. "Look, we're brothers. We shouldn't be at each other. I don't want us to be, no matter how much mother wants that. We should be closer. But you do have to respect Deirdre. She's going to be my wife in ten days. My wife, Benjamin. Anyway, she and all women deserve your respect."

Without words, Benjamin went into his rather large closet to get dressed. The closet had plenty of shelves and organizers. However, it was a total mess inside, with clothes and shoes strewn all over.

While Benjamin was in his closet, Nicolaus pulled the musty covers from the bed, onto the floor. He also pulled down the thick silk curtains with a yank, and piled them on top of the bedsheets on the floor. The luxurious bedroom smelled badly of sexploitations and sweat, as if an unkept teenage boy resided there.

Nicolaus stepped out the room into the upstairs corridor and dialled the lead housekeeper. The mansion staff was available to the family twenty-four hours a day, every day of the week, and lived in quarters in the mansion. "Ms. Lucy, this is Nicolaus."

"Yes, Mr. Nicolaus, how may I help you?"

"I was wondering why my brother's room hasn't been cleaned. It smells awful in there."

"So sorry, Mr. Nicolaus. Mr. Benjamin does not let my staff in to clean."

Nicolaus could hear the family still chatting below, waiting on the brothers. "No, that's not acceptable. You have my orders and my permission to go in and clean it daily."

"Yes, sir, but … what if …"

"If he protests, just tell him you have orders from me, and go in and clean it. Listen, I've pulled off his bed-

161

covers and the curtains. It's a mess in there. I need someone to come in and clean it for him right now. He has another guest, and ..."

"Yes sir, I understand, we'll be right on it!"

"Thank you, Ms. Lucy. I appreciate it."

As Nicolaus completed the call, Benjamin stepped out of the messy room. Nicolaus smiled at him, touching him on his shoulder. "All right, already," Benjamin told him, "You have your forgiveness."

Nicolaus gratefully nodded, "And Deirdre?"

Benjamin nodded, "Yeah, I'll ... do better," he was not able to read the look on Nicolaus' face, but he thought he didn't believe him. "I will," he reassured him. "Doesn't mean I don't love her though. But I can be respectful of you."

"Thank you," Nicolaus said simply. Time would tell if Benjamin was being truthful.

Nicolaus let Benjamin lead down the steps. Glad tones were heard for Benjamin's better appearance, as he'd lost his inebriated buzz and was able to get down the stairs just fine on his own. He grabbed Slit's hand and introduced her to Ceil, who was less than pleased.

As the family headed into the dining room, Nicolaus swooped Deirdre outside onto the terrace in the warm summer breeze. He quickly swung her around then dipped her backwards, making a joyful cackle escape her lips before he planted a romantic kiss on her. From inside, Benjamin watched the scene and saw how happy they were, bringing prangs of jealousy to him. As Nicolaus lifted Deirdre, her arms were on his shoulders, pulling him in for another kiss. She liked how he was becoming a little bolder with her. She was ready to fully become his wife. Quickly, they rejoined the rest of the family before it was noticed that they were absent.

At the end of the night, Nicolaus walked Constance and Deirdre to their rooms, first dropping off Constance. He held Deirdre around her waist outside of her bedroom door. "Honey, I've decided you need security detail, for your safety. You remember Roddy?"

"Your Roddy? Strictman?"

Nicolaus smiled at her, "Yes, Roddy Strictman. I'm going to get him to be your security. At least until we're married. Benjamin is busy tonight with his lady friend, so he shouldn't be around to bother you, but I'll ask Roddy to start tomorrow. I trust him with my life, and I know he'll totally protect you."

Deirdre touched Nicolaus' face, with love. "You sure this is necessary?"

Nicolaus nodded, "Yes. Once we're married, you'll be in my bed, and I'll have to see how Benjamin is, but hopefully, once we're married his behaviour will stop. I did talk to him, and he told me he'd be more respectful of you, but …"

"You weren't convinced?"

"Hmm … not really. I don't trust his word, not until he backs it up. Anyway, Roddy will be professional, and will not flirt or anything. He's very straight with his work."

"Okay, whatever you think best."

"For tonight, if you need anything, don't leave the room without me. Just call me, and I'll escort you, okay?"

"Yes, darling."

They parted with a sweet kiss, and a lock of Deirdre's door.

Chapter Thirty

With a drink in her hand, and her sexy, satin night-gown on, Ceil brought papers to bed, as she snuggled next to Nigel. She removed the finance book he was reading from his hands, and laid on his chest. She looked up at him, and kissed his chin. "What did you think about Nicolaus and Benjamin tonight?"

Nigel hugged his wife to him, thinking it odd she got into bed to snuggle, and with papers in her hands. "Hmm, you mean when Benjamin came in stumbling?" He gently took her wine and drank some. "I didn't think much, glad to see them seemingly getting along today. Why? Did you have an issue with it?"

"No, not particularly. I was glad they did not fight."

"Yes."

"Well," she sighed, as she was not sure how to present the contract to Nigel, but she thought it was just easier to drop it on him. "I have something for you."

"You seemed to have enjoyed your trip to Tallin. Did you get on with Francesca okay?"

"Oh yes, all was fine. And yes, I did enjoy the trip. I appreciated seeing the Drone operations, and talking to the staff. In fact, this is what we came up with." She handed him the contract folder.

"Oh, that's what this is." Nigel briefly glanced at it without reading anything, thinking it was a report of ideas. He then closed the folder, "Okay, thank you! I'll look it over tomorrow." He placed it on the nightstand.

Ceil finished her wine, and shook her head, "No, dear, I really want you to look at it tonight, especially page forty-two."

Nigel chuckled. "It can wait …"

"No," Ceil insisted.

"Okay." Nigel picked up the folder, and glanced through it again. Suddenly he realized it was a contract. He frowned when he saw all the contract elements were present. Then he went to page forty-two, to see what the hoopla was about. He briefly scanned it, and Nicolaus' name caught his attention. He frowned. Why would Nicolaus' name be in the business contract? He sat up and backtracked and this time he read it. Frowning, not believing he understood what he'd just read, he read it again. "Ceil … what is this?"

"What do you mean? It's the Drone Pharma merger contract."

Nigel went back to the very beginning, making sure it was indeed the merger contract. Yep, it was! Then he went back to page forty-two, the page that included the marriage arrangement between Nicolaus and Marguerite Drone. "Ceil … what is this?"

"You like?" now it was Ceil's turn to chuckle. Indeed, she was getting a kick out of Nigel's reaction.

Not taking his eyes off the paper, Nigel jumped out of bed. "Ceil …what have you done?" He felt a little panicked. It was not Ceil's place to close the deal on the merger. Suddenly, Nigel realized why Ceil insisted on taking care of a stock transfer, and why she suddenly wanted to go to Latvia, alone. He felt tricked, deceived, and duped.

"You are welcome!" she said happily. "I have sealed an unwavering deal with Drone Pharma. We will make profits galore! Make sure you tell that to the board when you explain the terms of the contract to them."

"How could you do this? Nicolaus to marry …"

"Yes, create a long lasting relationship between our two companies? Marvellous, isn't it? Not even you would have thought of it."

"Oh, my God, Ceil …"

"What?"

Speechless, Nigel sat himself down at her vanity table. He looked around the room dumbfounded. How was he going to fix this?

"Don't worry, you'll appreciate my work when you've had more time to read through the contract." Ceil yawned, as if nothing were wrong. "Don't stay up too late, dear, good night." Ceil turned off the lamp on her side of the bed. With a huge smile on her face, she laid down to go to sleep.

Chapter Thirty-One

Nicolaus and Roddy met early in the morning, before dawn, and went running together, ironing out the details of the security arrangement. Roddy was to guard Deirdre's safety in Nicolaus' absence, and Nicolaus would ensure Deirdre was not out of his sight when she was with him. Nicolaus would pay Roddy a handsome fee out of his own savings, and the length of the arrangement was contingent on Benjamin's behaviour after the wedding. Upon their return to the mansion, Nicolaus knew Nigel would be up and about, and interrupted his morning coffee to introduce Roddy and their plans. Nicolaus also introduced him to the staff, and provided him a suite for whenever he wanted to use it.

Nicolaus thoroughly enjoyed his morning run, and had missed such activities. He decided to call up several of his mission buddies to set up regular morning runs and workout routines, to not only keep them fit, but also to keep them bonded together.

As the day wore on at the VMC headquarters, on the twelfth floor, in the downtown glass walled skyscraper, Nicolaus' large muscular frame is studious at his desk, meticulously raking over financial documents. A wall of windows behind him carries the view of downtown Austin. Alexander enters his office without knocking, and lands himself in a chair across from Nicolaus. Nicolaus barely looks up, trying not to lose his place in the mass of figures. "Hey Alexander! I'm getting a workout team together for early mornings. You should join us."

"Early? How early are we talking about?"

Nicolaus shrugs his masculine shoulders, keeping his pen and his eyes on the figures, and enters some numbers into the calculator. "Four thirtyish."

"Whoa! Too early for me, but thanks." Alexander looks over Nicolaus, and sees that he seems to be fitting in the role they've been given. "Well, how are you liking this so far? Trading in your military career to run our dad's company?"

Nicolaus smiles at the question, "It's not easy. That's for sure." Nicolaus makes a mark on the paper, and puts everything down, rubbing his neck. He stretches his tired neck muscle, looking up to the ceiling, and sits back in his chair, giving Alexander his attention.

"What about the wedding? You two ready?"

Nicolaus leans the chair backwards with a smile. He sighs, "I am so ready. Eight days and counting."

Alexander nods. "Yeah, you know, I've known you for so many years now Nicolaus, and I know that you are ... pure, at least that's the word, but ... how are you going to know what to do?"

Nicolaus smiles and frowns at his best friend. He crosses his arms, wondering what Alexander is up to. "What do you mean?"

Alexander chuckles, "You know what I mean. For your wedding night. If you've never seen a naked woman, or done ... anything ... how will you know what to do?"

Nicolaus laughs to himself, he looks at Alexander's mischievous eyes, "I've seen naked women. I've seen pictures. And Deirdre and I have been known to skinny dip at Hippy Hollow for years now. In fact, we were just there."

"What? You got Deirdre to skinny dip? You're joking, right?"

"No. We were just there."

170

"Wait a minute. You've seen Deirdre naked, and you've never …" Alexander uses his hands in a rolling motion instead of words.

Nicolaus chuckled at him. "We're both virgins. We're saving ourselves until we're married."

"Yes, but … have you seen Deirdre?" he seemed amused.

"Alexander, what are you trying to say?"

"Ah, that she's so beautiful. How can you be naked with her, and not …?"

Nicolaus chuckled again. "She's my angel. That's how."

"Uh, I don't think I could do that!"

"Frame of mind, my friend, frame of mind."

"I guess. Okay, but how will you know what to do on your wedding night?"

"I've studied, and read up."

"Studied? Studied what?"

"Medical journals. Reputable sources …"

"Nicolaus, are you kidding me?"

"I'll be ready. I'm more than prepared. Anyway, I imagine we'll both learn as we go. Traditionally, isn't that how it works anyway?"

"No. You need practice."

"Practice? You're not going to turn me into my brother!" They both laughed, "I'm just fine, thank you. Anyway, what's the point of staying pure all these years, if I just go and practice on someone? Nope. I'm good."

"All right, all right. As your best friend, and your best man, I just want to make sure you have everything you need." Alexander threw his hands up in the air, defeated in conversation.

Nicolaus laughed lightly with an eye roll, and a loud

throat clear.

"To change the subject, have you seen Benjamin? I sent for him hours ago."

Now it was Alexander's turn to frown, "You still trying to give him a position?"

"Yes. We need help in accounting. He must be good at something, and I figure he could help with the numbers."

Alexander relaxes in the chair. He knows Nicolaus' heart is in the right place, but this is a time when he must step in to steer him in a different direction. "Oh God, no! You want Benjamin to handle an accounting job? Bad idea ... bad idea! That would most likely be a huge liability for our company. We'd never get him to be responsible with such a heavy job.

Look, why don't you leave that to me? As your co-partner, when you need something, just let me know and I'll take care of it."

"Alexander ... don't you have enough on your plate?"

"Look, we're in this together. I want us to do an even better job running this corporation than our fathers did. So please, let's work together on everything." Nicolaus nods. "I'll tell you what, if we can possibly get Benjamin to step his foot through the doors, let's put him somewhere else, where he can't do us any harm, like over warehousing. Let me look at staff, and see what I can do about accounting."

Nicolaus nods again with a smile, "Agreed!"

A knock at the door presents Dwight. "Hello, my sons, is all going well?"

Nicolaus and Alexander smile at the greeting. They both nod.

"Alexander, I have a task for you, please son."

"Sure, dad! I'll see you later Nicolaus."

Dwight beckons for Alexander to follow him, and they walk to his office. Once inside, Dwight closes the door, and hands Alexander a large document. "Son, I need you to put your lawyer hat on, and review this."

Alexander looks over the document, with a frown. "Is this the Drone Pharma contract?"

Dwight nods, "Yes. There's a problem with the contract. I want you to review it with our team of lawyers, you take the lead. You'll quickly see the problem. But I need you to poke holes in this contract, see if you can find a way around the problem."

"Okay, sure, dad! I'll get the team together. When do you need an answer?"

Dwight loosened his tie, and sat at the edge of his desk. "We have an emergency board meeting at six this evening to discuss it. I'll need you to present your findings."

"Okay, that's plenty of time. But dad, Nicolaus won't be here at six. He has a dinner meeting with Shaquille and Mary."

"Perfect! I asked Shaquille to help us clean up that interview debacle. And now we have this other mess!" he pointed to the contract. "Nicolaus is not needed at the meeting this evening. It's fine."

Alexander looked at his father strangely, "Okay." He briefly looked over the contract and got to work on it.

Chapter Thirty-Two

Elsa's desk is outside of Nigel's office at the VMC headquarters. Suddenly, Benjamin appears clean shaven and looking handsome. He is dressed suited for entering the company building, knowing he has to compete with the neat and suave appearance of Nicolaus and the always professional looking Alexander. Benjamin had not seen or thought about Elsa for some time. The last time he spoke with her was on Deirdre's idea to get his mind to pay attention to Elsa, however, that plan did not work.

Smelling sexy, and feeling his usual horney self, he walked right up to Elsa's desk, as now she'd caught his eye. "Um-mm, who's this pretty thing?" he flirted with her. Benjamin inappropriately places himself on Elsa's desk, just to the side of her.

Elsa, having had a crush on Benjamin for some time, becomes flustered at his direct flirtation. She could feel Benjamin's sexual aura, and wasn't' ready, but knew if she wanted to get this man, she had to act quickly. She stands close to him, feeling daring, and drawn to him. She felt her body get excited as he looked at her. "Aren't you a sight for sore eyes!"

"Sore eyes? Why? You've got my brother to gawk at all day, just like all the other women do," he responded rudely, challenging her.

Elsa bites her lip flirtatiously. "Mmm, maybe I only have eyes for you, Benji."

That got his attention, "Really? Now that's intriguing. Tell me more."

Elsa makes strong eye contact with Benjamin. "There's … something about you. Maybe I have a strong attraction to you."

"Really?" Benjamin's eyes don't leave hers. He draws closer, and grabs her around the waist with one hand, roughly pulling her to him, without her permission, making her gasp. He smiles when she doesn't resist him. He breathes in the scent of her, and moves himself inches from her lips as if he were going to kiss her. His mood changes to a seductive nature, for which he does not try to disguise.

This moment lasts for several minutes, making Elsa's body temperature increase. Her heart is pounding to where she can feel it inside of her chest. Her breathing gets rushed, and she feels heated in his arms, his mouth inches from hers.

Elsa smiles, and rests her hands gently on his chest, wanting his kiss. "Here to see your father?" she softly asks him.

"Actually, I'm here to see my brother, but..." he pauses to observe her face and her beautiful lips, "when I get done," both of his hands encircle the small of her waist, "I'd like to play with you some more."

Elsa remains calm, smiles flirtatiously, fluttering her eyelashes, "Mm-mm, I'd love that, Benji." Elsa turns from him, removing his hands from her. "Follow me, I'll take you to Nicolaus' office."

With obvious flair, Benjamin examines Elsa's back side, in her tight A-line skirt, as she walks like a model, switching her hips all the way to Nicolaus' office. As they round the corner to Nicolaus' office, Nicolaus is putting on his suit jacket to leave. He looks up to see Elsa and Benjamin coming towards his office. He frowns at Benjamin's behaviour as he ogles Elsa's backside.

As they enter his office, Nicolaus smiles and nods, "Thank you Elsa." She nods and leaves the brothers, closing the door to Benjamin's wink. "Benjamin! Alexander and I were just talking about you. Did you get my messages?"

"You gonna blow up my phone every day now, or what?"

"I want to know what type of work you are interested in doing. We can really use your help around here."

Benjamin is surprised at his question, as he feels Nicolaus should already know the answer. "Work? No, that's not what I came to talk about."

"Okay, well, what is it, I was about to leave. I have a meeting."

Benjamin sighs, hating having to ask anything of Nicolaus. He paces, then sighs again, much like Nigel does when he's nervous. "Well … I need …" he sighs again, hesitant to ask.

He paces more, then sighs again.

Nicolaus frowns at his brother's nervousness, and tries to put him at ease, without babying him, "Benjamin, just tell me. You need me to help you with something? No problem."

"I need my credit cards replaced," Benjamin blurts out.

"I'm sorry … what? I … I don't get it."

"My credit cards got stolen."

"Oh no, well did you cancel them?"

Benjamin looks puzzled, "Cancel them? I don't know how to do that."

"Benjamin, you just call the number on your credit card statement. Tell them what happened, and they will cancel them and issue you new ones."

Benjamin shrugs his shoulders, "I don't have that. I don't pay those bills."

Nicolaus frowns, "Wait ... how many credit cards are we talking about?"

Benjamin shrugs again, in an uncaring manner, "I don't know. Ten ... or twelve."

"But ... you don't have the statements? Well, who pays them for you? Mother?"

"I don't know. I guess the bills come here, somewhere."

"Wait a minute ... they're company issued credit cards?"

"Yeah."

Nicolaus is taken aback. "You have ten or twelve company issued credit cards?"

Benjamin shrugs again, as if it is no big deal, "Yeah."

Now Nicolaus is shocked, "I don't have any company credit cards. How much money are we talking about?"

Benjamin is beginning to get tired of the questions, "I don't know. I ... just charge 'em."

"You don't even know how much money you're charging the company?" Nicolaus feels himself getting ticked off, but he tries to control his emotion, though the unjust treatment between him and his brother is gigantically glaring at him, and it stings. "Well, when did the cards get stolen, Benjamin?"

"I'm not sure, maybe a week or two ago."

"Two weeks? And you're just now saying something?" his voice was getting elevated.

Benjamin had enough of the questions. He feels that Nicolaus was about to pass judgement on him. He shrugs his shoulders again, as if he doesn't' really care. "Look, just take care of it for me. Don't tell father, and don't concern mother. Just … take care of it. All right?" he demanded of Nicolaus.

Nicolaus is speechless at Benjamin's reckless behaviour. He doesn't answer him as his mind plays through the scenarios of the request.

"You can do that, right?" Benjamin asks sternly.

"Yeah. Yeah, I'll … take care of it," Nicolaus finally answers him.

"All right. Thanks." Benjamin turns and leaves the office, leaving the door open, feeling that he is benefiting from his brother's position in the company. That Nicolaus is finally doing something for him.

With a frown, Nicolaus picks up the phone and dials the accounting department, the irony not lost on him as to the earlier conversation he had with Alexander. "Yes, this is Nicolaus Ravenell. I need some discreet research done." He provided the details, then left the office to get ready for his meeting.

Chapter Thirty-Three

At the Ravenell mansion, Nicolaus quickly showers and changes his clothes. He has one hour to get to the restaurant for his meeting, and he must pick up Deirdre. As he descends the grand staircase, he sees his mother playing up to television cameras, with several reporters. Having reporters in their home was truly unusual.

A reporter calls attention to Nicolaus, "There he is now! Nicolaus," he calls to him.

Ceil squashes the diversion and places the attention back onto herself, "No, no, no! He has an important meeting. Don't you dear?" she asked of Nicolaus, not waiting for his answer. "Go ahead, go to your meeting. Don't be late."

Nicolaus nods, but looks at his mother with suspicion, as she has never addressed him as "dear". As he leaves out the door, he hears Ceil say, "Yes, well, we must all make sacrifices sometime in our lives."

Deirdre is dressed beautifully, in semi-formal wear, that is also sexy. She loved that Nicolaus couldn't seem to take his eyes or hands off her, respectfully. She loved his essence, and was thankful for having him in her life.

Nicolaus pulls his car into the valet area at the swanky hotel in downtown Austin, arriving about ten minutes before their dinner meeting. Both Nicolaus and Deirdre leave their phones in Nicolaus' car, as requested by Shaquille. The valet attendant assists Deirdre out of the car, and Nicolaus swoops her in his arms in his usual fashion. As they walk into the famous hotel restaurant, many camera flashes appear, as people take pictures of the lovely couple. Nicolaus proudly escorts the beautiful Deirdre to the table, where they greet Shaquille and Mary. The couples exchange hugs and kisses.

"This excitement must be all about you two," Mary tells them. "We don't get all this attention anymore.

For us, it's more like folks waive and keep going," she lightly laughs. Shaquille nods in agreement, "Get used to it. You're both in celebrity status now."

Mary touches Nicolaus' arm, "Especially after that interview. Whew! Your brother, Benjamin! He must be a handful."

"Yes, he certainly is," Nicolaus stated.

Suddenly, the sweet sound of a soulful singer's voice flows through the airwaves of the loudspeakers, when the hit 'All This Love' is aired. Couples flock to the dance floor at the sound of the song.

Deirdre lights up, "Oh my God! This is our song!"

Nicolaus takes Deirdre's hand. He asks Shaquille and Mary, "Do you mind?"

Shaquille has the hugest smile on his face, "Oh, I insist!"

Nicolaus and Deirdre join the other couples on the dance floor. Nicolaus holds Deirdre close, while dancing to the song. Suddenly, they are alone in the middle of the dance floor, with the other couples surrounding them, celebrating them. Nicolaus twirls Deirdre, never letting his hand leave her, then brings her back close to him in a loving embrace. Deirdre is enjoying their dance. Their concentration on each other is interrupted by delightful fervour in the crowd on the dance floor, as suddenly, the singer, himself, appears before them with a microphone, singing the words to the song. A popular celebrity media magazine host and camera crew follow him to the dance floor as he begins to sing to the couple. Deirdre gets frazzled, and the charming singer encourages them to keep dancing as he serenades the couple with the sweet song.

Cameras are flashing, and people all over the restaurant live stream the happenings onto their social media platforms.

Shaquille is happy at the crowd's reaction to the famous singer, "Our plan is working!" he tells Mary with a big smile.

However, while Nicolaus and Deirdre are enjoying their time on the dance floor, back at the VMC headquarters, the board members are chatting and gathering for the emergency meeting. They fill their sturdy paper plates with snacks of fruit and nuts.

Dwight takes Alexander just outside the door. "Okay, you ready? Your findings?"

Alexander holds up the contract with a disappointed look about him, "Dad, it's solid. There's no way to get around it."

Dwight holds his head down, tight lipped, arms crossed. "That's what I figured."

Alexander was quite bothered by all this, "When are we going to tell Nicolaus?"

"Nigel will tell him at the board meeting in the morning."

Alexander was shocked, "He's going to find out at the board meeting? That's really harsh, isn't it?"

Dwight held Alexander by the shoulder, "And Alexander, you cannot tell him. It's not our place! It's Nigel's call. Nigel is his father," he explained.

Alexander nodded, "I understand. I don't agree with it, but … I understand."

"If something of this magnitude was going to be dropped on you, I'd want to be the one to tell you. Let's give Nigel that respect. Right now, my job is to sell this to the board." They walked into the conference room. Dwight closes the door to begin the board meeting.

Meanwhile, back at the hotel, after the song is finished, the singer gives private words of encouragement to Nicolaus and Deirdre, then chicly floats away just as magically as he appeared. Nicolaus and Deirdre are swamped by couples on the dance floor who talk with them and congratulate them.

Shaquille gets a phone call as he and Mary are at their table observing the scene on the dance floor with joy. "Oh, oh, that's the emergency line!" he says looking at the phone. He answers the call with a frown. "Hello!" He pauses to listen, then answers, "Yes, success so far. What?" He sits forward, a deep frown on his face. "She did what?" He looked at Mary with concern. "Oh geez, well … that sucks." He shakes his head, then gives a hard sigh, "No, we'll keep them here. Don't worry about it. I'll take care of it. Okay, no worries."

When the excited couple return to the table, Shaquille is whispering to Mary. The bewildered look on her face changes when she sees Deirdre. She smiles at them, reaching across the table, she takes Deirdre's hand, as Nicolaus helps her with her chair.

Deirdre is still excited, and she puts her hand to her face, "Did you see that? Can you believe it?" She feels hyped up. "Oh my God! That was incredible!"

Shaquille smiles and waves his hands in the air, "Yes, and now you are going to be our guests here at the hotel."

Nicolaus smiles with a frown at the unexpected offer, "Oh Shaquille, I can't let you do that!" He looks around the wonderfully beautiful and expensive hotel.

"Already done, my friend. Sometimes, you have to stop to make memories. And this is one of those nights."

Deirdre knows this is a big deal, "Wow! But we don't have a change of clothes."

Mary waves her hand. "Oh, that's easy. I'll take care of that for both of you. Don't even worry about it. I know it's getting late, and you're both probably tired. Anyway, just please, think of it as gifts from us. We want to do this for you."

"Exactly," Shaquille agreed with Mary's point, "So, I imagine you'll want separate suites, unless you're both too hot, after that love song, to remain virgins until the wedding day," he laughs lightly at his purposefully bad joke.

"Uhp!" Deirdre laughs and chokes on her drink. "No", touching Nicolaus' leg, "we want separate suites, please!"

They all laugh, and food is placed on their table. Loud chatting and excitement in the hotel restaurant remain high. While eating, Shaquille and Mary discuss increasing their investments in VMC with Nicolaus.

After a great meal, the couples are led to their suites by hotel staff. Oddly, the staff members remove all media, such as the televisions, and the alarm radio. Nicolaus thought this strange, but he remembered that Shaquille did have rules for better living, which was why he told them to leave their phones in the car. Nicolaus nods at Shaquille, "Another one of your rules?"

Shaquille gives him a big smile, happy Nicolaus did not question him, "You catch on quickly, my friend." The men bump chests and do a brotherly handshake.

Nicolaus ensures Deirdre is locked in safely and instructs her not to open the door for anyone but him. He hears her secure the door.

Mary hugs Nicolaus to her. "Nicolaus, you are such a good person. Stay true to yourself, no matter what happens."

Nicolaus nods and bids the couple a good night.

Chapter Thirty-Four

The morning brought hurried rushing to both Nicolaus and Deirdre, as they needed to get to work after having breakfast with Shaquille and Mary. They enjoyed their stay at the fabulous hotel. Nicolaus and Deirdre noticed they had several calls on their phones when they turned them on, but had no time to pull the calls. After getting through the stacked up stop and go traffic of the city, Nicolaus dropped Deirdre home, as she had to pick up her vehicle and computer equipment. They kissed passionately on parting, then he got himself to the office.

When Deirdre entered the house, she was surprised that her mother met her with great upset. Upon seeing her daughter and how happy she was, Constance knew Deirdre had not heard the news, which surely meant that Nicolaus had not heard it either. She wasn't sure what to do.

As Nicolaus entered the VMC headquarters, his phone was continually ringing, as he has not yet checked it. Walking up to the building he sees that his phone has over a hundred calls. As he enters the building, there are rows of staff on both sides of the entrance with handmade VMC signs, and hero signs, and other signs with various sayings acknowledging him as a hero. In astonishment, Nicolaus looks up from his phone, not sure what is happening. About a hundred staff members, some familiar to him, and some he did not recognize, clap for him upon his entry. Suddenly, they swarm him and thank him, grab his hand, and shake it, some pat his back, some women hug him, some kiss him on the face.

Different staff approach him, "Thank you, sir," one tells him.

Another person is before him, "Thank you for saving our jobs and the company, sir. I have a sick son, and ... if I were to lose my medical insurance," the woman gets emotional, "... I don't know what I'd do." She takes his hand, "Thank you so much!"

Yet, another staff, "Yea, thanks for saving our jobs. My elderly parents live with me ... they depend on me. If I lost my job, it would really be tough. Ya know?"

Nicolaus has a confused look on his face, as he is gracious to the staff.

The gratefulness continues to flow, "Thank you sir for making such a sacrifice. I know it must be hard."

"You're a hero, sir, marrying that horrid woman. How is Deirdre handling all this?"

Nicolaus frowned at the young man, "What? What are you talking about?"

Elsa suddenly appears from within the crowd. She whisks Nicolaus away from the staff, as she can see he does not yet know the news. "Nicky," she grabs his hand and pulls him away from everyone, guiding him into the elevator. She stands on the opposite wall from him, facing him.

"Elsa ... is something going on that I should know about? That young man said ..."

"Uh! I'm not sure sir," she stalled, following the strict instructions from Nigel. "Your father wanted me to bring you to the emergency board meeting this morning, as soon as you arrived," she told him with a smile, trying to hide her stress. She'd been trying to call Deirdre since last night, after she saw the news reports, but had not been able to reach her. However, she then understood why she couldn't reach her, when she saw the celebrity news coverage of them dancing while being serenaded by the soul singer.

Nicolaus frowned again. He couldn't seem to stop frowning, as he had the looming feeling that something was terribly wrong. "Emergency board meeting?" He looked at his phone again, to check the text messages.

Abruptly, Elsa takes the phone from his hand. "Sir, please prepare yourself, we are about to enter the meeting." She turned from him, knowing he was shocked at her action, but not giving him the chance to ask anything. The elevator opens, and they are met by Alexander.

Alexander grabs Nicolaus by the arm and takes him into his office and closes the door.

Nicolaus puts his attaché case down, and straightens his jacket. "Alexander, is something happening? I have over a hundred calls on my phone ..." he looks around, "the phone that Elsa just took from me ... the phone that won't stop ringing." In panic, he turns around in thought, "Oh my God, is Deirdre okay? I just left her a few minutes ago, and ..." Alexander grabs Nicolaus' arm again, to stop him talking. He sits Nicolaus down in his chair at his desk, and begins to walk in a circle pattern, thinking.

"Alexander, what is it? You seem concerned about something." Nicolaus sighs, tired of asking and getting no answers. "If something is happening ..." Nicolaus' words fall off, as he notices a newspaper on Alexander's desk. He sees a picture of himself beside a picture of a woman who is unknown to him. He quickly picks up the newspaper. "What is this? What ..."

Alexander quickly snatches the paper from Nicolaus' hand, before he can read it. "You're about to be ambushed. You have to stay calm and think clearly."

Nicolaus feels that everyone is behaving strangely today, he frowns, "Why did you take the paper like that?" He sighs, "Ambushed? What are you talking about?" Nicolaus stands, tired of the game. Sternly, he asks Alexander "Are you going to tell me what is going on?"

A knock on the door is heard, followed by Elsa's voice. "Sirs, you are wanted in the conference room now. The board members are waiting for you."

Alexander opens the door, and they follow Elsa to the conference room.

Before entering, Nicolaus composes himself, not sure what is about to happen, but not liking the air of things. As he enters, he sees all twenty-five board members present. "Hello everyone. Forgive me, I was not aware of this meeting."

Nigel stands, and greets his son with a half hug, and hand gestures for Nicolaus to sit in his usual chair beside him, across from his mother. "No worries son, please ...." Alexander sits next to Nicolaus, across from his father. "We had to call an emergency meeting this morning," Nigel continued, "we weren't ready for your presence until now, as this meeting concerns you."

"Oh! Really!" Nicolaus looks at the board members, with a kind expression on his face, while wondering what they have been up to.

On the other side of town, Deirdre answers the door to her beautiful, luxurious home in an upper middle-class neighbourhood in Austin, to find Rachel and Francesca standing before her. Media crews inconspicuously begin arriving outside her home. She seemed frazzled, "Auntie Rachel! Francesca! Wow, I'm not sure why you're here, but I'm so glad you are. I cannot get mother to stop crying, and she won't tell me what's wrong."

Francesca grabs Deirdre to her, and hugs her tightly. Tears welling in her eyes as well.

Rachel sits next to Constance, and tries to console her.

Deirdre frowns with great concern, "What's happened?" She gasps with fright, "Is Nicky all right? Has something happened?" Suddenly, she thought the worst. Was he in a car accident? Was he critically injured?

Back in the conference room at VMC, Nigel begins to lay out the major event that has brought about the emergency board meeting. "As you remember, we were in contract negotiations with Drone Pharma Group."

Nicolaus nods, "Yes. Were we successful?"

Nigel tries to break the news easily. "Well … your mother expedited the negotiations."

"Hmm." Nicolaus briefly eyes his mother. He notices she has a smug look on her face.

Nigel continues, "And … Ceil achieved most of what we wanted as far as the pharmaceuticals. However …" Nigel sighs heavily, and then pauses, staring at the folder before him on the glossy wooden conference table. He felt stressed. How does one do this?

"Yes, father, what is it? "Nicolaus urged him, frowning. "Are we ready to implement the contract?" Silence encased the room. All eyes were on father, son, and mother.

Nigel breathed out, trying to relieve some of the stress. He believed, he'd just better get on with it. Get on with the inevitable heartbreak. There was no way around it now. His son, his dear son, Nicolaus, was the only one in the room that didn't know what life changing news was held on the pages of the paper in the folder before him. He breathed again, "There is a clause in the contract that has a lot of weight and" Nigel pauses again, in thought of how to continue. What words does he use to soften the blow? He wanted to protect Nicolaus from this mean and evil doing of his mother, but no, too late. Can't be undone.

Nicolaus sits back in his chair and eyes his father's unusual behaviour. His forefinger to the side of his mouth. "Clause? What kind of clause?" he asks patiently, urging his father to continue.

"Well... I believe your mother was trying to find a way to strengthen our partnership with Drone Pharma. A way to solidify the contract, you see."

Some board members chime in with agreement, of the unreasonable contract, breaking their awkward silence. "Yes. Solidify," one board member repeats Nigel's words.

"Yes," another board member simply agrees.

"Good contract," an older, grey-haired member offers.

"Solid."

"Yes, good conditions."

Nicolaus frowns, finding the board members' comments odd, and strangely, all from men, as the women board members remain silent. He briefly ignores them, and returns his attention to his father. "Father, what clause?" he returns them to the matter at hand.

Nigel sighs, "Well, that there should be a marriage between families. Our family to their family. Our first born ... to their first born. You to Marguerite Drone."

Nicolaus sits forward, his eyes show disbelief. "What? That's in the contract? That's the woman the papers are talking about? A marriage? In our contract?"

Nigel nods, sighs with stress, and looks down at the contract with closed lips.

Nicolaus looks amongst the board members in the room, with a nervous light laugh. "Who would approve this? Father, surely, you don't need me to tell you to simply have the lawyers strike that clause!"

Nigel takes hold of Nicolaus' arm. "Wait a minute …" Nicolaus sits back in his chair to listen, and Nigel explains, "Of course, we have had the lawyers review it. We had several lawyers of different persuasions review the contract."

"I led our team to review it, Nicolaus. It's solid. No way to break the terms," Alexander told him.

Nicolaus frowned at Alexander, "Alexander, you knew about this and you didn't tell me?"

Alexander opened his mouth to state that he couldn't tell him, but was interrupted by Ceil as she hit the table as if in victory, attracting the attention to herself.

Ceil smiles and gloats, "This contract is unbreakable!"

Nigel briefly gives Ceil a disparaging look, and continues the explanation, "Yes, unfortunately, this is true. It's legal, and its solid. And my son, if the marriage does not happen, we lose everything. The company, every dime, everything."

Alexander agrees, nodding, "That's true," providing the legal opinion for the board.

"What? Why would anyone do this?"

"Not anyone. Your mother!" Nigel corrected him, eyeing Ceil suspiciously, knowing she purposefully schemes against Nicolaus. "Your mother did this behind our backs, I might add. We knew nothing of these terms."

"But … how can mother negotiate a contract on the company's behalf? She doesn't have legal authority!" Nicolaus felt himself getting upset.

"Yes, she does," Nigel told him.

"No father. She doesn't! She'd have to own the largest number of shares …"

Without words, Nigel drops his head, with closed lips and another sigh. He feels utterly defeated. He should have known Ceil was up to something when it came to those retiree shares.

"That's right! So, you do know something about our business after all," Ceil announced sarcastically. "Yes, I do own most of the shares of our company."

Nicolaus racked his mind, thinking of all the figures and monthly reports he'd gone over. He did not remember seeing a share transfer or changes. "Since when? How is that possible?"

"Since I bought all the shares of two retiring stake holders two weeks ago. I bought them out," Ceil continued to gloat. Inappropriately, Ceil taps the table with her fingers, "That contract is solid and legal."

Nigel continued to lay out the terms, "The marriage must take place in seven days, with consummation in six months, or Drone Pharma will own our company, all our stocks, all our money, all our clinics … everything!"

Nicolaus looks shocked and is speechless. Ceil watches with a smile on her face.

Nicolaus grabs the contract from his father to look it over. He sees the bookmarked page forty-two which shows the terms of the marriage. He goes to the signature page. He shakes his head in disbelief. "But all of you signed off on this! How could everyone agree to this?"

"The contract was effective five days ago. The time to reverse the contract has already expired. We only found out about the contract yesterday." Nigel felt sad to tell Nicolaus, because of course, he felt the sting of letting his son down and letting Ceil win over him.

The weight of realization sets on Nicolaus, "No, this can't be! No."

"Nicolaus," Nigel touches his arm, as does Alexander.

Nicolaus tries to maintain some composure for the twenty-five board members who are present to witness this tragedy. He pushes the contract away from him, and sits back into his chair, placing his forefinger to his lip, as before. "So, you are telling me, that if I don't marry the first-born daughter of Drone Pharma, then we lose everything!"

Nigel nods once, "Seven days."

"And everyone signed off on this because it's too late to reverse course. You signed off on it whether or not you agree with it?"

Dwight felt this was a good time for him to interject and assist Nigel, "What I can tell you Nicolaus, as painful as it may sound, as the board, we actually believe this is mostly a good deal, excluding the marriage, of course. What we don't agree with is losing the company."

A long-time board member added, "What choice do we have? Time is expired to make any changes. "

Nicolaus looks to his mother, trying to disguise his hurt. "What choice did you give them?" He shook his head, "This is all because you want to stop me from marrying Deirdre? This is all about Deirdre?"

"This is about the future of this company!" Ceil said happily, the only happy person in the whole room. "You are being groom for Vice President now, for after your father retires. Stepping in where Benjamin should be. So, you want that role, you need to take it all the way."

Nicolaus shakes his head again in unbelief, "Benjamin?" He scoffs. "What are you talking about? Where is Benjamin, mother? Where is he? Really? He surely isn't here! I can't get Benjamin to enter this building to do one task, let alone for him to take over the company!"

Ceil is offended at his comment, hatefully she tells him, "Don't you talk about my Benjamin like that."

"If this is so important to you mother, why isn't his name on this contract? Why isn't your most beloved son named to marry the Drone heiress?"

In controlled anger, Ceil yelled through gritted teeth, "Don't you question my motives!"

Nicolaus nervously challenged Ceil and the Board. His pious spirit would not let his mouth say what his mind was actually thinking. "With a contract like this, frankly mother, I'm questioning a lot of things!" He put his attention on the board members, "You all know darn well Deirdre and I are planning to be married in exactly seven days. We've waited ten years to get married." Nicolaus shakes his head, and places attention back on Ceil, holding up the contract, "Why would you do this? You're putting the company on the line for your little vendetta?"

Nigel reacts sternly, "Okay, okay this is getting us nowhere."

Disgust and upset envelopes Nicolaus. He throws the contract onto the table. "I don't know what everyone is expecting. That I'm just going to roll over and do mother's bidding? It's clear that she should not have authority to make these kinds of decisions!"

Dwight opens his portfolio and tries to find a path for Nicolaus to accept the obvious. He stands and goes to Nicolaus with excited steps. "Look at this Nicolaus! Since the announcement of the merger, our stock price has doubled! And it's expected to quadruple once the marriage takes place! Isn't that wonderful!" As Nicolaus looked at the figures, his mind could not comprehend the relevance to what his mother was purposefully doing to him. "And you just have to understand, this is going to strengthen our company, not only financially, so we can expand services to many more underprivileged people, but this merger will also allow us to be part of biomedicine! It's terrific! I know it seems hard to understand right now, but your mother does know what she is doing!" Having stated his case, Dwight re-seats himself.

Ceil nods and smiles to Dwight, "Thank you Dwight!" then she places her attention back to Nicolaus. She wants to fully expose him publicly. "Nicolaus, why don't you tell us why you haven't married Deirdre? You have known her since you were a child. You have been engaged for ten years." She touches her collar bone, "Ten!" she shouts. Harshly she demands, "Why aren't you already married?"

As Ceil does her best to embarrass and publicly shame him, suddenly, time seems to slow to a stop for Nicolaus, and he can hear his own breathing. He sees the atmosphere of the room turn into slow motion as his anxiety rises. Sweat beads on Nicolaus' forehead. His mother's behaviour makes him feel helpless and stricken with the anguish that only she brings about, as when he was a child when she was abusing him. Memories of childhood abuses flow through his mind: the time she crushed his leg bone, the many times she harshly struck him across the face, the many times Ceil mocked him and laughed at him, the time she threatened to physically remove his manhood with shears. And he remembers Deirdre's reactions to Ceil's cruelty, and how it terrified

197

her, which is why she has been hesitant for them to marry for so many years. And now, this.

Nicolaus' eyes move from side to side as he views the board members waiting for his answer. He eyes his mother. Sweat drops from his brow as his anxiety further heightens. He grows pale with sick nerves.

The loud sound of Ceil's voice harshly yelling at him and insulting him before everyone, brings him back to reality. "Tell us! If she is so important to you, and you love her so much, why haven't you married her?"

Nigel touches Ceil's hand, for her to stop, "Ceil."

Ceil jerks her hand away from Nigel, refusing to stop. "The board deserves to know why." Ceil sharply looks at Nicolaus, and yells again, "Tell us!"

Nicolaus is startled by her demeanour, as she resembles an evil caricature to him, fully displaying the hatred she has for him. "Because ..."

"What? Speak up!" she demeans him, the military hero, in front of the board.

Nicolaus feels the sweat drop from his forehead, as the sickness rises. He is determined not to vomit in front of everyone. He can feel the eyes of the board members on him as silence fills the room, waiting for his answer.

"She hesitates."

Alexander is uncomfortable with Ceil's public shaming of Nicolaus, as she tries to turn this on him, though it is her doing. He wants to say something, but he sees his own father slightly shake his head for him not to intervene. Dwight has often warned him not to get in the middle of disputes and arguments where Ceil is concerned.

"Speak up!" she says in a hateful tone. "We cannot hear you!"

"She hesitates because of you." Nicolaus says the words as the reality grips him. "It's because of you, mother!"

Ceil sits back in her chair, as if in satisfaction. "My, my! Yet, if I were in love with a person, that I claimed I could not live without, there would be nothing stopping me from marrying that person. Just goes to show, I am right about her. She does not belong in this family. She is not fit to be part of us. And she brings nothing to the table."

"That is just not true, Mother," he sternly states, frowning. At this point, Nicolaus is not sure what to do. He absolutely wants to do something, he wants to say more, do more to defend Deirdre; but the look of his mother's eyes forbids him.

Nicolaus struggles against the high anxiety draped over him, being paralyzed with the dread and childhood fear of his mother, uncertain what more she would do to him. Would she harshly strike his face before everyone if he disagreed or challenged her further?

Nigel is silent. The Board members are silent, mostly looking away or down at the table, anything to avoid eye contact with either Nicolaus or Ceil.

With a smile, Ceil leans forward, over the table, eyes locked directly on Nicolaus, her behaviour escalating. She publicly wields the power she knows she has over him. In a harsh but calm voice, she tells him, "No. You will honour this merger. You will marry Marguerite Drone. And nothing more is to be said. Do you understand me?"

Sickness rises to Nicolaus' throat, but he refuses the urge of his body to project his vomit in the room. Nicolaus takes a shaky breath, with eyes stayed on Ceil. In a calm tone he tells her, "Don't do this. Please … don't do this." He shakes his head, "If you want me to step down, I'll step down. Just don't do this."

"It's already done. You will honour the merger." Ceil sits back, and smiles with satisfaction.

Nicolaus looks down, away from Ceil's eyes, trying to shake the spell she has over him.

His commander mind takes over. He knows he's got to get out of this room. "Uhm, I will get back to everyone. Let us, please, table this discussion for now." The board members agree, what else could they do? This has been a shocker to all of them. Nicolaus retrieves the contract from the table and leaves the conference room, as everyone is standing and chatting. Nicolaus heads directly for the men's room. He enters the stall, and vehemently vomits his guts.

Chapter Thirty-Five

After a while, Alexander has not seen Nicolaus, and he is worried. Alexander seeks out Nicolaus, knocking on his office door, then entering, without waiting for permission. He closes the door, seeing Nicolaus in a chair in the corner, staring out, looking devastated and sickly pale.

"Nicolaus, how are you doing? I've never seen you like this."

Nicolaus is extremely distraught, barely aware of Alexander's presence, he suddenly looks up. "What?"

"It got pretty heavy in there." Alexander pulls up a chair and sits next to Nicolaus. "What are you going to do?"

Nicolaus leans forward, his elbows on his knees, his hand rotates over his mouth, face, and eyes. He shakes his head, "I don't know." He sits up straight in resolve, "I'm not gonna give up Deirdre!" Then retreats back to his previous leaning position. "I ... I ... can't be without her." He gets emotional, deeply frowning, "Do you get me? I cannot exist without her. The mere thought of it just kills me. It's like ... I can't freakin' breathe. My life ..."

Alexander touches Nicolaus on his shoulder, "Nicolaus you know what will happen."

The thought of what will happen fills Nicolaus with anger, "This is all such bull crap!" He sighs, "I don't know what I'm going to do."

"Did you call Deirdre yet?" Alexander tries to navigate Nicolaus through this chaos. Nicolaus lets out a breathy scoff, "What am I gonna tell her?" He frowns even deeper if that was possible, "She tried to warn me.

What would I even say?" He scoffs again at a loss, "How am I supposed to explain this?"

Alexander stands, nudging Nicolaus, "We should go over there. She's probably heard something by now. I'll drive you."

When Alexander pulls up to Deirdre's beautiful home, press are camped along the street.

Manfred and Roddy are already there. Manfred has a team of security keeping the press away from the house. Nicolaus sadly nods to Manfred in appreciation, patting his shoulder.

As he and Alexander walk up to the front door, it flings open, and a crying and distressed Deirdre is before him. She sees his tears as she jumps in his arms. His loving, strong arms wrap around her. The flashing cameras of the press is overwhelming.

"What's happening to us? What's happening?" she asks him.

Nicolaus continues to hold her, the contract still attached to his hands. He buries his face in her shoulder, unable to look at her for the moment, "Please don't hate me," he whispers to her. "Please, don't hate me." They enter the house. Alexander closes the door to shield them from the eyes of the press.

Rachel is consoling Constance who is overwhelmed with consoling Deirdre from this tragedy that Ceil has created. Francesca takes over for Rachel when Nicolaus walks in. Rachel kisses his forehead with the love of a mother. She is concerned for Nicolaus as he holds Deirdre to him, comforting her, while appearing sickly upset himself. "Nicky," she says lowly, looking upon him with deep empathy.

"Auntie Rachel, thank you … I … I …" he can't think right now.

Rachel brings Nicolaus and Deirdre to sit on the sofa. "I heard about what Ceil has done. You must be strong through this, Nicky. Most of all, you cannot let Ceil break you."

"Why is she doing this, Auntie Rachel? Why doesn't she want us to marry?"

Rachel shakes her head, "It's Ceil. She has always done things like this to you, in one form or another."

Nicolaus frowns, the anger resurfacing, "But why this? Why?" he slightly yells.

Rachel is at a loss to explain the complexities to the couple at this emotional time. Also, she knows Nigel would not want her to try. Anyway, no one can really explain Ceil's behaviours. She sighs, "I don't know, sweetie. But look, no matter what happens, the love you two have for each other is special. That is very evident."

Nicolaus shakes his head, as if Rachel is not grasping the situation, "She doesn't know what she is demanding of us."

Rachel kneels before the couple, who are hugged up, as if the world is against them. Francesca and Constance join near, Constance is more composed. "Nicolaus, remember the pictures Francesca showed you of our Estonian ancestors? You resemble Nicohls, and you are named after him, as he was a great warrior. And Nigel, well, he has African American roots of free people joined with his Moorish roots. Your ancestors have given you strength through their blood and strong determination. But Nicky, it is you who must carry forward the torch of all our ancestors. Both sides have lived through many struggles, and we never give up. Our family history is long, and many sacrifices have been made over many decades for us to be where we are now."

Rachel stands and sighs, wanting to reveal truth to Nicolaus, but knowing it is not the right time. "When you were born, I had a premonition that your life was not going to be easy, and I was right about that. You cannot let Ceil break you, or destroy our fortune, or give away everything our families have sacrificed to build," she tells him sternly, looking to lift him up.

Deirdre lays her head to Nicolaus' shoulder, tears streaming from her eyes as she holds onto him tightly. "We know Auntie Rachel, we know. This is heart wrenching! It's our love ..." tears cut her words.

Rachel kneels before them again, taking both Deirdre and Nicolaus' hands, but speaking directly to Nicolaus. "Nicky, your father needs you. He wants to retire. And Nicky, I want to see you run the company. Is this a high price to pay? Yes. But honey, one day you will be head of the family; making all the decisions for all of us, including Ceil."

Nicolaus nodded in understanding, but her words did not diminish the sting of hurt, unjust action, and heartbreak that is occurring. Is everyone expecting him to abandon Deirdre?

Chapter Thirty-Six

Cleary eyed, and a little calmer the next day, Nicolaus and Deirdre are attempting to find a way out of this contract. Deirdre asked her long-time friend, and lawyer, Frank, to assist them to review the merger contract.

"Deirdre, you're a lawyer, too. What do you think about the contract?" Frank asks her.

Deirdre tries to be strong, however, she cannot make the tears stop falling from her eyes.

"I can barely believe what I am reading, Frank. And I'm too close to it. That's why we asked you to review it. This is the worst merger I've ever seen. Drone Pharma gets all the advantages. Everything hangs on that marriage clause."

Frank nods in agreement. "Yes, that is true, the marriage is the agreement. I am very sorry, but there are no loopholes in this contract. Alexander was correct. Whoever drew this contract up, covered all the bases. And Nicolaus, your father is correct, the deadline for reversal expired many days ago."

Nicolaus takes Deirdre's hand, and sighs heavily. He shakes his head in disbelief, not getting the break he was hoping for.

Deirdre stands and speaks with emotion. "Babe, remember I told you, your mother was adamant about us not marrying. During the fundraiser, she told me she was going to decide who you would marry. This contract makes sure of that!"

Nicolaus nods with pain, holding his hand to her, so she could reseat herself. "So Frank, give us the full run down."

"Okay, well, the contract specifically names you, Nicolaus, as the party to marry Marguerite. If you don't marry the Drone heiress within the next six days, VMC belongs to Drone Pharma Group. I'm talking all stocks, monies, offices, clinics, staff, research, everything.

And there must be consummation within six months of the marriage. If Marguerite doesn't marry you, she will lose her inheritance and her trust fund. The contract states that her recently deceased mother set a condition in her will, that Marguerite must marry a rich American before receiving her trust fund money.

If you two marry and divorce or attempt to annul the marriage, your family will lose the company, and her trust fund will be rescinded. If there is no consummation, your family will lose the company and her trust fund will be rescinded. The contract also states there can be no amendments or changes added. I am sorry Nicolaus, there is just no upside to this contract."

"And what about Deirdre?"

"The contract does not mention Deirdre."

"Nicky, you cannot let your family lose the company," Deirdre points out. "The work that is done to help so many people is too important. And who knows what Drone Pharma will do with all the research, and the assets."

Frank nods in agreement, "Nicolaus, your mother knows you very well. This is such a huge gamble. I'm pretty sure she is certain you will not sacrifice the company."

Nicolaus was incensed, "Isn't this extortion? How can I be forced to do this?"

"It's not extortion. It could certainly seem that it might be, but in actuality it's not, because it is your mother, the leading partner, who set the terms, and this fact is clearly stated in the contract. Now, if Drone

Pharma came up with these terms, then yes, that would be different.

Unfortunately, the contract lays grounds for the strengthening of the corporate partnership through marriage of the families. Similar to royal arranged marriages. Therefore, it is not illegal. However, Nicolaus, as your lawyer, I will tell you that since this is not extortion, you do have the option of NOT doing this." Frank sits back into his chair, pausing, giving Nicolaus a moment to think about what he is saying. Then he continues, "You are an adult. You do have rights. You do not have to be forced to marry anyone. If you don't marry this woman, the consequences are great in that your family will lose the company, but you are not obligated to alleviate that consequence, Nicolaus."

"Oh my God, this is so unfair!" Deirdre knows there is not really an option here.

Frank continues, trying to persuade Nicolaus not to endure this. "As your lawyer, I am directly advising you not to go through with this merger. Do you even know of Marguerite Drone?"

"No. I know nothing about her. Why would I?"

Frank frowns, but happy to have a way to drill this home, "Nicolaus, you will be miserable. That woman is awful! She's not a nice person. Do some research. You should run from this, and let the chips fall where they may. Your mother took a huge gamble, and there are consequences to these kinds of decisions."

Nicolaus feels saddled in disappointment, not sure what to do. He turns to Deirdre, taking her hands in earnest, pulling her to him. "Deirdre, let's just leave now. Come away with me. Let's get married today. Right now!"

Deirdre slowly touches his face, kisses his lips, and holds his face gently, so he could really hear her words. "I love you so much. You know I do. And I thank you for offering that, Nicky." Slowly, Deirdre sits away from him, tears uncontrollably falling from her eyes again. She shakes her head in disbelief, "I cannot be responsible for the fall of your family's empire! It's too much!"

Another sting. Another blow. Another defeat. "You're right." He looks at her, what was he thinking? "You're right. I'm sorry for asking that of you."

Deirdre and Nicolaus hold each other's hands.

"Nicky, you are my heart! You're my love! I will be here for you, no matter what you decide." Deirdre straightens with dignity and stops crying. "If you decide to let it all fall, six months after the dust settles, then we'll get married. If you decide to marry that woman, I will still be here for you to support you in whatever you need."

Nicolaus tenderly kisses Deirdre's hands, as if she were a queen.

Deirdre wipes her tears, stands, quickly gathers her things, and leaves the room in quiet grace, dignity, and beauty. She has to work hard to hold herself together. She enters the elevator across from Frank's office. Deirdre is alone in the elevator as the doors close. Emotionally, she falls apart.

Chapter Thirty-Seven

In the Ravenell mansion drawing room, it is just after noon when Benjamin enters. Having just gotten out of bed, his hair is tousled, his face unshaven, he is bare-footed, and wearing a silk robe. He goes straight to the side bar, for a fresh scotch. His only concern seems to be that scotch.

Both Ceil and Nigel are present. Nigel is quickly upon him, "Benjamin, have you heard from your brother?"

Benjamin frowns, "Surprisingly, no. I usually get messages from him every day trying to recruit me for some kind of work at the office. I haven't heard from him in three days now. I supposed that is because mother is trying to railroad him into that marriage."

Ceil plays fake appalled at such a notion, "Railroad him? I am doing no such thing. I'm merely trying to expand our company."

"Expand? Mother really? I can hardly believe that you so callously set this all up, just in time to interrupt his marriage plans to Deirdre."

"Callous? What you must think of me Benjamin!" she replied jokingly with a light laugh.

Benjamin smirks, while taking a drink of the smooth scotch. "Mother, you do know you are literally ripping Nicolaus' heart out? I hope he hasn't flung himself off some cliff somewhere."

Ceil sighs, "Don't get my hopes up!"

Benjamin takes offense, not finding her comment tasteful or funny, "Jesus, mother! Have you no mercy for Nicolaus at all?"

"I'm sorry, Benjamin. I didn't mean to upset you." Ceil walks over to touch him to calm him, more worried about upsetting him, than her awful thoughts about Nicolaus.

Nigel frowns, bothered by her attitude, "This is no joking matter. We need to find Nicolaus to make sure he is okay. And the clock is ticking on this merger."

"This marriage merger is a huge action to stop Deirdre from coming into this family," Benjamin observes.

"That woman does not belong in this family."

Benjamin frowns, "Why is it that you dislike Deirdre? She's always been around us, ever since I can remember. She's practically part of our family anyway."

Ceil sighs and shakes her head, "I'm tired of taking care of her and her mother."

"On the contrary, as I keep reminding you, it was Constance that took great care of my mother when she was dying. Surely, you remember that, Ceil."

"Yes, yes. And as I keep telling you, it is we who took care of Constance when she lost her husband, and have taken care of her ever since."

"Yes, because that was your doing, Ceil. We owe that to Constance! We owe her!" Nigel yelled.

"When the hell does that debt get paid, Nigel? Never?"

Benjamin was confused. He had not heard this argument. "What happened? I haven't heard about this ..."

"Never you mind," Nigel snapped at him.

"Don't worry about it, Benjamin."

"Well... regardless, you have miscalculated one fact, mother."

Ceil looks upon her son, "Really? And what might that be?"

"You forgot that I too love Deirdre. And now that she can no longer have Nicolaus ..."

210

Ceil rolls her eyes in disbelief, "Oh no, we're not going there. I forbid it!" She points her finger at him as she gives him this directive. "You hear me, Benjamin? I forbid it! I will find you a suitable wife. You leave Deirdre alone!"

Benjamin smirks at Ceil again for trying to place a demand on him. "Not likely mother, not likely." Benjamin quickly refills his drink and exits the room.

"Benjamin," Ceil calls after him to no avail, "Benjamin!"

Constance steps into the room, hearing all the yelling. She suddenly appears before Ceil and Nigel, who have fallen silent at her presence. She nods to each of them in greeting. "Nigel. Ceil."

"Constance!" Nigel greets her with a kiss on the cheek and a slight hug. "I'm surprised to see you here!"

Constance nods, "Yes … well, I'm here standing in for Nicolaus. He sends word."

Nigel breathes a sigh of half relief, but he does not know what Nicolaus is going to do.

"Constance, please tell me, do you know where he is? Is he okay?"

Constance looks at Nigel with a frowned surprise, "Nigel, he's been with me and Deirdre. Surely Nigel, you must know he is not in a good way. Sometimes I wonder if you even know your own son."

"I just thought …"

Constance interrupts Nigel and looks to Ceil, ready to defend Nicolaus and Deirdre.

"We have been discussing this ugly business you've manufactured. This is cruel, Ceil, even for you."

"I don't know what you are talking about…"

"Why are you tearing Nicolaus and Deirdre apart? You know they have always been destined for each other. Truly, I don't understand why you think you need to run Nicolaus' life.

And I certainly don't understand what you have against my daughter! Not less than two weeks ago, Deirdre fund raised over a million dollars for your company mission."

"Well, I ..."

Constance walks away from Ceil, not letting her finish, and she looks to Nigel.

"This is all so hard for me to understand! How could you even let this happen, Nigel? Letting things get this far out of hand! I really think you do not understand who your son is. You really truly, do not know who he is." Nigel looks sheepish, not having answers for Constance.

"Constance, I do appreciate you looking after Nicolaus, especially at a time like this. Where is he now, do you know?" Nigel asked her, feeling desperate to hear from his son. Nicolaus literally holds the fate of their family in his hands.

Constance nods, "He is at the office. He asked me to let you know he is ready to speak with the board."

Nigel sighs with nervousness, "Okay. Okay."

It was about two o'clock that afternoon, by the time the board members were gathered to meet. Everyone was on edge, not sure if Nicolaus would agree to Ceil's cruel scheme of forcing him to leave Deirdre at the altar to save the company.

Alexander sits next to Nicolaus, who sits next to his father, and across from his mother.

The board members give Nicolaus their undivided attention and hang onto his every word.

Nicolaus sighs, emotions still raw. "It has been a trying time for me. This decision is heavy. Put yourself in my shoes, just think if it was yourself that was being asked to make this decision, or your son, or family member.

When I left my military career to take the lead here alongside Alexander, to follow after my father, at his request, I was sure that leaving the military was the biggest life decision I'd ever have to make. It's a sacrifice. And of course, I want to support my family and the business in any way possible. But now, I'm being asked to make an even greater sacrifice … one that seems … unfair."

Ceil rudely interrupts him, "Stop whining! You think you're the only person who ever had an arranged marriage?"

Nigel remains silent, nervous, but inward he is beaming with pride in his son, seeing he has pulled himself together, feeling he will make the expected decision.

However, a board member, feeling a little more sure of himself today, steps in, "Ceil… please. The board would actually like to hear what Nicolaus has to say. Please, let him speak."

"Thank you," Nicolaus replied, surprised that the board member spoke up for him. Nicolaus' eyes meet Ceil's gaze of hatred for him, as he takes a breath to regather his thoughts and continues. "It was not easy to come to a decision about what is being demanded of me.

This merger, this contract, while not illegal or extortion, is really close to being just that." Nicolaus eyes Ceil again, feeling the upset return. "And frankly, it's completely unjustifiable. Marriage has nothing to do with merging companies. This merger, for the pharmaceutical benefit, could have easily happened without the marriage clause. While some of you in this room have tried to convince us that this merger is good for the company, I wholeheartedly disagree with you.

Although we may be getting some benefit of biomedicine, that is not our company mission. Our company mission is to serve underprivileged communities at the local level, through health insurance and medical care in our clinics, and we have done this well.

This merger puts an albatross around our necks, and is going to bog us down with massive regulations, especially because it's an international merger.

On top of that, the very existence of our company is now hinged on the actions of a few people. And if those people fail... including myself, we will lose everything. So, no, I do not agree with this merger, and it should have never been binding.

Also, we have to think about other aspects this merger touches. What about our 15,000 employees? They have livelihoods and families. And what about the thousands of patients we serve every day? And the stockholders?" Nicolaus pauses to eye Ceil, then the board members, then continues. "This vendetta merger is a dangerous game being played with people's lives."

Nicolaus takes a breath. "Having said all this, we are now down to decision time.

And I want everyone in this room to understand, that it is a decision. Some people thought this was a done deal, well that is just not true. I am, after all, an adult... and an American citizen, and... I do have rights! So, in honouring my rights ..." The board members are intrigued, hanging onto his every word for his answer. "I have conditions of my own before I would ever agree to honour this merger. Alexander has assisted me with legalities and terms."

Ceil chimes in, "You cannot add conditions to this merger. It's already signed, its legal."

Another board member interrupts Ceils rant, "Ceil … please. Again, we are going to ask you to refrain from interrupting Mr. Nicolaus. Go ahead Mr. Nicolaus."

Nicolaus gives a slight smile. "Thank you. I am aware that I cannot add to the contract, but we can institute a policy, right here and right now. I propose that we ensure this kind of action can never happen again! All contracts over the amount of five thousand dollars must go through four levels of approval: Alexander will be the first line of approval, then myself, then Dwight, and then my father. In the policy, which Alexander and I have drawn up" Alexander stands and passes copies to the board members, "… for you to read and for your signatures, we name the positions of authority, for future use. Only, with unanimous agreement, from everyone in this room, today, will I then move forward with the arranged marriage, so that we can keep our company, our money, stocks, and assets."

Ceil retorts, "Five thousand dollars? That's absurd! It's such a low threshold. That is only going to cause more work for everyone. We will not agree to this!" Nigel touches Ceil's hand in an effort to get her to hush.

The board members discuss the policy and are murmuring amongst each other.

Nicolaus replies to his mother's concern, "I know the threshold sounds low, mother, but it's the only way to protect our company assets."

Ceil balks at him, "You are ridiculous! Protect them from who? We …"

"Ceil, the board agrees with this proposal," states one of the board members that asked Ceil to stop interrupting Nicolaus earlier, now interrupts her ranting. "It is not unreasonable at all. Nicolaus, I will be glad to be the first to sign this well thought out policy."

Dwight also replies, "Nicolaus, I have to say, I respect what you said about sticking to our mission. And I appreciate that you have thought about our stakeholders, and our employees in your decision. This policy does make sense, and really, we should have already had such a measure in place for quality assurance. Nicolaus, you and Alexander are showing us that you are both in the right place at the right time. I will be honoured to sign this policy."

Several board members agree loudly as well, "I will sign it!" one says.

"Me too, I think it's a brilliant idea."

"We can't just have rogue contracts being formed without our consent," comments another board member, indirectly criticizing Ceil's actions. "We do need something to protect our assets and our stocks."

With the needed support to keep his mother from making any such future moves, Nicolaus looks to his mother, "As I said, mother, I must have unanimous agreement, from everyone, and I mean everyone, in this room, today, in order for me to move forward."

The board members quickly sign off on the policy without hesitation or complaint.

Ceil is the last to sign. Begrudgingly, she jerks the pen from Nigel, and signs the paper with grunts and masked complaints. After signing, she angrily storms out of the conference room, without speaking to anyone.

Though Nicolaus won this battle against his mother, and is unsure of the consequences it will bring to him, the heavy price of giving up Deirdre still drapes around his neck. "Thank you all for your support on the new policy," he tells the board. He stressfully sighs and sombrely confirms to them, "As I have given my word, I will now move forward with the agreement."

Nigel grabs Nicolaus on the shoulder, "Thank you son. As Dwight has said, you have proven to this board, yet again, that you should lead our corporation into the future, with Alexander by your side." Nigel looks at all the board members with a sigh of relief, and nods one time, "This meeting is adjourned."

Nigel calls Elsa on the conference room phone. "Elsa, go ahead and make the arrangements we discussed earlier for Marguerite Drone and her family. Get them on the first available flight, we need her here immediately!"

As they are gathering their papers, and Nicolaus hands the dreaded contract back to Nigel, Alexander looks up in surprise. "Oh my God, look whose here!"

Nicolaus looks up and is also surprised. "Benjamin!"

"Don't get excited!" Benjamin tells them. He is dressed professionally, shaven, and smelling good. "I just came by to check on you", he tells Nicolaus. They briefly hug. Benjamin frowns, glad he is not in his brother's shoes. "You look like shit! You okay?"

Nicolaus looks down with a frown, then at his brother, "No. Not really."

"So, you're seriously going to let mother take Deirdre from you?"

Nicolaus nods slightly, without joy.

"He did great in the board meeting, though. You just missed it!" Alexander tells him.

Nicolaus crosses his arms, "I have given my word. And anyway, there really is no other option without us losing everything. Mother made sure of that."

"Your word?" Benjamin looks at him surprised, as if that were an outdated thing to do. "Shheww! If it were me, I'd let this place burn. I'd strike the match myself before I let mother do me so wrong. She knows it too, that's why my name is not on that contract." He crossed his arms and observed his brother in a similar stance as Nicolaus, feeling sorry for him. "I can't believe you still let mother push you around like that!"

Nicolaus shakes his head, "It's more complicated than that, Benjamin."

"Like hell it is."

"Mr. Nicolaus," a board member interrupts the conversation, "what you said is profound and true. I think we all needed to hear it. Thank you for your thoughtful decision."

Another board member comes right up to speak to him, "Nicolaus, you are very brave. I know this cannot be easy. Bless you, sir! Bless you!"

"Thank you," Nicolaus tells him.

The next board member in line to speak to Nicolaus, kisses him close to his mouth.

"What you are doing is brave. And yes, you will save many jobs and livelihoods." She pats him on the chest with a smile, and leaves.

"Thank you for your support," Nicolaus tells her.

Benjamin continues their conversation, amused at the interaction of the women on the board with his brother, "How is it you are a decorated military major, who commands units of men and women - who would die for you- by the way, but you can't stand up to your own friggin' mother?"

Nicolaus briefly thinks before answering. "It's … not that … cut and dry."

Benjamin teases Nicolaus, "My brother, the mighty warrior, who can't stand up to his own mother."

"Look, I did what has to be done," Nicolaus' tone was that of ending this conversation. "Now if you really want to help, it would be great if you would start contributing to the company. We really need you! I'm more than sure we can find something for you to do."

Benjamin steps back, half joking, half not, index finger in the air, "And that's my cue to leave!" Benjamin turns quickly and walks out the conference room.

"Benjamin!" Nicolaus calls after him, "Benjamin!"

Alexander rolls his eyes and shakes his head.

Chapter Thirty-Eight

Andrejs loaded his daughters into his private jet, for their journey to America. They would be staying in Texas for three days, and he planned for him and Penelope to leave immediately after the wedding ceremony, as he imagined the environment would be hostile towards them. Already, they had been receiving calls from the media for interviews, which he declined.

Unfortunately, one of the media members got ahold of Marguerite, and she was upfront in letting them know about her unhappiness to marry 'this Nicolaus Ravenell', whom she "hated". Furthermore, she "did not care about 'that Deirdre', and she could keep that ass Nicolaus and go to Mars to never be seen again, for all she cared". Sadly, these quotes were printed, and already causing issues for the Drones, as Nigel called Andrejs and asked him to keep his daughters away from the media.

Also, his family was directly receiving nasty letters and comments from Americans, as Marguerite disparaged the beloved couple. There were hundreds of thousands of single American women who would gladly step in to be the good wife of Nicolaus Ravenell. The American women let Andrejs know that the attacks on their beautiful and innocent Deirdre were unnecessary and would not be tolerated.

"And I'll tell you another thing," Penelope fed Marguerite lies about Nicolaus, knowing her sister would take whatever she gave her, hoping to make the marriage fail so that she, who was the one who actually loved Nicolaus, would be the replacement to keep the contract intact, "that Nicolaus tells lies. And don't think he won't cheat on you with Deirdre." She put her hands in the air as she spoke in somewhat broken English, "Oh, he's going to cheat, cheat, cheat! That's why his mother not trust. And believe me, Marguerite, if the mother not trust son, then not you too!"

Marguerite brooded as she listened to her sister, knowing this marriage was a horrible idea. She looked at the pop magazine before her, as even their own local media carried the story. It showed a picture of Nicolaus and Deirdre, the happy couple, enclosed in a broken heart frame, with a picture of Marguerite between them. Angry, Marguerite closed the magazine and slammed it on the floor of the jet, getting her father's attention, who was sitting across from them, reading through the Latvian Financial Times newspaper. He smiled broadly, as he saw that the stock in Drone Pharma was through the roof, more than any time in the history of the company. He knew it was because of the impending marriage, for which he sent a press release yesterday.

"Turn this plane around! I'm not doing this!" she yelled at her father. "I hate that bastard, and I'm not going to marry him!"

"Stop it, you two," Andrejs ordered them. "This is a done deal." He looked at his older daughter as if she'd lost her mind. She'd been acting more horrible than usual lately, "Do you know how many women want to be in your shoes, Marguerite? You are getting a good man. And this is already helping our company."

"Good man? Ha! No papa, he is a liar and a cheat!"

"Really?"

Marguerite pushed at Penelope's arm, who was sitting quietly next to her, "Tell him, Penelope, tell Papa how he lies." When Penelope remained quiet, Marguerite looked at her astonished, she pushed her again, "Tell him!" she orders her sister.

Andrejs did not want to hear it anyway, he waived the concern, "All men lie about something. You mean you have never lied to me, Marguerite?"

"What? I … I …, that is different Papa!"

Out of patience, Andrejs closed the paper and sat forward to address his daughter.

"Let me make this clear for you, daughter. You going to marry Nicolaus. You going to be good wife, and love and honour and cherish. You going to make it work. If not, you bring shame and dishonour on this family, and I will never, never take you back." He sighed, as he saw the look of submission on her face. He sighed again, sitting back in the chair. "Now, I suggest you get that manual I bought you and study the customs of America. I don't want you look stupid at your own wedding," he told her rudely.

Tears of abandonment fell from Marguerite's eyes, as Penelope helped her get the manual. She remained silent, understanding she had no choice but to go through with this marriage. She resolved, within herself, that she was going to make everyone in America miserable, especially that Nicolaus. He was the reason of her abandonment, and she was determined to make him pay.

Chapter Thirty-Nine

There was so little time to make preparations for the huge wedding. The Drones arrived Wednesday night, and the wedding was to take place on Friday at noon. Everything about Nicolaus' and Deirdre's wedding remained the same, except the bride was swapped. Deirdre was a superb wedding planner, and so much of her work remained in place.

There was no time to uninvite people who already had plane tickets, and there was no way to cancel venues or caterers, or cakes and snacks, or flowers. And to add insult to injury of Deirdre, the wedding was to take place in the same church, as previously planned. It was expected that over two hundred guests, including several celebrities, lawyers and colleagues, and socialites of Austin, were still going to attend.

Ceil found herself running around, calling in favours from prominent people to get the marriage certificate arranged, immigration papers in order, find marriage rings, get the gift registry up and filled, get to the salon, find a hairdresser for Marguerite, get new gift bags to her own taste, get a new guest book, get the wedding announcement to the papers, change the music, and change her and Nigel's reception speech. By the end of Wednesday, she was completely exhausted.

The next morning, Ceil remembered that she forgot one important thing. "Oh no, her wedding dress!" Ceil bumped right into Deirdre in the mansion, as she made this realization.

It was Thursday morning, and the formal reception of Marguerite was to take place at six with dinner. She and Nicolaus would meet for the first time, the day before the wedding.

Over one hundred guests were expected at the mansion for this occasion. Ceil had to get everything ready.

"Do you need help, Mother Ceil?" Deirdre offered, sadly, trying to be strong.

Ceil looked at her astonished, as she had not seen Deirdre all week. She was speechless.

"Would you like for me to assist Marguerite to get her dress?" Deirdre offered.

"What ... why are you here?"

"Nicky wants me to meet Marguerite." Deirdre felt an overwhelming urge to attack Ceil for ripping her love away from her, but then turned from her, blaming herself for having made Nicolaus wait such a long time to marry her. If they had just gotten married before he left for the military, as he'd begged her .... Deirdre stopped, and looked down, her back to Ceil, waiting for her answer, or for her to throw her out of the house. "I thought I'd come early to assist." She gathered her small ounce of strength that she hadn't cried away in the previous days, and faced Ceil, wanting her to know that she was not going away, that she was not going to be out of Nicolaus' life. "Things seem a little ... frazzled," she stated, then waited. Rachel and Constance told Deirdre that she must do this, that she must face Ceil alone, and not back down. And she must not let Ceil see her cry.

Ceil thought about the offer, and realized, there was no way she could take Marguerite, and there was no one available to send, as she needed all hands on deck for the reception preparations. Ceil frowned, feeling she was being played, but was out of options. After all, Marguerite wouldn't know what to do or where to go. She nodded, "Yes, Deirdre, that is very kind of you," she frowned, trying to understand. "Yes," she accepted her offer, "please I do need help. Would you take Marguerite to get her dress? She must have everything to-day. They are staying at the hotel at the arboretum."

Deirdre smiled at Ceil and touched her arm, "Don't' worry Mother Ceil, I'll take care of it. I'll make sure she is ready for this evening as well."

The beautiful smell of Deirdre lingered as Ceil watched her elegantly leave out the mansion door. Ceil was momentarily touched, and then got back to her frenzied chaos.

Chapter Forty

When Deirdre entered the lobby of the luxury hotel, with Roddy in the distance, but close enough to help if needed, she was immediately greeted by Andrejs, who recognized her. "Ah, Ms. Omari! What a surprise! We waiting for Mrs. Ravenell's team."

Deirdre nodded with a smile, pointing to herself, "Yes, I'm the team!"

Marguerite stepped up to her, frowning and offended, "You? What you doing here?"

Penelope moved her sister out of the way, and offered a hand to Deirdre, "Ms. Deirdre! Pleased to meet you. I'm Penelope, Marguerite's sister."

Deirdre shook her hand briefly, "Nice to meet you. Well, Ceil ... ah, Mrs. Ravenell, Nicolaus' mother, asked me to assist you today. Marguerite needs her wedding dress, a dress for the reception tonight, and all her accessories for tomorrow."

"You?" Marguerite, was still stuck on this.

Deirdre nodded, "Yes, uhm." She noticed right away that this woman had no class.

She could see why Ceil chose her, it was easy, and would make things difficult for Nicolaus. Deirdre couldn't even imagine the two of them together. "Unless you'd rather go yourself! I just thought you might like some help of where to go, what to get ... you know ..."

"Of course," Penelope moved Marguerite out of the way again, frowning at her rudeness to Deirdre ... to the one and only Deirdre. Not fully realizing that the lies she had been feeding Marguerite was affecting her behaviour. Penelope was thrilled to meet the beautiful

Deirdre. "We so very happy you are here to help! Of course we accept!" She bowed in gratitude.

Deirdre slightly bowed as well, not sure if this was a Latvian custom. "Well, ladies ..." Deirdre stood by the front door, for them to follow her.

"Ms. Omari, this is very nice of you, I mean ... consider the circumstance. Thank you," Andrejs said as sincerely as he could. "And please, I give Penelope the charge card for pay."

Deirdre smiled and nodded, and headed for the waiting limousine. It was all she could do to keep from crying. Quickly, she took her mind off herself, and remembered this was for Nicky. Even if he weren't marrying her tomorrow, she did want everything to go as smoothly as possible for him. She knew this was already extremely difficult for him. Her love was going to be his beacon. She wanted him to know he could always depend on her, despite them being torn apart.

Marguerite and Penelope followed her into the limousine.

Unsettling as it was, Deirdre took the Drone sisters to the same shop she bought her wedding dress from. This store had all types of formal wear for women, so it was perfect for a one stop shop. Especially since it would take hours for the sisters to find what they wanted.

Deirdre let the sales attendants help the sisters, while she fielded calls, as she was still receiving several calls from around the country. Earlier she talked with Ms. Winfree. Her words of wisdom gave Deirdre the strength to get through the day. She'd noticed that the closer it got to Friday, the day she was supposed to marry Nicolaus, the more emotional she became. She was pretty sure this was a normal reaction, for being on the receiving end of such cruelty.

From a distance, Deirdre observed the sisters. She noticed how different they were. Marguerite was tall and thick with flowy hair, but her demeanour was rude and huffy. Penelope was short and plump, with her hair done up, and she was more kind and deliberate in her manner. Deirdre watched as Marguerite treated the sales attendant with rude indignation, as if she was so much better and the sales lady was some kind of servant. Deirdre was sending a text to Nicolaus to prepare him for Marguerite's attitude when Penelope plopped down beside her.

Penelope touched her arm. "Ms. Deirdre, I am so sorry for you. I understand because I too love Nicolaus." Without missing a beat, and ignoring Deirdre's strange look, Penelope continued, "I want to ask you. Because I love Nicolaus for so long time, and it's my sister who hates Nicolaus. She hates him. If you have word with Mrs. Ravenell, and tell her to trade us – me for my sister. That I marry Nicolaus instead." She stopped talking and waited for an answer.

Deirdre was a little shocked at this request, and suddenly felt like she was in some strange type of alternate reality or a gimmick television show. She wondered if the sisters were going to fight over Nicolaus. Deirdre put her hand over her chest, "Penelope, no," she shook her head, "I cannot tell that to Mrs. Ravenell. No, she would be upset. I don't have that kind of influence."

"Influence?"

"Say in the matter. None!" she spread her arms open for animation.

Penelope nodded in understanding, "Oh… well … then," she said sadly.

Deirdre thought Penelope might cry from the look on her face. She touched her arm, "You should ask Mrs. Ravenell yourself. She will listen."

Penelope's expression changed to a frowned resolve, and then she got up and went back to dress shopping.

The ladies shopped for about four hours, but purchased everything that was needed for the reception and the wedding.

On the drive back, Penelope did most of the chatting, asking Deirdre many questions about Nicolaus, such as his food preferences, his favourite colour, and of his character. Then she asked her for some beauty tips. Marguerite mostly stared at Deirdre, taking note of how uniquely beautiful she really is, and now realizing this is whom she is going to be competing for Nicolaus' affection. Affection she did not care for. She did not like this whole situation, but she was powerless to change any of it, least she loses all her financial security. She observed Deirdre's beauty and felt very inadequate. She did not speak, but listened to the beauty tips. Deirdre felt the cold, hard stare of Marguerite and it made her uncomfortable.

Once they arrived back at the hotel, Deirdre did not join them, but left the ladies to ready themselves for the reception. She headed to the mansion, satisfied that she'd lived up to her offer of help.

Alexander assisted Nicolaus as the time for the reception drew near. He made Nicolaus leave the office at a decent time to shower, change, and get ready. Since he was officially the best man for the previously planned wedding, he still took his duty seriously, and he knew Nicolaus was going to need help navigating this horrid situation he was in.

Nicolaus' chiselled body stepped out of the bathroom, wrapped in a towel. He'd half dried himself, and water droplets were glistening off his smooth, moisturized, caramel skin.

Alexander handed Nicolaus a drink of brandy because he looked pale sick again. Nicolaus wasn't able to eat anything all day, but Alexander figured the alcohol would help ease his nerves.

"Dude, we've got twenty minutes to get downstairs, and I already hear guests arriving."

Nicolaus took the two-ounce glass of brandy and downed it, as if it were water.

He looked at the empty glass and handed it back to Alexander. "Guess I'll need lots of these tonight." He turned in a circle, feeling confused. "What am I …" when he circled back around to Alexander, his grey suit and a dark mauve shirt was extended before him. "Oh. Thanks."

"Yep. No tie. You don't want to be too formal."

"Right."

"I already put your shoes out, too. Look, I'm going to go check on Deirdre, I heard she is here. I'll be back in ten. And… please Nicolaus, be dressed."

"Okay," he answered, grateful for the assistance.

Alexander went downstairs to find Deirdre. He was surprised that she was holding together pretty well. "How did the shopping go?"

Deirdre nodded, "They got what they needed. I did make some observations, though."

Alexander nodded, seeing more guests arrive, and not wanting her to say what she was thinking out loud. "Yes, I saw the texts you sent Nicolaus."

"How is he?" she asked, with great concern.

Alexander shook his head and sighed. "Not great, not great. But … we'll get him through this. We have to." Alexander looked up beyond Deirdre, "Hey!" he waived and shouted across the room at one of their famous donors to the foundation. "Excuse me." Touching Deirdre, he left her side and went to chat.

Deirdre busied herself with straightening things that didn't need straightening, such as the dinner cloth napkins, and the plates and silverware that the kitchen staff had perfectly set.

Deirdre soon heard Ceil behind her greeting the Drone family. Andrejs complimented the mansion, and Penelope made comments on almost everything she saw, calling them exquisite or luxurious or rich. After a while of Penelope's childish behaviour of naming items, Andrejs stopped her from doing so. The Drone sisters eventually made it over to Deirdre, and began to cling to her, as they didn't know anyone in the house, and soon the mansion filled up with guests, celebrities, and dignitaries. Marguerite's dark, thick hair dangled in loose curls at her shoulders. She wore the satin blue designer dress she had picked out earlier. It outlined her shapely, medium sized body. As the guests entered the home, they came to greet the ladies. kissing and hugging Deirdre, offering their sorrows and apologies for her having lost her true love, making tears fall from her eyes. Incredibly, the guests found Marguerite to be quite curious, extremely rude, and an incomprehensible match to Nicolaus' kind spirit.

After about another twenty minutes, Nicolaus swiftly came down the stairs and jumped right into the crowd, joining his father greeting the guests, and accepting their condolences on having to give up Deirdre. Their words pranged his heart, and he found it difficult to re-

234

turn their smiles. Many of the women gave him hugs and the usual kisses. Alexander busied himself gathering food from the buffet set up, that preceded the sit-down meal. Benjamin appeared in and out of the main room. No woman on his arm tonight, as he watched Deirdre, and noticed her security guard was still hanging around. The board members made sure to speak with both Alexander and Nicolaus, and quietly provided their opinion on Marguerite. Most were disappointed, not certain she would represent the company in a positive light.

Nicolaus was downing another drink while chatting with a bank executive when suddenly Penelope grasped him in a full side hug, laying her head on his chest. She gave herself over to the fantasy of loving him, holding him tight, even though they had not been introduced.

"Hum," Nicolaus tried loosening her grip without hurting her, but Penelope wasn't having it. "Ah, Miss?"

Not letting go of him, she looked up at his face. That gorgeous face! "I'm Penelope, Marguerite's sister."

"Oh!" Nicolaus didn't want to hurt Penelope. He tried to loosen her grip again, as she tightened up more. "Okay," he told her, as if to say that was enough. "Umh!"

Deirdre stepped in, "Penelope, what are you doing?"

"What? Is that the bride to be?" Francesca asked in her boisterous, accent ladened voice. "Has she come to you with love?" Francesca teased Nicolaus, knowing there was nothing funny about all of this.

"No, this is Penelope, Marguerite's sister," Deirdre corrected her. "Penelope, I think this is a good time for you to go see Mrs. Ravenell, about what we spoke of earlier."

That seemed to do the trick, as Penelope's arms fell from Nicolaus. "Nicolaus, I will be your family now. And I plan to be so much more." She blew a kiss to him, and left him momentarily.

"Oh my God!" Nicolaus said in a panic, grabbing another drink from the passing tray, upheld by a waiter. He downed the drink, not even knowing what it was.

"Nicky, you're drinking too much! You need to slow it down." Deirdre, frowned, chastising him, touching his torso. She looked around for support from Francesca, but she had already moved on and was chatting it up with a celebrity. Nicolaus looked at Deirdre as if he wanted to kiss her, suddenly, sexual tension between them was strong, the hope of ever being together was waning. Their moment was interrupted by Andrejs.

"Nicolaus!" He put his hand out. Nicolaus took his hand, a slight smile on his face, as much as he could muster, recognizing the foreign accent. "I am Andrejs Drone, the father of Marguerite and Penelope. I want to welcome you to our family. It's little but, hey."

Nicolaus nodded, "Thank you." He sighed, not sure what to say. "I wish I could have met you under different circumstances."

"Well, this is happy occasion, no? Marriage and mergers!"

Nicolaus frowned deeply, not liking that comment. Deirdre half hugged him, touching his chest, trying to keep him from saying something he would regret to his soon to be father-in-law.

Suddenly Andrejs realized what he'd said, and why Nicolaus looked upset, Deirdre by his side. "Oh, look, it may seem difficult, but I promise you, it will get better. I put Marguerite in the large room over there," he pointed to the drawing room, "she waits for you. You will see, I gave you the pretty one." Andrejs left them, knowing that Nicolaus would have to man up and accept his daughter, or his family was about to be even more rich than he could have ever imagined. He'd be richer than the stock market was predicting.

Penelope caught up with Ceil, whom she was surprised provided her undivided attention. "Well, you see, Mrs. Ravenell," Penelope chose her words carefully, as she'd been driving herself to practice her English for such a moment. "It is I who loves your son, Nicolaus," she put her hand to her throat, "and I want to ask that you to switch me for my sister. My sister is very miserable, you see. She cried all night," she embellished the happenings, as Marguerite did not cry all night, but she surely had mad fits. "I would be honoured to step in for my sister."

Ceil thought about what she said, and realized Penelope may be useful to her purposes in the future. "Well, Penelope, that is just not possible. But I'll tell you what, you and I will make a partnership to work together in the future." Penelope wasn't sure exactly what Ceil was talking about, but the two ladies shook hands in agreement, and for now, this satisfied Penelope, because anything regarding her involvement with Nicolaus was satisfying.

Nicolaus grabbed another drink that was floating by, and he downed it. He took a deep breath, "Well, let me get this over with." His lingering hands left Deirdre, his only true love, and he went into the drawing room to meet Marguerite.

Nicolaus quietly stepped into the drawing room, where he found his wife to be. Purposefully, he left the door open. Marguerite was staring out the window, and he could only see the back of her medium built but shapely frame, and long, curly, dark hair. Her designer dress landed just below her knees, and accented her body. He observed her in silence.

Marguerite could feel the presence of someone. Quickly she turned, knowing it was probably Nicolaus. With contempt in her eyes she glared at him.

He saw that she was no beauty, but she was not ugly, either, just plain looking. She might be prettier if she could change that mean expression about her face. In Nicolaus' mind, she was no comparison to Deirdre. But then again, no one could compare to Deirdre Omari. Quickly he observed that Marguerite was not open to him.

Marguerite noticed Nicolaus' slight limp as he walked towards her. When she had seen his image on television or in magazines, his handsome looks did not impress her. However, now, seeing him in the flesh was different. She felt herself get overtaken by his charm, overtly aware that this man was going to be her husband. She was drawn to him, like most women were.

He is strikingly handsome, with kind and inviting eyes, a strong, muscular physique, and he smelled intoxicatingly masculine. He is the type of guy women dream of. Marguerite felt herself be pulled in by him, though he did nothing to cause it, he was just … there. Her uncontrolled reaction to him made her angry, and she cut off her feelings. She narrowed her eyes to glare hard at him, trying to reel away her body's chemical reaction to him.

Nicolaus stepped forward and attempted to lift her hand to shake it or kiss it as a gentleman would. At the touch of his fingers, Marguerite harshly jerked her hand away.

Coldly, she moved away from Nicolaus to the other side of the room.

His eyes followed her. "I am ... "

"I know who you are," she snapped at him, cutting him off. "You no think for a minute I am pleased to know you. I want no part of this!"

Nicolaus smiled lightly, understanding exactly what she meant. "Marguerite, it would appear that you feel about this matter the same as I do." Nicolaus sighed. "I hope we can try to make the best of this."

"I want no part of you! I know all about your conniving self! I hate you! Hate you!" she yelled at him, making her stance clear. Her voice carried across the hall to where the rest of the family, and distinguished dinner guests were chatting, making Ceil smile.

Nicolaus frowned, realizing this was going to be more than difficult. "You hate me? Well, at least you will get along very well with my mother." Not willing to give up so easily, Nicolaus approached her. He offered his hand to her again, trying to reason with her.

"Do not touch me!" she harshly yelled at him.

Nicolaus took a step back from her. "Look, obviously neither of us chose this, but we are stuck. I do not want to be your enemy, I just ..." Marguerite spit in his face, and she ran out of the drawing room. Naturally, Nicolaus was alarmed and offended at such poor treatment. He went to the small sink next to the alcoholic beverages, and he washed his face. He was now having trouble controlling his emotions. Why was such a burden being placed on him?

The first one next to him was Deirdre, then Rachel and Nigel rushed in.

"Nicky," Rachel and Nigel could see the meeting did not go well. Marguerite had pushed past Rachel as she fled from Nicolaus.

Deirdre wasn't sure what emotion she was seeing on Nicky's face, but she was very sure she had not seen it before.

"What did I do to mother to make her hate me this much?" Nicolaus point blank asked Rachel and Nigel. "I've been racking my brain for years trying to figure out why she hates me."

"Nicolaus …"

"Tell me! What did I do? It's something I can't re-member. Must have been when I was a kid. Did I hit her? Insult her? I threw something at her? I broke some-thing she cherished?"

Speechless, Rachel shook her head. She was hurting to see him in this awfully painful situation. She wanted to tell him the truth. Nigel touched her to stop her.

"Nicolaus, it's not you," Nigel told him.

"No," he said, not believing his father. "Just tell me what I did."

"You've been drinking too much, Nicky," Deirdre repeated, trying to get him calmed.

"I know what I'm saying."

"It's not you, son … it's me."

Nicolaus scoured at Nigel, "What the hell does that even mean?"

Nigel was reluctant to answer, but he knew Nicolaus rightfully deserved an explanation. But he was only willing to tell so much. "I did something that has caused your mother to go after you. And for that, I'm sorry," he added.

Nicolaus sighed in disbelief, still thinking his father was not being straight with him, "Well then fucking undo it!" He uncharacteristically yelled at his father, then put his hand to his head, "Oh my God, did I just curse? I'm so stressed out over all this. I am sorry father."

Rachel grabbed both his hands. "Nicky, remember our conversation the other day? You are not going to let Ceil break you. You are going to remember our ancestors."

Nicolaus nodded at her words. "Right, right."

"You can do this! It's going to be okay."

"It's easy when you're on the outside of this thing to tell the person on the inside that it's going to be okay. It's not going to be okay Aunt Rachel! There is just no scenario where any of this is going to be okay! I'm not going to be okay. I have to give up Deirdre for that creature?"

"Nicky, don't talk about her like that," Deirdre told him, frowning, "not if you are going to marry her."

"Marry," Nicolaus repeated. Suddenly, he grabbed Deirdre to him, and kissed her head.

"Look son, the choice is still yours. Like you said, it's a choice. You just have to remember, if you choose not to go through with this tomorrow, we will lose everything. This very house we are standing in, all our money, our assets, our stock, our company, our clinics, our employees, will all belong to Drone."

"Don't worry father, I'm not going to forget. It's all I can think about!" he told Nigel in his upset.

Feeling he could do no more, Nigel held both of Nicolaus' shoulders, "I'm counting on you to follow through on your word, son." Then Nigel did what he usually does when Nicolaus is in distress, he left the room.

Rachel took his hands again, "Nicky, you just need to focus on tomorrow. Just get through the dinner, then focus on tomorrow. Where's that military courage? You've faced much more ominous situations than this, and those were life and death situations. You can get through this. I know you can." Rachel kissed Nicolaus, then left the room. She felt horrid, knowing that she and Nigel caused this to fall on Nicolaus.

There was motionless silence between Nicolaus and Deirdre. Nicolaus pulled her to him, and placed their foreheads together. He looked in her eyes. "Promise me, you'll never leave me," he told her, his hands to the small of her back.

"Nicky, you've been drinking too much," she told him softly again, trying to resist his silly demand on the night before his marriage to another woman.

"Stop saying that, Deirdre. I'm not that drunk yet. I very well know what I'm saying. Please. Promise you'll never leave me."

"Nicky…"

"Please, Deirdre. I can't do this without you."

Her eyelashes fluttered as she met his gaze, her hand to his chest. "Yes, I promise. I'm not going anywhere."

She knew that no matter what, her heart belonged to him.

Chapter Forty-One

Ceil called the dinner to order, sitting each of her guests. She sat Marguerite next to her, and Nicolaus sat next to Marguerite. Nicolaus' stress level increased as he sat next to Marguerite. She spitefully stared at him, half turning her back to him. The knot in his stomach tightened, and he attempted to loosen it with more drink. How was he supposed to marry and live with a woman who absolutely hated him? This seemed the worst trade off to him, to have to sacrifice his love for Deirdre for this woman.

When all the guests were seated, Francesca quickly saw that Ceil had purposefully seated herself towards the end of the table, away from Nicolaus, and there was no seat for Deirdre at all. Francesca was not having this. Quickly, she asked guests to move down, and had the servers bring an additional chair and plate setting. She sat Deirdre on the other side of Nicolaus, and she sat next to Deirdre. At this point, Francesca did not care that her Auntie Ceil was going to be mad or make a scene, she only knew that they had to be there to support Nicolaus through this ordeal.

Unfortunately for the guests, Marguerite's behaviour did not improve during dinner. Every chance she got she insulted Nicolaus, slighting him, which went unanswered. She was also successful at embarrassing Ceil and Nigel.

"But dear, aren't you excited at all about the wedding?" one of the donors asked her. She was a busy body elderly woman who still maintained her natural hair colour. She knew all the latest news of each and every city, and made sure everyone else did too. Marguerite did not know any of these people, and did not care to know them, as she had told Ceil earlier when she tried to introduce her. As far as Marguerite was concerned, this was a gawk show. Her father and Penelope sat across from her. Andrejs often frowned or shook his head at Marguerite's remarks.

Marguerite looked over at this woman, as she sat towards the middle of the table.

"Would you be happy to be traded like a sheep?" she asked loudly and rudely. Andrejs was frowning.

Many of the guests gasped at her question. "But look who you are getting!" the woman pointed towards Nicolaus with a smile. Many guests at the long dining table verbally agreeing with her.

Marguerite looked upon Nicolaus with that same disdainful look, as earlier, "A man that I hate! A man I do not want! You want him? You can have him!"

The look on people's faces was of disgust for Marguerite, and disbelief at Ceil. Much murmuring began. Nicolaus knew he had to do something, as his mind saw their company stock prices falling. The thought of the business made him realize his inebriation was wearing off. Before he could speak, Marguerite continued with her insults, this time against Ceil and her father.

"What kind of parent sells their own children away?" she yelled above the murmuring, bringing silence to the room. "What kind of ..." she began to cry, unable to finish her sentence, feeling much the same as Nicolaus did earlier.

"Now wait a minute ..." Ceil started at her. Andrejs looked like he was going to stand in anger at his daughter's words, for trying to publicly humiliate him.

"I've got this mother," Nicolaus cut Ceil off, knowing she was only going to add to the nasty atmosphere already present in the room. "What Marguerite is trying to say …" Nicolaus stopped and looked at her. She was bawling into her cloth napkin, about to go into hyper-ventilation. He wanted to touch her, to calm her, but feared what her reaction would be. "She is only saying that although this is very difficult for both of us, we promise that we will protect your investments and your donations. Truly, I thank all of you for being here to-night." Having pulled himself together, putting on his Vice President hat, he stood, grabbing his glass. "I'd like to make a toast." He looked at his father to lead everyone to raise their glass. Nigel took the cue and did so, and everyone followed his actions. "I'd like to toast all of you for believing in VMC … and for supporting our efforts to help the underserved communities in our nation." Nicolaus drank his glass, and everyone fol-lowed. "Marguerite, and her family have travelled a long way from Latvia to join us, and I'm sure they are very tired. Lots of excitement. So let us please clap them out as we all retire, and get ready for tomorrow."

Suddenly, the heavy cloud that hung over the room was gone, as everyone had a smile, stood and clapped for Andrejs and his daughters. Andrejs stood and bowed. Nicolaus signalled the staff, who then assisted Andrejs and his daughter, and escorted them out to their limousine.

Francesca grabbed Nicolaus around the neck, "Oh my God, you are amazing! You fucking saved the din-ner. Although I didn't get to eat a bloody thing!" She kissed him repeatedly on his face, and he hugged her, needing her love.

Many people came to Nicolaus to shake his hand, hug him, or kiss him, and they left the family. Shaken, Nicolaus sat down at the table after all the guests had left. He asked the server for another drink, his only solace. Nigel grabbed onto his shoulders again, but said nothing, and left the room, coaxing Ceil out with him.

"That was genius!" Alexander told him. "What made you think of it?"

Nicolaus shook his head, "I don't know. I just saw money leaving out the window every time she opened her mouth."

Alexander let out a hearty laugh. "Yeah, I wasn't sure what to do! Look, she will be different once you bed her. She'll treat you differently."

Nicolaus looked at him as if he were crazy, scoffing, "I doubt that!" Deirdre had disappeared from his sight, but was now returning. He grabbed her hand, "You ready to turn in, babe?"

Deirdre looked down, then at him, "You can't call me that anymore," she told him softly.

"Oh yeah, right. Ms. Omari, you ready to turn in?"

She smiled at him, "Why yes, Mr. Ravenell, I am. Would you mind escorting me to my door?" she joked with a southern drawl that she did not normally have.

"Alexander, you are staying, right?"

"Don't' worry, I'm already settled into my room. I'll be two doors down from you. I'll see you both in the morning."

"Okay. Thanks Alexander. I really appreciate you."

"No worries."

Just as Alexander left, Benjamin appeared. "Benjamin, you okay? I haven't seen you all evening," Nicolaus asked of him.

"Oh, I've been here for this little show. Deirdre ..." he held his arm out to Deirdre, as if he were going to escort her somewhere.

Nicolaus chuckled at him, with a frown, "What are you doing?"

"I'll escort Deirdre. No reason for you to cast a shadow on her now that you are engaged to be married tomorrow. I mean, after all, you are off the market now, aren't you?" he rubbed the salt in the fresh wound.

"Thank you Benji, but Nicky will escort me. I'll see you at the church tomorrow." No way was Deirdre taking chances on thinking Benjamin would behave like a gentlemen with her.

Looking a little hurt, Benjamin left them, knowing he was going to have ample opportunity to win Deirdre over, now that Nicolaus was out of the way.

As Nicolaus and Deirdre slowly walked arm in arm by the library, the light of the full moon glistened through the window. Nicolaus showed Deirdre the hidden door that led to the stairway to the veranda above the library at the back of the mansion. The balcony contained furniture, which he led her to sit next to him. Without hesitation, he gathered Deirdre in his arms, knowing this would be the last night he would be able to hold her in such a manner.

The light of the moon fully lit up the balcony, as no other lights were on. They sat quietly for a several minutes, listening to the cool breeze and to each other's heartbeat. They enjoyed being alone, being so close for the last time. Nicolaus felt like he was in a nightmare that he just couldn't wake up from. He held Deirdre closer, against his body, feeling she was literally slipping away from him, the very thing that was unthinkable. Deirdre basked in the warmth of Nicolaus' body, silent tears falling from her eyes. She would be there for him, no matter what. She had to help him get through this marriage tomorrow. Though if tonight was any indication of how he could pull himself together at a moment's notice, he might be all right. She figured it was his military training that brought on that stand up/chin out measure tonight.

She looked up at him and kissed his chin, the very thing she was thinking of. "Now, Nicky, you cannot move too fast with Marguerite tomorrow. Don't even try to consummate." He was looking at her dazed, as if he were going to kiss her endlessly. "Nicky," she touched his face, and he nodded. "You need to court her first. Give her flowers. Take her on dates. Build a friendship. Remember, she doesn't know you. If you move too quickly ..."

Nicolaus couldn't hear a word Deirdre was saying, he could only concentrate on that sweet mouth of hers.

Suddenly, his lips caught hers, devouring her. By no means could she resist him. His hands moved over her body, respecting her womanness, though he wanted to touch her everywhere. He wanted to take her, and make her his, to be her first and she be his first, as was always meant to be. He could not imagine Deirdre with another man, that thought was too painful for him. If she were with another man, it would kill his heart, but now ... who was he to stop such a thing? The built-up passion he had for her was evident, as they kissed without coming up for air for some time. When he released her lips, they were both out of breath, still he repeated his actions, as if trying to prove his love for her through the act of kissing. It was Deirdre who tore away from his scorching, endless kiss. She found strength to stand up and move away from him. Didn't he know what he was doing to her? Her heart broke with his every touch. The way he looked at her, with such love, was unbearable to her.

He was right upon her, wrapping her in his loving arms, making her weak. Their pain was so raw, so hurt-

248

ful, so undeniable. How were they going to get through this when they couldn't stand to be away from each other? Nicolaus lovingly kissed her neck under the moonlight, wanting to make her his. He knew the neck kisses aroused her body. She sighed, her arms lifting to hold the back of his neck to draw him closer. In this moment, his body was not under his control, and was harshly demanding to be inside of Deirdre, to be as close to her as heavenly possible.

For the first time ever, Deirdre felt his manhood grow hard against her. She knew what he wanted, what he needed, what he desired. She was so weak for him, would she be able to deny him? Should she deny him? Or should she give in to what they'd both waited ten years to experience? He held her in silence, his arms wrapped her tightly. She felt his warm, silent tears fall onto her neck, and drip down her chest. The warm Texas breeze cemented them together, in this moment they would never forget.

Taking deep breaths to calm his body, Nicolaus gathered himself, and walked Deirdre to her room. He stopped at the door, though he wanted to carry her in, throw her on the bed, and make mad love to her, to sear his imprint upon her body and her mind. He put his arm up on the door frame to stop himself from entering, not wanting to soil Deirdre's body, nor her reputation. He would never do anything that would hurt her.

Gently, but passionately, without words, he kissed her one more time. Then, sadly, he let her go. Hearing the door lock, he turned to see Roddy at his station. They shook hands and half hugged in a manly fashion. Then Nicolaus went to his room, where sleep would elude him, and depression found its way to his heart and his mind.

It was midnight when Benjamin rounded his way to Deirdre's bedroom in the mansion. Roddy was surprised, but not unaware of Benjamin's antics towards Deirdre, as Nicolaus had filled him in.

"Ah, you are still here?" Benjamin asked surprised.

"Well, yes, I am." Roddy straightened his stance in front of the bedroom door to the room that held Deirdre. "And Ms. Omari is not taking any visitors at this hour, nor is she taking any visitors in her bedroom," he said sternly, expecting not to be questioned.

"Okay, I understand," Benjamin replied. He took a step closer to Roddy. "But you know, you're not going to be around forever. I'll get my time with Ms. Omari."

"Well, whatever. It will not be tonight. So, you may retire back from where you came from Mr. Ravenell." Roddy remained in place, not budging at Benjamin's challenge.

Benjamin smiled, and left the area, muttering under his breath.

Roddy took a swig of his coffee to make sure he was alert for the duration of the night. Nicolaus had the staff provide him his own coffee pot, with all the necessities.

Chapter Forty-Two

It was early in the morning, the day of his wedding, after his run with his buddies, when Nicolaus received another call from Ms. Winfree.

"Hello. Yes ma'am, I ... thank you for calling," he still sounded a little distraught. "I'm surprised to hear from you."

"No, no, don't be surprised," she told him. "You know, I have a lot of stock in VMC, because I believe in the mission, and I like your father. Now Ceil, your mom ... she's a mess. I don't agree one bit with what she is doing to you and Deirdre. It's not fair, I know, baby."

"Thank you Ms. Winfree."

"Yes, well, usually, I can make things happen for people, in their lives," she referred to the power she had in the community, the state, and indeed in the nation, "but baby, I just can't undo this thing! And Nicolaus, if it makes you feel better, when the vote came to us stockholders, for the record, I voted against this measure. I'm pretty sure most of us did. I know our vote doesn't change anything, but we wanted to go on record to show we just don't agree with it. We couldn't have changed anything because that darn contract was already in effect. But of course, I'm sure that was probably part of Ceil's plan."

Nicolaus listened to what she was telling him to get a full understanding of what was happening. He sighed heavily, not having had to face such a heavy weight throughout the whole of his military career. "No ma'am, there isn't a way out of this without us losing everything."

"No, Ceil made sure there was no way out for you. I just want you to know that I support you and Deirdre.

Your love is precious. And listen Nicolaus, just because Deirdre cannot be your wife, doesn't mean she cannot be in your life."

"Yes ma'am, I had figured that part out already. Deirdre is not happy about having to step back, but I believe our bond is strong."

"After all these years? Your bond is strong. And Nicolaus that is what you have to hold onto. No matter what. In fact, I think you should make a statement at the wedding ceremony."

"A statement?"

"Yes, well, I see that we weren't uninvited to the wedding, so I imagine everyone is still invited. Am I right?"

"Yes ma'am, it was too late to make those kind of changes."

"Well, that's what I thought. You should make a statement before the preacher begins. Tell everyone what is going on, in your own words. Explain your position. Express your love for Deirdre, so people will know this is not her fault. The public doesn't know what is happening. They don't know what Ceil has done. Say whatever you want. It's your wedding, you can make whatever adjustments you feel like making."

"I see."

"Yes, take the power back."

"Ms. Winfree, that's actually a great idea! I hadn't thought of it. Thank you."

It was after Nicolaus took that wisdom from Ms. Winfree and wrote out his statement, that his nerves ceased his body, causing him to retch so badly, it seemed his guts would soon appear. The thought of what his mother was doing to him, and the thought of being wed to the creature that hated him without cause, exacerbated his depression and brought about his sick nerves. He couldn't hold back when he realized the doom the future held for him.

Alexander panicked and had the staff bring in Rachel, who had arrived a short time ago. Rachel didn't know what to do so she called for Nigel, who also knew not what to do, except ... to call for Deirdre.

When Deirdre entered Nicolaus' room in her bathrobe, as she was not yet dressed, Alexander rushed everyone out. Deirdre found her Nicolaus looking sickly grey, sitting on the bathroom floor, after having retched his guts. She took a towel, knelt next to him, and wiped his face, and the sweat from his forehead. He seemed to be devastated, and he wouldn't look at her. Deirdre called for the staff, and had them draw him a warm bath. They did so, and left them. She led him up, and began to undress him.

At first Nicolaus stopped her from shedding his minimal workout clothes, but then he let her undress him. It was pure torture. He figured he deserved it. Perhaps he deserved everything that was happening to him.

Deirdre paused when she dropped his bottoms. She looked his beautifully chiselled body over. She adored how the pubic hairs lightly danced around his beautifully carved penis. If she didn't know him, she'd swear he was a Greek god statue come to life; or an Arabian prince statue, or whatever beautiful man statue a woman could think of. She'd never seen Nicky in such emotional pain before. She knew it was taking everything he had to go through today, to save his family's fortune. Deirdre bit her lip as she became even more keenly aware of what she was being forced to give up, as her eyes tried to remember him as he was, naked before her.

Those times they'd skinny dipped together, they really had not gazed at each other's underwear clad body, only held onto each other in purity after the cleanse. Now, as he stood in front of her, he was out of her reach, and she could not be with him.

Taking his hand, she led him into the perfectly warmed bath water. The staff added a nice smelling emollient to the water. The luxury tub sat in the middle of the bathroom, surrounded by steps. As Nicky sat back in the tub, Deirdre was able to sit on the steps to his back, and she gently bathed him in an act of love, the last intimacy they'd share. This was something she'd never done for him before. She cradled his head against hers, and she gently washed his temples to calm his nerves, then his chest, slowly, trying to remember his every manly curve. His ribs were stacked and muscular. Nicolaus' eyes were closed, and he was unmoving. Even the slightest touch of her fingers to his body put a stab wound to his heart. He suffered it. No words passed between them. No words were needed. The love they would always have for each other, no matter what happened, spoke volumes. She kissed his neck, and eased herself away from him, having calmed him.

Tears fell from Deirdre's eyes as she quietly left the bathroom. Her own pain was increased tenfold now if that was even possible. In her own devastation, she found her way back to her bedroom, laid on the bed, and cried some more. Deirdre was not exactly sure how she was going to get through the day.

Chapter Forty-Three

Deirdre had to get out of the Ravenell mansion, she just had to. Certainly, she did not want to run into Ceil. She knew that Ceil would only gloat to her face, for having dislodged her from Nicolaus. She would say mean things to her and make her cry again, and then be glad for it. Deirdre knew she could not withstand such a scene, so she left for the church earlier than anyone else.

When she arrived, she sat outside for a few minutes and stared at the outer walls of the church. Today was supposed to be her day. Today was the day she and Nicky were going to make good on their promise of ten years of love and purity. She looked at the engagement rings on her finger. She touched them, and moved them around her finger, deciding to never take them off. Nicolaus gave her the first simple, little band when he was sixteen and she was fifteen, with a promise to marry her whenever she was ready. On their five-year anniversary, he upgraded that simple engagement ring with a beautiful diamond band, in hopes of prompting her to say she was ready to marry. Regret filled her tears. She looked at the church, realizing she'd just lost her future with Nicolaus, the only man she would ever love. There was no one else on earth like Nicolaus. He was irreplaceable, just as she knew she was irreplaceable to him. Two young people, whose hearts had been purposefully ripped up and wounded, for no good reason.

Deirdre entered the church, wanting to get inside before the press arrived. She wore a sexy black dress, though she was not trying to be sexy. Black symbolized her loss. After all, what does one wear to a wedding that was supposed to be your own, but now someone else is marrying your beau? The church pews were decorated in the flowers and lace she had meticulously chosen. The volunteers placed it just as she wanted it, lining the aisle for the bride walk.

In a flash of mental blindness, Deirdre began snatching the flowers and lace away from each pew, on both sides. The church was rather large, and the decorations began in the middle. She snatched it off, threw it to the floor, and stomped it. She worked until she was so tired because crying and working brought on fatigue. It was the bishop that stopped her. She had one last pew to attend. She reached for it, but the bishop pulled her into a hug, trying to comfort her. Deirdre fought against him, but then relented, as he half carried her into the back space of the church, sitting her frenzied self down.

"I'm okay, I'm okay," she cried, "I'm okay," she repeated, not even aware of what she was saying. "I'm o ... o ... o ... kaaaaaaaay," she cried. The uncontrolled emotion poured from her. Her Nicky. Her heart. She was devastated.

"There, there," the bishop sat beside her and patted her arm and back. He wiped her face with tissues, then gave her several in her hand. "There, there," he told her gently, and patted her more. "I'm so sorry this has happened. You will get through this, Deirdre."

She nodded, hyperventilating, still crying.

"It's all right. Take a breath," he told her. "Just breathe, dear."

Deirdre nodded, and took some short breaths. She could feel herself begin to calm down. While she was breathing, the bishop made a call, and instructed to whomever he was speaking to clean up the aisle, and to remove all the flowers and lace, and whatever else was there. Deirdre nodded to him.

The bishop chuckled, "You see, I'll have someone take care of that. You don't need to worry about it. We'll make it all bare!" The bishop patted her again, "There is something I want you to do, though. When you start feeling like you want to scream, or cry, or that you cannot handle things today," he paused to hand her a rosary, "I want you to use these beads, and just start praying. It doesn't matter what you pray, just pray. You can pray for strength, or patience, or love, or forgiveness, or peace of self whatever you need, that is what I want you to pray. Will you do that, Deirdre?"

Deirdre received the rosary, she nodded, "Yes, Bishop," she replied calmly, "thank you. I'm sure it will help." She took a deep breath, and felt more herself. She began to work the rosary immediately.

The Bishop saw this, and remained a little worried. "There is something else I want to tell you." He paused, looking for the right words. "The love between you and Nicolaus, is a special kind of love. I don't see love like that very often these days. And I want you to remember that no one, not even Marguerite, can take that love away from you. Now, I'm not saying that you should go make a fleshly sin, but the pure love you and Nicolaus have in your hearts for each other, well, that love can never be taken from you. Do you understand what I am saying, Deirdre?"

Deirdre slightly smiled to keep from bursting into tears again, as she fingered her engagement rings, "Yes, Bishop. I've already thought about that." She stood with the Bishop. "Thank you." She hugged him. "If you see my mother, please let her know I will be upstairs. I want to be out of sight of the press."

The Bishop smiled at her, and nodded.

Chapter Forty-Four

Time for the wedding grew near, and everyone was arriving to the church. While Constance tried to comfort Deirdre, watching her daughter work the prayer beads, she wondered what she was praying for. Across the hall, Ceil joined Marguerite and Penelope, as Marguerite prepared to walk the aisle. Marguerite was in her white, designer wedding dress. The beautician was styling her hair, as she watched in the mirror. Ceil pulled up a chair and sat next to her soon to be daughter-in law.

"What a beautiful bride you make, Marguerite," Ceil told her gleefully, happy that her plan was working out.

Marguerite pouted her mouth and did not respond.

The look on her face was that of scorn. She knew it was going to be hard to resist Nicolaus, and she had been thinking about how to handle the night.

"I want you to know that no matter what Deirdre throws your way, I will always support you, I'll always back you up."

Marguerite was quick to hold a glance to Ceil. She frowned, "What you mean? What of Deirdre?"

"Well, you know, she will be hanging around. Pretending to be helping, but no, she is not going to let him go that easily. She will try to come between the two of you. And well… you know what that means." Ceil maliciously sowed seeds of mistrust to try and move Deirdre out of the picture.

Marguerite's frown grew deeper, "What it means?"

"Well, Marguerite, you know if you cannot make this marriage work then you will lose your money, just as we will." Ceil dramatically grabbed Marguerite's arm, "Are you going to let Deirdre make you lose everything you have?"

Marguerite bit her lip and looked at Ceil wildly. She looked at Penelope, and with a sweep of her hand through the air, she motioned for her and the beautician to leave the room, so she could talk to Ceil privately.

At the sound of the door closing, Ceil moved closer to Marguerite. "It is Nicolaus who has her around. He will never tell her to go. You will have to do that, Marguerite. You have to make him tell her to leave. If you do not, Deirdre will be a threat to your inheritance."

Marguerite nodded in understanding. "Very well.

You confirm your son is a scoundrel, and it is I who will tame him. I see now, why you brought me."

Marguerite pounded the small vanity table, just as Ceil would have done. "No one is going to lose me my mother's will. No one!"

Ceil was happy to see Marguerite riled up. She discussed timing with her, and felt that she would be able to mould Marguerite into her purpose against Nicolaus. When Ceil left, Penelope and the beautician returned, but saw that Marguerite had an angrier change about her.

Chapter Forty-Five

The traditional wedding music played as Andrejs escorted Marguerite down the church aisle. She was not smiling. Her walk was stiff and somewhat resistant, as she glided down the aisle into her new and unwanted life. She was fuming mad at what Ceil had shared with her about Nicolaus and Deirdre. She refused to be made the fool.

Andrejs pulled his daughter along, with a smile on his face, as he knew the business world would be paying attention to what was going on. He was oblivious to the depth of Ceil's scheming, but did not really care, because he knew Nicolaus was a good asset not only for his family but to his company. Also, he knew what he could potentially gain if this did not work out in the outset. Six months would tell if he would be rich beyond his wildest dreams.

The handoff of the bride to Nicolaus did not go smoothly, as Nicolaus held his hand out to assist Marguerite onto the platform steps, she pushed his hand away, refusing his help. She stepped up on her own. Neither of them had support, except for Nigel, who was to be the official witness to the actual marriage, as required by the company lawyers. Neither the bride nor groom wanted the best man or bride's maid scenario, since this was not a happy occasion.

Nigel stood to the side of the platform, closer to the bishop than to his own son. He looked out to see the church was completely filled. Many press were present, and the camera bulb flashing was continuous and out of control. One would think a prince was getting married. Nigel saw that Nicolaus looked extremely stressed, and he was sorry for such pressure that had been placed on him. However, Nigel had no doubt that Nicolaus was going to do the right thing for the family.

Nicolaus and Marguerite stood opposite of each other. She angrily glared at him, no bridal veil present. Nicolaus breathed through the awkward situation. His slight smile to her went unreturned. Suddenly, Nicolaus steps off the platform, to the front, away from his father and away from Marguerite. "Before we begin, there is something I'd like to say." He looked around the crowd of the two hundred faces that stared back at him. "Deirdre," he called, sighing, trying to relieve some stress, "are you here? Please ...." He waited a minute for her.

Marguerite slowly, and angrily placed her hands to her hips. How dare he call for Deirdre during their wedding ceremony.

Deirdre knelt down and hid to the floor of the pew in the back. Only the people on the same row could see her, and she begged them to stay quiet and not to say anything. She was already humiliated, barely holding it together, and she didn't want to make another public spectacle. Besides, she didn't know what foolish behaviour Marguerite might display if she did go up there before everyone.

After a minute of waiting, Nicolaus continued, "I want to make a statement, for all of you that are here, and for all the reporters. I'm sure you must be wondering what is actually happening ..." he used an open hand to point towards Marguerite. "Well, what you are about to witness is a business transaction. This ceremony has nothing to do with love or marriage," he said sadly, frowning. "If I were marrying for love, Deirdre would be by my side right now, as was originally planned. Deirdre Omari is the only woman I have ever loved." He stopped to sigh, trying to hold himself together. "No. No, instead, I have …" he points to Marguerite to include her, "we have been, our lives have been reduced to a business transaction. An unfair one at that. However, as I have given my word to the VMC board members and to Miss Marguerite Drone and her family, I will move forward with this business transaction. But I want to be clear to everyone present, this action I am about to take today, does not diminish one ounce of love I have for Deirdre.

And Bishop, I would ask that as we proceed through this business transaction, that we leave out such words as love, cherish, and until death to part." Nicolaus knew that some people in the audience would be shocked by his statement, and he did not look up at them. He felt the hand of his father on his shoulder, as Nigel wanted to support Nicolaus, but did not want him to say anymore. Nicolaus obeyed, and rejoined Marguerite on the platform. She looked upon him with eyes of hatred, stinging him with her stare.

As the ceremony got underway, Deirdre bolted for the nearest door that entered the outside corridor. She just wanted to get away. Her eyes were full of tears, and she did not know where she was running because she could not see properly. She just knew she wanted to run. Suddenly, strong arms grabbed her into a nearby door. She fought against the blind force, until she couldn't fight anymore. Exhausted, and unable to stop crying, she folded against Benjamin's chest, as he genuinely comforted her.

"I am here for you Deirdre". When she heard Benjamin's voice, she actually relaxed against him, unable to do anything else at the moment. He knew this must be the worst day of her life. He was glad to be there to hug her and touch her.

Deirdre bolting out the door caught Nicolaus' eye. His attention was on Deirdre. He had hoped she was in the church all along and had heard what he'd said. After the Bishop asked him twice if he took Marguerite to be his lawful and wedded wife, the Bishop touched his arm to return his attention to the matter at hand. "Sorry," Nicolaus muttered. For the third time, the Bishop repeated the question. Nicolaus looked at Marguerite, then to his mother in the front row of the audience, then to the audience, then to the Bishop. Feeling himself grow ill again, sweat begin to bead his forehead. He looked at Marguerite and nodded one time, "Yes, I do," he said, holden to his word. With a cold meanness, Marguerite agreed to have Nicolaus as her husband. With the exchange of the plain gold wedding bands, the Bishop had the couple repeat his words, having to adjust what he originally had planned, as they each placed the ring on each other's finger, and the Bishop held their hands together, as they did not seem to be willing to hold each other's hand.

'I take you to be my (wife/husband), and offer you my solemn vow to be your faithful partner for better or for worse, for richer, for poorer, in sickness and in health, in good times and in bad, and in joy as well as in sorrow. I promise to honour and respect you, for as long as we both are together.'

The Bishop then insisted they take holy communion, which they did. Then he led them to light the unity candle that was in Deirdre's favourite colour.

Bringing them back to the centre of the platform, the Bishop held their ringed hands together, and reminded them, "These rings are a commitment of faithfulness to each other, no matter the circumstances of this marriage." Still holding their hands, trying to bring some normalcy to this wedding ceremony, the Bishop then declared, "By the power vested in me by the state of Texas, I now pronounce you husband and wife. You may now kiss the bride."

Without putting his hands on Marguerite, Nicolaus quickly kissed her on the cheek that was closest to the Bishop. The audience made a hesitant clap, because they weren't sure to be happy for the couple, as when they faced the audience, they both looked horribly miserable.

The Bishop smiled trying to make things a little lighter, "Well folks, I now present to you Mr. Nicolaus and Mrs. Marguerite Ravenell." He swooped his hand in front of the couple, and blessed them as they walked together, unsmiling, not touching, Nicolaus stopping to chat with friends in the audience. Only suddenly did Nicolaus notice the flashing of cameras, and the murmuring of the hundreds of people that filled the numerous church pews.

Alexander was the first to come to Nicolaus, on this unhappy occasion. "You did it, you did it! You made it through." He shook Nicolaus by the shoulders.

Nicolaus shook his head negatively, "I need a drink. Where's Deirdre? I saw her run out. I need to check on her."

Francesca, Constance, and Elsa fled the path that Deirdre had ran prior to the ceremony.

They were extremely worried about her. They found her in Benjamin's arms, crumpled on the floor. They lifted her, thanking Benjamin. Elsa stayed with Benjamin; no way she was letting him get away from her at a wedding, no matter how awful it was. Elsa was dressed in a sexy champagne coloured short dress, which left one shoulder bare, and shaped tightly to her model body and curvy hips. Benjamin couldn't help but notice her, despite his lust for Deirdre.

As Nicolaus headed towards the front of the church, Francesca and Constance led Deirdre down the corridor and out the back. They were able to get to their vehicle, unseen by the press.

Nicolaus gentlemanly grabbed Marguerite by the arm, and quickly walked them the rest of the length of the church aisle, and out the front doors. He was shocked to see a large number of reporters at the entrance of the interior church, and then hundreds of people outside the church, waiting to get a glimpse of the couple. Some people he recognized from the office, most he did not. There seemed to be even more press, from around the world, to cover their wedding.

Marguerite yanked her arm from him, watching what he would do. She would not have him commanding her about. This move caused cameras to flash at a phenomenal speed to get pictures of the divided couple.

Nicolaus sighed, wanting to leave to find Deirdre, but now with all this press, there was too much pressure for him to stay by Marguerite's side. He saw that suddenly, the expression on Marguerite's face changed when she noticed all the press, and all the cameras, and the hundreds of people that were screaming for Nicolaus, as if he were a celebrity. Marguerite seemed scared.

Nicolaus stepped up to her. "It's okay", he told her. "Come on, let's greet the crowd for a minute." Without touching her, he held his hand out to the crowd of people that were on the sidewalk to the church, and in the parking lot, as the limousines were in the rounded driveway. Marguerite was frightened of the large crowd, and didn't move, so Nicolaus slowly walked towards the people, looking for her to follow, which she did. He greeted the many ladies in the crowd with handshakes, autographs, and selfies. As Marguerite watched him, he invited her to join him, "Come on wifey, get in this picture." The fan asked her to please join in, and she did.

They began taking many pictures with the fans together, and Marguerite seemed to enjoy this, smiling and laughing with the people in the crowd. She received many compliments on her dress, and her hair, and her makeup. She was told that she was beautiful, and oh so lucky to have Nicolaus. She was asked several times if she would be friends with Deirdre.

After about five minutes, Nicolaus felt he'd had enough, and he ushered Marguerite to the waiting limousine, touching the small of her back, having forgotten not to touch her. When he realized his hand was on her, and she did not protest, he breathed a small sigh of relief, but did not want to read much into it. As Marguerite got in the large car, she realized she'd just had fun with her new husband, and wanted to thank Nicolaus for involving her. However, she could see he was on his phone, trying to reach Deirdre, not paying attention to her, despite sitting next to her. Instead of engaging him, she stared out the window. They did not speak for the ride to the reception hall, which was held in the grand ballroom at a large hotel chain.

Inside the reception hall, after giving Deirdre the support she needed, Deirdre and Francesca were trying to make sure everything was ready for Nicolaus, as so little time was allotted for needed changes. Deirdre refused requests to return home. She felt it her duty to be present for Nicolaus.

Deirdre saw to the wedding cake set up. The cake that was supposed to be hers.

It was the one she had meticulously picked out, with real flowers, and the design of her and Nicolaus' initials intertwined. When she saw they forgot to change it, tears fell from her eyes.

Immediately, she got the knife and scraped off the design. It was Francesca who stopped her from destroying the cake, holding her hand back from the stabbing motion, making her drop the knife. Deirdre, wasn't aware of what she was doing. She collapsed again, this time against Francesca.

"Love, you shouldn't be here! It's too fucking hard! It's too fucking hard for me, I know it's too hard for you." Francesca quickly looked around for Rachel. "Oh God, where's mum?"

"No, no, I'm alright. I have to do this, for Nicky."

"Nicky would want you to be okay, Deirdre. And clearly, you're not okay. Believe me babe, this ain't no picnic for him either. I thought he was going to run after you when you ran out the church."

"No, I can't see him. I can't," she cried, trying to keep it together, wanting the day to be half decent for Nicolaus. "I just want to do this, and then I'll leave. I'm okay."

Francesca sighed, "Okay, then maybe to the kitchen, love. Let me handle the cake. Okay babe?"

Deirdre nodded. She wiped her face, and went into the kitchen to see how she could help. As she entered the kitchen, Nicolaus grabbed both of her hands in his, with an undeniable look of pain on his face. "Oh, my Deirdre... love, are you all right?" They'd made it to the reception hall. Marguerite loudly cleared her throat, as she stood behind them, lifting her wedding dress off the ground, with each hand to her side. Nicolaus glanced at

Marguerite, over his shoulder. As he looked away, Deirdre bolted from him, unable to stand his touch.

As a natural reaction, Nicolaus made a move to go after her, but his body was stopped by Marguerite's voice.

"Am I going to have a problem with the two of you?" she asked in a threatening manner, reminding him of his mother.

Nicolaus looked to her, choosing his words carefully, "No," he simply answered her.

"I know all about you, and what you trying to do," she stepped up to him, "I promise you, I will not let you make me a fool. I make your life living hell, I promise," she told him angrily. "Living hell," she shouted at him, making the dozens of kitchen staff stop to look in their direction to see what was going on. "I tare her eyes out!" she seemed about to get out of control now that she had an audience.

Frowning at the physical threat to Deirdre, "No Marguerite," Nicolaus told her, looking into her eyes. "I just made a commitment to you. I will keep that commitment. I will be faithful," he told her, "you have my word."

Marguerite sighed harshly, trying to calm herself, backing down.

In his gentlemanly manner, he again took Marguerite by the arm, and they entered the reception hall to the loud clapping of the guests, as many people had arrived right behind them.

Nicolaus tried to instruct Marguerite on how to greet these famous, and high-powered guests, as much as she would listen, even telling her to just nod without speaking. Marguerite felt out of place and frightened, as some celebrities she recognized, and didn't understand why they attended their wedding. She was so anxious, she did not leave Nicolaus' side.

After the long line of guest greeting, Ms. Winfree appeared and congratulated Nicolaus on his effective statement. Nicolaus ushered Marguerite to their table, as he was sure her feet were probably hurting. Though a wedding happened, there would be no traditions of speeches, or well wishes, or dances. The guests ate their food, drank their drinks, and mingled. There was no shortage of visitors to their newly wed table, and as usual, the woman provided hugs and kisses to Nicolaus, and he was sure to respectfully introduce Marguerite to every one of them.

Just after the meal was served, Andrejs and Penelope bid farewell, as they were scheduled to leave on his jet back to Latvia that afternoon.

Andrejs took Nicolaus, his new son-in-law aside, placing his hand sternly on his shoulder. "Just because I leaving, means not I gone." He wagged his finger close to Nicolaus' face. "You treat my Marguerite the way a wife is treated." He nodded at Nicolaus, expecting and receiving Nicolaus' nodding agreement. "Now, you let me know when you will come to Latvia to see the operations," Andrejs laughed nervously, "I want us to be strong, very strong partners. No?"

Nicolaus nodded again, "Yes."

The men shook hands with a smile. Andrejs had already bid Nigel and Ceil goodbye.

He saw Penelope heading towards Nicolaus and guided her away from him towards her sister.

Marguerite already knew of their flight and that they would be leaving. She refused her father's hug, still upset with him for her predicament, and more so now that he was abandoning her. Penelope briefly gave Marguerite an unreciprocated hug, and the pair left the ball-room.

Two hours of additional awkwardness had passed, and Nicolaus deposited Marguerite with Ceil, Nigel, and their guests, and he found Alexander and his comrades, who went to the bar to enjoy drinks, anecdotes of wedding nightmares, and jokes. The guys made bets on whether Nicolaus would make it through the night with his balls intact or wake up a sissy from his new wife having raked his virgin ass across the sexual coals. As the wedding observance ended, Nicolaus was filled with alcohol, and the dreaded thoughts of failing at his new mission of saving the family fortune. He still had one more task to secure the money, and the business. This task is what his mind was focused on.

The family returned to the mansion. As Nicolaus and Marguerite entered the prepared suite in the unused west wing of the mansion, he giggled at the absurdity of the large wedding bow that covered the door to the bedroom. He jerked it off and threw it to the floor. When they entered, he saw that the bedroom had most likely been prepared for his night with Deirdre. Rose petals made into the shape of a heart covered the top bed covers. Without feeling, Nicolaus wiped them off the bed and onto the floor.

Marguerite watched him, her anger growing yet again. Was he so callous? Not even caring about what she thought. She began pacing the room. "You not to touch me," she told him harshly, as he mechanically turned down the covers of the bed, not listening to her, focused on the mission at hand.

The only thoughts going through Nicolaus' mind was that of saving the family fortune. He knew Marguerite would need help getting out of her wedding dress.

Without words he offered his hand to her. Frowning, she turned her back to him, lifting her hair, and he began to undo the hooks that ran along her spine. As he gently undid his wife's dress, the smell of Jasmine escaped her hair. His thoughts were racing about sexual techniques to get through this as fast as possible. Slowly, he pulled her dress off, without protest from her, letting it fall.

Suddenly, Marguerite found herself on the bed, underneath Nicolaus, clad only in her silk undergarments. His hands touched her body at her waist, then softly at her breasts.

Her mind grew confused at the intoxicating smell of him, his gentle touch, and the gentle eyes connected to that handsome face. Nicolaus worked quickly, undoing his own pants, ready to get the consummation over with.

Unfortunately, his actions brought rage upon Marguerite. Harshly, she clawed the side of his face with her manicured tipped fingernails, creating instant deep cuts that burned. Then in response to his attempt at taking her, she used her knee to wallop him in his groin as hard as she could. Nicolaus moaned in pain, just as he received another hard wallop. Then, in the fastest instant, Marguerite grabbed hold of his erect manhood, twisting with all her might, digging her fingernails into him, as if she were trying to separate it from his body.

Intense pain ceased upon Nicolaus, and escaped his mouth. "I'm sorry, I'm sorry", he begged her as she tried her hardest to tighten her already tight grip on him, as if to rip him apart. "Please ... please! I'm sorry!" He was motionless, waiting for her to release him.

Having a little pity, Marguerite harshly let him go.

In pain, Nicolaus rolled over onto the bed, away from Marguerite, his hands cupping his member. He wanted to yell at her, but all his brain was telling him to do was to get away from this woman. It had been years since a woman attacked him; the last being Ceil. In haste, he was out of the room, finding it hard to walk. With great distress, Nicolaus eased himself into one of the other rooms in the mansion wing, where he spent his wedding night, away from his new wife, behind a locked door. Truly, he was wounded in body and spirit.

Chapter Forty-Six

When Deirdre did not see Nicolaus among the breakfast attendants, only being Nigel, Ceil, Benjamin, Alexander, Rachel, and Marguerite, she went to look for him. She would do anything not to sit at that breakfast table, as she heard Marguerite entertaining them to some laughter and gasping at her harsh actions towards Nicolaus. She found him in his own bedroom, and could tell that he'd been sick this morning. He looked pale and weak. "Nicky," she whispered to him in a worried tone, wiping the sweat from his brow with a nearby towel.

She saw the large marks across one side of his face, and frowned, "What happened to your face?" she asked him.

Nicolaus touched his face, and stood away from her. "Marguerite, that's what!" he said with agitated annoyance, the cuts still burning his face. "This is not all she's done to me," he stated.

"Perhaps you moved too quickly last night. Remember, I told you to court her first."

"Well, she's my wife now, and I just …

"Please do not finish that sentence," Deirdre cut him off, eyes closed, hand in the air, not wanting to hear which way his thoughts may go, under these circumstances. She felt a little stronger today than she did yesterday, and was able to deal with all this. Her unfulfilled wedding day was over now. She had to face a new reality. She was determined to remain a part of Nicolaus' life, after all, he was still the love of her life, and even though his mother rejected her, he had not, and she was sure he never would.

He sighed, "I am sorry," he tried to calm a little.

Deirdre nodded, "I count it as you not feeling well." She turned to leave, "I'll get some ointment for your scratches. Why don't you get cleaned up?"

Deirdre returned to his room in about fifteen minutes time, and found Nicolaus showered and sitting on the bed, a large towel wrapped about his waist. His agitated mood had not changed. She sat on the bed next to him, the irony not lost on her. She used her index finger to smooth the ointment on his facial cuts. "This will burn a little," she told him, as she laid it on thick.

When she was done Nicolaus took her hand and kissed it.

"This is all so wrong," he complained, irritated.

"Nicolaus, you need to calm down. Eventually, this will all work out. You have to give it time, just the same as you would if it were me."

"If it were you, we would not need time."

Deirdre had not seen this side of Nicolaus for quite a while, as he was truly angry and worked up. She was not sure how to help him. "Tell me, where else does this need to go?"

He looked at her, and gently took the ointment from her. "Where this needs to go, your beautiful hands cannot." Deirdre felt herself blush, and wondered what Marguerite had actually done to him. He went into the bathroom, where Deirdre heard him make sounds of angry discomfort. Not sure what else to do, Deirdre sat in silence and waited, in support of Nicolaus. He appeared from the bathroom half dressed, but then quickly dressed himself. He took Deirdre by the hand, which she did not fight against, or recoil from him, and they walked to the breakfast room together. He released her hand before they entered the room.

"Look, there he is now," Marguerite said loudly, pointing at Nicolaus, gaining boisterous laughter from Benjamin, Ceil and Nigel. Ceil pointed to his face, and laughed uncontrollably, Nicolaus the obvious butt of the joke. Neither Alexander nor Rachel were laughing, but looking quite uncomfortable. Rachel shook her head in disapproval.

In hurt, Deirdre left the scene. With Nicolaus in his angered mood, she did not know what he would do, and she just didn't want to witness his wrath. It was obvious that Marguerite told everyone a story about what transpired last night.

Nicolaus did not find any of this disrespect amusing.

Controlling his anger, he moved towards Marguerite, and short of slapping her, he harshly pulled her chair away from the table, her weight going with the chair. All at once, the laughter stopped, everyone watching. "You are dismissed, Marguerite," he said with authority, through gritted teeth and eyes of fire.

Everyone was still, waiting for her response.

"Ha!" was all she said, and tried to scoot her chair where it had been. The chair did not move because Nicolaus still had a hold of it.

Nicolaus harshly lifted her by the arm, not letting her out of his grip, "You are relieved of my presence," he told her, guiding her towards the door. She turned to say something, however, Nicolaus took her by the arm, and forced her towards the door. "I said get out," he yelled at her, pushing her out the door, outside of the room. Quickly, he closed the French doors on her.

"It would appear that you fall short on how to treat women, as you do in other areas of life," Ceil said sarcastically.

"You brought this upon me, mother, upon all of us," he said, highly agitated.

Benjamin and Alexander stared into their plates. Alexander did not think things would go so badly for Nicolaus. Benjamin frowned, actually feeling sorry for his brother.

"Here we go again. Whining and complaining, and blaming others for your troubles. Grow up Nicolaus!" Ceil rose from her chair and left the room.

Nicolaus felt distraught, and imagined he would be, at least until his injuries stopped bothering him. He did not know what he was going to do with Marguerite. Nicolaus left the mansion by himself. He did not go into the office. He needed to think. He sped his sports car down the highway.

Chapter Forty-Seven

Nicolaus found that dismissing Marguerite when she exhibited bad behaviour worked for now, as it made her feel embarrassed and treated like a child, which she did not like. It only took two more episodes of this, one in the presence of Deirdre, to tap down her disrespect towards him. Her behaviour in the airport for their trip to Latvia was fine, however, she was a little bothered by their airplane seating arrangements, as Nicolaus sat between she and Deirdre. Francesca sat between Alexander and Rachel, behind Nicolaus. Rachel decided to join them at the last minute, as Nicolaus implored her to go with them.

When they arrived in Estonia, their first stop, Alexander went on to Latvia to vacation ahead of their meeting with Andrejs. At the Ravenell castle, Aunt Clara was overjoyed that the family came to see her. She was immediately drawn to Nicolaus, hugging him, and touching his face. It was beyond her imagination how much he resembled Nicohls, their ancestor. And she looked very shocked when she saw Deirdre, exclaiming a joyous noise to look upon her. She was happy to see Rachel again, and Francesca. She was stopped in her tracks when Nicolaus introduced Marguerite as his wife.

Clara frowned deeply, "No!" she exclaimed loudly. "No!" making a cross out gesture with her hands towards Marguerite.

"Aunt Clara, it is okay, Marguerite is my wife," Nicolaus said without touching Marguerite, as was the couple's custom.

"No! This not right. No."

Nicolaus looked to Francesca and Rachel for assistance, only to be taken by his great Auntie Clara, as she

279

pulled him forward, closer to her. She touched his face, the scratches still visible, then she looked to Marguerite, as if she knew Marguerite was the cause of this pain to her nephew. "It's all right, Aunt Clara," Nicolaus tried to reassure her.

"No!" she told him again, slightly shaking him. Then in the Estonian language, she said, "Siin pole midagi (There is nothing here)," she pointed between him and Marguerite. "Ta ei tohiks olla su naine. Tähtedes kirjutatut ei saa muuta. (She should not be your wife. You cannot change what is written in the stars)." Nicolaus understood his Auntie Clara, because Rachel made him learn the Estonian language when he was young, and he'd mastered it while in the military. Nicolaus looked at Marguerite, who now stared at him with folded arms. He slightly smiled at her, hoping she was not able to translate this conversation. Clara shook Nicolaus by the arm to return his attention to her. "Miks sa selle tüdrukuga abiellud? See on Deirdre, DeeDee, mis kuulub teile (Why you marry that girl? It is Deirdre, DeeDee, that belongs to you)." Clara grabbed Deirdre, pulling her forward and next to Nicolaus, as she had been standing behind him. She smiled and nodded in approval.

Nicolaus nodded with a frown. Suddenly, he felt that heavy weight of saving the family fortune return upon his shoulders. Rachel stepped in. "Clara tädi, see pole tema tegevus. (Auntie Clara, this is not his doing)," she told her in Estonian. "Ceil sundis selle abielu. (Ceil forced this marriage)."

"I know you talk about me!" Marguerite said in anger. "I demand to know what is said."

Nicolaus turned to her, "Ah, my great Aunt Clara knew about my engagement to Deirdre, and she wants to know what happened. That is all," he told her.

Marguerite did not unfold her arms, but she accepted what he said. Losing interest, she turned from him, and looked over the beautiful castle. When she came upon the ancestral painting of Nicohls and DeeDee, she was taken aback, having further understanding of his aunt's questioning.

Deirdre stood next to Marguerite, also to see the painting. She was shocked at what she was looking at. Francesca's words reverberated in her mind about this woman looking exactly like her, and Nicohls looking exactly like Nicolaus. It was uncanny. Deirdre was lost in the painting, and did not notice that Marguerite was eyeing her with a mean glare.

Marguerite had enough of everything always being about Deirdre. She was feeling left out, despite being Nicolaus' wife. Marguerite ceased upon the moment to pounce Deirdre, as the rest of the family was on the other side of the enormous room, talking to Aunt Clara.

Marguerite harshly grabbed Deirdre by the wrist, twisted it backwards, making Deirdre shriek. "You think you so beautiful and so in love," she harshly shook Deirdre, "you better know he no longer is yours!"

"Let go, Marguerite. You are hurting me!"

Marguerite tightened her twisted grip on Deirdre's small and delicate wrist, making her lean with the twist. "He belongs to me. You need to leave!" she shook Deirdre.

Deirdre clawed at Marguerite's hand, but was unable to get out of the tight grip.

Marguerite shook her again. "I'm his wife now. You got that?" she yelled at her.

At the commotion, Nicolaus was quickly upon the ladies, and he pulled Marguerite off Deirdre, releasing her hand, and pushing her to a nearby corner. "What is wrong with you, putting your hands on Deirdre like that?" he asked her frowning.

Marguerite turned from him, heading back toward the direction of Deirdre, who was being consoled by Rachel and Francesca.

Nicolaus stopped Marguerite, pulling her back towards him, into the corner. He grabbed hold of her shoulders, "Stop it," he yelled at her, frowning, "stop it," he repeated, as she tried to get away from him again. "You don't touch her!" he told her harshly.

His words got her attention. Marguerite stopped and looked him in the eyes, "Who is your wife?" she yelled at him. Striking him, she began to fight Nicolaus, repeatedly striking his chest, trying to strike his face. Nicolaus grabbed ahold of her wrists and turned her back to him, putting her in a restraint hold, as he'd done for many a soldier that got out of control. He held her tightly to him. She was unable to withstand his strength, and gave in, out of breath from fighting against him. Being wrapped in Nicolaus' arms did something to her. She gave in, but he didn't release her for several minutes. She laid herself against him, not understanding why he made her feel bewildered.

Aunt Clara yelled at Nicolaus, "She is no good. She will not last. You cannot change what is written in the stars," her Estonian language veiled to Marguerite. Nicolaus looked at his Aunt, while holding onto Marguerite, as he could clearly see his Aunt Clara was upset with him.

Once Nicolaus got Marguerite calm, he had the house staff take the two of them to their guest room inside the castle. He closed the door, after the staff brought in their luggage.

"What was that all about?" he asked her, agitated, yet again.

Marguerite stood away from him, her arms crossed.

She looked down, "No, not to discuss."

"Oh no, you're gonna discuss. What the hell was that? You know I'm not going to let you put your hands on Deirdre. Don't ever do that again," he told her sternly, without yelling.

"What was the argument about?" he asked more calmly, then waited for her response.

Marguerite looked up at Nicolaus, her husband, who was starting to get next to her. Her husband whom she liked it when he held her tight. Her husband, whom she wanted to be next to. She sighed, "It was about you," she yelled at him, "okay, it was about you!"

Nicolaus was not amused by her behaviour. It was actually upsetting to him. He stepped closer to her, slowly pacing himself until he was right upon her. He frowned at her, shaking his head, "No more of this," he told her softly, "no more." He took her hands, and she did not pull away from him, so he went with it, wanting to get through to her. Their eyes met, "Deirdre is not your enemy, nor am I. My wife would never act the way you did," he tried to reason with her. When she didn't pull away from him, he kept going. "Please understand, I will always love Deirdre. I will. But …" he held her hands a little tighter, "you are my wife now. And I have promised to respect you as my wife. And I am a man of my word." He put his forehead against hers when he saw a tear seep from Marguerite's eye. "Can we agree there will be no more fighting?"

Marguerite nodded in silence.

"You owe Deirdre an apology," he added, "my wife would make that apology, and she would mean it, and she would not make that mistake again," he told her softly, but sternly.

Marguerite tried to sniff away her tears, but it wasn't working. He embraced her, and left her to join the others.

As soon as Aunt Clara saw Nicolaus descend down the stairs, she continued her rant, "What is that? Why have you done this? That woman no good!"

"Yes, Aunt Clara, I understand," he told her in Estonian. "Auntie Rachel, will you please help me calm Aunt Clara?" Rachel went to Clara. As she did so, Nicolaus went to Deirdre, "Babe, are you all right?" he gently took her hand to examine her wrist.

Deirdre jerked her hand from him. "Stop calling me babe!" she yelled at him. "You're a married man now."

"I'm sorry. It's a habit."

"Well, get a new habit," she snapped at him, and walked away, holding her sore wrist.

"Wait, Deirdre ... I'm sorry ... Deirdre," he was astonished.

"Good Lord man, you've got woman troubles, haven't you? You've even upset Deirdre," Francesca observed.

Nicolaus shook his head in disbelief, "We've never had words like this. We've never argued."

"You mean to tell me that over ten years' time, you and Deirdre have never argued? Not once?"

"No, never."

"And now look what you did! You've got poor Aunt Clara crying. Nicky, you'd better handle this."

Nicolaus went to Clara and kneeled before her, as she was sitting. He took her hands in his. He apologized for Marguerite's behaviour, "Mul on kahju, et mu naine on valesti käitunud. Ta ei tee seda enam", (I'm sorry my wife has misbehaved. She won't do it again). He apologized for disappointing her, "Ma palun andeks, et valmistasin teile pettumuse," (I beg your forgiveness for disappointing you).

Clara touched his head, and then she touched his face where the cuts lay. She nodded, accepting his apology, and then told him, "Teie teekond saab olema keeruline, täpselt nagu Nicohls, sest olete nüüd oma tõelisest elukursust kõrvale kaldunud", (Your journey is going to be difficult, just like Nicohls, because you are now off your true life course).

Then Clara stopped crying and wiped her face, and she called for Francesca. She kissed Francesca dearly, then spoke in broken English. "I want you have something," she told her. Clara lifted a large, thick book, which held the Kiviste family history, Rachel and Ceil's side of the family tree. "You now keeper of our heritage. Our legacy. You must read and know everything. Nicolaus going to need help. You must record everything that happens. Francesca, this huge, huge responsibility, but you chosen by the stars to be keeper of the family legacy."

Francesca was in awe of the responsibility being bestowed on her. "Me?" she asked her. Clara handed her the book. Francesca, hugged the book to her chest, as if it were a child.

"I will do as you ask, Auntie Clara. I will make you proud."

Clara smiled at her, and reached to kiss her cheek. Then Clara reached for Rachel, "You have done well," she told her, "your children are wonders," she told her, speaking of Francesca and Nicolaus. Nicolaus frowned at the comment, thinking Clara was confused, but said nothing.

Then Clara called for Deirdre. Deirdre kneeled before her as well, and Clara touched her face and her hair. "Beautiful," she told her. "You must work to fulfil destiny. Nicolaus yours. Not other. You!" she reiterated. Deirdre looked down, tears filling her eyes. "Ah," Clara lifted her chin, "no. You. Just wait. You see," she assured her, as if she had some way of seeing into the future.

Deirdre nodded, and kissed Clara's hand, "Thank you, Auntie Clara. I'm so glad to have been here to spend time with you."

Clara chuckled, "Yes, time. Time." She sighed loudly, "I tire now. I rest. You go. I rest," she told them all, shewing them away with her hands.

Nicolaus leaned down and kissed his great Aunt Clara. Clara took his hand and patted it. They bid her goodnight, knowing they would see her tomorrow, to continue their conversation.

Chapter Forty-Eight

When Nicolaus returned to his guest room, he found Marguerite was calm. She had changed clothes and cleaned up her face.

"I'm sorry," she told him, "I'm ready to apologize to Deirdre," she rolled her eyes and chuckled, "after all, she did help me prepare to marry you."

With a slight smile, Nicolaus held his hand out to her. She took his hand, and they went to the room he'd seen Deirdre led to. Deirdre opened the door, but did not let them inside.

Nicolaus thought this odd, but understandable, since Marguerite did attack her. "Ba ...," he stopped himself, "ah .. Deirdre, Marguerite has something she'd like to tell you." He pulled Marguerite forward, but stood next to her to stop any sudden movements she might make towards Deirdre.

At first Marguerite looked down, having to swallow some of her pride, then her eyes looked at Deirdre. "I'm sorry. Was mistake to grab you and yell at you. I apologize," she told her, then her eyes were on Nicolaus, where they remained. Deirdre noticed this.

Nicolaus nodded to his wife, then to Deirdre, waiting for her response.

Though Deirdre realized the apology was probably forced, she nodded in acceptance. "Sure," she said gently.

"I'm sorry," Nicolaus added. "I don't want us to be ..."

"What, Nicolaus?" Deirdre frowned at him, not wanting to hear his words. She was still upset. Now Deirdre stood with her arms crossed before her chest, a stance she'd never given to Nicolaus. She saw the shocked look on his face. It took all she had to remain in her stance.

"Ah … at odds with each other. Please, Deirdre."

Deirdre sighed, still frowning, "Okay, I'll think about it. I have to get some rest now." She closed the door, then crumpled to the floor, her tears flowing. It killed her to see him with that woman.

Chapter Forty-Nine

One bed was in the guest room that Marguerite and Nicolaus were assigned to. The situation was tough for Nicolaus, as he was not sure what to do, and did not trust being in the room with Marguerite. They had not shared a room together since she attacked him on their wedding night. Though the room was elegant, there was not extra furniture, such as a chair or couch that he could sleep on. When they got into the bed, Nicolaus placed pillows between them, and his sleep was uneasy.

A few hours later, Nicolaus was easily awakened when he felt rustling of the covers next to him. Marguerite was cold in the drafty castle. And despite a fire going in the bedroom fireplace, the room was still cold. She'd gone around the bed and climbed in on the side where Nicolaus was sleeping. He awoke to Marguerite snuggling herself next to him. "Marguerite, what are you doing?" he asked her, trying not to sound alarmed, though he was extremely alarmed.

"It's freezing in here!" She grabbed him around the waist and snuggled against him.

Nicolaus stiffened at her actions.

"Do your job!" she griped at him. "I need my husband to warm me."

With quick thinking, Nicolaus grabbed a pillow and placed it over his groin to protect himself. Then he took his wife into his arms to warm her against his torso, and with his feet, her back against him. He felt awkward and sad at the same time, and was glad when Marguerite quickly fell asleep.

More uneasy sleep awakened Nicolaus to Marguerite, facing him and rubbing his chest and staring at him. "What's the matter?" he asked her, frowning with concern, thinking something was wrong, and wondering why she was awake. It was still dark.

"Why the matter? I can touch my husband, no?"

Nicolaus frowned as Marguerite proceeded to touch his face, where she had left the scratch marks. He wasn't sure what was happening, but he did notice the pillow was gone from his groin area, and seemed to be replaced by her body. Marguerite's hand continued at his chest, and then began to descend down his body. Once she passed his belly button, Nicolaus grabbed her hand to stop it from going where he feared it might.

"What?" she chuckled, resisting his removal of her hand.

"No. Last time you touched me there … I did not have a good experience."

"Ahhh! You scared of me?" she started to tease him, but then thought about what she had done to him. "I'm sorry. I should not have done that, it hurt you. But you should not have touched me," she justified herself, not wanting to seem weak.

Nicolaus took her hand in his. Marguerite turned her back to him, and he held her to keep her warm. For a fleeting moment, he thought the action was nice. However, he'd much rather be holding Deirdre to him. He worried that Deirdre may also be cold in her room, and it was hard to keep himself from getting up to check on her. Eventually, sleep fell upon both he and Marguerite.

Chapter Fifty

In the early morning hour, there was knocking at the bedroom door. "Yes, you may enter," Nicolaus said loud enough to penetrate through the thick wooden castle door.

"Master Nicolaus," the head house staffer called to him after opening the heavy laden door.

"Yes, what is it?" Nicolaus half set up in the bed.

"Sir, I am very sorry to inform you … that … Mistress Clara … sir, well, she has passed away, sir … in her sleep," he said sadly.

"What?" Nicolaus was shocked. "I … I'll be right there."

Nicolaus quickly dressed, washing up in the cold water supplied in the room. Nicolaus sighed before entering Clara's room, where the staff were gathered in the hallway just before the bedroom door. He went in, and sat next to Clara's body, taking her hand, as if it were a precious artifact. It was cold and lifeless. She looked as if she was peacefully sleeping. He observed the room and her surroundings, nothing seemed out of place or out of the ordinary. Rachel then entered the room, having also been alerted. Nicolaus stood and hugged Rachel to him, as she began to mourn her aunt, who was the last living of that generation of Kivistes.

By noon, Rachel, the closest living descendant to Clara, decided she was going to let Nicolaus be in charge of the funeral and burial arrangements, with her guidance. She wanted him to learn this important task that all adults must eventually perform. Without hesitation, Nicolaus accepted what she wanted, and he immediately got to work. Rachel notified Nigel, and she was sure he and Ceil would arrive as soon as they could get a flight to Estonia.

Marguerite watched Nicolaus as he respectfully spoke on the phone with her father, and postponed their visit for one week. He touched her shoulder, and handed her the phone so she could speak with her father. Marguerite folded her arms and turned from Nicolaus. Being reminded of her predicament suddenly made his charms wash off her, and brought her anger back to the surface. She looked at Nicolaus with darted eyes. Nicolaus didn't like what he was seeing, and frankly didn't have time to deal with Marguerite's childish behaviour. He made excuses for her, and continued to rush around to make funeral arrangements, after also notifying Alexander.

It was not long that Nicolaus was at the historic St. Nicholas church in Tallin, with Deirdre in tow. The extended rafters and beautiful stained glass took their breath away, and they were overtaken by its beauty. They were stopped in the middle of the aisle by the bishop on duty.

"Nicolaus Ravenell!" he shouted from the front of the large church, his voice echoing in its emptiness.

Nicolaus was surprised, "Yes."

The bishop met them halfway, first taking Deirdre's hand and kissing it, then shaking Nicolaus' hand. "I am Bishop Moratey. I am so glad you came to see your Aunt Clara. She has been very worried about meeting you and your sister, Francesca."

"Oh, yeah, Francesca is my cousin. My Aunt Clara had that a little confused."

"Oh," the bishop moaned, without other words, as if there was more to the story.

Nicolaus arched an eyebrow and smiled, "Wow, that sounds like you may know something I don't know."

The bishop waived the awkwardness away, as it was not his place to tell. "What brings you about? Your Aunt Clara is worried about you. She says you will have some trouble in your life. Nicolaus, do you have the faith?"

The bishop grabbed hold of Deirdre's hand as he spoke to Nicolaus.

Nicolaus nodded, "Yes, yes, I have faith. As does Deirdre."

"Yes, Father," Deirdre confirmed.

"Good, good!"

"Bishop, what is this trouble that everyone keeps talking about?"

The bishop shook his head, "We cannot see in the future, Nicolaus. Clara felt that she was having some premonitions of something. She could not tell for certain, but understood it to be trouble, or a troubled path for you."

Nicolaus nodded. "Bishop, actually my Aunt Clara passed last night, and ... "

"Oh no, I am sorry for such a loss. Wow! You know, your Aunt Clara is well known here in town. Many people will be affected by her passing."

"Yes, I heard she was a bit famous."

"Well, she has already written everything out, exactly the way she wants it. We literally worked on this two weeks ago. And you do not need to worry, she also has her will and trust in order." The bishop stopped in thought, then touched Nicolaus on the shoulder. "I am so glad that you made the journey to see Clara. It is what she wanted most."

Chapter Fifty-One

The funeral services for Clara happened fairly quickly, within two days' time as she wanted. Just before the start of services, Francesca led Nicolaus to see her discovery of mausoleum tombs that held their family members, their names etched into the walls of their place of rest. She was moved to tears when she saw Nicohls and DeeDee were buried side by side.

They had made announcements of Clara's passing in the customary fashion in the city of Tallin, and to the surprise of the family, the church was packed with community members who wanted to pay their respects to Clara. Nicolaus is shocked to see the large number of extended family members present. People who looked like them, first and second cousins, even aunts and uncles, all he's never met before. Nicolaus also noticed plenty of press was in attendance as well. The press seemed to be a part of their lives, in every aspect now.

Nicolaus led all the family into the church. As he walked the historic church aisle, he could feel the presence of his ancestors. He felt as though he was walking in their exact steps from a time past. Ceil and Nigel walked behind Nicolaus, followed by Benjamin and Francesca, Rachel and Constance and then the extended family members.

Ceil was annoyed as she saw that Nicolaus seemed to be balancing his marriage with his long-term relationship with Deirdre, as the ladies flanked him. His right arm was around the waist of the crying Deirdre, her tears for Clara; and his left hand tightly gripped Marguerite's, without any trouble from her.

Clara, who had no sons or daughter of her own, was to be placed in the church mausoleum, next to her husband.

The reading of Clara's will was conducted quickly after her burial. All family members were astonished to learn that Clara left the castle, the massive grounds including the waterways, property and assets, such as buildings, structures, animals and livestock, to Nicolaus and Deirdre. The family historical records were officially left to Francesca. Rachel and Ceil, and their direct descendants were left the financial inheritance of the family. Clara also left a large monetary donation to the historic church, which of course held her family members posthumously, where she now lay. Altogether, the estate is worth more than three hundred million dollars.

Chapter Fifty-Two

It was in the airport, when Marguerite was alone with Nicolaus, as they waited to board the plane for Latvia, that she decided to act out again. As they stood in line to board first class, Marguerite harshly jabbed Nicolaus in his rib cage with her elbow.

The unexpected attack made him half bend his torso, in pain. "Ouch!" he said loudly. "What was that for?" he frowned at his wife, pain coursing up through him.

Marguerite crossed her arms and got out of line, as she had been quiet most of the morning.

Nicolaus followed her. "What happened?"

Marguerite pointed her angry finger at him, "You think I don't know what you do?"

Nicolaus was flabbergasted, "What'd I do?"

"You try to make me look a fool. You think I don't know?"

"What? What are you talking about, Marguerite?"

"You and your fancy suit, all over Deirdre. You think I don't see?" she pointed at him again.

"Deirdre?" Nicolaus sighed, already tired of this scene, his hand on his rib, a reminder that Marguerite was easily willing to physically hurt him. "We're not doing this. Come on, we've got to get on this plane. Your father will be waiting."

"No, I'm not going." She crossed her arms and turned her back on him.

Nicolaus sighed, closing his eyes, wanting to wish this never-ending nightmare away. "Marguerite, please."

"No!" she yelled at him, getting attention from other passengers, who were waiting to board the plane. "Go by self. Leave me!"

Nicolaus stood close behind her, "Look, I told you ..."

"No!" Marguerite tried to leave and was captured by Nicolaus, he pulled her close. However, she did not want to be charmed by him. She tried not to look at him, but it was no use, his touch was intoxicating her, just as his eyes do to her. She struggled against him, pushing at his chest, only to be held tighter in his arms. She could feel his taunt muscular body against hers.

"Wife, please." He frowned at her refusal and struggle against him. He held her tighter. "I'm sorry," he whispered in her ear, hoping it would calm her. "Wife, I'm sorry," he told her, not knowing what he was apologizing for. He felt her relax against him, as Marguerite gave in. He wrapped her in his arms, unable to figure this woman out. She did not return his hug, but she laid her head against his shoulder in surrender. Marguerite was confused by this man; she knew she didn't want him ... but then, why did her body seem to want him? What was he doing to her?

They had little talk on the short plane ride, though Nicolaus did try to tend to her.

Once they arrived, Andrejs had separate itineraries for the couple. Marguerite was to spend time with Penelope, while Nicolaus and Alexander were to spend the day at the factory, and Drone headquarters. Nicolaus and Alexander were impressed by what they saw at the pharmaceutical factory. Andrejs had his staff present numbers and projection reports to them as well. By the time the men returned to Andrejs' mansion, it was close to eight at night.

Right away, Nicolaus saw that Marguerite was further closed off to him, back to not wanting him to touch her. Alexander was surprised by the predicament of his best friend. He was hopeful his relationship with Marguerite would get better with time.

Nicolaus had no way of knowing that Penelope had received a call from Ceil to goad her into doing her bidding, to get Marguerite agitated against him. Nor did he know that Penelope had been feeding lies to Marguerite and was behind the change that had come about her. Marguerite refused to share a room with Nicolaus, which left him a little despondent, because he saw all the progress he'd made with Marguerite wash away so easily.

In the separate bedroom, Nicolaus studied the reports that were provided to him and Alexander, since he could not sleep. They were scheduled to return to Austin in the morning.

Marguerite remained cold towards both Nicolaus and Alexander, all the way to Austin. Nicolaus was not sure how he could get her back.

Chapter Fifty-Three

Five months of marriage misery followed Nicolaus, with no relenting of rude and avoidance behaviour from Marguerite. Nicolaus felt as though he was at war in his own home, being made to feel constantly uncomfortable. He wondered if things could get worse.

As a wedding gift, Nigel gave Nicolaus the deed to the west wing of the mansion as living quarters for the couple, as it was almost separated from the rest of the house, only joined by a long, narrow corridor. Nicolaus and Marguerite adopted separate bedrooms, as Nicolaus did not see any path forward nor did he even want to deal with the consummation issue.

He treated Marguerite cordially, only formally escorting her to breakfast and dinner, without touching her, because she still refused his hand, and would rile up if his hand graced her in any way. He rarely conversed with her, only when it was necessary, or to give her husbandry instructions, suggestions, or to give her permission for something. He did sit next to her at dinner, and across from her at breakfast, but his eyes did not look upon her.

Sometimes, Deirdre was present at dinner which really perked him up. However, Deirdre no longer provided the family her full support at the mansion, as she had done in the past, though Nicolaus begged her to stay with them.

Deirdre stayed in the background of things, mostly. Nicolaus' heart pined for Deirdre. His body wanted her more than anything. He wanted so much that she be his wife. Every fibre in his being, knew she was the only one for him, which increased his aggravation and defeatist attitude toward Marguerite.

His heart was pained at the misery his mother purposefully drowned him in, his obvious loveless and hopeless marriage, but he no longer complained or gave voice to his feelings. What is done is done, and Marguerite is his wife now, and he intended to remain a man of his word.

Deirdre could feel Nicolaus' magnetism, so strong at times, it scared her. She talked him into sending fresh flowers to Marguerite's room on a regular basis. She wanted them sent daily, but could only get him to agree to send them weekly. What usually happened was that Marguerite would receive one rose from Nicolaus, and the other eleven would mysteriously appear before Deirdre, whether she was at her home or the mansion. Constance and Rachel were not sure what to make of all of it, or how the two would navigate this difficult time. Rachel was proud of how Nicolaus was gracefully handling everything, especially when observing the hard time Marguerite regularly heaped on him.

Nevertheless, it was at times like now that Deirdre could feel Nicolaus wanting her, when she talked with him, no matter who was present. His eyes never left hers. He sat very close to her. His hands never left hers, but he remained the utmost gentleman, and respectful to both Deirdre and Marguerite. "Nicky, Marguerite's birthday is in two days. You should give her a grand party ... you know like a coming out party."

"No," he simply disagreed, shaking his head, without further comment. Deirdre's lovely scent enveloped him, making him lose his senses. He pulled Deirdre close to him. They were standing by the window of the drawing room, as the light from the stars was clearly visible in the Texas night sky, through the nine-foot-tall windows.

Without thinking, his arms encircled her, catching Deirdre by surprise. His lips were inches from hers.

Deirdre turned her head away. "Nicolaus!" She twirled herself away from him, her back against his chest as his arms went tighter around her. Her breathing grew heavy. Didn't he know what he was doing to her? "Nicolaus, what are you doing?" Her soft voice became a whimper, "What are you doing?"

Slowly he released her, realizing the predicament he was placing her in. He frowned to himself, shaking his head. "I am so sorry." He sat himself on the large window seat. "I would never do anything to dishonour you, Deirdre. Please forgive me! I just ... love you so. I ... need you so much."

Deirdre was quickly beside him, comforting him. "I know it's hard on you, Nicky."

He took her hand and kissed it. "I'll watch myself, I promise. I'll never do that again. Please forgive me."

Deirdre touched the back of his hand to the side of her face. "Of course," she whispered. Her precious Nicolaus was suffering.

Chapter Fifty-Four

Marguerite found life as a Ravenell wife to be utterly boring. Although Nicolaus did not take her anywhere because of her awful and insolent treatment of him, he did make sure she had anything she wanted. He ensured she had a driver to take her anywhere she wanted to go, and plenty of money to buy whatever she wanted.

Marguerite took Nicolaus' advice and joined the local country club, where she met other women, some of whom were foreigners, like herself. This helped her network and make friends, which led to shopping extravaganzas, sometimes even in other cities, like Houston, Dallas, and New York. However, Nicolaus forbade her from leaving the country, having taken her passport; and he forbade her from talking to the press. He warned her that if he learned that she talked to the press, he would revoke her freedom and she would not be able to go about without him. This threat was more than enough to keep Marguerite in line.

Since Nicolaus had not made plans for Marguerite's birthday, Ceil asked Deirdre to help her plan an event. Although it was short notice, people did not turn down a Ravenell invitation. Ceil held the huge party in a lavish downtown hotel, to accommodate two hundred guests.

Marguerite's behaviour was the best Deirdre had ever seen, most likely because of her girlfriends, each of whom had their eyes on Nicolaus, as if they wanted to sexually devour him, as soon as he and Alexander walked in. Nicolaus greeted his wife with a hand to her shoulder, and told her she looked pretty. For show, Marguerite jumped up from her seat and surprised Nicolaus with a hug, which he didn't know what to do with.

He smiled at her, glad she seemed happy, and left her to her friends after introductions.

To even out the guests, Deirdre made sure Nicolaus' military comrades were present as well. She saw the relieved look on his face when he saw them. However, many celebrities and high-powered people also attended, as well as the VMC board members. Nicolaus, Alexander, and Nigel made the rounds to talk to everyone. Drinks flowed, musicians provided live music, and an over-the-top banquet was served.

With Elsa on his arm, Benjamin did not miss a chance to pursue Deirdre, grabbing her by the hand in passing; pulling her into a hug when she least expected it; offering her a drink at an inappropriate time.

Elsa became annoyed with Benjamin making passes at Deirdre. She got his attention by grabbing him by the chin, "Hey ... you owe me a dance, don't you?" Though Elsa was doing her best not to jump in bed with Benjamin, which was a monumental task, their relationship had moved to the next level, as they were now exclusive to each other. Elsa had to manage Benjamin carefully, as her father, Jonathan Baird, a former diplomat, and current secret agent Elsa suspected, had an extreme personality. No one knew what work her father actually did, though he often travelled to other countries. If Benjamin's actions angered her father, there was no telling what he might do. Benjamin's obsession with Deirdre did greatly worry Elsa, and she did not want to be used or abused by this man she was in love with.

Benjamin smiled at his lady, and grabbed her around her hourglass waist, and gently twirled her to the music, joining the other couples on the makeshift dance floor.

Nicolaus and Marguerite seemed perfectly happy in their separate worlds, hanging with their friends, drinking and laughing. Nicolaus watched from the other side of the room when it was time for Marguerite to open her gifts. She seemed like a different person, happy and grateful. "See, there's hope," Alexander told him, nudging him as they watched Marguerite. Nicolaus truly hoped the generosity of others would do something to change her.

At the end of the celebration, the Ravenells, Alexander, and Deirdre stood at the door, and thanked each of the guests, giving them direct attention.

"I'm surprised you are not pregnant, Marguerite. Hasn't it been six months?" Ceil pried, between guests.

"Pregnant! We do not do that!"

"What do you mean?"

"No, he's not going to touch me!" Marguerite told Ceil, rather too loudly.

Nigel overheard the conversation. He looked horrified, and pulled both Marguerite and Nicolaus out of the line, and into a private room. Ceil following behind.

Benjamin shook his head, "My brother! The only married virgin in town," he chuckled.

Alexander was shocked at Benjamin's comment. He looked back at the closed doors, "Oh my God, that's really bad," his mind immediately on the merger contract.

Inside the private room, Nigel was panicking because he knew it was close to the six-month deadline. "Nicolaus," he half yelled at his son, "is this true what she is saying? You have not consummated your marriage?"

Nicolaus folded his arms in defence of himself, "What's the matter, father? It's not funny anymore?"

Nigel looked to Marguerite, who turned from him without words. Nigel waived to Ceil to take Marguerite out of the room. Once the ladies were gone, Nigel began pacing the floor.

"Oh … this … this is … unacceptable, son. Six months? Six months, Nicolaus. You know what will happen if you don't consummate before the deadline."

"I never asked for this. It's all been forced upon me. And she is …" he had trouble trying to find a kind word, "incorrigible. How do you expect this marriage to work? I'm doing the best I can," Nicolaus frowned, hating that he had to defend himself like this.

"No, it's not good enough, son," Nigel stood his ground, though he saw that Nicolaus was visibly upset. "Without consummation, we still lose everything, and all your suffering will have been in vain." Nigel briefly side hugged Nicolaus, "Get a grip on yourself, son." He stood away from him, "Listen, all you have to do is be with her just one time. One time. That is all you have to do."

"And how am I to do it? She refuses me."

"Well, don't let her refuse you. Take her. Force her. Get her drunk. Whatever it takes, son. Our family fortune is at stake here."

Nicolaus stood away from his father, in shock at his words, "For Christ's sake, father, I am not going to force her! I will not do that!" he was adamant.

"Well you had better do something. The clock is ticking down."

Chapter Fifty-Five

The following day, Deirdre nourished the other side of her life away from the Ravenell family. Not only had she decided to leave her position at the Capitol, but she also decided to take up charity work at a local foster children's home. She had previously intended to get to this work, but had put it on hold to prepare for her wedding event. Her wedding that did not happen. And then this work was delayed again for helping deal with Nicolaus' problems. However, she had not missed a day for the past two months since.

This work was helping her move forward from her all-consuming love for Nicolaus. Although she would never stop loving Nicolaus, she poured her raw heartache into spending her time with the children who needed much love and attention. And Helena, the owner and Head Mother of the children's home became her confidant, and an additional best friend, as Elsa was occupied with holding Benjamin in line, which was an arduous task.

Deirdre bounced a little baby in her arms. She hugged the baby girl, who was abandoned four days ago. "Really Helena, we must get you some help," she expanded on the ideas she had been thinking of to help the children's home. "Write a list of everything we need. Surely the church will help, Nigel and Nicky, and anyone we can think of."

"Okay, but only if you agree to become my assistant, and get paid for your time here. I am more than certain you spend more than forty hours a week with me."

"You can barely pay your staff now, and anyway I do not mind helping. I love the children."

"Yes, and they love you. They take to you so easily. They know your heart Deirdre. Besides, you're a natural."

Deirdre frowned, unable to respond, feeling the sting of having wanted to be a mother to Nicolaus' children.

Helena was right beside her, "Oh honey, I'm sorry. I didn't mean to …"

Deirdre shook her head, "Oh no, it's okay," she finally managed, having swallowed back her tears, willing herself not to cry anymore. With a smile, she held the little baby in the air, "These little ones have helped me face reality, in more ways than one." The baby cackled, making both Deirdre and Helena giggle.

Deirdre received a message from her mother that she was sleeping over at the mansion tonight, as she was to assist Rachel with a project in the morning. When Deirdre arrived at the mansion, she was surprised to find Alexander, as it was late. He seemed to be helping Nicolaus drown his sorrows in alcohol.

In silence, unnoticed across the room, Deirdre watched as Nicolaus and Alexander downed their shots of whisky together, then Alexander refilled their glasses, and they swallowed the shots down again, without hesitation. They cooed and gasped as the strong whisky went down their throats with a grown man's burn. Deirdre frowned, wondering if Alexander was up to something as he pressured Nicolaus to keep drinking, though after seven shots, Nicolaus was half strewn across the table, giggling at things that were not funny, and slurring his speech. Suddenly, one of the staff escorted Marguerite to the men, and after a hearty challenge of who could hold their drink better, Marguerite could not resist the test, and joined the men.

Alexander checked Nicolaus' drunkenness by making up silly talk as if he were telling a joke. Nicolaus laughed uncontrollably, and Marguerite was not amused. She pushed at Nicolaus to remove him from across the table.

As Benjamin walked in to investigate the boisterous noise, Nicolaus beckoned for him, "Bent! Benjil" he called, with silly drunken laughter, as Alexander poured him additional whiskey, for which he drank happily. "More drink for Marguerite." She swished the drink back, and slammed the glass on the table, feeling as though she were winning the challenge. Deirdre noticed that Alexander had stopped drinking.

Marguerite's spirits lifted quickly, as she had been bored out of her skull. She was happy for this excitement. The next drink, she and Nicolaus entangled their arms. She giggled at him, and they slammed their glass on the table at the same time.

Alexander talked the couple into going with him, and they both agreed. Deirdre rushed over, not liking what she was seeing.

"Alexander, where are you taking Nicolaus? He shouldn't be going anywhere like this."

Alexander was stopped in his tracks and surprised that Deirdre was before them. He looked back and noticed the couple had not seen her. "Ah, no, it's fine. We're just going out."

Deirdre pulled him aside, away from the couple, as Nicolaus helped Marguerite into her jacket, barely able to stand himself. "Alexander, you don't understand, Nicky gets ill when he drinks like this. He needs to be cared for. And people shouldn't see him like this. Now, please ..."

"Deirdre, I'll take care of him. I promise." He looked at her with an apologetic look on his face, "This must be done. I'm sorry," he whispered to her.

The words brought understanding to Deirdre's mind, making it clear what he was doing. She grabbed his arm to stop him. "No, … no, no," she said frowning, devastated, not sure what to do. "No, please, Alexander. He cannot go. He …"

"Deirdre," Alexander held her by the shoulders and told her as bluntly and as clearly as he could, in his lawyer frame of mind, "he's not yours, anymore. He's a married man. He doesn't have to answer to you."

The shock and hurt that appeared on her face at his words broke his heart, but he needed her out of the way. He sighed, "I'm sorry, Deirdre."

Alexander tried to take leave of her, but Deirdre grabbed him again, not letting go. "Please! Not like this for Nicky's sake, not like this."

Alexander turned to Benjamin, "Benjamin, please, help her."

Benjamin quickly lifted Deirdre and carried her out of the room before Nicolaus could notice her presence or that something was happening. Deirdre fought against him, and he swiftly lifted her over his shoulder and carried her as if she were a doll. "No! Nicky!" she yelled for him. "Nicky! Please! No, please, Nicky!" her yells became cries, then tears, then silent tears. "Nicky," she struggled against Benjamin. "Let me go, Benji! Put me down!"

"Jesus, woman! No one will ever have love like this for me." Not wanting to deal with her, Benjamin placed Deirdre onto her feet, delivering her to Constance.

Constance opened her bedroom door frowning, "What on earth?" Deirdre fell into her mother's arms.

"I didn't do this!" Benjamin defended himself. "Alexander is taking Nicolaus and Marguerite to consummate, you know for the six-month deadline, and … I don't know, I don't think Deirdre was supposed to find out yet."

Constance looked at Benjamin as if he were crazy. She hugged her daughter to her. "Deirdre, did he hurt you? Did he touch you?" Deirdre shook her head no. "Okay Benji, thank you for bringing her to me. It was the right thing to do," she told him with a smile.

Benjamin nodded, "Yeah. Goodnight, ma'am."

Constance closed the door and comforted her devastated daughter.

Although Nicolaus had been married for almost six months, as long as he had not consummated his marriage with Marguerite, it seemed in some small way that he still belonged to Deirdre. However, now, even that little glimmer of hope had been snuffed out.

Chapter Fifty-Six

Alexander was afraid that he'd made Nicolaus drink too much whiskey, and he'd be rendered useless when it was time to perform sexually. He worried, and on top of that he was not sure how he was going to get Marguerite to do what needed to be done.

At the luxury hotel room, Nicolaus sat in the recliner, his head back, as his mind drifted on the alcohol. He felt warm and fuzzy, ready for sleep. Marguerite had become furious when she realized that Alexander was not taking them dancing as he had told her in the limousine.

"I am no whore!" She attempted to strike Alexander across the face, but he jumped back, and she missed.

"I never said that! But you are your mother's daughter. Don't you want to honour her? Marguerite, you know you and Nicolaus have to consummate this marriage." He moved as she started to go after him, while Nicolaus was oblivious to what was happening. "Marguerite, stop, please, just hear me out. Hear me out." She stopped chasing him to listen, crossing her arms. "Look, Nicolaus is not the only one who loses here. You will also lose your inheritance if you do not consummate. Remember? You lose all the money your mother has set aside for you, as well. Why should your father get everything? Anyway, I thought you were upset with your father for this marriage in the first place."

"Yes, I am angry at him."

"Well then, why get cheated out of your inheritance?"

"Hmm." She rolled her eyes, as what he said made sense.

"Sex is what married couples do anyway, right?"

315

"Hmm," she repeated. "He doesn't even know what to do," she flung her arm in the air toward Nicolaus' direction.

"Okay, but that doesn't matter right now, does it?"

"Hmm." Marguerite turned from him, knowing he was right. She grabbed the whiskey Alexander had brought, took a swig, and went over to the half sleeping Nicolaus.

Roughly, Marguerite unzipped Nicolaus' pants and took out his member, before he could react to her, as his mind buzzed with the alcohol, and he was slow moving. Roughly, she rubbed him. "You not going to steal my inheritance from me," she angrily told him. Her act of touching him in this way quickly woke Nicolaus' senses, and he remembered the last time she touched him there, she tried to separate it from the rest of his body. He was shocked and a little frightened at her actions, and not sure what to do. Her actions did not exactly feel good to him. Finally, he sat up to protest and to remove her hands from him. Marguerite pushed him back, keeping her hand going on his shaft, as it was already stiff and erect. "You not leaving this room a virgin," she said, with certainty.

Having on a dress, she quickly straddled him, her back to him. Moving her underwear to the side, she sat on his large manhood, moaning as he filled her. She heard Nicolaus moan at the feel of her vagina surrounding his virgin flesh, as well. Marguerite got to work to satisfy herself, not caring one iota for what he was feeling. She felt her orgasm quickly, as his large size was certainly rubbing against her g-spot. Once she was done, she got off him without words, and laid on the bed as if to go to sleep.

Not aware that Alexander was keeping an eye on them, Nicolaus needed full sexual release, as she'd left him hard and erect, so he followed Marguerite to the bed. They remained clothed. He was glad when she didn't resist him as he began to enter her in the missionary position. Nicolaus moaned and worked to bring her to orgasm again. Her arms and legs wrapped around him, pulling him close, as she enjoyed her husband, surprised that he had effective techniques, and happy to take what Deirdre could not ever have - his virginity.

Marguerite thrashed beneath his muscular frame as he filled her completely with each intense thrust. After several minutes, Nicolaus' body released ten years of pent-up sexual frustration as he ejaculated hard inside of Marguerite, with a loud moan that he was not able to hold back. He uncontrollably shook with orgasm, and experienced what he never had before. As endorphins washed over Nicolaus, doubled with the alcohol, he lost himself.

In his orgasmic blizzard, Nicolaus realized this experience was only supposed to be shared with his beloved Deirdre. The thought of it brought him to tears, crying escaping his mouth, which he also could not control. Raging anger returned to Marguerite because she knew why Nicolaus was crying. Harshly, she pushed Nicolaus away, and she closed herself off, turning from him. Nicolaus laid alone on the other side of the king-sized bed and cried until sleep fell upon him.

Chapter Fifty-Seven

When Nicolaus opened his eyes, he was astonished to find himself in Marguerites' bed at the mansion. He frowned, not remembering how he got there. Next to him, Marguerite lay asleep, her back to him. They were both fully dressed but under the bed covers.

As Nicolaus sat up, sickness seized him. A glass of juice was extended from Alexander's hand. Alexander smiled at him, and spoke in a whisper, not to awaken Marguerite, "Here, my friend, drink this, you'll feel better. I promise. A special little something."

Nicolaus took the glass, and drank. It seemed like more than just juice. Nicolaus felt the beginnings of the huge hangover, he touched his head, and Alexander was again by his side, this time with aspirin. "Here you go."

Nicolaus smiled slightly, and swallowed the pills with the drink. He drank slowly.

Alexander sat in the chair next to the bed, beside him. "I promised Deirdre I'd take care of you."

Nicolaus looked around, feeling as though he was dreaming. He looked to Alexander, "What's happening?"

"You are just home, that is all."

"But … we were drinking … and … what … how … did I fall asleep in here?"

"Wait, Nicolaus, you don't remember?"

Nicolaus frowned, trying to remember, it hurt his head. He sighed, "We were drinking, next to the kitchen. You and me, and Marguerite."

"Yep, and then?"

"Well, I don't know. You brought us in here? She let you?"

"Nicolaus you seriously don't remember?"

319

Nicolaus looked at Alexander with a blank stare. He shook his head, "I drank too much. I was asleep. Right? I remember laying on the table. Oh God, I feel so sick," he touched his stomach. "I don't think I'll be drinking again. I need to get to the church and ask for forgiveness. Please tell me I didn't do or say anything stupid."

"Nicolaus, no, you consummated. Remember? The hotel …"

Nicolaus frowned, "I did?"

"Nicolaus, you mean to tell me you don't remember consummating?" Alexander sounded a little disappointed. "Well, it's a good thing I stayed. Exactly why I stayed, so she couldn't lie and say something else happened."

"You stayed?"

"Yes, I was there. She didn't even notice me. Anyway, neither of you undressed, so don't worry, I didn't see your wife. Let me tell you what happened."

Marguerite stirred at the whispering. She turned, and opened her eyes to see her husband and Alexander, in her bedroom, and Nicolaus in her bed! Anger flooded her mind, as the soreness of her vagina would not let her psyche deny what happened at the hotel last night. She was only glad that now she could have her own money, and not have to depend on either Nicolaus or her father ever again. She also never had to lay with Nicolaus again.

"Good morning, Marguerite," Nicolaus offered, reaching for her hand.

Without words, Marguerite only gave him dart eyes, turned her back on him, and left out of the room.

Alexander shook his head at her behaviour, and continued. "I booked a room at one of the five-star hotels downtown. Marguerite was furious at first, but then I talked her down."

"Really? Where was I?"

"You were drifting, but there. Anyways, Marguerite tells you that you are not leaving that room a virgin, and then she gets to work on you. And she finishes, and then you go to work on her, and you finish, and then you start bawling like a baby. I mean ugly bawling, man."

"What ... the hell?"

"Yep, you did."

"I cried, in front of Marguerite?"

"She was pissed!"

"Oh, God!"

"Yep. And then you both fell asleep. But I stayed the whole time so she couldn't say you raped her, or some nonsense like that. And then, I called your dad, told him it was done, and we brought you back here."

"You stayed there, for me, Alexander. Just like a brother, watching over me."

"Of course. I know you'd do the same for me."

"So, we consummated?"

"Yes! Twice! And I can't believe you don't even remember."

"But why did I cry? What was that about?"

"I don't know. I think maybe you realized she wasn't Deirdre. I ... I really don't know."

"Alexander, thank you for helping me get it done. I sincerely owe you. Please, anything I can ever do for you. And I mean it. Thank you."

Chapter Fifty-Eight

Benjamin was attempting to get access to his lady friends, for which he paid Fiona's escort service, formerly known as the famous Austin Brothel, despite his exclusive relationship with Elsa. His problem was that his relationship with Elsa was sexless, though she drove him wild with her body, and her looks. His excuse was that her teasing drove him to Fiona's place.

It was the middle of the day, and Fiona was blocking the door, not letting Benjamin inside. He used to be one of her best customers, until he abused her rules of the house as well as the girls who accompanied him.

"No, Benjamin, your credit is no good here anymore. You keep my ladies longer than we agreed, and have the nerve to bring them back hurt and bruised. You think I'm going to let you abuse my girls? You're no good, Benjamin Ravenell."

"Come on, Fiona," Benjamin whined. "You can't just cut me off like this. Have a heart. Please. I need Kristy or Raven, or Slit, or …"

"You're no good, Benjamin Ravenell," Fiona yelled at him, repeating her words, trying to make him hear what she was saying.

"Ouch!" a woman's voice said behind him. "That must really hurt to hear such a thing from Fiona, who is the sweetest."

"Hey there Ms. Helena!" Fiona called to Helena, who was on the curb behind Benjamin. "How are your little darlings today?" Benjamin briefly looked over his shoulder and out of the side of his eye he saw the figure of a woman. However, his mind was occupied on getting into Ms. Fiona's.

"We're all good! I just wanted to thank you for the baskets of fruit. It really helped us out Fiona."

"Oh no problem. Oh, hold on, I have more." Fiona closed the door for a few seconds, then appeared with a large basket of apples, bananas, and cantaloupes. She dropped the basket into Benjamin's arms without asking. "Here," she told him, "make yourself useful and help Ms. Helena. This is for the children." Fiona waived at Helena with a smile, then went inside, closing the front door on Benjamin.

When Benjamin turned around, with the large basket of fruit in his arms, he saw a beautiful, middle-aged woman, who had a shapely body and a black eye. Helena recognized Benjamin, but also, Deirdre had described him. She looked at him with a frown, "Uhm, aren't you Benjamin Ravenell, Nicolaus Ravenell's brother?"

Benjamin hated it when people recognized him that way. He shook his head in disdain, "Yeah, well, what of it?" he asked her rudely.

"What are you doing at a place like this? You mean to tell me you cannot get a date, with a real girl?"

Benjamin frowned back at her, not liking her question. "Well, I …"

"A nice girl. You've got to be kidding me."

"Look lady, I don't have to answer to you. Where do you want this basket?"

"I'm just across the street. I can carry it if it's too heavy or too much trouble for you."

"I've got it. Of course I can carry it."

They began to walk, but Helena did not let up on him. "You should be ashamed of yourself, begging to be with a call girl. I'll bet your mother doesn't know your down here doing this. What is wrong with you?"

"Who are you to question me?" he stopped, getting angry, mainly because he couldn't defend what she said, because she was right. "I'll bet your man hit you in your face because you won't stop talking," he threw at her, wanting to hurt her feelings.

Helena touched her eye, stopping at the front door of the children's home. "Actually, he hit me because I didn't make his dinner fast enough. But I'm sure you wouldn't know anything about using force or hitting a woman to make her do what you want. Surely, you're not like that Benji, now are you?"

Benjamin looked at her, speechless. It was as if she knew him. He frowned at her. "Well ... here you go," he tried to hand her the basket.

Helena laughed at him, "Oh no, you can bring it into the kitchen. You can help the cook put the fruit away." She entered, leaving the door open for him to follow. Follow he did.

When Benjamin entered the children's home, he was amazed at what he saw. Immediately, he understood the concept. He went into the kitchen and helped the cook put away the fruit, after introducing himself.

Once he was done, Helena was right on him. "You know, I could really use your help around here. Instead of spending all your money and time chasing tails and vaginas, you should come here and help me with these abandoned children. I even have teen boys here that need some mentoring. You could use this place to turn over a new leaf, Benjamin Ravenell, and change your life. You know you need to." Benjamin frowned at Helena as she left the room.

She returned with a newborn baby boy, and gave him to Benjamin, who did not shy away from holding the baby. "This is Nathan. He was born addicted to drugs, and was given up on by his parents."

Benjamin looked at the little baby whose skin was red, and he was very fussy.

Helena led Benjamin to a rocking chair. Benjamin sat down with the baby, with no words.

He smiled at Helena, and attempted to comfort the baby. It was only a matter of minutes before the baby took to him, accepted his comforting ways, and quietly went to sleep. Benjamin looked upon the little guy as he cradled him in his arms while he slept.

Chapter Fifty-Nine

Nicolaus was hoping to avoid Marguerite most of the day, for he knew she was going to land into him for crying during their sex capade. Instead, it was Deirdre he bumped into, as he was leaving for the office, his head still spinning with alcohol, making him swear it off.

"Nicky, are you okay?" Deirdre's voice sounded concerned, as she touched his arm.

"Hmm, yes, yes, I'm fine. Thank you." His heart leaped at the sight of her. She took his breath away, even now. He had to stop himself from reaching for her and pulling her into a hug. His life wasn't the same with her distant from him. There was a huge hole, as if a chunk of himself was missing. His mind thought of her often. He could not sleep without dreaming of her and their times together. Everyone noticed that Nicolaus was not happy as before, did not smile, and seemed melancholy, though he tried not to show it.

"Alexander was so mean to me last night, just really out of character."

"Mean?" he asked her flatly, frowning. Moving closer to her, wanting to hold her.

"Why yes. I tried to stop him taking you, and …"

"Deirdre," he interrupted her, taking her hand, "no, he helped me. Alexander helped me do, what I couldn't get done myself, for us to keep the family fortune. Ya' know. I'm sorry. I apologize if he came off mean to you, I think he was really more focused."

"Well … okay," she didn't like that Nicolaus seemed to be making excuses for Alexander, but maybe he was right. "But Nicky, are you okay?" She took her hand from him, unable to bear his touch, as it sent her mind in a frenzy, making her want to throw herself to him, knowing he'd gladly hold her in his arms. She stepped back from him, trying to maintain distance.

Nicolaus smiled at her concern for him, and he noticed that she was trying to help them both keep their heads about each other. He loved her so much. "Yes," he said, "I'll be fine."

"What was it like?" she inquired in a whisper, out of curiosity. "What you expected?"

He was taken aback by her question. "No, because it wasn't with you!" He looked down, putting his hands into his pockets, then looked at Deirdre, "To be honest, Deirdre, I actually don't remember anything."

"Nicky, you don't' remember?"

He shook his head, and chuckled.

"Oh my God, Nicky, too much drink."

He nodded in agreement with her, "Yes, too much for my own good."

"And where are you going?" she had noticed the keys in his hands, which were now shoved into his pocket.

"To the office," he said as a matter of fact, as if she should know.

"On Sunday?"

"Is today Sunday?"

"Nicky, are you sure you should be driving?"

Knowing she was right, he chuckled again, took her hand, and placed his car keys there. He shook his head again, "That's why I love you so much."

Chapter Sixty

In contrast, later that day, Nicolaus did meet up with Marguerite. She was still cold and closed off to him. Nicolaus knew he had to face the music of his crying episode with her. He fully expected Marguerite to mock him and make fun of him. However, he hoped this was a way in for him to reconnect with her. "Marguerite, please let's talk."

"Why? I have nothing for you."

"Marguerite," he softly touched her arm, hoping to reason with her now that they had consummated their marriage.

Marguerite was quick to get away from Nicolaus. "Don't touch me," she snapped at him.

Nicolaus scoffed with a frown, feeling offended, "That's not what you said last night."

"Shut up!" she yelled at him. "I used you. Only to get my money. I promise, I will not be with you again!"

Nicolaus felt a little hurt and disappointed, as Marguerite stormed out the room.

This made his heart more engorged with love for Deirdre, if that was even possible.

Both Nicolaus and Deirdre focused their time on their work to keep their sanity. On the rare occasions they were at the mansion at the same time, they intensely focused on each other, wanting to know all about each other's worlds, with short light touching or hugs.

"The children's home needs a full makeover, wall repairs, the roof, new flooring. And the playground could use new equipment and ..." Deirdre stopped talking when she noticed that Nicolaus was extremely close to her. He looked like he wanted to kiss her. A nervous giggle escaped her. She worried about who might be watching. "And the little babies …," she continued, "they're so precious. Helena needs to hire more staff. The state keeps coming in to inspect and I think they want to close her down. She's adamant of not letting it go."

"Anything you want," he simply told her, happy that she was happy.

"What?" she asked softly, hoping he was saying what she thought he was saying.

Nicolaus shook himself from her trance. He took a deep breath, wishing his life was different. What if he'd re-enlisted instead of staying back to help his father? What if he'd left, like his mother wanted him to do, would Deirdre be his wife? "Anything! How much does Helena need?"

"Nicky!"

He smiled and nodded. "I'll be glad to support any of your projects."

"Well … you've got to meet Helena first. You can't just dole out money …"

"I can meet her later. Will three hundred thousand be enough to start you off?"

"Nicky, that's … too generous."

"Not at all, it's for the children. I can have contractors there tomorrow to see what needs to be done, and get that work started as well. By the time I'm done with that place, the state will close their books and their mouths, and leave Helena alone."

"Nicky …"

"You know I'd do anything for you, Deirdre."

Chapter Sixty-One

The next day, Deirdre was shocked to see Benjamin being bossed around by Helena. Deirdre giggled as he followed her directions to change a baby boy's diaper. "Benji?"

"Look who I found next door, begging to be let into the brothel," Helena told Deirdre.

"Ha! I was not begging. I dropped off a lady friend, and ..."

"And Fiona wouldn't let you in," Helena explained, laughing at him.

"All right, all right!" he giggled, letting her win the argument.

This was such a strange occurrence for Deirdre. "Benji ... I ... I ...."

"What? I like babies. Helena dragged me over here, and I got interested. So, what's wrong with that?"

"I've just never seen this side of you before," Deirdre said slowly, not believing her eyes.

Benjamin lifted the baby to the air, playing with him, making him coo. He carefully brought him down to hold him in his arms. The baby seemed very content. "What? You think I'm just a sex crazed guy?"

Deirdre frowned, "Well, actually ..."

"Oh honey, Benji is great with the kids. He'll make a great father!"

"Thank you, Helena. I appreciate that." Benjamin talked to the baby, "Yes, we do, don't we William, we appreciate it!" Benjamin continues to give the baby boy his undivided attention.

Deirdre looked to Helena, and then gasped at her injury. Gently, she touched Helena's black eye, "Oh, Helena! What happened?"

"Oh, that ain't nothing. You know Joel can get a temper sometimes."

"Yeah, he probably hit her to shut her up," Benjamin said out loud. The baby boy shrieked, and Benjamin responded to him, "Ain't that right, little buddy. Women just talk too much sometimes." He picked up the baby and played with him, making him laugh loudly.

Deirdre was very confused by all of this. She had never seen Benjamin with any child whatsoever!

"Oh, you hush up, Benji! You're no match for me. I'd flip you right on your backside."

Benjamin held the baby's arm out, and spoke in a baby voice, "Oh yeah, want to try it?" Both he and Helena laughed at teasing each other. Deirdre understood they seemed to be in some kind of state of friendship. She assumed Helena was physically okay.

"Well, you won't believe this!" She handed Helena the check for three hundred thousand dollars, signed by Nicolaus.

"Oh … my … God! What?" Helena couldn't believe her eyes. She'd never had that much money at one time before. "Three hundred thousand!"

"And Nicky is sending contractors over today to see what work needs to be done."

"My God! Deirdre!" Helena hugged Deirdre tightly to her, and began to cry. She wiped her eyes, and then frowned at Benjamin. "Why haven't you offered me help like this Benji?" she chided him. "Your brother is already one up on you."

"Oh Helena, I'm sure Benji is offering help from his heart. That little one seems to really like you, Benji."

"Hell, Benji has offered us left over scraps from the dinner parties. I mean I'm grateful for the offer Benji, but damn," she hit the check to her hand, "Nicolaus understands my vision and I haven't even met him."

"Sorry Helena, I don't have access to that kind of money."

Helena went over to him, and smack kissed him right on the lips. "You're a blessing to me anyway baby. As long as you stay out of Ms. Fiona's house, I won't have to kick your butt." She touched Benjamin's shoulder, tousled William's hair, and went about her work.

Deirdre watched Benjamin and horribly wondered if he had an ulterior motive for being there. She looked to see that Helena was not in the area before she made her comment to him.

"Benji," she touched William's back. As soon as the baby recognized Deirdre, he flung his body to her arms. Deirdre gladly held him with a smile. "I hope you are here for the right reasons. These children have already been abandoned at least once, and ... Helena is not going to sleep with you, she doesn't do that."

Benjamin nodded, not mad at her, but loving the smell of his Deirdre. "I promise you, I'm only here for the good. I think I can help with the older boys, you know. Since I've been here today, I've been thinking about it."

"The older boys? Benji, are you sure you're ready for something like that? I mean, they cannot see you going next door if you want to mentor them."

"I know," he sounded a little offended. "Look, I'm not Nicolaus, okay. I'm not like him, won't ever be, and don't want to be. But I am me ... and I do like children. I want to help Helena, anyways, she asked for my help."

"Okay. Just please ... be honest about it all, is all I'm saying. And gosh ... if you want children, I think you need to go ahead and marry Elsa. She loves you, Benji, and has for some time. I'm not sure why, but she does."

Benjamin chuckled, and nodded his head, "Oh no, I'm not getting married, to anyone."

"Not even Elsa?"

He thought for a moment, then William leapt back into Benjamin's arms. "I like Elsa, I really do, but she's not you."

"Benji!"

"You're the only woman I would ever consider marrying, Deirdre. Only you," he told her, his eyes not leaving hers. As Helena entered the room, he provided her an offer. "Helena, why don't I set up a luncheon or something for you to meet my mother. And then the two of you can talk about a fundraiser. When my mother finds out that I am interested in helping you, I'm very sure she will be glad to assist. I'll bet we can triple my brother's check."

Helena put her hand over her mouth out of such surprise. She realized this has all come about because of Deirdre, sweet Deirdre. She hugged both Benjamin and Deirdre to her, "My God, that would be so wonderful. Thank you, Benjamin."

Chapter Sixty-Two

The following day, Nicolaus went to Helena's children's home to meet her, and to scope out the full situation, as he'd already received some estimates on the work that needed to be done. When he arrived, Deirdre was present as well. Helena went to him, taking his hands, as she immediately knew who he was. She was beyond grateful to him. "Wow, you're very handsome!" she told him unabatedly. She hugged him, and rubbed his chest, "I cannot tell you how grateful I am that you are helping us. You, Deirdre, and now Benji, too! It's really remarkable."

"I'm glad to do it," he told her, "not only to help the children, but to help you grow this organization. I'd like to offer the full support of our company if you'll have us. By that I mean that we'll take care of all the repairs, remodelling, and improvements. We want nothing in return, only that your organization be successful for the children."

Helena was taken aback. She gasped, speechless. "Nicky!"

"Also, we'll provide full healthcare for the children, at no cost. But I don't want to get ahead of myself, it's your decision."

Deirdre and Helena grabbed hands in joy at his offer. Deirdre nodded to her to accept the offer. "Yes, yes, of course," Helena told him, "my God, Nicky, thank you. Thank you."

He sighed with relief. "Okay, so, the three hundred thousand is for your operation expenses. You can hire staff, and buy whatever you need for the children. Between you, me, Deirdre, and Alexander who is our company Vice President and a lawyer, let's come up with a budget so that we can provide funds for you monthly. Oh and Helena, you can have anyone on your team to represent you and present ideas as well. How does that sound?"

Helena shook her head in disbelief, seeing her dream come true before her very eyes. She would really be able to care for these children the way they should be cared for. "It sounds wonderful! Too good to be true!"

Some men were brought into the room by Helena's receptionist. "I asked a few contractors to meet me here so we can get started on repairs, I hope that's okay. Mind if we look around?"

"No, of course not. Please!" The men left the room, and began to show Nicolaus their findings and they went into detailed discussions.

Deirdre hugged Helena to her, knowing what she was thinking. She knew her dreams of having a pristine children's home was coming true.

"Deirdre, how can I ever thank you?"

Tears fell from Deirdre's eyes, "We'll just keep taking care of the children."

Chapter Sixty-Three

Before Nicolaus left, he asked to speak to Helena alone. "All the work described to me is doable, with just light disturbance to the children's rooms. You may need to move them for a day or two until paint fumes or glue fumes diminish. I've instructed the contractors to be sure to consult with you before they start anything, and you can guide them on how much area you want done at a time. You can also guide them on their work hours, so they do not disturb the children. And Helena, I will be sure that everyone that comes through here has had a background check and has been fully cleared through security, so that you and the children are protected."

"Nicky, how am I ever going to thank you for all of this?" she seemed overwhelmed.

They were standing close to each other, and he touched her shoulder, "Helena, like I said, just making your organization successful for the children is enough for us. Truly." He sighed and smiled at her. "I noticed your eye ... did your husband do that to you?" he meddled, purposefully, with a frown.

Helena looked him in his gorgeous eyes. She was taken with him, and seemed to be unable to lie to him, for some reason. Suddenly, she understood Deirdre's love and captivation for him. "Yes," she admitted, "he did. He gets angry over little things, and sometimes really jealous about my work."

Nicolaus crossed his arms, standing as the strong, tall man he was. "Wow, that's a shame. I'm surprised your husband is not more present to help you here. This is beautiful work. And you ... Helena, are too beautiful of a woman to be treated like this. No woman should be treated like this."

He looked at her in earnest. "Helena, if you want, I can help you with your husband."

"What ... what do you mean?"

"Well ... I've done my research. I know your husband is Joel Gaulkven, the architect. Right?"

Helena was taken aback again. She nodded, curious to see where he was going with this, "Yes, yes, that's my husband."

"And ... I happen to know he's actually looking for work right now."

Helena giggled, and nodded again. "Yes. He's actually upset because he cannot get on projects, and the unemployment office wants him to look into another line of work."

Nicolaus nodded. "Well ... I've got five clinics that need to be built from the ground up, in five different cities. I need them designed, and built."

"Nicky..." she was in awe, "what are you saying?"

"I admire your husband's work. I like his taste in design, and I really think he could help us. I am willing to give him these lucrative contracts, except, he cannot work for me if he's an abuser because that just will not look good for our company. And really Helena, it does not look good for your company, either. But I know it's hard to control something like this on your own, I understand that."

"Oh, Nicky." She was on him, hugging him again, she wanted to kiss him. "You'd do that for me?"

He nodded, "For you, and Deirdre, and the children .... I can use leverage to get him to change his behaviour." He looked at her earnestly again. "And I think you'll know what he's willing to do, by his decision."

"Nicky," she said softly, under her breath, she felt her eyes well up, her bruised eye hurting. Nicolaus gently wiped her tears with his fingers. It was a tender moment between them. There was something about Helena that Nicolaus adored, though he'd only just met her. He felt that she needed love and caring for, and protection, and somehow, he wanted to provide for her. They hugged.

"Just tell him about the clinics, and send him to me next Thursday, around two. I'll talk to him and see what he thinks."

The kiss happened, because like many women, Helena couldn't resist kissing on Nicolaus Ravenell. She hugged him to her, knowing he was special, and their relationship was going to be special as well.

Chapter Sixty-Four

The following week, Marguerite was surprised to find Nicolaus and Deirdre talking in the drawing room by the fire, at four in the morning. Though she wasn't feeling well, she was angered at this situation. "Nicolaus," she called to him, interrupting their talk and light laughter about the children and paint colours, "what are you doing? It is four A.M.," she snapped at him.

Nicolaus looked at her, surprised. "Four A.M.? Wow!" he looked at Deirdre. "We lost track of time, we were just talking." Nicolaus frowned, seeing that Marguerite did not look so well. He went to her. "You need something? Are you feeling okay?"

"Do not touch me!" she snapped at him again, in her usual go to phrase to get him away from her. "I am fine. I go to Jeane's now."

Nicolaus cocked his head in amusement, as Marguerite had never risen from bed this early. "At this hour? Are you going out of town?"

Marguerite crossed her arms, trying to be in control, "Maybe." She didn't want him telling her what to do.

"Well, let me know what you decide. I'll be available most of the day."

"Hm!" Marguerite jerked herself out of the room.

"Wow, not much has changed with her I see," Deirdre commented.

Nicolaus put his hands in his pockets, and shrugged, "Nope. I guess it won't get better unless she wants it to. She has to make an effort, you' know?"

"Yes," Deirdre nodded. "I'm sorry it's so hard for you."

Nicolaus smiled, "Nah, I've still got you!" He held his hand out to help her up. "You need a nap? It's four A.M. my lady."

Deirdre giggled, oddly, she did not feel tired at all.

Chapter Sixty-Five

Nicolaus was surprised when Marguerite returned from Jeane's earlier than planned. She could not make the shopping trip to Albuquerque. She was just too sick to go. Marguerite did not understand what was wrong with her, as she'd never been sick like this before.

"I think we should get you to a doctor, Marguerite," Nicolaus gently told her across the dinner table, with all the family present. Nigel, sitting next to Nicolaus, nodded in agreement.

When a dinner plate was placed before Marguerite, she recoiled at the smell, having to cover her nose, as the gravy smothered chicken and rice increased her nausea tenfold.

Ceil heartily laughed at her reaction to the food. "Oh, she needs a doctor all right, an obstetrician!"

Nicolaus looked at Ceil, shocked by her words, "What are you saying?"

"She's pregnant, that's what!"

Marguerite's nausea momentarily turned to tears of hatred for Nicolaus, "I hate you!" she loudly shouted at him, not caring that everyone was watching them. "You have me one time, one time," she repeated to reiterate her anger, "and now I'm pregnant? Uhh, I hate you!" The nausea returned, making her flee from the room to the nearest bathroom.

Ceil and Nigel laughed heartily. Nigel grabbed Nicolaus on his shoulder, proud father he was at this moment, "Well done son, well done."

Though his father seemed proud of him, it was strange for Nicolaus to be celebrated on the result of being forced to perform a sex act against his will. Nicolaus' thoughts were immediately on Deirdre. In sadness, he felt loss for what could have been between he and Deirdre; what should have been their future together.

Francesca saw the look about Nicolaus, and knew he was sad about Deirdre.

She touched his hand, "Love, it'll be all right."

Chapter Sixty-Six

Joel Gaulkven was a man that was too arrogant for his own good, which is why he'd get into physical altercations with Helena. They were both strong willed people, but Joel was determined to remain the man in their relationship, and was not going to take what he called 'back talk' from his wife. He expected Helena to do what he told her without question, and to be there for him in all aspects, including in a traditional sense of making his meals, cleaning the house, washing his clothes, and to react at his every beckon call. He didn't give a flying flip about her work of running the children's home, or that she may put in twelve and sometimes fourteen-hour days.

From the time Joel walked into the VMC headquarters, he was impressed. Their meeting took place just as Nicolaus finished up a meeting with the accounting team. Their handshakes were firm, as they eyed each other.

Joel was rugged, mountain man looking, with spikey hair, a goatee on his chin, and tattoos on his forearms. He didn't bother to put on a suit for this important meeting. He was dressed blue collar style, in jeans, work boots, and a blue shirt with red and purple stripes. He had the shirt sleeves halfway rolled up his muscular arms, giving the impression that he was ready to immediately go to work.

Joel noticed that Nicolaus was suave, tall, with nice looking features, muscular, fashionably dressed in what appeared to be an expensive suit. Nicolaus was clean shaven, hair neatly styled, and he smelled fresh and affluent. The straight, white teeth smile that appeared across Nicolaus' face upon their meeting gave Joel a prang of jealousy, as he'd already heard so much about Nicolaus from Helena's nonstop talking about him. He had to meet this guy that he was afraid his wife was having feelings for. For Joel, this meeting gave him mixed emotions. On the one hand his jealousy was present, but on the other hand, Helena told him that Nicolaus wanted to help them, and wanted to talk to him about a generous employment offer.

Nicolaus invited Joel to sit across from him at the oval conference table in his office. Nicolaus explained the projects he had in mind. Joel seemed very interested, and was actually surprised that Nicolaus knew what he was talking about when it came to buildings and construction. Nicolaus showed Joel documents, and rough draft plans. This gave Joel a better understanding of why VMC was interested in Helena's children's home, setting his mind more at ease about the enthusiasm of his wife.

"So, what do you think? Is this something you'd be interested in handling for us?" Nicolaus asked him.

Joel looked at him, for the first time finally smiling back, "Yeah, yeah, sure! I can get this done for you. I'm already getting design ideas in my mind," he almost sounded excited.

"Great! I'd like to have each clinic roughly the same square footage, two stories, the clinic on the first floor, and the offices and suites on the second floor. And I want the designs to compliment the local communities."

Joel nodded, liking what he was hearing. He rubbed the rough hair on his chin, in thought, as money had not yet been discussed. "And cost?" he asked.

Nicolaus sat back in his negotiation stance, because now was the time to hammer home the expectations that would bring about a change of Joel's behaviour towards

Helena. "These clinics have to be a labour of love, not only because they will serve local children, but also because the funds are coming from our national partners. So, I've got to be clear with you, that if I choose your company and you decide to accept the contracts and the contract terms, everything has to be above board, not only with you and your leadership team, but also with each of your staff members, and you have to be sure they understand the values I expect. This standard of excellence will be the same for any company I choose to take on this build."

"Okay, what exactly are we talking about here?" Joel sat forward.

"I have budgeted one-hundred twenty million for each site, but I'd like to see us come in around eighty-five million max for each."

Joel made a whistle sound at the numbers, as the most he'd ever worked to build with was closer to fifteen million. His level of impression increased again.

"Yes," Nicolaus nodded. "So, you see, I cannot have any improprieties, whatsoever.

For instance, I asked Helena about that huge bruise on her left eye. And she told me the typical excuse of walking into a door," he covered for her. "Now, I'm not accusing anyone of anything, Joel, but come on, a woman like Helena, of her stature, and her stance in the community with the work she is doing, should not have to lie about something like that, nor should she actually be experiencing such a traumatic event. How does that look to the children, both boys and girls? And then, once I involve the both of you, with this kind of money, should any improprieties like that creep up, my donors are not going to be pleased, because, frankly, it makes us all look bad. And bad publicity is not acceptable. I would immediately stop the work and cancel the contracts." He stopped talking to give Joel a chance to respond.

"Yes sir, I get what you are saying." Nicolaus was surprised at the fast change of his attitude. Right away he knew Joel understood the depth of what he was saying. "Mr. Ravenell, I am honoured that you are considering me to take on these projects. I want you to feel that you can fully trust me and my team to do what is right. From beginning to end."

Nicolaus nodded. "I want to be able to fully trust you. You've got to make things right at home first, with Helena, before I can move any farther in my consideration of you and your team. Now Joel, believe me, I understand that couples have issues in marriage, God knows I have my own marriage issues, and it's not always perfect, but ..."

"Yes sir, I totally understand what you are saying," Joel reassured him.

"I have two other architects I'm interviewing, one from Canada, and the other from California. I'll tell you, I really like your design work the best, and I really want to give these contracts to a local architect. I only hesitate because ..."

"Mr. Ravenell, you have my word. I will make everything right with Helena, and I will get everything in order. In fact, even though you want to interview the others, not to be presumptuous, but I will provide you a rough draft of my design idea for the first two clinics by noon tomorrow."

Nicolaus crossed his arms, and nodded with a smile. "That'd be great!"

Chapter Sixty-Seven

Helena asked Deirdre to go with her on a surprise visit to VMC headquarters. Not only did she have to see the operations first-hand, but she was headstrong about talking to Nicolaus.

Elsa greeted both Deirdre and Helena with a hug. Elsa knew all about the children's home, and had bought and donated a slew of new fashionable clothes and new undergarments for the girls.

Elsa escorted the ladies to Nicolaus' office. Nicolaus was happy to see them both, greeting them both with hugs, and a gentlemanly kiss to their hands. He asked Elsa to bring them coffee, which she quickly did. "Great timing, but I have a meeting in about fifteen minutes," he informed them, joining them at the conference table.

"My God, this place is extravagant!" Helena stood and looked around the office, and out the glass wall of windows. She could see Lady Bird Lake below, and the people that were canoeing looked minuscule, because they were so high up. She giggled. She noticed the nice furniture in the office and the artwork. "Nicky, I had no idea …"

Nicolaus offered her a seat at the table. "This was all here before I arrived," he told her with a chuckle. Helena also noticed how handsome Nicolaus appeared, the same as at her place. He seemed to be so together. She also saw how he looked upon Deirdre, though he tried to be subtle, she saw such love he had for her.

She grabbed his hands across the table, "What did you tell my Joel?" she asked him, then took a sip of her coffee after adding crème and sugar.

Nicolaus chuckled again, happy to have these ladies in his life to bring a lightened mood, joy, and some laughter. "Why, what did he do?"

Helena smiled at Deirdre, as she hadn't discussed this with her yet. "Nicky, he brought me flowers. Flowers! He's never done that before. And he profusely apologized to me. Promised me he'd never hit me again. Said he'd have to think of me differently, that he had to respect my role in the world, like I respect his."

Nicolaus nodded, "Good. I'm glad to hear that!"

"Helena, that's great!" Deirdre was thrilled.

Helena shook her head, "He seems changed."

Nicolaus nodded again, "Good! Hopefully, he'll come through for me business wise as well. Now Helena, sometimes change is hard for people, and sometimes they need support. So, you may have to be patient if there is backsliding, ... but ... hopefully the work will be a major influence on his behaviour. That is my goal. A win for all of us." Nicolaus had a big smile on his face, hoping his plan would work for VMC, as well as for Helena.

The three of them clasped hands. Helena was so grateful for this newly found support. She loved Deirdre, and she was having some kind of unusual and different feelings about Nicolaus, which was undeniable.

Chapter Sixty-Eight

Two days later, Nicolaus called Joel to offer him commissioned work. "Alexander, my Vice President, will go over the contracts and paperwork with you. And just as a formality, we'll schedule you to meet with our board members, just to give them a brief summary of your design ideas. Nothing set in stone."

"Thank you so much, sir! I appreciate the opportunity!" When Joel hung up the phone, he grabbed Helena in his muscular arms and twirled her around and around, lifting her up, and bringing her down to kiss her lips. Because of his wife, he now had a chance of a lifetime, and they were going to be rich.

The next few months went by quickly for Nicolaus. Nigel and Dwight mostly turned over all decisions to Nicolaus and Alexander. It turned out to be just as Nigel imagined, their sons made a great team of Vice Presidents to lead VMC into the future. They were serious about the business, and kept everything and everyone right on track.

As Marguerite went through her pregnancy, Nicolaus was the ire of her scorn. The sight of him gave her explosive anger, coupled with her out of control hormones. They mostly isolated from each other. Though both Nicolaus and Deirdre made attempts to comfort Marguerite, her behaviour just made it impossible. It was easier to leave her alone, or to let her girlfriends or Ceil be of help to her.

Marguerite even refused a visit from Andrejs and Penelope, which highly offended them. Early on, Marguerite decided she would never love the baby, and in fact she did not want it. She was not shy to let Nicolaus know her thoughts. Nicolaus was concerned about what Marguerite might do, or if she would harm the baby.

In the meantime, the development of the five clinics was progressing, with one fully completed. Also, the improvements to Helena's children's home had been completed. Because of Nicolaus' generosity, Helena was able to hire more staff to care for the children.

Nicolaus developed a volunteer program for the VMC administrative staff. They could rotate to volunteer at the children's home or any other community organization that helped children. For a few hours a month, he encouraged them to do all kinds of things, especially at the children's home, such as clean or paint the playground, help with the laundry, help the children with homework, beautify the lawn, or decorate for holiday time.

The volunteer help really took a load off Helena, and gave her time to rest on the weekends. She was happy that Nicolaus and Benjamin visited with the children often, and she still had Deirdre as her close assistant. She was now anxious to meet Nigel and Ceil, who brought about VMC in the first place, as well as had created Nicolaus.

As time moved forward, Nicolaus knew he had to get back to the Estonian property and he wanted Deirdre to go with him. "We need to make a trip back to Estonia and see about the property. We need to do inventory and secure and insure any valuables, and I want to look over the land, the boundaries, the maps, everything. We can't just let it sit."

Deirdre understood what he was saying, but she knew she shouldn't go with him alone. Not that she didn't trust Nicolaus, but the appearance of them together in such a situation would not look right. What if the press got involved? "By we, you mean you, me, and Marguerite?"

Nicolaus smiled at her, knowing she was again taking care of their relationship.

"Well .. I mean … sure. To be honest, I haven't discussed this with Marguerite."

"Nicky, don't you think you should?"

He sighed, not really wanting to. "Well … I suppose."

"Maybe she'd like to see her family"

"No, I don't think so."

"Okay, well, let me know what she says," Deirdre did not finish her sentence, as she was at the children's home, and became preoccupied with a few babies.

Later that night, Nicolaus did bring up the subject with Marguerite, despite her foul mood. "I'm planning a trip back to Estonia to inventory the property. I'd like you to come along. Deirdre will probably go as well," he told her in the sitting room of their wing of the mansion. Nicolaus was well across the room from her, the dividing space seemed to be the definition of their actual marriage.

"Oh, there it is! You want to cheat with Deirdre! You asking me permission?"

Nicolaus frowned at her, not having heard this ridiculous accusation before. "Marguerite, I'm asking you to go with me."

She cut off his words, "You know I go not with you!" she yelled at him in her broken English. "You know this!"

"I want you to go with me," he told her.

"Now you lie!"

"Marguerite."

"No! You cheat with Deirdre! I will tear her apart!" she threatened.

Nicolaus frowned. Why did she always turn to violence when she didn't get her way? "Marguerite, stop it! Just calm down. Please. I'm not cheating or asking for your permission. I told you, I am faithful to you. I'm asking you to go with me. If you don't want to go, I'll ask my Aunt Rachel or Deirdre's mom."

Marguerite gave a hard sigh. "You do that," she told him.

Nicolaus found conversations with Marguerite to be unnerving, which is why he mostly avoided having any with her. He could not imagine what was going to happen once the baby was born. He worried about the environment for his child. It greatly annoyed him that his mother didn't think about these things while she was concocting this arranged marriage scheme. Additionally and sadly, their one-year wedding anniversary went uncelebrated and unmentioned, as if it didn't even matter. Marguerite did not pretend happy on this event for her girlfriends, who were astonished that nothing was done to acknowledge it. Marguerite was content to bask in her pregnancy misery.

Nicolaus called Deirdre to report back, "Well, Marguerite is not going with us. And you are right, we do need someone with us, she immediately accused me of cheating with you."

"Oh no, Nicky."

"Don't worry, I set her straight," he sighed with aggravation. "How about Francesca instead?"

Deirdre shook her head, "No, her classes have already begun. I don't think she can leave her students so abruptly."

"Your mom, perhaps? And Auntie Rachel?"

Deirdre giggled, "I think that's a good idea. Let's ask them."

The next week, Nicolaus and Deirdre were escorted by Rachel and Constance to the Estonian property. Constance was thrilled to be asked to go, and Rachel was happy for her company. The castle staff made high preparations for their visit, as they were worried if they would be able to remain working, since no family members were living there now.

The first thing Nicolaus did was call a meeting of all the staff. He wanted to hear from them and know what their jobs were. After the first hour of discussions, one of them brought up the subject of keeping their jobs.

Nicolaus was quick to bring comfort to their minds. "No, we don't plan on any layoffs. From what I've heard today, I think each of you are still needed, including the kitchen staff to provide meals for the workers. And we will continue to honour your current salaries."

The castle workforce of thirty people all clapped with relief. After their meeting, Nicolaus and Deirdre worked together on going through all the rooms and conducting inventory, which had never been done before. They wanted to know about everything that was on the property. It took all day to complete half the rooms, ending with Aunt Clara's room.

She had a large box of diamond and gold jewellery. Nicolaus did not feel comfortable leaving it laying about. The staff helped them learn about the castle safe, and how to access it. Nicolaus worked on changing the digital combination, while Deirdre reviewed the contents.

Once done, they placed Clara's jewellery inside, and Nicolaus shared the safe code with Deirdre.

At the end of the day, they were exhausted. They joined Rachel and Constance for dinner, which was served formally, making them feel special. They were provided separate bedrooms to retire for the night, and Nicolaus had no trouble getting to sleep.

The next day, he and Deirdre completed the inventory of the rooms inside the castle, focusing on their work.

The following day, they explored the grounds. At first Nicolaus thought they could walk the grounds, but when he saw the map, he realized there were several hundred acres. He could hardly believe it. He and Deirdre were provided calm horses for the trek, and the stable manager went with them, to ensure their safety and that they would not get lost their first time out.

The weather was pleasant for their exploration. Nicolaus noticed how the sunshine beamed off Deirdre's beautiful hair, as they rode side by side. She saw him looking at her with that gaze of love he'd always had for her. She giggled, "Are you going to look over the land or just stare at me?"

He chuckled at her comment, "Both!"

Deirdre thought it would be so easy to fall into his arms while they were out on the property, under the beautiful Estonian sky, with the cool breeze, and the smell of nature all around them. How easy it would be. Her thoughts were interrupted by their guide as he pointed out landmarks of the property. After about an hour, they came upon the water way that was on the edge of the property line, and which Nicolaus had a high curiosity to see.

They dismounted, wrapped the horse reigns to the nearby fence, and went to the water together. The stream was crystal clear, and looked quite deep, as the water calmly rushed over the grey rocks underneath.

"Oh, this is just beautiful," Nicolaus commented. He leaned down and put his hands in the cool water. Deirdre did the same. He sighed, and looked at her, his love for her overflowing. "I just can't help but think about why Aunt Clara gave this land to both of us. She knew we were supposed to be together." He felt emotion come to his throat. "It's hard."

Deirdre nodded in silence, feeling herself wanting to cry, as their lost future presented itself to them again.

Nicolaus sighed again, trying to get ahold of himself. He breathed in the crisp air. "You being here with me means so much, Deirdre. Thank you," he told her.

Deirdre's heart ached for the man she loved. She prayed he would swoop her up in his arms and carry her away. She knew it was wrong to wish it, but she just couldn't help it. She smiled at him, those automatic tears dropping from her eyes.

He grasped her hands, then hugged her to him. They stood, and hugged some more, then in silence, got back on the horses and returned to the castle, enjoying the nature scene around them.

The ladies enjoyed two more days in Estonia, while Nicolaus went to visit Andrejs for a day. Deirdre was adamant about taking her mother to see the historic church for a closer look. When they entered, Constance was taken aback by the beauty of it. Bishop Moratey greeted them, remembering Deirdre. He hugged her, and she introduced her mother, and Rachel.

"Rachel! Yes, very good to see you again. How are you?" the Bishop grabbed her hands. "You know, Clara spoke of you often!" Constance and Deirdre drifted away to look at the stained-glass windows.

"I'm fine Bishop, thank you."

"And your wonderful children, Francesca, and Nico-laus?"

Rachel smiled at him, understanding that Clara told him much, "Yes, Francesca didn't make this trip, but Nicolaus is with us, and is in Latvia today, visiting his father-in-law."

He looked at her confused. "Latvian father-in-law?" He looked back at Deirdre.

Rachel chuckled to herself, looking down, then back at the Bishop, "Bishop, it seems my Aunt Clara spoke to you about our family."

He looked to Deirdre again, and frowned, his mind remembering that Deirdre and Nicolaus were to be wed. Rachel pulled the Bishop to sit on a pew with her, as Deirdre and Constance continued their self tour of the historic church.

"Yes, yes, she told me ... everything, really." He frowned for a moment, "At least I think she did. She wanted to be sure there were records ..."

"Sometimes Bishop, things don't always turn out the way we want them to. I had to learn that a long time ago; the day I gave birth to Nicolaus." He stopped to lis-ten. "Sometimes, we are forced to take a different route. My Aunt Clara believed that was a bad thing. To be off your life path ..." she paused in thought, "and ... I think she may have been right." Suddenly, Rachel began to cry softly. "I've made a mess of things ...for Nicolaus and Deirdre."

"Oh now, now," the Bishop told her, taking her hands.

"I ruined their lives. Oh God, the day Nicolaus was born, he didn't have a chance."

"Oh now, now. That can't be true. I met Nicolaus. He seems to be an astute young man. He led the family during the funeral. Clara left the land to him."

"Him and Deirdre," she corrected him.

"But don't you see, that's just it. They will be tied together in heartache forever."

He frowned, not understanding, "Heartache?"

"They cannot marry now. Nicolaus was betrayed. Betrayed because of me. Don't you see?" she cried. The Bishop patted her hands trying to comfort her, still not understanding, but he let her talk. "Nicolaus and Francesca don't even know they are brother and sister!" She cried, putting her head in her hands, needing the release. Constance appeared from nowhere, and went right to Rachel, hugging her, to let her get that crying out.

The Bishop nodded to her, and went to Deirdre who seemed upset. Tears seeped from her eyes, seeing the pain Rachel was in. "Is Auntie Rachel okay?" she asked him.

He seemed more confused that Deirdre referred to Rachel as Auntie. The Bishop put his arm around Deirdre. "Yes, all will be fine. She just needs to cry, she has a lot on her mind. You okay?"

Deirdre nodded, "Yes," then thought about it. "No." She sat on the pew and started crying as well.

The Bishop did not expect this. He sat next to her, and took her hands, trying to comfort her. "Is it Nicolaus?" he asked her.

Deirdre nodded. She felt comfortable crying in this beautifully historic church. It seemed right to cry here.

"I love him, Bishop, I do. With all my heart. And I know he loves me too. And we are meant to be together, but no, his mother doesn't want us to be, so she fixed it so it can never be. And Bishop … I just … I just …"

grief overcame Deirdre. The hurt and the tears that she'd been socking away for the last year, came all flooding out. Also, she left the Bishop more confused than ever, because he knew Rachel to be Nicolaus' mother.

Suddenly, the women all coalesced together. The Bishop found that he was also moved to tears from this emotional event, although he didn't understand the full situation.

They remained at the church for several more hours. After their crying spell ended, they had tea and cake with the Bishop. When the women left, Bishop Moratey was still not clear on the whole matter, but knew he'd need to talk to Rachel alone. They had exchanged phone numbers and she'd promised she'd fill him in later, so he would have the information for the church historical record.

Meanwhile, in Latvia, Nicolaus had lunch with Andrejs and Penelope, and of course, Marguerite was the first topic of discussion.

"I worry that Marguerite not travel with you," Andrejs told him. "How is she?"

Between bites of the salmon meal, Nicolaus knew he had to be delicate in his characterization of Marguerite. "Well, she is okay. I did try to get her to travel with us, and visit with the two of you, but … she refused. Physically she is okay, I just think she was not up for traveling."

"Have you been nice to my sister?" Penelope forthrightly asked him, as her eyes had not left Nicolaus since they were seated. Though she wanted to create trouble, she was still very much in love with him.

Nicolaus smiled at her, "Of course!"

Penelope smiled, and shook her head. "She says no. She says you and Deirdre …"

Andrejs talked over Penelope, cutting her off, not wanting her to attack Nicolaus, "How is Ms. Deirdre? I never forget her kindness she gave my girls."

He was satisfied when Penelope stopped talking and focused on her meal.

"She is well. She is here with me, my Aunt, and her mother. She sends greetings to both of you, actually."

"Very nice! Very nice!" Andrejs replied. "Nicolaus, I want to inquire you the foundation. How is money raised? Much is given?"

Penelope obeyed her father as he turned the conversation over to business talk. She listened, and watched Nicolaus. As he explained how the foundation worked to Andrejs, she wanted to learn, but instead her mind was focused on Nicolaus' mannerisms; the way he moved his strong hands when he spoke, and the way his mouth moved when he chewed his food. The smooth sound of his voice mesmerized her. The way his chuckle was deep in his throat when he lightly laughed at her father's joke. The intoxicating scent of him that was carried by the light breeze on the restaurant veranda. The way his caramel skin was smooth and glistened in the sun. Those eyes.

"Penelope, perhaps you would like to run it?" her father asked her, interrupting her study of the man she dreamed of.

"What … huh?"

"You daydream again?" Andrejs asked her, annoyed she wasn't listening.

Nicolaus chuckled at her, "The foundation, here in Latvia."

She smiled at him, "Nicolaus, will you be involved?"

He returned her smile, "Sure, I'll help wherever is needed."

"Then yes, I will do what you want. Yes!"

Andrejs did not seem to like her answer, or perhaps it was the way she answered. He frowned at her, then returned his attention to Nicolaus and they discussed stock prices.

The lunch was ended with the chilled Latvian berry dessert of debessmanna.

Nicolaus decided to take the last flight back to Estonia, instead of staying over with Andrejs.

He wanted to spend the last day of the trip with his family, and be close to Deirdre.

Andrejs and Penelope went to the airport with Nicolaus, in Andrejs' American luxury car, for which he had a driver. They went to the departure gate with Nicolaus.

"When the baby born, you call me and I come see about my Marguerite," he told Nicolaus, patting him on the back.

"Yes sir, I will call you."

Penelope, was quick to latch onto Nicolaus. This time, he returned her hug. Penelope basked in his arms. She could feel his muscular body through his clothes. She believed her sister a complete fool for not taking advantage of her situation with Nicolaus. Penelope loved the smell of him. She longed for him and wanted so much to be with him. After about one minute, she released him, as a normal person would, except she made sure her hands ran down his buttocks.

Chapter Sixty-Nine

A little while after being home, Rachel had that chat with the Bishop so she could explain what was happening with their family, as she'd promised him. They spoke by video.

"So, Francesca and Nicolaus are siblings?" he started off to get this clarified in his mind.

"Yes," she answered.

"When I spoke with Nicolaus just before the funeral, he did not seem to know this. He told me they were cousins."

"Yes, because Nigel does not want him to know. He is afraid Ceil will use it against him in some way."

"So, both Nicolaus and Deirdre believe Ceil is his mother?"

"Yes, Bishop."

Bishop Moratey sighed, feeling counsel was needed here. "Rachel, my dear, after what Deirdre told me, and from what you are telling me, it appears that Ceil is using this information against him already. Don't you agree?"

"You mean to keep them apart?"

"Well, yes. She has stopped them from marrying. Most likely in retribution against you. At the church you told me Nicolaus was betrayed. Is this the betrayal you speak of?"

"Yes Bishop," the pain surfaced for Rachel again, bringing tears to her eyes.

He was silent for a moment in thought, knowing this was not good. "With this truth untold, I fear that Ceil has the potential of further betrayal, Rachel. You must tell Nicolaus the truth. Don't you think he deserves to know that you are his mother?"

"But Nigel …"

"As his mother, Rachel, you need to make the choice, not based on what Nigel wants."

"Oh Bishop, I don't want to hurt Nigel."

The Bishop nodded in understanding. "But are you hurting Nicolaus more in the long term?" He sighed. "Rachel, love can be a tricky thing sometimes."

"But … if I tell Nicky, he will hate me for having kept this from him all this time. And he's going to want to know the whys. And what will Deirdre think of me?" She shook her head, wiping her face with a tissue. "I just don't think I could take it, Bishop. I cannot lose them."

The Bishop was silent for a moment. "Rachel, what if Ceil is the one who tells him?"

"Oh no! That would be awful! I'm sure she'd be very ugly about it."

"Yes, and that is what you're up against. Rachel, the truth is always better."

"Yes, Bishop," she accepted what she already knew.

"You just need to weigh your options, find the right time, and sit him down and tell him the whole truth. Your way. With the love you have for him, I know you'd want to spare him having to learn this from Ceil."

"Yes, Bishop." Tears began to flow from her again.

"Now, Rachel, are you and Nigel still involved?"

"No, Bishop. It was too difficult."

"Yes, and … a sin against God," he said gently, unable to let this glaring issue pass.

"Yes, Bishop," Rachel agreed, silently.

"We must ask for that forgiveness, Rachel."

"Yes, Bishop."

Together, they prayed.

Chapter Seventy

Marguerite was at the country club when her pregnancy water broke, and in real drama, she was transported to the hospital by ambulance. Nicolaus immediately went to the hospital once he received word. He texted Deirdre to meet him there. Nicolaus was treated like a celebrity, as the nurses and Marguerite's girlfriends swooned over him. When he went to Marguerite, she outright rejected him, "Don't touch me!" she shouted at him. "Get out, I don't want you here". One of the older nurses rubbed Nicolaus' back, and offered him to stay in the waiting room, that they would bring him word on any changes.

As he and Deirdre were waiting, Nicolaus seemed nervous. Ceil and Nigel soon arrived, as they wanted to be present for the birth of their first grandchild.

When Nicolaus explained why he was in the waiting room instead of the birthing room, Ceil shook her head. "Well, what do you expect?" she asked him, pointing at Deirdre.

Nicolaus frowned at his mother, but said nothing.

Ceil left them to go support Marguerite in the birthing room. Marguerite was in labour for several hours. Finally, she gave birth to a healthy boy.

The nurses alerted the family, and Ceil stayed with Marguerite, who made it through her childbirth strong and just fine. Nicolaus was overjoyed to have a son, and he hoped that Marguerite would change her mind about not wanting him.

Ceil arranged for two nurses to care for Marguerite, and to assist with the baby. Marguerite refused to even touch her son, and had not done so since she pushed him out.

She didn't even want to look at him.

Now that all was cleaned up, and the baby was assessed, clothed, and warm, he was being formula fed by one of the nurses, which Ceil did not appreciate. Ceil felt that her grandson should have his mother's milk, as breast milk has protective properties for the baby.

Nicolaus and Deirdre entered the room. The nurse placed the baby boy in Nicolaus' arms, for which he was somewhat unprepared to hold this brand-new human.

He and Deirdre observed the baby. Nicolaus held his son in awe, as the baby looked up at him with his similar eyes that were staring back at him. He couldn't believe that this baby came from him, due to a night that he couldn't even remember. However, the child was undoubtedly his, as Deirdre quickly confirmed.

"Oh my God!" Deirdre exclaimed, "He's so beautiful," she carefully grabbed onto Nicolaus' arm, "he looks exactly like you!" She stepped closer to Marguerite, "Marguerite, I hope you are doing okay. The baby is so beautiful," she told her.

Deirdre's words did not appease Marguerite. "No!" she yelled. "Give her the baby. Give her the baby," she told Nicolaus, as if she was almost near hysteria.

"Marguerite …"

"Give it to her!" she shouted at him.

Nicolaus gently placed his son in Deirdre's arms. Deirdre did not take her eyes off the precious little one. She smiled at him. He brought her joy. Nicolaus watched as Deirdre immediately heaped love upon his son with her smiling face, her gentle touch to his head as she carefully cradled him, and kissed his forehead. She told him, "You're so beautiful, yes, and just a precious jewel to be treasured, yes you are," she affirmed him.

"There. Now you have what you wanted," Marguerite told Nicolaus.

"Marguerite, please."

"You can have him. I don't want him," she snapped at them.

"It's okay, I don't mind," Deirdre said sweetly, trying to make the best of this awful moment, as the baby wiggled and cooed in her arms. Her eyes never leaving Nicolaus' son's eyes, "Marguerite needs a break."

"Marguerite, please, don't do this," hurt was on Nicolaus' face and in his voice at her rejection of his son. His son is being rejected, just as he had been rejected by Ceil, as a child. The thought of the generational abuse, tearing down of esteem, and lack of motherly love brought up raw emotions for Nicolaus.

"Take it away! Get it away!" Marguerite was referring to the child she had just birthed.

"Marguerite, he's just a baby, he needs his mother. He needs you," Nicolaus tried to reason with her.

"Get out!" Marguerite shouted. "All of you, get out!" she shouted loudly, closer to hysteria than a few moments ago.

Nicolaus wanted to go to her, but Deirdre stopped him. She knew he would only make things worse, and it was clear to see that Marguerite was more unstable than usual.

The nurses ushered them out of the room, saying they would attend to Marguerite, as she quickly spiralled into a hysteria fit. One of the nurses retrieved the baby from Deirdre, and tended to him. She told them they could return once they settled Marguerite down.

Nicolaus left the hospital room in a brain fog. Somehow he found himself inside the hospital chapel. Tears dripped down his face as he felt this is some kind of cruel joke God is playing on him, or a cruel heavenly test of character. How could it be that he is married to a woman who hates him, who gave birth to his son who she does not want, only to have the only woman he truly loves, whom he cannot have, take to his son as if he were her own.

Nicolaus was not aware that Deirdre had followed him to the chapel. He turned at the sound of the squeaky chapel door to see Deirdre, looking as beautiful as ever.

"Don't worry darling," she told Nicolaus, "I don't mind. I will take care of Little Nicky. He won't even know his mother is missing. I promise, he won't even notice." She looked upon Nicolaus with great love, ready to step into the role of mother for his child, as she would do anything for her most loved and precious Nicolaus Ravenell.

TABLE OF CONTENTS

Chapter One; 11

Chapter Two;... 21

Chapter Three;.. 25

Chapter Four; 31

Chapter Five;... 37

Chapter Six;... 43

Chapter Seven; 45

Chapter Eight; 49

Chapter Nine; 55

Chapter Ten;.. 61

Chapter Eleven;... 65

Chapter Twelve;.. 73

Chapter Thirteen; 77

Chapter Fourteen;... 81

Chapter Fifteen;.. 85

Chapter Sixteen; 89

Chapter Seventeen;..93

Chapter Eighteen;..97

Chapter Nineteen;..101

Chapter Twenty;...107

Chapter Twenty-One;...111

Chapter Twenty-Two;..117

Chapter Twenty-Three;..121

Chapter Twenty-Four;..125

Chapter Twenty-Five;...133

Chapter Twenty-Six;..137

Chapter Twenty-Seven;..145

Chapter Twenty-Eight;...149

Chapter Twenty-Nine;..157

Chapter Thirty;...165

Chapter Thirty-One;...169

Chapter Thirty-Two;..175

Chapter Thirty-Three;..181

Chapter Thirty-Four; 187

Chapter Thirty-Five; 201

Chapter Thirty-Six; 205

Chapter Thirty-Seven; 209

Chapter Thirty-Eight; 221

Chapter Thirty-Nine; 225

Chapter Forty; 229

Chapter Forty-One; 243

Chapter Forty-Two; 251

Chapter Forty-Three; 255

Chapter Forty-Four; 259

Chapter Forty-Five; 261

Chapter Forty-Six; 275

Chapter Forty-Seven; 279

Chapter Forty-Eight; 287

Chapter Forty-Nine; 289

Chapter Fifty; 291

Chapter Fifty-One; 295

Chapter Fifty-Two; 297

Chapter Fifty-Three; 301

Chapter Fifty-Four; 305

Chapter Fifty-Five; 309

Chapter Fifty-Six; 315

Chapter Fifty-Seven; 319

Chapter Fifty-Eight; 323

Chapter Fifty-Nine; 327

Chapter Sixty; 329

Chapter Sixty-One ; 331

Chapter Sixty-Two; 335

Chapter Sixty-Three; 337

Chapter Sixty-Four; 341

Chapter Sixty-Five ; 343

Chapter Sixty-Six; 345

Chapter Sixty-Seven; 349

Chapter Sixty-Eight; 351

Chapter Sixty-Nine ; 363

Chapter Seventy 365